A Fallen Man

A Fallen Man

Tom Levitt

Tom Levitt is a former Member of Parliament in the UK. Since 2010 he has been a writer and consultant on responsible business and has been the author of several books and two plays.

Other books by Tom Levitt:

Responsible business:

> *Welcome to GoodCo (2015)*
> *The Company Citizen (2018)*

Biography:

> *The Courage to Meddle: The Belief of Frances Perkins (2020)*

Political fiction:

> *The Spine Politic (2020)*

Copyright © 2022 by Tom Levitt
ISBN: 9798433217324
Kindle Direct Publishing

Cover photo by Daniel Mačura via Upsplash

  The characters and events portrayed in this book are fictitious. Any similarity to real persons, living or dead, is coincidental and not intended by the author.
  No part of this book may be reproduced, or stored in a retrieval system, or transmitted in any form or by any means, electronic, mechanical, photocopying, recording, or otherwise, without express written permission of the publisher.

This fiction is dedicated
to all those who strive to make the world a better place
through politics, often with too little thanks

A Fallen Man

Prologue: Tuesday 24th May 1983

39 Years Later: Saturday 7th May 2022

Watching the Detectives - Alison & Ruth: Saturday 7th May

Scratching the Surface: Sunday 8th May

Charles Mallory, Chief Whip: Sunday 8th May

Paul Roe, Honourable Gentleman: Friday 22nd April

Pub Quiz - Henry & Paul: Friday 22nd April

Kate Mellor has a Plan: Monday 25th April

Money Talks - Lee Hardman: Monday 25th April

On the Bench - Kate & Lee: Thursday 28th April

How Things Were - Kate & Damon: 2000-2002

Paul's Dilemmas: Saturday 23rd April 2022

Lee Investigates: Friday 29th April

Hazel with Hazel Eyes: Monday 25th April

The Candidates' Weekend: October 2009

Mayo and Ketchup – Kate: Tuesday 3rd May 2022

Central Lobby - Lee & Damon: Thursday 5th May

Chilli sin Carne - Paul & Damon: Thursday 5th May

At Home with Kate & Mark: Thursday 5th May

Adolfo Seeks Advice: Wednesday 11th May

Deception? Alison & Ruth: Wednesday 11th May

Taking Stock – Paul: Wednesday 11th May

The Interview (Paul): Thursday 12th May

The Interview (Kate): Thursday 12th May

Lee Plans his Escape: Friday 13th May

Hazel to the Rescue: Friday 13th May

Kate's Story: Friday 13th May

The Chief Whip Negotiates: Friday 13th May

Ruth Ploughs On: Friday 13th May

Alcohol Stimulates the Brain: Friday 13th May

Action Replay: Saturday 7th May 2022

Prologue:

Tuesday 24th May 1983

It is Tuesday, 24th May 1983, shortly after 6 p.m. The studio floor at Lime Grove is a hive of semi-organised activity as the BBC TV's nightly topical magazine programme, *Nationwide*, is broadcast to the attentive nation. Only 16 days remain before the country will go to the polls in a crucial general election.

Large cameras move effortlessly, silent hovercraft gliding over the floor, guided by lean and intense young operatives. Without exception they are men, sporting wispy beards and spectacles with heavy black frames, each with a microphone protruding from his headphones. In topical silhouette each unit appears like a Dalek fused with a Cyberman.

On set, opposite the presenter's desk, is large a bank of square screens. One is huge and four are minor, which together match the larger one in area; upon each, a living bust of a selected member of the British public, briefed and prepared to contribute to the peak time flagship show. It is their personal minute and a half of fame. When they are called to interrogate the most important woman in the land they will switch from their cosy minor to the exposed major screen. The whole exercise is designed to portray the BBC as 'in touch', delighting the friends and families of these several guests from communities across the nation, even though such exercises in face-to-face politics rarely change the allegiance of a single voter. Maybe this year will be different…

On one screen, labelled 'Bristol', the oldest contributor-in-waiting closes her eyes whilst a busy young make-up artist, her hair in a ponytail, dusts the woman's face with powder on a soft brush, thus reducing the glare and reflection from the studio lighting. Tonight, the programme is expecting its highest ever viewing figures - even the smallest out of place glint or gleam could mar the visual aesthetic. Although the programme started some minutes ago the studio is almost silent as viewers are treated to 'the news where you are'. Any moment now this regionalised section will end and the show's national host - tonight it is the experienced Sue Lawley - will resume her place at the helm.

Here she comes; a petite woman in sober dress and fixed, sporty coiffure, bearing a confidence born of experience. She is followed by her guest who is also smaller than one might have expected. The older woman wears a dark, tailored business suit with a lilac blouse, and she walks with a slightly awkward gait. Her left fist is raised, but not aggressively: a shining black handbag dangles from her crooked elbow.

They take their seats.

'Ten seconds!' someone shouts.

Why are record audiences expected? Because, for the only time during this current election campaign, Margaret Thatcher, Prime Minister of the United Kingdom since 1979, will be answering questions directly from the public, live on television.

Now.

The tannoy speaks: 'Quiet, studio... thank you... Three, two...'

Everything is going according to plan: Sue introduces her guest, who smiles serenely and bows her head to graciously acknowledge the presence of the Great British Public. Any deference on Sue's part is, however, token as the Prime Minister takes charge of this exercise. Sue expects this to happen; it is one of those things that a Prime Minister must do if she is to be re-elected. A robust but fair debate is anticipated, and no fireworks are planned. Utterly confident, Thatcher sets about delivering her answers with deadly efficiency. She fires her bullet points as though they were real ordnance, searing across the airwaves and aimed at the heart of the matter, appearing to answer each question in authoritative, unchallengeable detail. Her advisers have correctly anticipated the general thrust of the challenges; an ever necessary exercise.

The fourth question, however, will go down in history.

The elderly lady from Bristol is Diana Gould. After growing up during the second world war Diana studied the South Atlantic as part of a geography degree. After graduating she worked in Navy Signals throughout the 1950s before settling, with husband, Cliff, into school teaching. They made their home and brought up their children in the pleasant Cotswold town of Cirencester. Diana taught her subject at secondary level whilst Cliff rose to become a primary school Head. Diana has long, greying hair, tied back into a neat bun; she has always worn it like that in public. From the evidence of her skin and her cosy woollen jumper viewers could get the impression that the lady is soft and gentle and, in general, she is. Sue Lawley now briefly introduces Diana, who poses her question with confidence. It relates to the Falklands Campaign of a year earlier, a military engagement which, most pundits agree, is about to achieve its final political objective - securing Prime Minister Thatcher and her Conservative government an effortless re-election.

'Mrs Thatcher,' Diana asks in a clear but firm, school-teacherly manner, 'Why, when the Belgrano, the Argentinian battleship, was outside the exclusion zone and actually sailing away from the Falklands, did you give the orders to sink it?'

'But it was not sailing away from the Falklands', responded the PM, calmly. 'It was in an area which was a danger to our ships and to our people on them.'

Diana frowned, but only briefly. She was categorical, certain of her ground: 'It was west of the Falklands and sailing on a bearing of 280 degrees.'

The PM took offence at the women's temerity and railed upon her high horse: 'I think it could only be in Britain that a Prime Minister was accused of sinking an enemy ship that was a danger to our navy, when my main motive was to protect the boys in our navy,' was the first of several robust responses from the adamant, now defiant Premier.

Mrs Gould's final contribution to the exchange was: 'That's not good enough, Mrs Thatcher.'

It certainly was not. The Prime Minister had argued that the vessel was inside the 200-mile 'exclusion zone' that Britain had declared around the Falklands and that its bearing constituted a real and present danger. On both issues Diana Gould was correct - the Belgrano was outside that zone and headed for the mainland - and even the exclusion zone itself was of dubious legal standing. Only later would ministers argue that the zone existed to protected non-combatant vessels from other countries and that 'hostile' vessels could be attacked with impunity. As war had never formally been declared even that claim was questionable.

No television viewer had ever seen this Prime Minister - perhaps any PM - so rattled; and none would ever do so again. It grew to be widely believed that not only had the General Belgrano, a former US Navy cruiser which had survived Pearl Harbor, been sunk on 2nd May 1982, but the so-called Peruvian Peace Plan had been scuppered alongside it.

Perhaps, some commentators would wonder, the Plan had always been the real target of those British missiles.

The loss of 323 seamen that day, over a third of all Argentinian casualties of the entire ten weeks of the Falklands War, devastated that nation's morale and, arguably, brought a British victory, played out so very far from home, nearer. That happened just three weeks later, though not without political cost.

The controversy that followed would end several careers and enhance a few more in the world of politics though Margaret Thatcher would rule for seven further years. The story is an early example of a political leader deploying 'fake news' to win a political argument. The day the Belgrano was sunk was the day the war turned inexorably in favour of the British, enhancing an apparently pointless pursuit of the sovereignty of some God-forsaken rocks in a remote marine wilderness, rocks that the Argentines called Las Malvinas. Not until another decade had passed would Argentina drop its legal claim that the sinking had been a war crime; did they come to accept the reality of their loss, or did they simply realise that this judgment was never going to be made in their favour?

In 2011 Diana Gould took to her grave the certainty that the Prime Minister had lied to the nation, that the rules of war had been broken, and that men of two nations had died in the name of short-term political expediency.

39 Years Later:

Saturday 7th May 2022

If there was a sound, it wasn't heard.

The body flowed like molten lava over the edge, accelerating at almost 10 metres per second each second, a rate predetermined by that force of nature, that inviolate law, gravity. Its estimated journey time to its rocky destination was approximately two seconds. It was there already.

There must have been a sound: there's a transfer of kinetic energy when an object makes contact with another, in the absence of a vacuum. But the noise was vague and ill-defined, more an aspirated 'thud' than a proper 'crack' or 'crash', not as pure or clear as, say, the simple toll of a bell. Although flesh and clothing normally disguise the noise of breaking bones the skull affords relatively little protection when the drop is one of twenty metres, the substrate solid, and the body lands head first.

The skull had indeed taken the brunt, smashing onto the craggy limestone at the side of a farm track. The frontal lobe of the brain was smashed and most of the face was pulped beyond recognition except, perhaps, by those who loved him.

And there were precious few of them.

There was a twitch: was it caused by some final electrical discharge, by life giving up the ghost with a whimper following the bang of impact? More likely it was the inevitable settlement of muscles, of gravity finishing the job it had started seconds earlier; the completion of a complex and asymmetric origami involving limbs, head and torso. In the absence of major arteries in the face the pool of blood was small, expanding only slowly as it drained onto the rocks and into the porous ground; the pump once responsible for circulating it, now evacuating it, did not remain active for long.

It was Saturday, 7th May 2022, between five and six in the evening. The scene was set under a still, powder blue, almost cloudless sky in the proud, bleak, limestone countryside of the Derbyshire Dales.

The viaduct could be perceived as resembling a massive grin, but a macabre grin with a missing canine tooth. It had been built around 1850, when railways were in their pomp and iron horses ploughed their way; yet no behemoth, powered by steam or otherwise, had traversed it since the 1960s. Today no train could pass even if the tracks were still there to allow it as decay from lack of maintenance over more than 50 years had severed the bridge's western extremity from the hillside to which it once clung. The rail tracks themselves, together with much of their protective perimeter fencing, were now absent, recycled as scrap iron, probably piecemeal by freelance operators, somewhere along the way. The top of the long bridge could thus only be accessed by foot from its eastern end, more than 200 metres from where the body lay at the foot of the pillar which marked the start of the missing section of bridge.

The valley was broad, shallow, flat bottomed, its floor an alluvial plain. A farm track mirrored the route of the disproportionately small stream that meandered roughly along the feature's midline. Apart from the viaduct and the track there was little evidence of human settlement for as far as the eye could see, in any direction.

Immediately following the impact, the silence was restored completely, bar the occasional birdsong or the distant bleat of a lamb.

After about half an hour the quiet was broken by a gruff, baritone, playful bark. A middle-aged spaniel hastened towards the viaduct, approaching from the north. As he chased his pretend prey, a bouncing rubber ball, his attention was distracted.

The dog abandoned his quest in favour of the new toy. He made for the heap that should not have been there and carried out a swift and breathless nasal reconnaissance and then, finding a viscous liquid oozing from it, his tongue.

A man's voice: 'Kipper, here, boy! Here!'

The man turned his attention away from his mobile phone, its screen displaying football results on this busy, late-season Saturday. He had Bluetooth earpieces in place to listen to the post-match interviews; their content was almost as familiar as the barren limestone landscape around him. He had grown up with both.

'Kipper!'

Where was the dog? He was normally so good at bringing the ball back
'Come on, Kipper, come here!'

There he was! It was not in the family pet's nature to refuse to attend when called. Ever since he was a puppy, he had loved human contact; he would bring the rubber ball - or any other thrown object - back from the gates of Hell if it earned him a scratch behind the ear. So, what was distracting the dog today?

'Where's your ball, Kipper?'

The man made a beeline for the dog.

'What've you got there, Kipper? Kipper, what -'

As he approached it was clear what the dog had found. His first thought was that it was the body of a Guy Fawkes, out of season, its legs and arms sticking out in unnatural directions. The way the manikin had been finished off was, however, particularly tasteless: in place of the head was a lump of bleeding meat. It reminded him of the sheep's head that his mother used to bring home from the butcher's, stripped of fur and skin, ready to boil up for the dog's dinner.

'Oh! My God! Kipper, come away! Come away, boy! Come here!'

Watching the Detectives - Alison & Ruth:

Saturday 7th May

The Detective Inspector was not tall. She would acknowledge the description of 'thick set', others might say 'sturdy'. She was indisputably in her 50s and had recently negotiated menopause: thank God that was over. She did not miss the more debilitating episodes that were supposed to define her as a woman, she was glad that they were over now, too. If she had ever been asked 'How would you describe yourself? What are your distinguishing features?' She would probably answer: 'None', in line with what it said in her passport.

Alison Allyson had been allocated the late Saturday afternoon 'graveyard' shift and today that adjectival description was never more true. Her partner for the afternoon - and many others over recent time - was a rookie detective constable, recently graduated from uniform, Ruth Gaunt. Ruth looked as though she was about 16, as she had every year of the decade since she really was that age. She is slight, angular, some might even say 'gaunt'. If it were not for their hair, the two be-trousered women, standing to observe the corpse that mild May evening, could almost be represented by two images of the same body, reflected in complementary distorting mirrors in an ancient fairground attraction.

Fifteen metres away from the pair, parked next to Alison's car, stood an ambulance, its blue lights flashing to warn precisely no-one of the urgency of their mission. Although it was unavoidably blocking the narrow farm track that would be of no consequence: the route was rarely used by vehicles, least of all on spring Saturdays, approaching dusk. The senior of the two paramedics had already confirmed that the man was devoid of life, but they were not allowed to move the body until Alison, the senior investigating officer, said so. And she was busy. The medics confined themselves to the cab of the ambulance, each drinking coffee from a thermos, each doing their own silent crossword.

Gaunt had erected a makeshift barrier. It was a yellow plastic ribbon emblazoned with the words 'Crime scene - do not cross' repeated eternally along its length, placed at a respectful distance from the body even though there was no one around to be deterred. Nor was there any suggestion that any crime had been committed.

Kipper, the spaniel, though now having his owner on a lead, had been pleased to meet Ruth Gaunt, jumping up at her and demanding attention - duly received - whilst Alison noted that she herself was being ignored by the hound. Her theory, built on many years of experience and a lifetime of detecting, was that she was invisible to dogs, a hypothesis whose proof had never been found on her list of priorities.

'It's an odd name, isn't it, 'Kipper'?' said Ruth, but the dog offered no reply - save than wagging his tail to express his enjoyment at having his ears scratched. The man answered: 'My daughter was three when we got him. She couldn't say 'Skipper'.'

'Oh, right. Nothing to do with the smell, then?'

The man smiled weakly; he'd heard that one before.

The man confirmed exactly what time Kipper had discovered the body: it had been at the very moment that an interview with Jurgen Klopp was beginning on the radio, he was sorry to have missed it. No, the man had not seen the body fall and neither had he touched it, what did they think he was? He had nothing further to contribute to the sum of relevant human knowledge. Ruth made a note of his particulars and he was dismissed, released to search for a comfortable pee which would be followed, apparently, by a casserole which was almost certainly overcooked by now. The dog remained on his lead.

'We'll do a quick search for ID and what have you, Ruth, then I want you to pop up there' - the top of the viaduct - 'to look around the place where he either jumped, fell or was pushed.' Ruth looked upwards accordingly.

'Oh, and I've left my crampons at home!' She had the build of a rock-climber; there was nothing to her, her mother told her regularly. She did even climb rocks occasionally, with friends, a not uncommon Derbyshire preoccupation. But not today, not in her new shoes.

There was no access to the summit of the incomplete viaduct from this, the damaged end. Ruth would have to walk all the way to the far end, on the eastern side of the valley, climb up a steep path and walk all the way back along the top of the bridge. A few minutes later she would, no doubt, retrace every single step. Hey-ho, that was how delegation worked. One day she would be a delegator herself. Ruth Gaunt did not lack ambition.

'What am I looking for, Boss?'

'I don't know. If he was your standard jumper then you'll probably not find anything. If he's written a 'goodbye cruel world' it's more than likely going to be in his pocket or at home than up there, but on the other hand… signs of a struggle, maybe? God knows what they might be. Any indication that he didn't topple willingly, we need to know. If you see anything like that, we'll have to get SOCO in and, let's see, it's a good hour until sunset. We'll have to be sharp. Let's have a look at Sunny Jim first.'

Donning blue latex gloves Alison set about searching the body whilst Ruth took notes of any words she would utter. The inspector did not hold with new-fangled things like voice recorders.

'Let's see… ready? IC1 male, blond, make that grey haired? What would you say?'

'Bit of both, I guess. Thinning on top.'

'What's left of it… He wouldn't thank you for pointing out the thinning. Receding, too. Aged… 35 to 45. Medium build, not fat but not skinny either. Do you recognise him?'

It was a vain hope. Ruth looked where the face should be and recoiled.

'Not much to recognise.'

'True. He's wearing a suit on a Saturday evening, but no tie.'

She raised an eyebrow momentarily, wondering why he would be dressed up when it was not even going out time yet. Raised eyebrows did not, according to Ruth, merit recording in the official notes.

'So… He's lying on top of his left hand… if I lift him slightly, can you see? Here goes… anything?'

'There's blood on his hands… but no wedding ring, Boss. Is that what I'm looking for?'

Alison let the man lie back where he had been.

'Whatever. There are no right answers. No wedding ring doesn't mean…'

She tailed off. Alison never wore hers, either, not just for the past year but not for a long time before that. She went on: 'His suit's expensive, so are his… look, he's got a shoe missing. Can you see it anywhere? Maybe it's underneath him.'

'It shouldn't be, Boss.'

'Why not?'

'Because that would mean he'd fallen on top of it, so the shoe would've fell first. That's not very likely.'

Allyson pouted, considering. 'Fair point. Keep your eyes open for it.'

The inspector brushed a lock of unruly brown hair from her face, better to survey the remains of the man before her. Ruth wondered when her boss had last seen a stylist; not this side of Easter, that was certain. Christmas? The dark mop with grey roots was tethered with a broad, black, decorated band at the back but otherwise left largely to its own devices. Ruth wore her own coiffure, naturally blonde and almost supernaturally straight, in a tidy, functional, relatively low-maintenance bob.

The Inspector lowered her head towards the corpse's face, where Ruth could see a bloody jaw, a cleft chin. It looked for a moment as though Alison going to kiss him: surely not! There was no touching of lips. Alison inhaled deeply through her nose and then out again from her mouth.

She withdrew her face.

'If he's been drinking, it's not obvious. And he's not been here very long. An hour or two, I'd guess. Maybe less. No more.'

'There's quite a bit of blood…'

'It's all come from the head wound, as far as I can see. That's your cause of death. Blood on his shirt collar, too. Spatter marks… to be expected.'

Now Alison was taking photographs with her phone camera before twisting the apparently intact torso so that she could access the jacket pockets.

'They're normally like handbags,' she muttered.

'Eh? What are?'

'Men's pockets. They stuff everything in, never take anything out. And then they tell us *our* handbags are disorganised.'

Disorganised was a word that could never be ascribed to Ruth; to her it was the worst word anyone could ever attribute to a soul. The Inspector was a different matter: a police officer's job was to disentangle order from chaos, even if Ruth's boss appeared to believe that chaos was an essential and desirable prerequisite for life. Why not? Without it there was nothing to disentangle.

Keeping silent counsel was not Ruth's natural state but a habit she had learned. She was a young and often garrulous woman, but she knew to practice discretion when in detective mode.

'But not our boy, from the look of it. His pockets are virtually empty.'

'Posh suit, as you say, Boss. It's his goin' out suit. Not his day suit, full of all his shit.'

Alison paused and quietly gave a quizzical look towards the underling who was half her age and size. Just occasionally, the apprentice needed to have her decorum corrected. Had Alison ever had children herself she might have learned the art of correction better, but on this occasion the simple admonitory glance appeared to work.

'Sorry, Boss. I meant his accoutrements, not his… you know.' This word had only recently been added to her lexicon and, having pronounced it carefully, she was pleased to have found a use for it so early in their acquaintance.

Ruth completed the inventory: trouser pockets, one handkerchief, unused, jacket external pockets, nothing, jacket internal pockets, nothing, jacket breast pocket. Four pieces of card, three assorted business cards and one more, blank. Make that 'blank apart from a series of hand-written digits in pencil'. It was too long for a phone number, and it didn't begin with a zero. Alison lay the cards on the ground, gathered them together to pose them for a single photograph.

'Boss? How did he get here?'

Allyson gave her a withering look: 'Well, I think he fell. Or he jumped. Or he was pushed.'

'No, I mean… here. The middle of nowhere. Where's his car keys?'

'No keys of any sort, that's a good point. No wallet. No cash.'

'So, was he robbed?'

'I think you need to get up on top of that bridge and take a look at what's what. Take evidence bags and photograph anything you see. Oh, and pegs and tape in case you need to rope the area off.'

'Right-ho'. Get it over and get home, Ruth thought.

'Soonest done whilst we have the light. Have you got a torch?'

'On my phone, yes.'

'You might need it for the way back. We don't want you falling off the bridge, too.'

Sometimes Ruth felt it was almost as though her boss - who she admired and respected as a police officer - cared.

Ruth gathered what she required from the car and set off. Fortunately, it had been unseasonably dry in recent weeks so when she reached the makeshift steppingstones across the modest, shallow stream they were not only well proud of the water but most of them were stable. She could already make out the pedestrian access from the plain up to the far end of the viaduct. It was reasonably well defined, obviously much used by walkers seeking to re-join the former rail route rather than making the pointless trip along the viaduct. The bridge was now, to all intents and purposes, a pier.

Meanwhile, Alison Allyson continued her search, completing the pocket routine and wondering again how the man had got there. Should she let the ambulance take the body away now? Something made her wait. Let's see what Ruth finds, first.

She liked Ruth, though she was tough enough never to allow the junior ranks to bask in such knowledge. The Inspector was a great believer in starting off firm and making life easier later, as the rookies earned it - a management technique that was so much more effective than the other way round. She had an easy way about her, did Ruth, and she missed very little, she was full of confidence and would only get better.

Promising. That was the word.

Alison looked at her watch. Three quarters of an hour remained before the sun would set but the horizons were broad, the clouds few and high: a good hour of daylight remained. The man who had called this in - she had forgotten his name already, the one with the dog - would soon be tucking into his casserole. Ruth would remember his name. And the dog's. And what was in the casserole.

Unlike the man, Alison had little to go home to.

Alison Birkett was born in Manchester to Irish parents, a skilled carpenter and a nurse with ambitions. Unlike many of her compatriots in the streets where she grew up, she was an only child, and could never complain that she lacked her parents' attention. She tried hard at school but had few friends who lasted. Not the most academically gifted, she was not stupid: she had a quick grasp of information and learned to read people effectively from a young age. Marshalling facts and regurgitating them, as the school demanded, was not for Alison; with modest grades at 16 she went to a Further Education College to study English and Art. She met a female police officer at a careers fair, and believed immediately that she had found what she was looking for: reading people, making judgments every hour of the day, assembling facts - and having an external system to store and process them. Thanks to that woman - whose name she could never recall - Alison was able to tick her box labelled 'fulfilment'.

When she first married Eric Allyson the symmetry of her new name had been a novelty, a bit of a laugh, but better than her previous moniker: she was known as 'Burky' in the station at that time. Behind her back, she suspected, it was just 'the berk'. Nowadays her current surname no longer described her relationship with Eric, an antiquarian bookseller. It was six months since she had even seen him, but the feeling that she was married to him had been in decline for several years. Many would find nominal alliteration, such as she suffered, a barrier to being taken seriously but this was not the case for Alison Allyson: anyone who came across the Inspector knew, from the very first moment, that she was an officer who demanded to be treated with gravity and respect.

It was a year since their marriage had finally broken down, in spectacular fashion. She and Eric had shared their home but not their lives for a long time before that. They had no children to complicate things, though even if they had become parents the progeny would have fled the nest by now. Hopefully. They shared domestic bills fifty-fifty, perhaps the only advantage she gained from the arrangement - as her income was both higher and more reliable than that associated with Eric's core trade, rare folios.

Twelve months earlier, things had come to a head: a truce of half a decade had been shattered. Their rules of disengagement involved separate bedrooms, incompatible working hours and the minimum of neighbourly contact - apart for an occasional shared Saturday night television movie, Trappist style. Conversation was confined to the minimum necessary and there was no question of infidelity for either party - neither would have professed interest in touching another, and most certainly not by their former significant other. Been there, done that. Alison had forgotten what touching was like but did not think she missed it. On reflection, in the days leading up to their denouement, there had perhaps been a barbed edge to Eric's rare comments as the couple encountered each other, something which only happened when entering or leaving the bathroom or kitchen.

One night she returned from a hard day's work at eleven o'clock, resisting any temptation to sing a jolly 'I'm home! 'as she might once have done. She could hear that Eric was watching snooker on the TV with the volume turned up to an inordinate, grating, unnecessary level. Having no desire to watch this (or anything else) she wondered why a programme consisting mostly of silence had to be turned up so loud.

The house was warm. Too warm, even for spring; such a waste of money. She took off her jacket, hung it on a hook at the foot of the stairs, picked up the mail which had been ignored by Eric, surveyed the three envelopes and two fliers. Perhaps, she reluctantly accepted, on this occasion his dismissive judgment had been justified.

Alison entered the sitting room and, for reasons she failed to rationalise, thought to glance across to the grate. As the home was heated by gas the set of brass fire irons on the hearth - poker, tongs and brush, once belonging to Alison's grandmother - had but a token, decorative role. Wait... was it a few inches out of place?

She cursed her detective instinct, cut short her musing and headed for the drinks cabinet.

'If you must have that on so loud, I'll take my drink upstairs,' she declared, addressing her remark firmly, quietly but matter of factly, to no one in particular. She turned and bent down to open the cupboard which, by some existential combination of accident and design, was never more than sparsely populated. She removed a bottle of smooth, smoky 12-year-old malt, then silently cursed the sort of idiot who returned empty bottles to cocktail cabinets. It was just conceivable that the culprit had been Alison herself and, in any case, raising the issue with Eric would achieve nothing. Fortunately, an old bottle of blended stuff had, at some point in history, been pushed right to the back. She crouched to remove it but flinched when she heard a metallic clink that should not have been there. As she started to stand, turning to face the noise, she discovered Eric close behind her, right arm held high with a glinting object in his hand - the brass poker - aiming at her head. The ornament was less than full size and, again, her instinct came into play - telling her exactly what was about to happen. She twisted out of reach, deflecting the blow, such as it was, onto her shoulder. Eric dropped the poker upon impact and - silent up until now - started to yell furiously:

'You bitch, you've ruined my life! You've never loved me, just strung me along, all these years! You cow! You fucking, shitting -'. Taken aback, Alison simply listened as her mouth fell open; suddenly she felt no longer physically threatened. His barbed words, disarmed torpedoes, were meaningless.

It was amazing, as she often thought over the weeks that followed, how completely she remembered every syllable of that soliloquy. Every one of the twenty-two words was seared into her memory. Twenty-two. The dismissive, hateful rant contained fewer words than the alphabet had letters.

Eric made some incoherent noises as he raised his fist, in slow motion, now harmlessly bereft of any weapon. Then his whole body went into spasm, eyes and mouth agape, breathing in short, rapid, gasps: 'I haven't heard him make animal noises like that in many years', she thought wryly, as he collapsed in a heap. Despite his violent intentions of a few seconds earlier she caught him as he fell and lowered him gently to the floor. She checked that he had no tight neckwear - instinct and training again - there was none - and that his airways were clear. Confirming that he was still breathing she laid the limp body in the recovery position. She had, as ever, done the 'right thing'.

Twenty minutes later the ambulance paramedic told her 'It was probably a stroke'.

That was a year ago. She visited him in hospital every day for the next week, then weekly for three months; he was her husband, after all, it was the least she could do. It felt cold and calculating when she considered the phrase but 'the least' felt like an appropriate expression of her concern. Throughout the second trimester her visits were occasional, but since month six they had been non-existent.

This instinctive reduction in contact was not a deliberate act to sleight Eric, nor did it result from a decision to abandon her silent, non-communicative partner. In fact, it felt as though it was he who had abandoned her. At no time did his eyes focus on his wife when she entered his hospital bay and she disliked seeing him dribble, though she felt obliged to remove the evidence with a tissue. Rather it was because she herself had been put 'on the sick' in the aftermath of the attack, diagnosed with stress, over-work, the lot. She had needed treatment, counselling, the whole caboodle, which she had accepted without question, at least for a while. However, she refused to be reminded of the pain which she had both undergone and also that which she had, mercifully, avoided. Immediately after Eric's hospitalisation she had worked every hour she could, earning the promotion she had received a couple of years earlier, ten times over. Or so she reckoned. Looking back on it, Eric's 'incident' was the breaching of a dam; she had reached the limit of her tolerance of what life had to throw at her, had protected herself by succumbing to depression.

Which made no sense to her at all, as by then her incubus had effectively gone.

The doctors told her that she had suffered a nervous breakdown. How could that be? It was Eric that snapped, not me! The psychologist, whose focus was not with the most recent 50 weeks but the last 50 years, told her it was probably best not to visit Eric unless or until his condition improved significantly. She interpreted that advice as saying that Eric's presence would remind her of her complete failure to manage the key relationship of her life, though the shrink himself would never have been so bold.

After 14 weeks off work the police offered her early retirement on medical grounds, but that was the last thing she wanted to hear! To accept would be the end of her. She rested, resisted and negotiated. The authorities agreed, instead, that she would undertake six months of rehabilitation, 'light duties', to get her back into the swing and they would reassess the situation after that. Such work included, amongst other things, doing the quiet shifts, mentoring a particularly promising rookie, Ruth Gaunt, and avoiding Saturday nights. It seemed to be going all right, but Alison expected to hear any day now that her assessment was about to resume.

She looked at her watch. This particular Saturday shift was supposed to have ended an hour ago, but what the hell. She had nowhere else to go tonight.

Or any other night.

As a sinecure, the 'light' regime was going reasonably well. She had engaged in more community liaison than previously, even giving a couple of talks to groups of school children, which she had enjoyed. Ruth understood the situation and sympathised; the girl had been good company whilst learning at her superior's feet.

Alison put in more of her share of routine court appearances, too, finding senior officers particularly grateful that she was available to stand in for them or their staff. Having a capable, eloquent and experienced officer represent the constabulary before the magistrates was certainly better than relying on a busy, distracted and inexperienced constable taking 'Buggins 'turn'. Having an Inspector attend court also offset any frustration that magistrates felt whenever the 'wrong' officer turned up for a particular case. Again.

The Jason Graham trial of six months earlier was a case in point. The arresting officer was on leave and the case had already been postponed once; a court date had been set and no one wanted to delay proceedings further, especially as the pandemic had so disrupted schedules. Alison had not, hitherto, been involved with the case but she read the court papers diligently and spoke at length to the officer in charge. She concluded that two of the three alleged offenders were indeed villains, but that Jason had been caught in the metaphorical crossfire; unlike his friends, he had been in the wrong place at the wrong time. The supervising officer felt obliged to agree. In Alison's opinion senior colleagues had been too enthusiastic to close the case and had over-egged the pudding that they had sent to the CPS. The naive, almost certainly innocent lad should not serve time; an intervention was needed to avoid an injustice.

On the morning of the trial Alison found herself in the tea queue next to Jason's mother, clearly a decent and concerned woman. She casually suggested ways in which the boy might endear himself to the court. Off the record, of course, the line of defence which she advocated convinced both the boy's mother and the family's young and inexperienced solicitor; Jason received a token fine whilst his two friends went on probation with community service.

Jennifer Graham was hugely appreciative and massively relieved. An intelligent, sober and Christian woman, she was effusive when she bumped into the Inspector in a nearby car park at the end of that autumn day in court, anxious to explore anything that she could do for Alison in return for the good advice.

'Well, there is one thing…'

'Anything, Inspector!'

'You and I have met before, Mrs Graham…'

'Have we?' The woman was puzzled; she was not one for regularly engaging with the police and Alison's suggestion initially disconcerted her. She checked her conscience: it was clear. 'I'm sorry, I don't remember.'

'You're a nurse at the Infirmary, I think.'

'A Sister, yes… Have you been one of our patients?'

'No, but my husband -'

'Allyson? Oh, you mean Eric Allyson?'

'That's right.'

'I'm so sorry… It must be a terrible situation for you.'

Eric was verbally incommunicative and incapable of feeding himself. He responded only slowly to physical stimuli, mocking Alison's memory of whatever redeeming qualities he might once have had. Jen Graham, on the other hand, had never known Eric otherwise and she dealt with such cases all the time.

'Let's just say... I'm his next of kin, his only surviving relative. And that describes in full our current relationship.'

'Oh, I see...' said the Sister, though her concerned face suggested that she did not.

'It's been like that for several years now.' How deep did this excuse need to go? 'I mean our relationship, not his present condition.'

'Ah.'

'Quite honestly, Sister, I don't see the point in me visiting him regularly when he's... like he is. I don't see how it helps him or... or helps me. Maybe you could... let me know if and when there's a change in his circumstances. His condition. You know, any significant change. And then I wouldn't need to... so often.'

'Well, I suppose...' It was not right to discourage relative visits, the nurse knew; on one hand Eric had no other visitors that she could recall but on the other she could imagine how the situation must be affecting this decent woman of roughly her own age. It must make her feel terrible to see her husband like that. She knew how difficult it would be for her to cope if something like this ever happened to Mr Graham, a chartered accountant to whom she was totally devoted.

'Maybe you and I could... have a chat, you know, perhaps every month? Or so. About his condition. On the phone, maybe, just five minutes. Rather than me... keep coming in.'

'Of course, oh, that's the least I can do, Inspector. Look, call me Jen. Jen Graham. Sister Jen Graham. You know where to find me.'

The nurse was as good as her word. That five-minute phone call each month spared Alison the indignity - the anger - of seeing that useless shell of a pathetic human being stretched out before her, ever again. Until, perhaps, the day would come when she was asked to formally identify his body... No family matter would ever tempt Eric's brother back from New Zealand so there would be no one else available to perform that ritual. Unfortunately.

Jen Graham left the car park with a purposeful air and a sense of commitment to the woman who was her son's earthly saviour. Alison's final words to her had been:

'Yes, I know where to find you, Jen. Thank you so much; here's my card. I've written my personal mobile number on the back. Here you go.'

My card. My business card.

The dusk was advancing. Alison picked up and perused the four cards that she had found in the man's pocket. At first glance they had little in common: there was a journalist, a corporate lawyer of some kind and a politician. To be precise, it was that of a Labour MP. Alison thought his name rang a bell, but she was only an occasional follower of politics so could not be certain. She did not think that he was in the Cabinet, or rather the Shadow Cabinet; maybe he was. These business cards might as well have included Miss Bun, the Baker's daughter, for all the significance they held. And then there was the blank one with the fourteen-digit number. A bank account, perhaps? The numbers were handwritten.

'I can see you!'

Alison's reverie was broken by a voice calling to her from the heavens! She looked up. Ruth Gaunt was leaning over the parapet, twenty metres above her.

'Don't lean over, Ruth, for God's sake! We don't know how safe it is! He might have fallen rather than jumped, the edge might have crumbled or something!'

Shouting was an effort.

'It looks safe, honest!' Ruth bellowed back.

Alison took out her phone, held it up and pointed at it; Ruth got the message.

'It was right for me to come up here,' she said, once they had established a connection. The signal was relatively weak in this remote rural area, but it proved reliable enough.

'What've you found?'

'I've taped off the area... there are signs that might just about suggest a scuffle, maybe. If you have a good imagination. Something that might be a divot - is that what you call it? - kicked up. There's not a lot of grass here. Dust, spread about in a way that it isn't, six feet away to either side. But I wouldn't say it was conclusive. I have a fertile imagination, as you keep reminding me, Boss. The surface is too - what's the word? Too granular, almost gravelly, to get decent footprints. The missing shoe's here, though! It's scuffed. Brown, lace-up, four pairs of holes, burgers, some fancy patterns on them made of little holes.'

Ruth sometimes had a way with words which, on another occasion, Alison would have found amusing. But what was 'burgers' all about? She quickly realised that the word was brogues, not 'burgers', an unfamiliar word in that northern accent that Ruth normally hid much better than she used to.

'Right…'

'Check his wrists, Boss.'

'What do you mean?' Was Ruth suggesting that the man had slit his wrists before he jumped, just to make sure? There was blood from the head wound on the hands but there would have been even more if he had done that business properly.

'How many cufflinks is he wearing?'

'There's one on his right wrist. Hang on, I just need to lift him… his left arm's underneath.' Alison placed the phone on a rock while she performed a manoeuvre. 'OK… No, his left sleeve is hanging free, there's no cufflink.'

'So the right wrist has a silver cufflink with a four-leaf clover design, yes?'

'Correct. I can see signs of wear, so it's a favourite one - that also tells me it's EPNS, not solid silver.'

'A cheapo! That don't go with the fancy shoes.'

'Maybe…'

'And I've found a fern.' A fern? Were we plant spotting now?

'A what?'

'A phone. I've found his phone.' The northern accent was asserting itself again.

'Well done, Ruth.'

'It's locked, but it will open with facial recognition, so we can…' her train of thought tailed off. The face looked like it would be at home on a butcher's slab, so would probably fail to convince the phone's sophisticated artificial intelligence to reveal its secrets.

'Maybe not.'

'The guys in the lab will get onto the phone, tomorrow,' said Alison, reassuringly, but added: 'Or whenever.' What she was thinking was 'Sunday? No chance.'

During the following minutes, as Ruth was returning, Alison made sure her camera missed no angle on the corpse. She was, as ever, impressed by how clear its images appeared, given that the light was now fading. Satisfied that her work, for the moment, was done she finally gave the ambulance crew permission to take the body off to the mortuary.

The ambulance and its immobile passenger had gone, and it was more dark than light by the time Ruth re-joined her boss at ground level - which both had now instinctively labelled 'crime scene 'in their minds. The lack of trees or clouds and the open horizon helped the light remain helpful for as long as possible.

The returning Ruth was grinning like the cat that found the cream.

'Look what I got!' she said, holding up a small, transparent evidence bag.

'A car key?'

'That's the one!'

'Why didn't you say so?'

'I've only just found it - over there. I'd guess someone chucked it off the bridge.'

'Which suggests that his car might not be far away. Good. There's a small car park about half a mile back, isn't there? There was a handful of cars there when we drove past.'

'I bet there won't be many left there now it's going dark, Boss. His'll be the last man standing.'

'Last man in a crumpled heap, more like.'

'Unless it's a locale renowned amongst the local dogging community?'

Alison made a face: 'Ruth, please! Doesn't bear thinking about…'

Lacking floodlights, nor an obvious reason for remaining on site, they left. Alison drove south carefully and slowly, heading back the way they had come, along the pot-holed, pock-marked farm track. They travelled in silence for the short journey to the car park, both in evidence assessment mode. The detectives knew the score: if this was a suicide it was elaborate, unnecessarily anonymous. Every dead body is identified eventually, these days. An accidental death? It did not have the feel of one, not even close. Perhaps, if he had been dressed as a rambler an accident might have been more credible… As for murder or manslaughter, there was no reason to reach that conclusion although they were far from formally ruling out the possibility.

It was not worth expending emotional or intellectual energy worrying who the man was until they had checked the car park. Once they had established the ownership of any clearly abandoned vehicle they should be just minutes away from identifying the driver.

The car park had, once upon a time, been a small limestone quarry. In the failing light they saw that, as predicted, only a solitary vehicle remained in situ. As Ruth pressed the 'open 'button on the key fob, inside its plastic evidence bag, the shade of the evening, the exaggerated umbra of the hewn rock, was punctuated by two blinking tail lights and a noise like a tropical bird. The performance emanated from a dark blue Porsche, standing out like a welcome, flashing Christmas tree on a dark and cold December night.

'Not doggers but flashers, eh, Boss?'

The two women smiled at each other.

Scratching the Surface:

Sunday 8th May

9 a.m. was early for an office meeting, especially on a Sunday. They had agreed to meet at the 'incident desk', a piece of furniture in a small conference room which changed its designation on a regular basis, as officers required. A euphoric serial burglary team had vacated the room a few days earlier. After climbing the stairs upon her arrival Ruth diverted via the small kitchen. She put the kettle on to boil before shaking the rain off her coat, hanging it in the corridor and returning to the kitchen to prepare two mugs. She knew exactly how her boss liked to take hers: strong, black, with two sugars at any time before noon but only unadulterated herbal tea later in the day. A few minutes later Ruth placed two steaming liquid caffeine stimulants on the incident desk.

'Here you go…'

'Thanks, Ruth.'

'Gosh, you've been busy!'

Four black and white A4 portraits, hot off the office printer, were pinned to a display board. Why waste precious resources on colour?

Ruth sat down, removed a notebook from her bag followed by a pencil case, from which she selected a fountain pen, one of several quirks of her nature which appeared respectful of the *ancien regime*. Alison thought that such characteristics redeemed the girl's otherwise remorselessly modern approach to life.

Ruth stifled a yawn: this was a Sunday, for heaven's sake. By rights she should still be in bed. Alison, of course, noticed.

'Late one?'

'Not particularly, Boss, I knew I was coming here so I didn't drink too much and I was all tucked up by half one.'

Alison smiled: 'I was well away with the fairies by then, off in the land of Nod.'

Ruth thought that Alison could be just a little too much like her mother on occasion. This moment was close to becoming one such; best get started with the work. She did not resent the way the job impinged upon her night life, her social life, her love life, but nor did she welcome it. It was just a fact. Last night was a case in point: the young man she had been speaking to transpired to be a police officer himself, but whereas she would normally turn and run a mile when a colleague 'tried it on', this one was both hunky and pretty, far too good looking to do that. He was a stranger, but she had friends in common with his brother. The young man had not 'tried it on' in a conventional sense; he had been attentive but not clawing, interested but not obsessive, understanding when she explained why she could stay no later than twelve-thirty. He was up from London for a few days, staying with his brother, but would be going home later today. She could not quite remember his name, in the cold light of morning, but Alison was not the only one to acquire some business cards! She knew she had it somewhere, it was probably still in her going out bag.

The Inspector set out the situation as she saw it: 'The problem with this crime is… there's no evidence of a crime. We would need to establish motive, opportunity and means but that's all as nothing if no crime has been committed. Suicide's been legal since 1961 and, even if it weren't, there aren't many ways we can punish this chap now. But guess what, Ruth: our fallen man is… a Conservative MP.'

'No! Really?' Ruth's aghast response reflected genuine surprise.

'That makes the case politically sensitive, so we have to handle with care. There's going to have to be press involvement, probably later today. He was Damon Hough, rhymes with 'rough', 40 years old - 40 years and five days, to be exact. He was the Honourable Member for somewhere in the home counties, so what he's doing up here in Derbyshire, I don't know. No obvious connection. First elected to Parliament in 2010, twelve years ago. That's him, the picture on the left, although 'left' is a word that's never been used to describe our chap's politics….'

Ruth looked at the first of the four unlabelled black and white photographs pinned to the board, three men and woman. The man on the left was light haired, a rugged cut to his jaw. The photo looked official, perhaps from an election leaflet or, more likely, a website. The cleft chin was clearly the very one that had just about survived the impact. Although there was a twinkle in his eye there was a dastardly curl to the lip which would not have been amiss on a pantomime villain. The quiff of the man on the photograph had probably been subjected to some shape-holding 'product'.

Ruth tutted. 'Damon Hough. Not 'Hoff', then? Huff. I've not heard of him…'

'Huff, apparently. Not like cough, or through, but enough. He's not in the Cabinet, or anything like that. He's been a backbencher for 12 years. Single, always has been. On the right of the Conservative Party, one of the 'awkward squad', apparently. Some call him a populist, like Trump was, someone who will say anything to attract media attention or Twitter followers. Graduate. Solicitor, both before and during his time as an MP.'

'I didn't know they could do that, have another job.'

'Apparently they can. There are rules about it, but it's not banned outright.'

'You've been busy!'

'It's a wonderful thing, the internet.'

'Goodness! I thought stuff had to be written on vellum or papyrus for you to read it!'

'Oh, I'm quite used to paper these days, Ruth.' She waved a sheaf in the air.

'So, who are the other three?'

'These are the folk whose business cards were in Damon's pocket. I've not had long to check, but having done a very quick search I can't see what, if anything, they've got in common with Mr Hough or, indeed, with each other. Apart from their age… they're all hitting forty about now.'

Ruth took in the information, nodding. That could just be coincidence, after all people do generally mix with folk of their own age, given a choice. That was true of herself, except when at work. She could not imagine her boss going to the sort of club where Ruth and her contemporaries had spent time last night: loud, dark, steamy, with limited places to sit, pulsating music urging all to dance, dance, dance and the heating set to encourage them to drink, drink, drink. Nor could she imagine that Alison ever wearing a dress as tight and skimpy as the one Ruth herself had sported last night, the one her friend Stella had given her for her birthday. The strapless, flamboyant number hugged her petite contours like lycra, so red, so short. Perhaps that was what had attracted her suitor? No perhaps about it, job done. Having committed herself to this morning's meeting, however, Ruth had been abstemious with her drink, if not her dancing; her final tipple had been tap water, despite her friends' scoffing. So she had left the club early. Early? It was still less than eight hours ago. Jesus. She took another slug of coffee.

There needed to be something else. Alison went on: 'We can probably assume from the cards that they all knew - or knew of - our boy. And Paul

Roe - the second one along - is also an MP, but he's a Labour one.' The clean-shaven man's haircut was on the comfortable side of conventional, complementing a broad smile and an open-neck shirt. He appeared altogether more reassuring than the first one.

'Curiouser and curiouser.'

'Thank you, Alice.'

'Alice?' Ruth did not recognise the reference. Pausing only to think positive thoughts about her own education compared to that of 'young people today', Alison continued:

'That's where the stuff in common appears to end between these two, as far as I can tell, but I've only scratched the surface. Paul Roe is two weeks younger than Damon Hough - both grew up in the same part of south London, but London's a big place. They both left home at 18, took different directions in life. It's possible, not likely, that they knew each other as kids. This one, the Labour boy, has only been an MP for 7 years, elected in 2015. He used to be in advertising - communications, whatever they call it these days.'

'Comms, is that the word?'

'Comms, spin. Something like that. He's regarded as a highflier, likely to be a minister if Labour gets into government again any time soon.'

Ruth shook her head, bemused. 'I don't know him, either. The woman?'

'Kate Mellor, journalist. Went to the same university as Damon, worked most of her career in regional newspapers. She's married to an academic, a Professor Mark Shield, but she's kept her maiden name - professionally, at least. She has a column on a Sunday paper, a broadsheet. Happily married, if you can believe her column. She's what they call a lifestyle journalist, not a political reporter.'

'Same University, you say; at the same time?'

Alison consulted the Wikipedia pages she had printed off.

'Yes, exactly the same time.'

Ruth pursed her lips. 'And the last one?'

'Now, this one's interesting - he's known to us.'

'He's got a record?'

'No… no record, he's just known to the police. Maybe he should have a record, but he doesn't. This is Lee Hardman, he's a corporate lawyer and I can't see any direct connection to our boy, except…'

'Except what?'

'He was a Tory candidate in 2010, the same year that Hough was elected for the first time. Lee didn't win and doesn't appear to have tried again. Very sensible, if you ask me. I suppose they could have met through that political connection, back then - and possibly since, too, I guess. Why not?'

'Twelve years is a long time… and they're both lawyers?'

'Yes, but different types… Damon: solicitor in a small practice in a market town, doing, I don't know, small town solicitor stuff. Not full time, obviously. Well, I'd hope not! House conveyancing, wills, all that, I guess. And Lee's a corporate lawyer with MEKANICK.'

'Is that how we know about him? Where might I have heard that name?'

'It was before your time. MEKANICK is a finance company; quite how it still exists is a bit of a mystery. It used to be owned and run by a man called Guy Campbell.'

The name did not cause Ruth's brow to unfurrow. Diplomatically she asked 'Guy Campbell. Remind me?'

The older woman indulged her junior: 'In October 2010, after the economic crash, Campbell went to jail - a twenty stretch for fraud and money laundering. If it wasn't for the crash the evidence might never have come to light; at the trial his people argued that his was a 'victimless crime' and you can half see their point, but it didn't wash with the jury. It was a long case - fraud, laundering, and tax avoidance by Campbell personally as well, as I recall - and the sentence was pretty stiff, much more than anyone expected. Hardman, the lawyer, was one of Campbell's money men, though he personally appears to have been above suspicion. He was, however, a defence witness. Remember, not everything MEKANICK did was illegal and, of the bit that was not legal, not all the money involved was ever accounted for: several millions were missing. But enough was traced to put Campbell away, and that was the aim of the exercise. A lot of what was left was squeaky clean, so that's how the company manages to be still in operation, I guess. But it's smaller, quieter, perhaps more careful, I would guess, than it was back then.'

'Reformed sinners?'

'Better at not getting caught.'

This time Ruth looked at Alison and raised her eyebrows, asking for more. Alison understood the question implicitly.

'Perhaps I should have said' not proven' rather than 'squeaky clean'. There wasn't enough evidence.'

Ruth was thinking. '2010... 12 years ago. Could he be out on parole, Campbell? If he's been a good boy?'

It was Alison's turn to pause: 'I'll check on that. Good spot. But I don't know what it tells us about Damon. Any random thoughts?'

'Each of the three has one probable or certain or possible known link to Damon. Is he in touch with any of them?'

'The phone's gone for analysis, but it's Sunday today and it's not a high priority case... we'll be lucky to get anything back from the tech people by midweek.'

'What about the fourth card?' Asked Ruth.

'Fourteen handwritten digits. If it's six digits then eight more, or eight and then six, then my money's on it being a bank account, but no such account exists for either the 8-6 version or the 6-8.'

The two women were silent for a while, thinking. Alison broke the reverie:

'The press doesn't have the story of a suicidal MP yet, and we've only known his identity a few hours... the ambulance crew can't leak his name because they didn't know who he was, they'll have dropped him off at the mortuary as a John Doe. My first job is to bring the mortuary up to speed. As this is politically sensitive, I'm going to have to talk to the Super this morning, before we say anything to anybody else. And we need to find the next of kin. There's no obvious partner, nor any siblings that we know of. I don't know about his parents...'

Ruth was making notes in the form of a 'to do' list, in her notebook, with her fountain pen.

Neither Alison nor Ruth was rostered to work that day but both preferred to do so rather than spend what might otherwise be a grey and miserable day alone. They would adjust their hours later to recoup the time they spent on the case, in theory, though in practice they would probably never claw back all of it. And certainly not at Sunday rates, which required advance approval. As Alison busied herself on the internet Ruth spoke to local plods in Damon Hough's rural home counties constituency, testing the (justified) assumption that the MP had a residence locally, before repeating the exercise with the Met. Alison's meeting with her Chief Superintendent, by video link to his home, happened within the hour.

Time passed as the women set about their work diligently and with purpose. At one point Ruth's phone pinged but she ignored it. Later, *en route* to the loo, she found a moment to glance at it. 'Enjoyed meeting you last night! Let's stay in touch. Darren'. Aha, this must be the Adonis she had met last night, 'Met' in both senses of the word. No, it wasn't! He wasn't from the Met - the City of London police? That was it. She hoped his card was indeed in her handbag. Normally she would ignore such blandishments from strange men, but this approach had generated a slight tingle in the spine... 'How sweet', she thought, but only briefly. There was work to be done.

There would have to be a press conference, Alison was told, because of the political sensitivity, and someone needed to talk to the Government Chief Whip before anything went public. Alison, only vaguely aware of what the job of a Chief Whip entailed, offered to spend some of her empty Sunday preparing and then briefing the gentleman. Hopefully, this would be the preamble to passing responsibility for the media over to the political powers that be.

Dealing with the press was certainly one aspect of the case - and the job - that she could do without.

Charles Mallory, Chief Whip:

Sunday 8th May

Charles Mallory was known as a Chief Whip who took no prisoners.

Ill-discipline on the back benches had been at the heart of every wobble experienced by Conservative governments over the last decade. Accordingly, a year previously, the new man in number 12, Downing Street, had been determined to make such tremors things of the past. So far, agreed everyone who mattered, so good: the ship had been steadied. Over the several years that Mallory had spent in patient waiting, as Deputy Chief, he had learned where many political skeletons were buried. In a break with the policy of some of his predecessors he tried to get to know every single member of his flock personally, whilst meanwhile deliberately failing to shake off his reputation as a wolf in wolf's clothing. The approach was paying dividends: during his first year at the top of the whipping tree the government had lost not a single vote. On the downside, it was widely believed that peace had been only bought because Mallory had insisted on the PM dropping some of his more ambitious ideas. The less you try to do in politics the fewer mistakes you make…

'The most powerful man in government,' said a current affairs web site respected for its objectivity. 'Mallory not only keeps Tory nerves on edge, but he controls MPs' hormones, too: especially those concerning flight and fright.'

It was midday on the Sunday when the police switchboard located the Chief Whip at his home, and five minutes later when Alison got through to him. She started by reeling off a list of apologies: for disturbing the politician's day of rest; for being an Inspector, when this call merited being made by a superior officer (being a Sunday, she counted on his understanding) and finally, of course, for being the purveyor of bad news.

She gave him the briefest possible summary of Damon Hough's death. There was a silence at the other end of the good, old fashioned, telephone landline.

'Mr Mallory?'

'I'm sorry, I'm just composing myself. This is indeed sad news. Quite a shock, in fact… How much more are you able to tell me?'

How much indeed?

'I can tell you that we're not looking for anyone else in this matter - at the moment. There are some aspects associated with this apparent suicide that we don't quite understand, but I'm sure it's only a matter of time.'

'You say 'apparent suicide'? You mean -'

'I mean it appears to be a suicide. There's currently no evidence to suggest otherwise but it's still early days - we've found no note, for example, but we've not been to his home - homes - yet. He clearly fell from a high bridge onto rocks, it seems he landed head first. The odds against him surviving that sort of fall were slim and it's unlikely that he suffered. But with no eyewitness - and none has come forward - we can't be a hundred percent sure of exactly what happened. Yet.'

'My God... I've known Damon a long time. A very long time.'

'We found his car key close to the body, and his vehicle, a Porsche Macan, was parked not too far away. He had no identification on him, but we traced him through the ownership of the vehicle.'

'Do you have you any idea why...?'

'Why he jumped? No, sir, as I say, there was no note, either on him or in the car. Officers from his local constabulary are going to his home today to see if there's anything that might shed some light. The Metropolitan Police will be doing the same for his London address. To be honest, I was hoping you might be able to speculate as to his reasons for taking his own life. I understand that you're closely in touch with all of your Members of Parliament.'

'All of our Conservative members, yes. But really... I'm not sure how much I'm able to tell you... he wouldn't be the first Member to take his own life.' There was a pause, leaving Alison not quite sure what to say. Mallory, in his late sixties, spoke with professional authority whilst weighing his every word. He went on 'Being an MP can, of course, be a glamorous life, but despite appearances some people do find politics very stressful, even lonely. Damon... possibly falls into both of those categories. Lonely and stressed. Whilst, in his case, making the most of the glamour.'

'Of course. Well, I really ought to say, 'tell me everything you've got', please, then we can decide what may or may not be relevant, what's worth us exploring further. We would like to know why he did it and I'm sure his family would, too.'

Alison paused, but Mallory did not intervene. She went on: 'For example: he's been 12 years in Parliament but has never been a minister, 'on the front bench', is that what they say? Is that unusual? Is there an explanation for that?'

Alison thought she detected the start of a snort, stifled out of decorum. In other circumstances she might even have interpreted it as a chuckle. On this occasion being able to see her fellow conversee might have helped.

'That… no, that would not be a unique situation, Inspector. I'm blessed with having more than half of all the MPs in Parliament under my charge and, of course, we don't have scope to employ them all on the front bench. Not least as 'slimmed down government' is one of our guiding principles. It's not about taking turns. It's not a game.'

'But 12 years? He was a popular person, by all accounts. As a lawyer he must have had some degree of talent?'

Was that another grunt? Mallory cleared his throat.

'There's a difference, if I may say so, between popular and populist,' he said, stressing the final syllables. 'It's easy to be popular, in a very non-discriminating sort of way, if you are a populist, telling the masses what you have calculated that they want to hear - and nothing more. What's not so easy, in contrast, is to stick to your principles, to focus your talent on becoming popular by winning arguments or by impressing others with your dedication, your loyal, sincere and consistent performance.'

'So Damon Hough was a populist? Not loyal? You had reason to doubt his principles?'

This time the laugh was only barely suppressed. 'Not for repeating… But yes, you could say that.'

Alison awaited the clichéd rejoinder: 'but I couldn't possibly comment'. It didn't come.

Mallory went on 'You mentioned the talents of a lawyer: one of those talents is the ability to make a strong case without actually believing a word that leaves your own mouth - that's a measure of a good lawyer. And also of a cynical and manipulative populist.'

'You're saying that -'

'I'm talking in general terms.'

The Inspector raised an eyebrow; again, the limitations of telephone technology meant that the gesture went unnoticed. 'Maybe he needed a brief, guidelines to follow, the discipline of office.' She realised that she was close to telling a Chief Whip how to do his job, which was not her intention, so she continued 'But I'm sure you'd know best.'

Mallory did not take the bait - fortunately. She changed the subject.

'I wonder if you're able to tell me - who's his next of kin?'

Mallory hesitated. 'I would have to look that up for you.'

'He wasn't married, was he?'

There was an awkward silence. 'No. No, he wasn't married.'

'Was he ever married?'

'No.' More certain.

These momentary silences were hiding something, but she knew not what. Her discretion told her not to pursue anything that was unlikely to be relevant.

'Are his parents still alive? He was only 40.'

'I'd have to, as I say… but no, I don't believe… No, no, they're not. Just as well.'

For someone whose profession used words as its raw materials this man was suddenly tying himself in knots.

He went on 'I, erm… I said I'd known Damon a long time. Actually, all his life. I knew his father, Gerald, quite well. Both… well, both of his parents, actually.'

'So you're, what? Not just Damon's colleague - and his whip - but a friend of the family?'

'Chief Whip. His regional whip would be in day-to-day contact with him more than I was… But I was certainly a friend. A friend of the family. Technically, I'm actually Damon's godfather, but it's - what shall I say? It's an historic title, an honorary title, there's no… extended family-type relationship to back it up.'

'I see.' But Alison was not sure that she did.

'Gerald… He, er, he died. Gerald died, twenty years ago. That was suicide, too.'

The Chief Whip was at the epicentre of government discipline. He was a solid, dependable creator of confidence. Suddenly the man was giving a very good impression of a gibbering wreck who had just realised that two and two make four. Two suicides. It was as though Mallory was suffering from delayed shock, that he was only now responding emotionally to Alison's news. Father and son. Mallory also knew that both Houghs had leapt from bridges, but he judged it best to leave the woman to discover that parallel for herself; to volunteer that information would be too… macabre. Too involved.

Suddenly Mallory could not stop talking. 'That's why it's such a shock. It was May 2002 when Gerald… Exactly 20 years ago. Almost to the day… 2nd May 2002.'

Alison immediately thought that this was odd. It was an inconsistency, not a congruency: if Damon's suicide was supposed to echo that of his father, why had he not done it on 2nd May, last Monday, the anniversary? She suddenly thought she knew: three days earlier, on Thursday, 5th, she herself had voted in the local elections. A politician to the end, Damon would have known that the story of an MP's suicide in the national press on election day could only be bad news for his party. Two days after the election, however, the circus had moved on. It was an explanation, she supposed; time would tell if it was the correct one.

'Do you think he might have been aiming to emulate his father, but then delayed his suicide because of the local election?'

'Oh, come on!' Mallory was suddenly back in the world of reality. 'Actually,' he said, subsiding again and collecting his thoughts, 'that's not a totally absurd idea, about the election, but emulating his father? That I do very much doubt. He was a Party man to the end, is that what you're suggesting? I don't think I would dare to put that phrase in the *In Memoriam*. No one who knew him would believe a word of the rest of the obituary! But… we will probably never know, Inspector. Actually, now I think about it, it was Thursday evening, election day, when I last spoke to him.'

'Did he seem…'

'No. No, he wasn't suicidal.'

But he had been argumentative, stubborn, rude, two sheets to the wind at six in the evening, during working hours. Mallory judged that his interrogator did not need to know this; nor that Damon's condition had not been unusual.

'What did you talk about, may I ask? Any clues, hints, about that happened after that?'

'Just routine whipping stuff.' No hesitation this time. The Chief Whip was shutting down that strand of conversation effectively by lying about it.

'OK…'

'There was no mention of his father.' That was also untrue. 'You know, I wager he doesn't even remember the date on which his father died.'

Shocked he may be, and bound to him by history, but there was clearly no love lost between Mallory and Hough Junior, thought Alison. After a moment, she continued: 'Were there issues which were causing him political problems?'

'No, not that I'm… well, he's… Damon was a maverick. As I said, he's - was - a populist. He often gave the impression that he was choosing positions for maximum effect, and that sometimes got him into my bad books. He would usually come around, but he seemed to enjoy the chase, you know what I mean? A bit too much. He was fundamentally unpredictable, and you should never be able to say that about a half decent politician.'

'So he was a pain in the -' she stopped herself saying 'arse' just in time '- neck?'

'Sometimes. Look, I'm going to tell you something now, Inspector, something that really need go no further. It's a… throwback, if you like. In this day and age, it shouldn't be an issue. But, for some reason, it appears that it was - for him.'

'We've no reason to release any more information than we have to.'

She was proud of that reply. She should have been a politician.

'Damon was gay.'

As the man had said, why was that a problem these days? Practically every nick Alison had ever been in had a gay officer these days, either male or female. It was almost statutory. She had even heard of transsexual officers, some who preferred to be referred to using the pronoun 'they'. As broad minded as she considered herself to be, Alison could not get her head around that one.

'So why was that an issue?' she pondered.

'He wasn't 'out'. Is that the word for it?'

'He kept his being gay to himself? And his partner. Or partners.'

'Yes, that's right. He… certainly didn't have a regular, steady, partner. I think I would have known if he had. When I say it's a throwback, I mean 40, even 30 years ago, the Chief Whip would absolutely need to know where all the homosexuals could be found. They were regarded, particularly if they were anywhere near the security services, or defence, as a risk, potentially subject to blackmail, not to be trusted with classified information. Couldn't, therefore, become a senior minister, let's say. Banned by law in places like the FCO until the early 90s, you know. But since they've been 'out', what, 25 years now, there hasn't really been an issue around even senior ministers being gay. The weakness, the vulnerability, if there is any, comes from keeping the whole thing a secret. It's our job, as Government Whips, to know what our flock's vulnerabilities are; they're in the public eye, the media eye, whether they like it or not. We need to help them manage their secrets… especially if they can't manage them properly themselves. The press in particular are not always sympathetic to MPs with secrets… even Tory MPs with secrets.'

'So if they're out, if they admit to being gay, they're not a risk.'

'Not in the same way, no, that's right. Less of a risk, let's say. It's just habit, I suppose, that Whips continue to accumulate such information. But, as I say, Damon wasn't 'out', even if everyone - everyone in the House, at least, probably a few journalists, too - knew that he really was gay. And he was… prolific.'

'You mean he had lots of partners?'

'I believe so, one never knows these things for sure. I can't say I've spoken to him about it specifically. Big risk, what with AIDS and so on. And when someone is paying for it, paying for secrecy, in effect, that puts them into a different league again, security-wise.'

'And was he? Was he paying for it?'

'I'm not a hundred percent certain, to be honest. But I wouldn't be surprised. No, I wouldn't rule it out.'

'So what changed? He was living a certain lifestyle without -' again, she stopped herself from using a colloquialism such as 'topping' - 'without taking his own life, and then… he suddenly takes his own life. Why?'

The question was intended to be rhetorical. Mallory appeared to relax, but it was only an appearance. He entered reminiscence mode.

'You know, Gerald was fiercely anti… that sort of thing.'

'His father?'

'He'd been in the Navy, Gerald, he was a submariner. You know what they say about sailors, particularly submariners, but… well, I guess it takes you one way - or the other. With Gerald, it revolted him, the idea of men with men, and he wasn't slow or diplomatic in making his views known. I remember the last thing he said to me…'

'Sorry, Gerald? Or Damon?'

'Gerald. He was very pleased that Damon had a proper girlfriend. So much so that he rang me up, especially, to tell me. Damon was at university at the time, and she was a nice girl, Gerald said, very bright. He very much approved of her, though I'm not sure if he ever actually met her. This wasn't long before Gerald died. Apparently, they didn't stay together as a couple after Gerald passed away, which made me think, even back then, at the time, that Damon might have been, I don't know, putting on a show for his father. I'm sure it happens like that, doesn't it? Ever since then he's been exclusively into boys. Though he never boasted about it. Small mercy.'

'You don't remember her name?'

'After all this time? No. You know, I don't think I ever knew her name. I don't think Gerald ever knew very much about her, other than her being bright, and pleasant, and that she made Damon happy. Good wife material, he thought.'

Alison smiled ruefully: that was not her experience.

Mallory went on: 'They did speak on the telephone once, I believe, once Gerald had persuaded Damon to introduce her. That's about all I heard about her, just her very existence was what mattered to Gerald. He felt - I was going to say happy to have spoken to her, but that wasn't it. 'Happy' is not the word. Relieved. He felt relieved.'

Alison wondered if the odds on that connection being Kate Mellor, Damon's University contemporary, were shortening.

'May I ask how Gerald Hough…?'

Mallory's reticence was melting; he found himself telling the story he had earlier decided not to reveal.

'He jumped off a bridge, with a rope round his neck. Hung himself. In the middle of the day, a bridge over a motorway. Everyone that was driving by could see him… dangling, but no one who could see him could get to him… whilst anyone who might have been close by, on top of the bridge, wouldn't have seen what was happening beneath their own feet. He was hanging there for an hour, at peak time, apparently, before they got him down. Tragedy. A complete tragedy.'

'So, the involvement of a bridge is a parallel; how did Damon react to his father's death?'

The politician collected his thoughts, deciding how best not to answer the question.

'I went to Gerald's funeral. Damon wasn't there. I've never spoken to him about that. His mother died a couple of years later, she had cancer. Damon inherited everything, money, property, stocks, being an only child. Look, none of this…'

'I understand. Of course. This is all very valuable information for our investigation, though I see no reason to include any of this in any press statement. At this stage.'

'Is there anything else, Inspector?'

'Do you know for sure why Mr Hough, senior, killed himself? Was there a note?'

This time Mallory made no hesitation: 'Absolutely no idea. None. There was no note that I know of. I spoke to the mother, she was ill with cancer, as I said, but she had no idea either; she was totally shocked. I just assumed that his wife having terminal cancer had undermined his reason to live.'

If that was the case, it was odd that Gerald did not wait a little longer to see her off first, thought Alison. She could see no justification for pursuing that line of enquiry, but before she could redirect the conversation Mallory came out of his reverie.

'Look, Inspector, you rang me up to speak to the Chief Whip. I think that… I think that in fact you've been talking to the boy's godfather. I've told you… more than I intended to, and I suspect that's because… of the emotional connection that exists between - or used to exist - between myself and Damon's family. You will treat all this with discretion, won't you? Including about your sources…'

Alison was sympathetic: 'I see no reason why almost any of this needs…' she tailed off. Was that a sob she had just heard?

'Sir?'

'They've all gone, Inspector. None of the Houghs are left. They were a very fine, British family… Outstanding. Most of them.'

After a moment of uncomfortable silence decorum was resumed. There was only one issue left to sort. They spoke of the mechanics of a press release and Alison was more grateful than she let on when Mallory suggested that the Conservative Party would handle the media, rather than the police. He saw no need for a press conference as such at all, which was a further relief. Even if there were to be one, if there was a lot of media interest, which he doubted, there was no reason for the constabulary to be there. It would be better if they were somewhere else, Mallory said, catching villains.

This was the outcome Alison's Superintendent had hoped to achieve and which she was more than happy to accept.

'Thank you, Mr Mallory. Again, my condolences.'

'Thank you, Inspector. Thank you.'

Mallory put the telephone down.

Quietly seething, he muttered to himself 'Bugger. Bugger. Bugger!' Then, a little louder, loud enough to wake his wife's tiny Shih Tzu from its slumber: 'Fuck!' He stood, rising from the couch and sending the animal tumbling ignominiously onto the rug in front of a cold, grey, lifeless fireplace. He clenched his fists as the wise dog sought refuge behind the sofa, and his body shook. Images ran through Mallory's head, cascading, kaleidoscopic, historic but very real images that pierced his heart: Gerald, bold and handsome in his submariner's formal uniform. Jane, the night before she married Gerald, so beautiful, smiling but with a tear in her eye; Jane again, nursing the cutest little baby boy, who looked so like his mother. And then: the actual last time he ever saw Gerald, his hair smeared to his head to hide his pate, his moustache looking so bloody inappropriate. That had been the same night that Gerald Hough had told him, through gritted teeth, that the two men would never speak together again.

By dint of this history, and the difficult decisions he had been preparing to take, now rendered otiose, he cursed the lack of urgency by the testing laboratory in processing the DNA that he had requested, more than a week earlier.

'Fucking little shit!' he murmured.

Punching the air as he expelled each word through a rictus pseudo grin, Mallory yelled 'Fucking little bastard shit!'

The dog, still startled by his ignominious tumble, now sought refuge further away still, cowering beneath a table.

Paul Roe, Honourable Gentleman:

Friday 22nd April

Paul Roe was first elected to Parliament in 2015 and re-elected as a Labour MP at each election since. He was enjoying life immensely, apart from the obvious fact that the green, leather-bound bench upon which he habitually sat was to Mr Speaker's left, on the Opposition side of the Commons chamber.

Yet he had a positive outlook. He was, after all, the proud possessor of a safe seat in a freestanding industrial town west of London, a seat that had been in his party's gift, almost without interruption, since time immemorial. It was conveniently located a long way, geographically, from the disputed and volatile so-called red or blue 'wall' that was perceived to split the north down the middle these days. His five-digit majority, even in difficult times, was sound security - as long as he and his friends in the Party leadership played their cards right. Paul was a natural optimist: life would get even better, he knew, when a majority in Parliament would deliver him and his Party back into power! After a rocky few years, in which the newly established Member had kept his distance from the then leadership after his election in 2015, the road ahead now looked clear; but only as long as sense prevailed on the front bench and shoulders continued to be applied to the common political wheel.

He saw it therefore as a reward from the new people at the top - for his ideas, energy and commitment - that in the January 2022 reshuffle he had been granted access to the Holy Grail, a place on the front bench; he was now Labour's spokesperson on tackling poverty. It was more than satisfying to be a junior member of the team shadowing the ministers of the Department for Work and Pensions and he would be very happy if his position were morphed into that of 'Minister of State' after the next election. There could be no more important challenge than ridding the nation of unnecessary, degrading, life-draining poverty. Not only was it a matter of absolute principle but it was a perennially popular cause amongst the Labour demographics, too.

Paul believed that his appointment marked the return of the Party to the mainstream of politics; yes, he wanted to see the economy and society transformed in the direction of justice, equality and efficiency, call it 'socialism' if you like, but he saw that road as evolutionary and not revolutionary. What was it that the great free thinker, one of his heroes, Thomas Huxley, had said, in a letter to The Times in 1890? 'And what is socialism but an incarnation of the social question?' Quite. Every pitch Paul ever made, in every policy debate, was aimed at the centre ground. This was not to pander to indecision and ineffectiveness, qualities he associated with those who only occupied that space in order not to offend anyone, but to win the hearts and minds of those ordinary people who might have occupied it in the past. 'If we can't win over some of the people who voted Tory last time, we're lost,' was how he described his *modus operandi*. He was delighted that his Party now, at last, appeared to agree.

Paul had been 'pitching' ever since leaving university, early in the new millennium, initially delivering ideas to clients in the advertising world. His progress had been rapid, putting his English degree to use as he utilised language to promote and persuade, moving on every time the going in a particular office got… boring. 'Pitching' was such a wonderful word! In his favourite sport you pitched a cricket ball to confuse and deceive your opponent; you pitched your tent on your opponents' ground to claim territory for your own, a lovely political metaphor; but in recent years politics had seen too much pitching like a cork on the tide, a boat in a storm, as when cruel and terrible waves challenge your own sense of direction. At times it had felt like walking through pitch… At last, these days, they were in calmer waters.

Paul's rapid professional rise, during which he never stayed at one agency for more than three years, came to the attention of the Labour Party when the agency which employed him was commissioned to work for them over the period up to the 2015 election. Paul was able to take credit both for landing the account and leading the delivery team: a taste of heaven! He was a longstanding (though not over-enthusiastic) card-carrying member of the Party at the time, living in the constituency of Bill Grey, the former minister from back in the Blair years. Had he but known it, he was in both the right place and the right time.

In the February of 2015 a heart attack put the elderly Grey out of the running for the upcoming election, so the Party needed to find a new candidate in a safe seat, at short notice. Many big, well-known names, those who had spent the last year circling plum seats like vultures, had by then found the seats of their dreams. That cleared the way for two long standing local councillors from different wings of the Party to slug it out for the right to represent Grey's haven for the rest of their lives, should they choose to do so - if they played their cards right. Roe was but a mere branch secretary at the time, a role he had assumed six months previously on the not unreasonable grounds that he could do the job so much better than his predecessor, with half the fuss.

These skills plus a charming smile, boundless energy and a natural gift of the gab (aka a professional way with words), allowed the unknown young man to come through the middle. As different shades of councillor red punched each other black and blue in gladiatorial combat the patient, reasonable, Roe took centre stage: and the Party membership granted him the right to contest the seat on their behalf.

Truth be told, the branch secretaryship had been entered into as some consolation for his recent relationship status change, from 'occupied' to 'vacant'. In their five years of living together Rosemary, known as Rose or even Roe's Rose, had shown little inclination to become Rose Roe; nor was she as enthusiastic a Red Rose as he was a Red Roe. She, too, had worked in advertising: they had met in their early years in the trade, the hard working, hard drinking, hard shagging years that were standard at that time, in that London-based profession. Years later they had met again and fallen in… to the ways of a couple, before gradually falling out of them again. Then Rose's idea to emigrate to New Zealand suddenly emerged, with the purpose of… Paul could not recall if she had ever actually told him why she was going. Until three weeks before she left, he was sure she had never mentioned her plans. Or perhaps she had, and Paul had not noticed, which would explain a lot. It was probably for the best, for all concerned, for her to go, he reasoned to himself - and to anyone else who would listen. The house was registered in his name, not theirs, there were no children to worry about and no messy divorce was required. It was now many months since he had become free to commit his energy and passion entirely to his current loves: politics, Parliament and public life.

Damon Hough had been in the House for five years before Paul Roe came along. Paul was aware of this flamboyant, illiberal, right wing hot head from his own study of Parliament when working for the Labour Party and preparing for his candidacy. At first, he could not believe that this could be the same quiet friend in whose company he had spent several formative years. Although they had lived in different London boroughs, with different postcodes, the boys' homes were only a quarter of a mile apart and they were in the same year at both junior and comprehensive schools. Between the ages of 8 and 14 they had been - if not exactly inseparable - friends of significant closeness. However, when they chose different options for their public exams Paul had not been heartbroken to move on to friendships new. Damon had left school at 16 to go to a sixth form college which taught 'A' level law, which their local comp did not offer. It was not until 2015, 17 years later, that their paths crossed once more.

When they did meet again there was no embrace, no tears of joy, no laughter in common appreciation of times gone by. There was no 'Is it really you?' The encounter took place in the Upper Committee Corridor of the House of Commons in May 2015. It was Paul's third day in Westminster, early in Damon's sixth year.

Paul looked up as he carried a pile of documents towards the committee room which had been designated a temporary base for new members waiting to be allocated an office on the Parliamentary estate. Approaching him was a man with a familiar face, featuring a coiffured rage of blond hair with distinguished grey temples and long, narrow sideburns, which crept down his cheeks like fingers constantly caressing a lover.

The meeting was inevitable: despite being 'home' to 658 elected Members Parliament is still a small world. Paul had judged that this astral conjunction would occur sooner rather than later: and here they were.

'Hello there, Damon.'

Hough was scanning the front page of an early edition of the Evening Standard as he walked: he stopped short upon being addressed and looked Paul directly in the eye. Paul felt like he was being looked through rather than at; his visage clearly meant nothing to the more experienced Member.

'Paul Roe', the new boy prompted, feeling self-conscious in his brown work-suit with an open-necked shirt. The Tory was in immaculate pinstripe, silver braid on his waistcoat and a pale yellow, extravagant tie restrained by a silver pin. The tie was intended to stand out a mile on the television monitors which recorded and broadcast every moment of life in the Commons chamber.

'We were at school together?'

'Well… hello…' drawled Damon, realising that he ought to recognise the newcomer. He had almost forgotten that he had been to state school; his comprehensive origins were something to which he had never publicly admitted. 'Paul… yes, of course. Now, what are you doing here?'

The newly Honourable Member, his Parliamentary identity pass and lanyard clearly visible, nevertheless introduced himself properly.

'Just elected,' he concluded, smiling. 'Bill Grey's old seat.' His hands were full, clutching files, making a handshake impossible. But then, he remembered, MPs never shake hands with each other. Historically, shaking hands is a way of showing the other chap that you have no weapon, that you mean him no harm. Members of Parliament, Honourable Members, trust each other implicitly - or they did in the days of the civil war, when Parliamentarians were united against the crown - and thus they have no need to demonstrate such faith in each other.

'Well, well… Paul Roe. So, Bill Grey… that means you're working for the other side?'

It was a disappointing response, tinged with sneer - surely, they were colleagues now, of a sort?

'I guess I am!'

'Well, good luck,' said Damon, without even a smile. 'Look, I've got to go now, but we'll catch up, yes?'

'Yes, that would be -'

'We'll catch up. Got to go,' and off he went, with an exaggerated wink and an extended arm giving a 'thumbs up' sign. All this was conducted with no expression replacing that slightly relaxed, slightly offended bemusement which Paul's initial intervention had prompted.

A few yards further on, Damon stopped and turned to face Paul: who had by now disappeared. 'Of course,' he said to himself, then mouthed silently the word 'Pinko'.

They did catch up. They met outdoors on the Terrace overlooking the Thames, one summer evening a few weeks later, between votes. Looking back on it, the occasion - a pint of guest ale for Paul, a double vodka and tonic for Damon - achieved no more than confirming how little the two men now had in common. Over the next seven years their paths inevitably crossed from time to time - they had a common interest in footpaths and the All-Party Group on Rambling, the odd Parliamentary delegation, but little else. Occasionally they would nod to each other across a sterile committee room during the routine scrutiny of a government bill, such was the lot of the anonymous backbencher. None of this could be considered as rekindling a bond, but perhaps that was just as well…

Paul enjoyed the chamber of the House and tried to speak whenever he could, but the pecking order for speeches was long and the opportunities for a newcomer rare, once the ritual of the maiden speech had been performed. On one occasion, however, he managed four mentions in Hansard in one day! They involved a scheduled question to a minister, a time-limited 6-minute speech on planning regulations and two unplanned interventions on other speakers. In one instance he was friendly and supportive, giving a colleague the chance to breathe, think and then shine, whilst the other was a withering, hostile take-down of a government spokesman. The Chamber was an important public arena where it was necessary for Paul to be seen, but not all the time. There was so much else to do in this, his dream role of Member of Parliament. Damon, on the other hand, appeared to inhabit the gothic forum, he was as at home on the green benches as Dracula in his coffin. Hough was a perennial heckler, a joker on the Tory back benches, a provocative and witty right winger of disappointingly little substance, Paul thought. On one occasion Damon was speaking at length on the opportunities created by Brexit. From any other mouth the contribution would have been regarded as the gut response of a brainless politician, even a parody, but Damon's single positive, acknowledged attribute was his consistency. Several times Paul's request to intervene on him was shunned: there was no rule that said childhood friendships had to be acknowledged across the chamber. Being ignored was disappointing. On balance, Paul later reasoned, perhaps being ignored was better than being publicly splayed by the hostile scimitar that was Damon Hough's icy tongue.

Working with constituents was one of the most rewarding aspects of being an MP, Paul found, and he particularly enjoyed the advice surgeries which he held in various places around his patch. They were organised on two Friday evenings each month and the following Saturday mornings, and they took account of the security concerns that MPs could no longer avoid. Such a commitment, twelve months of every year and whether the House was sitting or not, would have played havoc with family life, had he had one. 'My constituents are my family,' he had been known to say, often sincerely. Representing a market town with a strong industrial base, relatively close to London, meant that his casework mountain was manageable: in charge of that task was Carol Hayes, his constituency office manager. Carol had been with Paul since day one and she gave similar support, albeit voluntarily and very part time, to her husband Joe, a longstanding Labour councillor and Paul's mentor in his early days in politics.

Paul's office was situated on a popular shopping street, convenient for all concerned, in a former shop. His staff would arrange 15-minute surgery appointments within a two-hour block, ensure that any pre-existing case files were available, take notes whilst Paul interviewed the constituents, write the notes up onto a database and oversee the technical production of any arising correspondence. Often these were standard letters, but Paul took a personal interest in every individual he met, and his input was often invaluable. He could usually add more coherence, contacts and insight to a case than constituents could manage without him. Notepaper headed 'MP' often facilitated the repositioning of a file from the bottom of a bureaucrat's in-tray to the top; this was perhaps the most important service an MP could offer to those who sought his help.

By far the bulk of all the MP's casework came not from these personal meetings but from mail. Much of it received a standard response - 'I am forwarding your letter to minister X (or council official Y)'. Those who had signed a particular petition might receive a common response processed by the office but anything that was specific to the constituent, or the locality, would be put aside for Paul to see before processing. In addition, councillors and other Labour activists would frequently pass on case work that was 'above their pay grade'. Thank heavens, thought Carol, she had two competent and attentive part time staff helping her to service this weight of correspondence!

In managing Paul's constituency diary Carol also worked in conjunction with Henry, the only other full-time member of staff. Officially Paul's 'Community Liaison' officer, Henry was a natural organiser who had worked for a student union for two years after graduating before joining the MP's team. Still only 25 years old, Henry's energy was already legendary; his ambition was to be a Labour councillor here, in the town where he had grown up, and where he was standing, for the first time, in the upcoming local elections. His job was to manage events, oversee anything that could be loosely described as campaigning and liaise with the media and the Party. Paul's Fridays would invariably include an hour's chat with Henry - either during the working day or, if the diary allowed, in the pub at the end of it - to review the week in politics. Their political views and their values were closely aligned, which was no coincidence.

The final member of the team was the recently divorced Hazel. She worked 20 hours a week in Paul's London office, much reduced in Parliament's non-sitting weeks, respecting her childcare duties. She oversaw Paul's Westminster activities, not least ensuring that he was wherever and whenever the weekly Whip required him to be. The 'Whip' was technically a coloured sheet of paper with each vote underlined once, twice or three times for emphasis. God help those who ignored, forgot or broke a three-line whip.

As a single mother, Hazel much appreciated the flexibility of working for an MP. For at least one session in each sitting week - often two - she would come into Paul's Portcullis House office in the House of Commons. Her boy was by now almost a teenager, her marriage was a dull memory, and her professional life was fulfilled; she loved her job.

Maureen Greatbach was one of Paul Roe's constituents. Maureen was 60 years old and married to Nigel, who was approaching retirement from his role as a senior manager in a supermarket. Maureen herself had recently retired as a civil servant in the Employment Service and the couple could reasonably be described as 'comfortable'. Neither had a particularly high profile, in their communities or elsewhere, and both were generally satisfied with their lots. They had two sons, one in Scotland and one in America, and often used their computers for family get togethers. But not too often. Maureen believed that privacy was precious, and their children were entitled to the same consideration as they would like to be granted themselves.

Maureen thought long and hard about how she voted at every election: she could see the sense in austerity as long as it did not impact her, her family or the poor people for whom she helped collect food parcels at Christmas, through her church. She was very keen on Labour's priority of helping all those children who were starving in developing countries - but the Party was under the thumb of the unions, she believed, nor had she known where they really stood on Brexit, that most important issue of the era. It was all very confusing. Such considerations had not helped her resolve her own lifelong equivocation about voting. At the last election she had considered both major parties' manifestos very carefully, reading both from cover to cover, and then done what she always did - voted

Liberal Democrat. Well, it was a compromise, and who could complain about compromise?

When Mrs Greatbach came through the office door at 6.45 p.m. on Friday 22nd April 2022, Paul greeted her politely, warmly and in a business-like manner. He introduced Carol, who was there to take notes, having briefly acquainted himself with Maureen's details on his iPad: name, address, gender… first time customer. Legal issue. Nothing else - such as that she could talk for England - was known.

'So… what can I do for you, Mrs Greatbach - have I pronounced that correctly?'

'Oh, yes.' Maureen smiled, timorously. 'Well, it's about my mother, I wouldn't normally bother you about something like this, but… well, it's annoying me, it's wrong and something needs to be done about it.'

'I see…'

'She's nearly ninety. She was widowed twenty years ago, when my father died…'

'Obviously', thought Paul, saying nothing. This was his last appointment of the evening and Henry would be waiting for him in the pub in half an hour. He was looking forward to their chat, marking the end of another busy week.

'And she's been in a care home for five years now.'

'So is that the problem, the care home?'

'No, no, they're fine. A very nice couple. They only have six people, six residents, the couple that run it, it's very pleasant. A tad expensive, I suppose, but mum can afford it.'

'I see.'

'She always did have independent means, you see, she always had her own account quite separate from my father's. Until he died, of course, and then she inherited his account, too. She was an only child and her parents - that's my grandparents, of course - well, they were quite well to do, you might say, in that they owned property.'

'OK…'

'Not a lot of people did in those days, not where they came from…'

Was the full 'rags to riches' story about to come out? Paul hoped not.

Maureen smiled, as though she was awaiting a prompt to carry on. Paul was already fighting an incipient frustration: get on with it!

'So this would be, the reason you're here to see me, is to do with… I'm sorry, you're going to have to guide me here.'

Carol intervened, helpfully, though it was not her normal practice to do so: 'What's your mother's name?'

'Hilda. Hilda Smith. She hasn't got a middle name.'

Carol continued 'And does she live locally?'

'No. No, she lives a hundred or so miles away.' She named another market town, on the other side of London. 'Enemy territory,' thought Paul, 'Tory heartlands.' He was sure that his judgment was right, but his nerd status was not sufficiently developed to be able to state exactly which blue-rinser represented that postcode. However, he felt wary: the mother was not his constituent, so he felt he would have to prove that any intervention he might make was in Maureen's interest rather than simply Hilda's. Either that or recruit Hilda's own MP to the cause.

He took the bull by the horns: 'And... what's the actual problem here? How can I help?'

'It's the Power of Attorney. You see, my mother has dementia, and - well, the money she has doesn't need a lot of looking after. It looks after itself, really. What happens is, one of the accounts, her current account, receives the income from her investments, along with her pension. She was advised to sell the property and put the money into investments when managing the properties got too much for her, you understand. And all together that's enough, you know, to pay for the care home. And a few little luxuries. And to pay the solicitor.'

'So your mother is not actually a constituent of mine, which... you know', Paul was trying to be tactful. 'It sounds like you might need to talk to a lawyer rather than an MP.'

Carol intervened again, this time to Paul: 'I think what Mrs Greatbach is trying to say is that her mother has dementia and can't handle her finances herself, so it's up to Mrs Greatbach here to do that for her, and maybe that's where the problem lies.'

'Yes, sort of,' said the woman, dropping her confused expression in favour of a smile in Carol's direction. 'That's the problem.'

Paul took back control of the conversation: 'You mentioned Power of Attorney - which is why I thought maybe a lawyer could help - you have Power of Attorney for your mother?'

'Well, no, I don't.'

'There's a Mr Greatbach?'

'My husband, Nigel? Oh yes.'

'Does he have Power of Attorney?'

Now the woman was showing early signs of frustration. 'No, he doesn't.'

'So... tell me about the Power of Attorney. What's the problem?'

'I have a brother, called Maurice. There's just the two of us.'

Thank God there aren't more! thought Paul. We could be here all night.

'He's a few years older than me. I've not seen him for years, to be quite honest with you. He lives in Norfolk. And when my father died - Maurice and my father didn't get on - well, nothing happened.'

Now it was Paul's turn to look confused.

'Nothing happened?'

'When I say nothing happened, I mean my mother has always looked after her own money, she used to move it around, you know, to take advantage of changing interest rates and so on, she had quite a broad... what do they call it? Portillo... no, portfolio, that's it. As long as there was enough money coming into that current account, the one I told you about, all the rest was just... accumulating.'

'Which you and your brother would eventually inherit? That doesn't sound like a problem to me!'

Carol flashed Paul a look which said 'She's worried. Don't belittle her concerns. We'll get there.'

Maureen went on 'As I said, my mother has dementia. She was diagnosed shortly after she went into the care home, I mean, we knew there was something, we knew she wasn't quite right, and it was quite a relief when we got the diagnosis. They're fine about it, in the care home, looking after people with dementia is what they do, so that's not the problem. She'll need a bit more care, of course, as time goes on, and they might well have to charge a bit more, but that's all right, as I said, she can afford it. Anyway...'

It was as though Maureen had stopped to think.

'Anyway... at that point we thought, what's the right thing to do? We should get Power of Attorney. The idea was that my brother and I would have it and between us we could decide whatever was best for our mum. But Maurice didn't want that: he told me he didn't want anything to do with her until the day came for the reading of her Will. I was quite shocked, I can tell you. Surprised. Upset! And he wouldn't tell her that, you know, not to her face. So, the idea was that I would do the Power of Attorney alone, and Maurice was happy about that, which also quite surprised me. I thought he was going to argue, it doesn't take much to get Maurice arguing. But he just said 'whatever you want, you do it, Mo.' He calls me Mo. No one else does and I don't really like it. It's not a respectful name, is it? Reminds me of that woman on the telly.'

Paul smiled directly at her, leaning forward in his chair. He only found himself wondering which 'Mo' she had in mind, very briefly, before dismissing the thought.

'This sounds quite painful, but I'm still not sure I see the problem... You were going to get the Power of Attorney - but it didn't work out?'

'No, because of the snow. It was snowing. Quite badly... I mean, we only have to drive a few miles, and then it's motorway nearly all the way, but it was snowing so badly that we were late. We don't normally get too much snow around here, do we?'

He ignored the question. 'Late for... when was this?'

'February, about three years back. I said we should cancel, but Nigel's a proud driver, he loves his car - I sometimes joke that he loves that car more than he loves me!' Maureen laughed quietly to herself. 'I couldn't even tell you what make it is. Anyway, Nigel wasn't going to let a bit of snow defeat him. And he was right; we did get there, in the end, but we were about an hour and a half late. It was thawing quite rapidly by then, so it was much less trouble getting home, even though it had gone dark. Nigel knows the roads very well.'

'Late for what?'

'We'd arranged to meet the solicitor, with mum, at the home, of course. Now that's Mr Steel: he's always been the solicitor for my mum's family, ever since I can remember. He's getting on a bit himself, actually. We were going to meet at the care home, that's me, Nigel, my mum and Mr Steel. As I said, she's got dementia and there'd be no doubt about that now, I mean if you saw her today, you'd know, straight away. I can't get a sensible word out of her these days. But back then, it was three years ago, on a Monday, I do remember it was a Monday. And we were late.'

'So the meeting didn't happen?'

'Oh yes, it happened. Well, my mother still had some wits about her back then and she told... well, it wasn't actually Mr Steel. I think maybe he's retired now, maybe he's not around anymore, Mr Steel, I don't know. It was the snow, he wasn't keen on going out in the snow, so a different solicitor came out instead. A younger man, someone who wouldn't find walking on the snow a problem. He didn't have to come very far, it's only ten minutes' walk from the solicitor's office - it's in the Market Place, I don't know if you know that area?'

Paul shook his head.

'No, well, he came, and he was on time, but we were an hour and a half late, as I said. We rang the home, of course, so they knew we were going to be late, and they told the solicitor, but he couldn't wait for us.'

Paul had a feeling that the story was reaching a conclusion, that he would soon know what was being asked of him. He would be patient. Carol was busily making notes.

'I'd written to Mr Steel and explained that my brother didn't want to do the Power of Attorney thing so that, if it was all right with my mother - which I was sure it was going to be, I would do it by myself. Nigel could help me, of course, if needs be. But I would legally be the Power of Attorney. It was time to do it, what with the dementia, the diagnosis, and so on.'

'That sounds reasonable…'

'But when we got there, he'd gone, the solicitor. He'd been there on time, he'd known we were on our way, but I guess the young man was busy and couldn't wait. Probably had other people to see. And my mum said it was all right, that everything had been sorted and that he'd been a very nice young man. So that was all right… it wasn't until we were on the way home - we stayed for a cup of tea with mum, but what with the weather and us being late, we didn't want to stop too long. On the way home, I said to Nigel: 'How can it be all sorted? I haven't signed anything'.'

At last, thought Paul, an air of mystery…

'So, the next day I rang Mr Steel, but his secretary said he wasn't available, and neither was the young man who'd come out to see my mum. I explained what the problem was, and why I was concerned, and why hadn't I had to sign anything? She said if there was any signing to be done then she would send me the form and I asked about having my signature witnessed, and she said she was sure that wouldn't be a problem. A couple of days later a letter arrived from the solicitor and I was shocked! Really shocked! It said that after discussion with Mrs Smith - that's my mum - it had been agreed that ideally the Power of Attorney should be held by both of her children - that's me and Maurice. Well, we knew that was true - ideally - but it wasn't going to happen. The letter said that whilst technically mum had been subject to a diagnosis of dementia it was early stages and she was still in sound mind, so it hadn't been necessary for her to be accompanied by a family member in the meeting. She was deemed to be capable of making a decision. And that decision was that because Maurice had said no then I shouldn't have the Power by myself; it was either both of us or neither, was what they said my mum had said.'

'You said her dementia is worse now, so who has the PoA now?'

'Well, at the end of the letter it said that the solicitor would have the Power of Attorney, and attached to the letter was a copy of a note, handwritten by her, saying that this was what she wanted. It was dated on the day we visited, it was signed by her and witnessed by the gentleman who runs the home. It granted the solicitor the Power of Attorney, and the note also said that he would be paid £100 for taking that on.'

'That sounds like quite a common arrangement, isn't it?'

'Well, that's right. And I didn't have a problem with it, not in theory. You do have to pay for a solicitor's time, don't you?' But not an MP's time, thought Paul. Maureen went on: 'We all knew that me and my brother would never agree to the ideal arrangement. I knew Mr Steel of old, he's always been my mum's solicitor, and always been very reasonable. I'm sure he would listen to any views I might have with regards to my mother's interests. I assumed this other chap would be the same - well, you would, wouldn't you? Even when I realised it wasn't just a hundred pounds, I wasn't too worried. As I said, she could afford it.'

Carol spoke: 'If it wasn't a hundred, what was it?'

'Well, it was a hundred pounds - but it was a hundred pounds a month.'

'For doing what?' asked Paul.

'Managing her portfolio. Making sure that she got the best possible return from her investments. It was a 'service charge', it said.'

Paul frowned.

'And then last week I got another letter, and this is why I'm here now, coming to see you. Nigel said I ought to. I did say Mr Steel's semi-retired now, didn't I? But it's still signed 'Steel and Partners'. They used to be called Steel and Grey, but Mr Grey's been gone a very long time. He was a nice chap, too. Look, I've brought it with me…'

Paul felt a lot of time could have been saved if this letter had been produced earlier, but he treated it seriously, taking it when the woman proffered it. He read it aloud so that Carol could hear.

'Dear... dar, dar, dar... your mother, Mrs Smith... here we go: 'In the light of the uncertain economic climate it has been necessary for us to carry out more work on Mrs Smith's investment than we had anticipated over recent months and -'

Maureen Greatbach was suddenly quite emotional. 'I wasn't having this. They're scraping the barrel they are, money for old rope, it's money for nothing. It's blackmail, Mr Roe. I spoke to the young gentleman, I got through this time, and do you know what he said?' She continued as she searched her handbag for a handkerchief; finding it, she dabbed her eyes. 'The contract that Mrs Smith signed, he said, allows them to vary the fees! And because she's now beyond the point that she can be responsible for things like this, and they have the Power of Attorney, there's nothing I can do about it!'

Paul was lost for words. Carol was not: she was leaning over and studying the document in Paul's hands. She turned to him and said under her breath: 'They've raised the fees'. Paul returned his attention to the letter. It said:

'We have found it necessary to implement a rise in our monthly portfolio service charge. As from the first instant Mrs Smith's charge will be £300 per calendar month, including VAT, collected as per the existing arrangement. We will implement this charge accordingly under the existing Power of Attorney that we hold.'

Paul felt a letter to the Law Society coming on; was this proper, was it ethical?

Eyes welling up with tears, Maureen said 'I told him I wanted the Power of Attorney back, that I wanted to cancel the contract, but he said I couldn't. It was all there in black and white, he said, I'm not - what did he say? I'm not a party to the contract, so I can't cancel it. And there was a copy of the contract - it's there, on the second page - and it's signed by my mum. It's dated the day after that meeting happened, three years ago. He'd gone back to his office, if you ask me, made all this up to suit himself, written it out and gone back there to mum and had her sign it the next day, without telling me.'

'Well,' said Paul, 'Even if there's nothing legal that can be done, I think we can try to appeal to this man's better nature, you know, family values, and get him to relinquish his hold over your mum - and over your money, because half of it's yours, after all.'

But there may be a price to that, Paul surmised...

'Let's hope we can do that, Mrs Greatbach,' said Carol.

'Thank you, Mr Roe, I'm just so pleased I've been able to talk to someone!' But the tears now running down her cheek were not tears of joy.

Paul took charge: 'May I keep a copy of this letter? Thank you. Carol, could you… oh, hang on…'

As he handed over the letter to Carol, who would make the copy using the machine in the outer office, he noticed a detail that he had previously overlooked. The letter was signed in ink but with little more than a large tick, above the printed name 'Steel & Partners, LLP'. In the small print at the foot of the page were the names of the partners: James Steel Snr, Alice Brain, Indira Sharma and Damon Hough.

It did not take a detective to work out which of the solicitors was the 'young man' who had done the dirty on Paul Roe's constituent.

Pub Quiz - Henry & Paul:
Friday 22ⁿᵈ April

'Mr Roe! One pint of foaming ale in a splendid baroque tankard is, at this very moment, heading in your esteemed direction!'
'Sorry I'm late, Henry.'
'You're supposed to say: 'if it's ba-roken then get me one that isn't'.'
'Am I? Sorry.'
'Broke: baroque. As Americans say it.'
'Sorry.'
Henry was already at the bar and the two pints were nearly poured - in conventional glass jugs - as Paul came through the pub door, slightly breathless after hurrying from the advice surgery.
'You were not late. You were serving the Great British public, my dear sir, their whim trumps my humble needs on every occasion - bar none. You may be behind schedule, but you are never late.'
Paul was not sure he liked this occasional affectation of unctuous humility, which he thought demeaned the young man unnecessarily, even if it was delivered with tongue firmly in cheek. But he also knew that it was a game that Henry sometimes played which, perversely, underlined the excess of confidence that he exuded at every other moment, when he was not playacting. And he did do it well. It could even be funny, in small doses. Together with his wispy, half-formed goatee, the beard that had grown not a centimetre in all the time the MP had known his campaign manager, verbal dexterity was the young man's defining feature. Usually, he would merge into the background, leaving Paul to occupy centre stage whilst ensuring that every logistical I had been dotted and T crossed. He was very good at his job, whether schmoozing reporters on the local rag, drafting a flowery press release or telling a shadow Secretary of State's office what time their Master or Mistress had to arrive in Paul's constituency - or else. He had a confidence and a gravity - when it suited him - that belied his 26 years, and he could talk persuasively for England on the detail of politics.

They each took their pint, navigating a slightly uneven, stone-flagged floor ('It's flat after a couple') in the former coaching inn. It was not difficult to find an unoccupied table.

There was an exchange of trivial pleasantries, even though they had been working in the same office barely hours earlier, and they dissected a few topics, ranging from the behaviour of rebels on both sides at the week's key vote, to Henry's mother's imminent and significant birthday and Labour's prospects in the forthcoming local elections. Paul was waiting to be told what he had already gleaned from the grapevine: that local polling suggested that Henry was in line to win a seat on the council in May at the first attempt, and he did not want to steal the young man's thunder. Sure enough, a suddenly proud and humble Henry told him the figures and Paul did not disappoint him by revealing that he was already acquainted with them.

The second pint, Paul's round, was going down nicely but it would have to be the last for tonight. He was suddenly ravenously hungry - as he often found at the end of a day in which the adrenalin had flowed, which was most days.

There was something nagging Paul that he had to get off his chest. There would be no opportunity over the weekend to have the ear of a confidant and he had to get this sorted in his mind before returning to the Commons.

'Henry, what do you think about MPs who have second jobs?'

The younger man put that mock puzzled look on his face, the one where he pursed his lips and his eyes swivelled from side to side before answering. There was no Scooby-Doo in sight.

'Why, has someone offered you a seat on the gravy train? How much?'

'No such luck! I mean, you see ex-ministers getting paid a hundred grand a year in consultancy fees for unspecified duties, five hours a week, with a big corporation, whilst still getting a pretty decent MP's salary. That's one level. I just can't see how you can give someone 120 percent of their MP's pay and then claim that their views aren't being swayed, to put it euphemistically. For Christ's sake, you've bought them, and that was the intention all along.'

'Yup. Guess so. I think 'bought' is the right word.'

'Indeed,' Paul agreed.

'It's worse in America. US companies spend over five million dollars a year per Congressman - on average - on their combined lobbying efforts.'

'Really? The state of the States is of little consolation, Henry. We're heading in that direction here.'

'Or a former PM can get ten grand for an hour's speaking engagement. It happens all the time', Henry observed. 'But not to you, Paul!' Mock sympathy.

'I'd do it for two grand!' This was a joke.

'Cheapskate! You're underselling yourself.'

'But that's not the point, Henry. I'm talking about big money, and it's not right.'

'So would you ban all outside earnings for MPs?'

'That's a really difficult question. There are rules that mean ministers can't earn loads that way - not whilst they're ministers, at least, though they make up for it when they leave office, more than often. On the other hand, you can't turn round and tell an established journalist who becomes an MP that he or she should never be paid five hundred for a column ever again - can you?'

'Well, I wouldn't. Covered this stuff in my degree. I wrote an essay on 'cash for questions', you know, Hamilton and all that?'

'1996? I started my GCSE courses that year! I remember, all right.'

'You're showing your age, Paul, that was the year I was born! Anyway, don't MPs have to report any extra income in the register of interests?'

'Yes, they do. I heard of one MP declaring three jars of honey he'd been given by a constituent who had an apiary, but I think he was taking the piss.'

'Bees-waxing lyrical.'

Paul took a moment to appreciate the pun and groaned appropriately, then returned to his theme.

'Seriously, Henry, in days of old the House of Commons never used to sit in the mornings - they always started at half past two in the afternoon. Do you know why?'

'Yes, I do.'

'Yeah, I knew you would! That politics degree serves you well - at pub quizzes.'

'So the MPs could appear in court in the mornings, so many of them were lawyers,' the young man confirmed.

'They weren't paid for being MPs in those days.'

'No, that started in 1911, when they got £400 a year.'

'A pound a day! I thought it was earlier than that...'

'No, Paul. 1911 Parliament Act. Paying a wage to MPs was a longstanding demand of the Chartist movement, to enable people on low incomes to stand for election.'

'And counter the corrupt influence of benefactors.'

'Indeed.'

'So even that took, what, 70 years to achieve? Anyway... Do you know Damon Hough?'

'Piece of shit, pardon my French, nasty little right winger. Monday Clubber. Do they still have a Monday Club?'

'Gosh, do I know something you don't? No, its links to the Tories were severed about twenty years ago. Anyway, Damon Hough's name came up in my advice surgery this evening.'

'You don't encourage your constituents to swear, do you?'

'Seriously...' that was enough. Henry got the message that flippancy was over. 'It's a tricky one. It looks like he's practicing as a solicitor in his spare time - that's another thing, how can these people even have the time to do two jobs? Being an MP takes me nine days a week already! It's not on his own patch, I think his is the constituency next door to where this lady's mother lives. We can check these things -'

'On it,' said Henry, taking out his mobile phone, 'I'll check the Register of Interests.' His thumbs raced furiously across its surface while Paul took out his own phone and typed 'Steel Partners LLP' into Google. The four partners and their office address were not only listed but their photographs were prominent on the site, too. 'It's him, all right', said Paul.

'And... here he is, Paul. Register of Financial Interests, Damon Hough, Category 1, 'Employment and earnings'... several figures. A few hours a month with the solicitor's practice, not huge. But add these figures up and it's about five grand since September! Not a bad hourly rate, why don't you pay me that much? No, I know why, you're all right. Oh, look, he's got two flats that he rents out in Eastbourne, too.'

'Really?'

'So, what's the story, Boss? I don't need the constituent's name, obviously'.

Paul outlined the bones of what he had been told and Henry did not need anything repeating. Twice the younger man asked succinctly for clarification; the two had a good rapport and the information was shared efficiently between them.

Paul concluded his story: 'I thought £100 a month was bad enough, we've no idea what he does for the money, if anything at all. A good investment doesn't need checking every month, particularly one financing retirement where you're looking for long term gains.'

'That's why a fee's better than a profit share for the solicitor: far less work.'

'That's right… but then to triple the fee without any notice - it's not as if they're offering a superior service.'

'Money for old rope.'

'That's what the lady said. She said it was a youngish man with blond hair.' Paul showed Henry his phone screen '- now, do you think that describes John, Alice, Indira or Damon?'

'Tricky. If only she'd said 'slick, greasy, balding bastard with a touch of vampire', then we'd know for sure which one she meant.'

Paul ran his fingers through his own receding hairline. 'So, what am I going to do?'

'Expose the bastard! Get a half hour adjournment debate in Westminster Hall on, I don't know, ethics in the legal profession, send him a note an hour before the debate saying you're going to name him. That's the proper procedure. Or - no, this is a good one - you get an appointment to see Mr Speaker, tell him you have reason to believe that a fellow Honourable Member isn't quite as honourable as he should be and ask his advice… tell him you want an apology for your constituent and her money back, keep it all hush hush, but say that you want it sorted. I bet you The Speaker will have a word with him and he'll come to heel.'

'These are options, I suppose.' Paul was downbeat.

'You say the town where the mother lives isn't in Hough's constituency - whose is it in?'

Barely ten seconds later Henry's phone had divulged the name of a cabinet minister.

'I doubt we'll get much help from her. But it's not as simple as that, Henry…'

'Why not?'

'We, er… we have a past, Damon and I.'

Henry resorted to mock exaggeration in his expression: 'A past?? You weren't once… don't tell me - a Tory, were you?'

Paul raised a finger and the flippant comment died on Henry's lips. Serious time.

'We grew up together. We lived ten minutes apart, went to the same primary and secondary schools, for a while. I think he came late, from maybe aged seven or eight? We were certainly in the top class at junior school together. He may even have been my best friend, that year, bezzy mate. And then at secondary, until I was 14.'

'You're the same age?'

'I'm either two weeks older than him or he's two weeks older than me, I forget.'

'Easily checked!' Henry's phone came out again.

'Don't bother, it's not important.'

'He's two weeks older. 2nd May.'

There was a wistfulness about Paul's speech. The pub was quiet enough that no-one was sitting near enough to them to overhear, busy enough that even those sitting two tables away would be unable to hear what was being said.

'You're saying he wasn't such a tosser back then?'

'We were friends. Politics was years away, for both of us. Anyway, at 16 he went to a sixth form college - I remember now - to do Law 'A' level, which our school didn't offer. I never saw him again, in the flesh at least, until my first week as an MP. It goes without saying, we've not exactly rekindled our friendship.'

'I should think not, he's a prat. I mean, I know some Tories are decent chaps and all that, 'top hole, don't you know?', but Hough's a wanker, isn't he?'

'He's adopted a certain profile, created himself a role to fulfil, it appears. Now I think about it, he was going to be a big shot corporate lawyer, not a rural solicitor in a one-horse town... I wonder what happened there?'

Henry looked at the MP in the silence that followed. The perennial brown suit looked as though he had been wearing it all week (he had) and there was an uneven five o'clock shadow gracing his chin. This was no surprise. The church clock across the road struck eight.

'Why do I feel that there's something you're not telling me here, Paul?'

His boss flashed him a momentary glance and the tiniest of smiles, more sympathetic than amused.

'Yeah, we were close. Cross country running; we were the best two runners in the year, aged fourteen. Sometimes he won, sometimes I did. In one important race not only could they not separate our timings but we'd both broken the school record. We were ten, twelve seconds ahead of the field, that's quite a lot. That run was a personal battle between us, all the way round the course... we were really strong rivals, as only friends can be. Anyway, we were walking home together after school that day, joint victors. We crossed the school fields, down a bank, through a hole in a hedge and down a track. When we reached the hedge, he said he couldn't remember the way through... of course he could. He was obviously pretending. Then he approached me by the hedge and said 'Well done, winner!' and gave me a hug. I thought that was all there was to it, the hug would be over in a second; but it wasn't. He carried on hugging me. I hugged him back, why not? Footballers do it, and... we were friends. But... you know that feeling you get when someone's hug, or handshake, goes on too long? Instead of relaxing he hugged me tighter, put his hands round me and grabbed my arse with one hand, forcing my head down onto his neck with the other, immobilising me.'

Henry listened patiently. This was no time for flippant comments.

It must have looked very odd, me the tall lanky one and him... a bit shorter, bit rounder.'

'Morecambe and Wise...' Henry said, wistfully.

Paul ignored the comment. 'I guess I trusted him, tried not to think anything of it.'

Paul was not enjoying the memory.

'I wasn't going to resist. I froze. And then... he started humping, you know, like a dog does. Fully clothed, but it was summer, we weren't wearing a lot. No coat. No jumper. He was pushing himself against my thigh, thrusting.'

'It's called frottage.'

'An innocent young child like yourself shouldn't know these things, Henry!' At last, Paul allowed himself a brief smile.

'I've packed a lot into my tender years. You were saying?'

'He was that close, and it was clear that... he'd got a hard on, and he was panting - I thought he was acting, but you can't just pretend to get a hard on, can you?'

'I don't suppose...'

'He grabbed my hand… and put it on his cock, which sort of confirmed… This was all outside his trousers, and he was still humping away. Then suddenly he pulled away from me. Opened his mouth wide in that - what would you call it? Demonic smile, almost laughing, not quite. He wasn't finished…'

'Wow…'

'I was… you know how snake charmers work? It's about the eyes, you get the look right and you can paralyse someone. I was 'under the influence'. Before I knew what was happening, he had his hands down inside my pants and… as I say, I felt hypnotised, frozen. 'Winner!' he said, a huge grin on him; I assumed he was talking about the race. Our race. The joint winners.'

'So… what then?'

'Nothing. It was all over in a minute, we didn't undress, didn't get down on the floor… I wasn't particularly enthusiastic, reticent's a better word. I was acutely embarrassed because… well, a teenager gets his cock touched, for the very first time. What do you expect? I don't know why I'm telling you all this.'

'Because you've never told anyone before?'

'Well, that happens to be true… I was fourteen, for Christ's sake. It was my first experience of… The first person to touch me, sexually, was Damon bloody Hough.'

'So, first attempt at rumpy-pumpy - what would you say, five out of ten? Six?'

'Ha! Not even two!'

'Things could only get better… as it were. Well, that's something!'

'Indeed. Not a problem these days… certainly not before Rose left, anyway. I think the sex was the only thing that kept her and I together until… until it didn't.'

'Too much information…!' Henry laughed, in faux embarrassment.

'I got really embarrassed with Damon, you know, as I said. The spell had been broken. I tucked myself in, sorted myself out and he just stood there… Mocking me.'

'How do you mean, 'mocking'?'

'His expression. Supremely confident. Superior. Arrogant. Lustful. Didn't take his eyes off me, whilst I couldn't look him straight in the face.'

'I'd never have guessed he was so versatile…'

'Anyway. It never happened again. I went through the hole in the hedge and thirty yards down the track he caught me up. He started talking, really normally, about running. We got to the end of my street - it would take him another five minutes to walk home - and he stood to attention, saluted like a soldier and offered me his hand to shake. I couldn't touch it. The hand that had just… Bastard…'

There was a moment of silence.

'Is there… another chapter?'

'Not really. That was summer 1996, like I said, and everyone was talking politics, even 14-year-olds. My family was backing Blair, everyone was. Literally, everyone I knew, except Damon. He was supporting Thatcher.'

'Well, she was very popular, especially amongst… Hold on. Thatcher? She'd been out of office, what, six years by then!'

'Not in Damon's eyes! Remember when Trump wouldn't accept that he'd lost the Presidency? Damon was the same about Thatcher. He didn't know what he was talking about, it was ridiculous. When people did challenge him, it was hilarious, he'd get really animated, defend her even more strongly! He didn't associate Toryism with grey, humble, meek Mr Major. Anyway, after that day he took to teasing me, calling me Pinko, which was supposed to be political, but I guess it was also sexual. Pinko, with - what do they call it? An aspirated 'p', he'd lower his head and fix me straight in the eye, then say 'pinko' as though he was blowing me a kiss… but no, he never came on to me again. Never.'

'Demon Damon, eh? How long did he treat you like that?'

'I got immune to it. It was just a word, and politically speaking it was unobjectionable, even if that wasn't how he meant it. But that day was the end of our friendship… two years later he went off to sixth form college, like I said. I didn't see him again, in the flesh, until the first time I bumped into him in Parliament. I'd known he was an MP, of course, but I never went out of my way to look him up online or anything. I knew of his reputation as a twat. Well deserved…'

'You're worried that he might think he's got something on you?'

'I don't know. I mean, is he actually gay? I don't think he's out, as such, is he? I just don't know, but I can't imagine that he's conventionally straight. Anyone who's seen him up close would agree with that.'

'Are you suggesting that if you confront him about the Power of Attorney stuff, and he doesn't like it, which he won't, he'll go round telling people that you… you know…?'

'I guess that's in the back of my mind.'

'And you being single, of course… You know what they say about men who are single in their forties…?' The air of teasing had returned.

'Come on, Henry. Not these days.'

'So, what are you going to do?'

'Do?'

'About your constituent?'

Paul pondered.

'Your idea of talking to the Speaker's a good one, maybe the Law Society first. I want to know if what he's doing is illegal or unethical. I've got another surgery tomorrow morning but after that the weekend's free. I might go back to the London flat, get a bit of complete quiet.'

'Is Hazel in London this weekend?'

'Why do you ask?' Something in his memory clicked. 'Oh, are you on about that again, Henry? You're a cheeky sod! She's my secretary, right? My PA. It's a totally professional relationship - and always has been.'

'You don't want to… prove a point, then? Prove Damon wrong?'

'Don't be silly.'

'So, when she said she'd shag you, given half a chance -'

'She was pissed! It was her birthday party, wasn't it? She was amongst friends! Anyway, I only have your word that she ever actually said it. She's never said it to me, we've never done - anything close - you know, and I hardly think -'

'Oh, she said it! Say 'She never will'.'

This was one area that Paul was not keen to discuss with his aide. He had his reasons, though they were going to remain hidden inside his head.

'Come on, Henry! You're better than that. But thank you, you've broken the trance I was in! It was sending shivers down my spine. That fucker did it again, like he did with his eyes…'

'One more pint? Shall I fetch a menu?'

Paul smiled. Henry was reading him well. 'Oh, why not?'

'Same again?'

'Please. Thanks. You know what, Henry, my constituent deserves some justice. What happened between me and Hough is in the past. It was just part of growing up, the very deep past, a quarter of a century ago. It's dead and buried. If, in getting justice for this woman, I just happen to bring that fucker down… well, perhaps there is some justice in the world…'

'I'll drink to that! Cheers, Paul.'

Kate Mellor has a Plan:

Monday 25th April

'Darling?' she called up the stairs, 'Yes, darling?' responded a mellifluous baritone.

'Darling, Sophie's going to Poops' after school, can you collect her from Helen's later?'

'Of course, darling! Usual time?'

'Usual time. Bye, darling!'

If Mark did call back 'Bye' then Kate did not hear him. It was fortunate that her husband was spending the week working from home, marking external students' scripts and recording a couple of podcasts on Ancient Greek themes. He might even start to write the book on contemporary mythology that he had promised himself (and his publisher) to produce. 'The Modern Minotaur' would be a worthy successor to 'Diagnosing Dionysus'.

Helen was Poops' mother. Twenty minutes earlier she had called round to collect their daughter, Sophie, before walking the girls to school. It was Monday, 25th April, the first day of the summer term, and Kate had not been quite ready for her daughter's escort - the two-week break in routine over Easter can disorientate a busy mum. Kate had still been in dressing gown and fluffy slippers, juggling toast, school lunch and her laptop in a state of barely disguised panic when Helen, the calm, ordered, earth-mother, had arrived.

The neighbour would be delivering the two 8-year-olds to school about now. She would have navigated Islington's tree-lined residential streets on foot, avoiding the congestion caused by Chelsea tractors queuing in the inappropriately narrow roads to discharge their small passengers. Eschewing ownership of an SUV, or indeed any vehicle, and walking on principle was a shared characteristic that bound Helen and Kate together from their very first encounter. Sophie and her best friend Poops (real name Poppy) occasionally questioned why 'everyone else' arrived at school in a tank - especially on rainy days - but they accepted their lot. Laments on the theme of shoe leather had certainly declined; the learning experience had taught young Sophie the meaning of the word 'inappropriate'.

'It's better for the planet that we walk, lovey.'

Kate was in a hurry to get to the office as she headed for the tube. She had a story which her editor would not be able to resist, but she also knew that it would take some time to pull together. It came with a natural, inbuilt deadline sometime in May - when it would land with maximum impact. She had two, maybe three weeks to complete it. But first she had to pass 'Go'.

After studying English at university around the millennium Kate had made steady progress up the career ladder. The year she had spent as a postgraduate on a journalism course sponsored by a popular tabloid had been invaluable. However, she soon left trivia (as she called the red-tops) behind. At first, she went to a London evening paper and then, for more than the eight years that had elapsed since Sophie's birth, to a Sunday broadsheet. She had started there full time, a desk-bound staff reporter but had moved to the slightly less chaotic world of features after becoming a mother; once back from maternity leave she had negotiated a contract with reduced hours, which suited her fine. This was balanced by her husband, now Professor Mark Shield, not only becoming a Vice Dean at the local university but having a reasonably compensated Higher Education advisory role in Whitehall, too. She retained her unmarried name, Mellor, for professional and most other purposes, not out of principle (though why not?) but for convenience.

Kate's regular weekly task was to write a column for the 'Family' section of the Sunday supplement. It was often deeply hidden in the plethora of paper that would be next week's recycling, but any disappointment that her opus could be hard to find amongst the dead trees (and sometimes even in a brutally sub-edited form) was compensated by the column having become an online hit. Oh yes, if anyone wanted a witty and moving insight into the trials of bringing up a talented six/seven/eight-year-old girl (and a jolly but fictitious dog called Richard) in the jungle of North London, then this was undoubtedly the column to follow! It felt as though she spent more time monitoring, promoting and adding to Richard's Twitter account then she spent writing the column itself. As a child Kate had loved her pet labrador and Rusty was Richard's role model, but it had nevertheless been decided that the puppy-loving

Sophie should wait until she was big enough to take responsibility before being granted any pet. That day was fast approaching.

Every now and again Kate's avid reading, plus an insatiable appetite for scandal, would discover a gem. This was a hangover from her tabloid days, and to her editor she was worth her weight in gold for the occasional leads that she shared with the 'Probe' team. Although her name rarely appeared on the by-line of such stories both Kate and, through her editor, the paper's owner were in no doubt of the value Ms Mellor brought to the title. On this occasion, however, she was heading into the office to ask to follow up a big story herself. One reason for this was that Kate had covered the original crime and trial, twelve years previously. Over recent days she had scrupulously re-read her cuttings and notebooks of that era.

By 10 a.m. Kate was in the office and two espressos to the good. She had fifteen minutes with the editor scheduled for 11 so she read her brief through yet again, thoroughly, twice, having honed its edges over the weekend. This was the updated document that she had been emailing to Nigella when Helen had appeared at the door in search of Sophie, catching Kate in her dressing gown and those absurd fluffy slippers. (Mark had always insisted Sophie had chosen them, but Sophie denied any involvement, dismissing them as 'just gross'. Out of the mouths… but at least they were comfy).

Nigella Taft was the editor in question and Kate had a good relationship with the worldly-wise Canadian. If this had been 50 years earlier her boss - had a woman acting in such a role been conceivable - would have worn a green plastic vizor, chain-smoked plain cigarettes and barked obscenities ever more foul as the deadline approached. The 21st century Nigella might appear more sophisticated but was still capable of turning the air blue. She was coming down after her regular high adrenalin decision-making session at the start of each working day.

'Yes,' said Nigella, 'I do remember the Guy Campbell story, fraud and money laundering on a grand scale. That's what this is, a boat?'

Kate did a double take: not 'a boat', but 'about'. The Canadian accent still fooled her at times.

'That's right, Campbell was CEO of a finance company, MEKANICK. It has so many capital K's he should have just called it 'Macho'. It was a major criminal operation, tied in with a legitimate cover, and I'm convinced that we - and the courts - only ever discovered the half of it. Campbell got a twenty-year stretch - which was massive, it included a tax charge, too - but we have a forgiving criminal justice system, so he'll be out in less than twelve - as early as mid-May.'

'Three weeks away… And you think you know where some of the unaccounted money can be found?'

'I am pretty sure I've found someone who knows how I might find that out. I'm very hopeful that I can persuade him to talk to me. He's a corporate lawyer close to the heart of MEKANICK. I intend to firm him up this week, if you give me the green light.'

'This isn't double jeopardy?'

'No, no, I'm not talking about re-trying Campbell for crimes for which he's already served time, rather these are the proceeds of crimes which never came to court the first time around. This is money that wasn't accounted for last time.'

'Statute of limitations?'

'Not for this type of crime.'

'Are we talking millions?'

Kate was less sure of her ground when it came to the quantity of money involved, but it was big. She was certain that it would be well into the millions.

'Yes.'

'Do you need a budget?'

Kate felt a thrill of anticipation. That question could only precede a 'yes'.

'I'll draft something for you. It won't be huge.'

'Go for it. We'll meet again early next week; you can update me then.'

Her body language said the meeting was over. According to the art deco clock on Nigella's wall, an anachronism in this stark palace of concrete and glass, it had lasted eight minutes.

'Thank you, Nigella.'

'No problem. By the way, Kate - loved your column this weekend. That dog, Richard - he really creases me up! Well done. You know my new husband's called Richard?'

'Oh really?' said Kate, hoping that her show of feigned ignorance would pass scrutiny.

Money Talks - Lee Hardman:

Monday 25th April

A finance company is not a bank. It's generally smaller, it's easier for a money business to work under the radar than it is for a bank. It can get away with... murder.

Metaphorically speaking.

There are rules of conduct, transparency, decorum - but they only go so far. Rules determine how one should behave in certain situations. But not every situation had a precedent, and financiers like Guy Campbell not only sought out unique circumstances in which to operate but they invested heavily in helping to bring such opportunities if not to light, at least into a silent, personal penumbra, where shade was an asset.

The global economic crash of 2007 happened because rules had either been relaxed or ignored. Relaxing some of them - in Britain, Europe, America - had sent out a subliminal message which led to other rules being overlooked; easing back on some guidelines suggested that almost every rule was ultimately arbitrary, flexible, temporary. And yet there were some to whom such signals meant nothing: if there was a way of achieving their goals, short term, pound, dollar, Euro-driven goals, then that was what they would do. And the rules could go and hike. Recruit clever lawyers and the world was your oyster. Recruit clever lawyers who were prepared to accommodate and work around the criminal activities of others - and the oyster became a giant squid.

MEKANICK stood out from the rest of the world of finance in the 1990s not just because its name never appeared in lower case but because it was a very slick operator: blink in a particular market sector where MEKANICK had an interest, and you would miss it. Selling products several times each minute - if intangible concepts created by linking lists of digits in different ways could be called 'products' - only made sense if you knew where you wanted to be, and how to get there, an hour from now.

Guy Campbell possessed that sense of direction. It pointed him towards a private yacht, a mansion with three swimming pools, a wife with an infinite wardrobe. The first two were easily obtained, but after several attempts at establishing the third he gave up and settled for buying female company. Ideally this would happen for a few months at a time but, where that was not possible, he would take it by the hour. Politicians are constantly reminding us that no 'magic money tree' exists, but no one explained that to Guy. He harvested its crop for several seasons - and out of season, too.

And that was the problem. There was a massive police investigation into MEKANICK at around the time of the 'crash'. The company was used to operating under the radar but with growing confidence had eventually become proactive, upfront and international. For two years Campbell's agile lawyers stayed ahead of the pack but when his senior legal adviser told him his number was up, he stepped back, restructuring and downsizing the legitimate side of operation significantly. If he was going to go down there was no reason why the company should, too. He needed to hold off incarceration for a year if he could manage it, buy time to hide assets whilst preparing sacrificial lambs, offer the police dogs red meat whilst putting his legitimate holdings on ice. Under his plan a five-year sentence would work out cost free as several dozen silent millions, invested at even a small percent compound, left untouched for five years, would create something worth coming home to.

Things did not quite go to plan.

In December 2010, after weeks of trial, Guy Campbell entered Wandsworth prison with a massive 20-year stretch hanging round his neck. As well as fraud and money laundering, he had been found guilty of tax irregularities, too. The way the judge overacted in delivering the word 'consecutive' reminded Guy of 'Trial by Jury', his favourite musical.

If Campbell behaved himself, as he thoroughly intended to, then much of his sentence would be spent in open prisons after an initial period of 'proper' incarceration - but that was of little consolation. Guy had never been one for the open air unless there was a pool or a yacht alongside him, a constant supply of sun cream and a pair of delicate hands to apply it. Two of his associates were also behind bars, but they did not 'go down' until well after his people had successfully insulated them from his dealings, deleted them from his address book, paid for their silence. By the time Madame Guillotine fell he had been successfully immunised against them. Whilst a guilty verdict might always have been inevitable the courts did not need to know everything…

Others within MEKANICK had always been distanced from criminality and that number included, unsurprisingly, several of the lawyers. One of these was Lee Hardman who, in 2010, had been an up and coming 28-year-old junior legal associate. Genuinely clean at the time of both the crash and the crime, Lee was tasked with hiding some of the remaining ill-, but also the not-so-ill-gotten gains. The overlap between the two profit centres was helpfully blurred. Essentially, Lee decided, shuffling the pack and then dividing larger sums into untraceable, ever smaller ones was the way to go. With Guy 'unavailable' how the money was handled would be Lee's call, and his alone. It was best that no one else knew what he was doing. Through Lee, MEKANICK would make payments for imaginary services, each in several instalments, rarely of more than a million pounds in total for any single or compound transaction. Such 'investments' would need to be hidden for quite some time. The 'deal' was that the recipients would look after the borrowed and disguised asset for at least five years. They would be given as much notice as possible of the requirement to return the capital which would be, at the earliest, on the day Guy eventually walked free. They would be 'encouraged', no more, to gift him a token in lieu of any interest or profit they had generated on the capital over the intervening period. In effect, all they were being asked was to say 'thank you' for an interest-free loan. Lee had taken it upon himself to tell his charges that the token need not represent a commercial level of return. The notice clause not only gave the 'foster parents' time to make sure their charges were in good health but, cleverly, nothing was carved in stone: the record keeping was minimal. Lee's packages were designed to ensure that no nosey authorities' attention would be attracted by a surge of big sums entering Guy's accounts immediately upon his release.

The first part of the plan worked. Lee found temporary homes for over thirty million pounds divided into eighteen packages of different sizes. Some was lodged with 'grey' companies, working on the fringe of legality, sheltered by registration in Panama or some other haven from tax or regulation. Some was paid upfront, in daylight, to businesses that were, to all appearances, providing a legitimate, if over-priced, service. In a few cases smaller amounts of cash were effectively put on deposit with Lee's friends and capitalist acquaintances. These were the smaller sums. One such destination saw three unequal instalments, a total of £750,000, paid to a rural law firm looking to expand into new premises. No one would ever spot that they never actually benefitted from fresh bricks or mortar, nor that they remained resolutely in the marketplace of a quiet and scenic home counties market town. Who was going to check? The firm was Steel & Partners.

Lee Hardman thought he knew what he wanted to do with his life. All this was happening shortly after his formative experience as a Prospective Parliamentary Candidate for the Conservative Party, in industrial Yorkshire, at the 2010 general election.

Now, in March 2022, Lee was almost 40 and his passionate desire to change the world, or at least that part of it which impacted upon himself, was unchanged. He had seen enough of high finance to last a lifetime, thank you. Once this job was over, and the loose ends tied off, it would be time for a change in lifestyle.

The veteran Kenneth Clark, former Chancellor and 'Father of the House', was Lee's political inspiration. The young man was genuinely middle of the road in his politics, though the road was not broad, and Lee was coming from the right-hand lane. Clark had been one of the few constants on the spectrum throughout Lee's politically aware life - and more. If Ken, his Hush Puppy shoes, his love of jazz, good wines and the odd cigar appeared to be - dare he say it? - slightly left of centre these days it was only because the world around him had moved to the right.

Back at the time of the crash Lee regarded David Cameron, Opposition Leader and future PM, as on the correct track but weak. He was also aware of a growing right-wing trend within the Conservative Party, a tendency with which he felt little empathy. 2010 might have been the last chance for moderate people like himself to make a difference inside that narrowing broad church.

When he had the chance to be selected to fight a Parliamentary seat in South Yorkshire he was delighted - even if he knew that he had not a cat's chance in Hell of winning it. The direct experience of politics, however, proved invaluable: he had made many good contacts and was conscious that those you met on the way up in political life could assist you when you were coming back down again, as everyone invariably would, before too long. He tended his contacts book carefully, regarding everyone he met through the Party as a friend until there was reason to consider them otherwise. In retrospect he was surprised how often 'otherwise' emerged…

Hardman went through the motions in 2010. He pressed the flesh, paraded the blue rosette, took part in community debates - and enjoyed giving speeches both to the faithful to the general public, even if on the hoof. Nevertheless, he eventually became aware that his corporate financial lawyer way of speaking, whilst technically correct, was dry and often went unappreciated. When other politicians were pounding the table Lee was always more at home tabling the pounds.

The candidacy was a learning experience beyond compare. He met future cabinet ministers, even the PM in waiting, identified and nurtured fellow candidates from the 'one nation' tradition who inspired him. He went to training sessions, soon regretting how he treated advice on public speaking as water off a duck's back. He even attended a mutual 'bonding' event exclusively for candidates. The idea of such gatherings was that those on the Tory front line should learn from each other, though a single weekend session would prove sufficient for Lee. Being a candidate was just wonderful in many respects, he considered, though in some ways the more he later discovered about being an MP, life in the political goldfish bowl, the more he found himself grateful that the good people of Yorkshire had spared him that fate.

There had been six first time candidates on that 2009 weekend retreat in Derbyshire, based in a 6-bedroom former vicarage, though only two would find their way into his address book. One of those, perversely, was the one from whom the tolerant, liberal lawyer felt the most politically distant: the maverick Damon Hough, who was already establishing a reputation as a rogue within the candidate fraternity. What the two men had in common were their legal professions, their single relationship status and the identical number of years of life under their belts. Having three things in common, Lee had always been taught, created a basis for partnership in politics as elsewhere. Although that idea would be tested over that weekend it would prevail sufficiently to include Damon in Lee's MEKANICK cash distribution scheme.

Being a fully paid-up member of the Ken Clark Fan Club did not define Lee's identity completely. Whenever he pondered the true nature of the Hardman being he saw a corporate lawyer, working for bent financial superstar Guy Campbell; he had made the best of it so far, he thought, and he could live with that. He knew too many people, in his own office and elsewhere, who could not say the same.

In their opinions of the law, Lee and Damon had a strong trait in common: lawyers were obliged to use it in whatever way might prove useful. They should avoid the law if it got in the way, and they should undermine it only when absolutely necessary. Like every other social structure, the law was respected for creating opportunities whilst being disdained for the obstacles it presented. Often the best way to tackle such obstacles was with a discreet sledgehammer.

It transpired that Damon, too, had aspired to be a corporate lawyer. For reasons that were not entirely clear to Lee, Hough had found himself attached to a rural solicitor's office instead. He was standing for a seat already held by the Tories but with a small majority and was working it hard. He had committed himself fully to the task. Perhaps that explained it? A corporate lawyer lives, breathes and shits work but that's not compatible with full time campaigning. Attachment to a solicitor's office puts your name onto a respectable, embossed business card, provides a decent source of income and serves as a great platform for working a patch, thereby creating a solid basis for winning. Lee found himself respecting Damon's approach.

Outsourcing some peripheral legal services from companies like MEKANICK to a small law firm was not unheard of in the finance sector. So, in late 2010, following the election, when Lee invited Damon to meet for a business chat, he was up for it. Several times in that discussion, over coffee just off Liverpool Street, Lee found he needed to bite his tongue: he did not regard Hough as a nice person but 'nice' was not on his list of necessary host qualities. The impression he had gained of Damon from the candidates' weekend - garrulous, disrespectful, bloated and capable of malice - was confirmed in spades. But Hough was also ambitious, ruthless and devastatingly capable of assimilating information, as any lawyer should be. The recently elected MP understood exactly what Lee was proposing and why discretion had to be the order of the day, without needing to have it spelled out. He was excited by the prospect.

Lee believed that secrets were part of Damon's make-up then, just as much as his natural quiff, cleft chin and prematurely greying temples were today. Those secrets were probably big ones, though Lee neither wanted nor needed to know what they were. A man who has his own secrets can be trusted with ours, reasoned Lee.

The implicit contract that emerged from that conversation, for Steel & Partners to develop its premises and deliver services to the Campbell empire, involved the transfer of £750,000, in three tranches, over several months. It was legally watertight and fundamentally meaningless. An interest-bearing client account was set up within the solicitor's portfolio and the money would be left to accumulate over at least five years; from this point on, everything was on trust. Lee had no means of monitoring the money directly nor controlling its fate; it was essential that he keep his distance from it. In the run up to the 2015 election, unknown to Lee, there was a significant withdrawal from the account. During the Brexit referendum of 2016, in which Damon Hough was an outspoken campaigner for Britain to leave the European Union, much to Lee's distaste, there was a second. Lee knew nothing of either; the money was no longer his responsibility.

The next few years were politically turbulent, with elections in both 2017 and 2019. Withdrawals were made from the account that did not exist on both occasions and as 2022 dawned the remaining balance was significantly lower than on day one. This was not how it was supposed to work, unless the cash was being replaced by a retrievable asset of comparable value. Had Damon been asked to repay the money immediately he would have been more than £150,000 short. But that was not a problem, because Campbell was going to be away for twenty years, was he not? There was plenty of time to get things back on track.

Make that twelve. Early in 2022 Lee, now employed at arm's length by the shell that still bore the name MEKANICK, thought it prudent to plan the pulling together of Campbell's errant millions. He had to be ready to bring the babies back when Daddy came home. It was money that, if it belonged to anybody, still belonged to Guy Campbell; or it was convenient to see it that way, as alternative explanations were too complicated. It looked as though Guy would likely be back in circulation in the forthcoming May, somewhat earlier than previously expected.

In early April Lee heard that Guy Campbell had a message for him, which caused him concern. It was his first message from that source in six years. Guy could not possibly want the money returned immediately, could he? All thirty million? It would - and should - take weeks, even months, to secure it all. Lee's intention had always been to dribble it back into the company, not flood it, which would only attract attention. He contemplated travelling up to Staffordshire, to the open prison where Campbell resided, but that proved unnecessary as Guy's personal lawyer and general right-hand man, Jacob Singh, announced that he would be acting as go-between.

Lee met Singh at a café on the upstairs shelf of Waterloo Station on Monday, 25th April 2022. The two had never previously met - Singh was a relatively recent arrival at the MEKANICK party - and Lee was not impressed by the clandestine nature of the assignation. 'Don't tell anyone who you're meeting or where,' Singh had said on the telephone.

Singh's flat cap looked horribly out of place, a Hackneyed affectation. If it was designed to render him incognito it was not working. He had a lazy eye, overly hairy ears, deep-set eyes and a face that was not built for smiling.

'Our mutual friend will be at liberty on Friday, the thirteenth of May,' Singh told Lee.

'Unlucky for some', thought Lee.

'On Tuesday, 17th, he will be in the usual office at his usual hour,' the lawyer went on, stretching the definition of 'usual' after a 12-year gap. 'By the thirteenth you will have provided us with a full account to show that all the elements of resource which you distributed are on their way home, is that clear? Not necessarily 'home', but accessible with a timetable for reacquisition. Mr Campbell will formally review your report over the weekend and may wish to talk to you on 17th, is that clear?'

'Yes, that's clear.' It was a big job to be accomplished in a short time. But he had been paid several years'-worth of generous retainer, helping keep the company on life support, to prepare for this day. He was reassured by having already started to plan this campaign, even covering aspects Campbell might not have anticipated.

'Jacob, I'm assuming that if all the resource can be positively accounted for then the post mortem would be brief. Would that be correct?'

'Remind me,' said Jacob, narrowing his eyes in thought as he stirred an additional sugar into his black coffee, 'your remuneration isn't tied to a positive outcome, is it?'

'No. I'm sorted, thank you.'

'As I thought.'

'If Mr Campbell needs me to meet, perhaps we could do that remotely?'

'I would have thought so, if there are no red numbers. I'll get back to you on that.'

'We'll set up a video conference then, if needs be, if that's OK.'

'You're not planning to be in the office, then?'

Lee swallowed and took a breath. He had been researching and rehearsing the next bit.

'You'll recall that I'm in receipt of a retainer in respect of my... janitorial services. I am not technically employed by Mr Campbell these days. My retainer expires - well, technically, it expires on the day Mr Campbell re-joins the outside world.'

'Oh, you mean the thirteenth?'

'Indeed. Midnight on the twelfth, to be precise.'

Singh's face expressed mild surprise, but he trusted his fellow lawyer to report accurately.

Walking away before meeting Campbell had not originally been part of Lee's plan, but the clause in his contract was a serendipitous recent discovery; by some oversight, any obligations that Lee had towards Guy would expire before the first feasible time they could possibly meet. This was not in the spirit of the contract, of course, which required all the pennies to add up and for Lee to be held properly accountable. Lee knew that if there were any 'red numbers' his conduct would not be forgiven, nor his laxity forgotten. That could be bad news. Very bad indeed. The books therefore had to balance or, better still, show a modest surplus. If all went well by May 13th they would balance and by 17th Lee would have wound up his work, discharged his obligations and placed himself a long way away from London.

Standing on the escalator that transported him down to the Waterloo & City underground line Lee took out his phone. It was an old one by mobile telephony standards, and he had several alternative SIM cards for it. The current one was only designated for use with one particular contact. He wrote a text message to the weakest link, the least reliable, of his key contacts: 'Daddy's coming home. We need to talk. Delete this message.'

It was years since he had last been in touch with Damon Hough, whose veer to the right in the past decade had been both embarrassing to the Party and personally offensive to Lee himself. He needed a screw which he could turn on the MP, should he prove unable to return 'Daddy's' money.

But he had done his homework and thought he had discovered Hough's Achilles heel... He had also tracked down a journalist, certainly no political ally of Hough, who had worked on the original Campbell case more than a decade previously. His plan was in place and the blessed day was in sight.

After that he need never see the shit again.

On the Bench - Kate & Lee:

Thursday 28th April

Kate knocked off Sunday's column on the Wednesday, a couple of days early, to get it out of the way. It was not one of her best, she might admit, but she knew her standards were high so it would have to do. Her desk was now clear to concentrate on MEKANICK. In particular, she had been contacted by someone she now knew to be Lee Hardman, a MEKANICK lawyer, but unless she could speak to him further, she would have no story. Although well informed about what was going on in the company a dozen years earlier, she knew that her current knowledge was insufficient to build a story upon. There was a pile of 'catch up' homework for her to do over the coming days. In just a few weeks Guy Campbell would slide quietly back into society and hide behind the resurrected, respectable facade of MEKANICK once more, where he would no doubt return to his carefully corrupt and egoistic ways - if more carefully than before.

24 hours later, on the morning of Thursday, 28th April, Kate was already exhausted before she even started on the heavier side of the work. She had her strategy planned and knew how to proceed. She had to be infinitely flexible, mentally prepared to find more dead ends than jewels.

The moment had come. She picked up her mobile, opened the contacts app, scrolled down to 'H' and paused. Since their first brief contact, she had sent this guy two personal emails and he had responded to neither. Had he developed cold feet? She winced: Hardman's contribution was the fulcrum on which the whole story balanced. She had guaranteed him anonymity, but did he did trust her? A proper journalist would go to the grave to protect their sources, and she was a proper journalist. On the other hand, he had warned her that he would be difficult to contact, whilst encouraging her not to give up. She sensed that the story was about to reach a tipping point, after which Hardman would no longer be on the scene, though he had not said as much. How big was the window in which she had to speak to him before it was too late? She thought that if she reached six failed attempts on the phone she ought to worry, maybe consider setting up camp outside the MEKANICK office. That was silly:

it would blow his cover. She had no doubt that he possessed the inside information that she needed. She had to know what was happening inside the not-quite-dormant Campbell organisation and what would change when Campbell reappeared.

She typed the text message and hit 'send'. Within a minute she had hit gold: all the reply said was 'Pret. London Wall. 2pm'. This could be the start of something big.

Kate recognised him as soon as she entered the coffee shop. Though never having clapped eyes on the man before, she'd found Lee's election literature from twelve years previously on the internet. He was exceptionally tall, thin, pale. He looked young for his age and his dark hair was more sculpted than the historic record suggested. He wore expensive-looking frameless spectacles, just as he had all those years ago. His simple suit did not stand out but was certainly not cheap; ditto the shoes and silk tie. There was something of a young Bill Gates about him, she thought. This was how to blend in, in this part of the City of London.

'You're Lee? Hi.'

'Hi. Kate?'

'Yes. You already have a coffee, shall we…?'

'Yes, let's go. Finsbury Circus?'

For a corporate lawyer Lee Hardman did not exactly exude power. If she could use a single word to sum him up so far it was 'ordinary'. Easy to overlook, despite his prodigious height.

As they made their way to the square Kate deployed small talk to break the ice.

'So, you fought a general election, Lee, 2010, wasn't it?'

'Yes. I was a Conservative candidate, unsuccessful, I didn't try again after that. I'm quite pleased not to be in the Commons now, I must say. Not that I would have been - I'm quite sure Johnson would have got rid of me in the purge!'

The incoming, pro-Brexit Prime Minister had stripped his ranks of pro-European dissent in the run up to the election of December of 2019.

'How long have you been with MEKANICK?'

'Fourteen years.'

'Since college, University?'

'No, not quite. I'm 40. I just look young.'

The same age as me, she thought, yet he could pass for thirty. If only I could!

'It must have been pretty quiet since Guy Campbell...'

'There's been lots to do, but fewer of us doing it. I was lucky to be asked to stay on.'

'By the way, how did MEKANICK get its name? Sounds a bit Kraftwerk, if you know what I mean.'

Lee smiled, for the first time, briefly. 'There's a German connection, yes. Guy Campbell's father actually set it up, in the eighties. His mother was German, Meka, his father was Nick. Simple, really. And meaningless.'

They reached Finsbury Circus and entered the gardens, where they had a choice of benches. Lee was the soul of good manners, inviting Kate to sit at the cleaner end of a convenient seat. His eyes were very pale blue; although they darted uncertainly around the park as he spoke, they were anchored tightly on Kate's face when she did.

'Would you mind if I recorded this chat, Lee?' Kate held up her phone, already open on the recording app. He hesitated.

'I'd rather you didn't.'

'Not a problem.' She put it back in her pocket. She would rely on her notebook, which she preferred to the electronic tablets that many of her contemporaries used. She sometimes wondered whether hers would be the final generation to learn Pitman.

For the first time Lee took a good look at his inquisitor: she was about his age, built like an athlete, a runner. She had ash blonde hair, wavy, collar length, worn with a fringe, grey eyes and dangling silver earrings. She had a serious but intelligent face, a small, discrete, silver stud in her left nostril. As she prepared her notebook, he noted that she wore a simple wedding ring. Although Lee's interest in politics, business and finance caused him to be an avid consumer of Sunday papers his reading did not extend to any 'family' section; Kate Mellor's was not a name that he recognised. He had seen cuttings of Guy's original trial, put some of the writers' names into Google and found her that way...

'So... you were working with Guy Campbell before he went to prison...'

Lee remained silent but could not deny her statement.

'And you were involved in the police investigation?'

'Well, in some way or other we all were...'

'What did they ask you about?'

'It was a long time ago... I try not to re-live those days.'

'They ended up with Guy Campbell being convicted of multiple cases of fraud and money-laundering.'

Lee did not challenge the facts.

'Can I ask what your advice to the company's leadership was, as a lawyer - you must have been aware of what was going on?'

'As they say, advisers only advise. I was quite junior. You must have read my witness statement.'

'I have. There's a school of thought that says… that the charges, which were serious enough to merit a very long prison sentence, didn't represent the totality of the misdeeds in which MEKANICK was involved.'

'Some people have claimed that, but if there had been evidence, I'm sure the authorities would have pursued it. You know how prosecution works; they concentrate on the charges they think they're most likely to win. Most people agree that the sentence was harsh, considering.'

Kate was aware that, statistically, the sentence was indeed long, but she believed that in putting away the spider at the centre of a corrupt web it was justified. 'You're not seriously still peddling the 'victimless crime' line, are you?'

'Some ones and zeroes got put in the wrong order, in the wrong place. Who suffered?'

If this was to be his line it wasn't going to get her very far. Or was his tongue in his cheek?

'Well, trust in the entire banking system, for one thing!'

'No, Kate, I'm not arguing that it was victimless. It was certainly an unfair accretion of funds by means which were, properly, not allowed. And I understand the trust argument, of course.'

'OK, but the harsh sentencing was down to the judge - and there was no appeal, was there? Why not?'

'That decision was taken way above my pay grade, by a different sort of lawyer. But I'm not surprised they didn't appeal the verdict, probably in order not to attract even more attention. My own view was that, yes, the sentence was worth challenging.'

'Do you accept that the company was operating illegally?'

'That's what the court found, in respect of some of the company's operations, but not, of course, all of it. Most of what went on was perfectly legal.'

'Fair point - otherwise you wouldn't still be there now, I guess,' Kate said, but she was thinking: that doesn't make it right. She continued 'So -

there was a strong belief that not all of the assets that had been acquired illegally were traced. Let me be frank, Lee, did people inside MEKANICK deliberately hide assets of which the police and the court were unaware?'

Lee's face showed no expression, but it was clear that he was thinking. The conversation had reached a turning point.

'That's not where you should be looking, Kate. Not at where the money came from. Can we go off the record? No notes, no attribution?'

Kate had already both sacrificed her opportunity to record the exchange and pledged that Lee's name would not appear in print. If not even writing stuff down was the only way to secure his trust… she made a show of retracting her pen and placing it on her lap.

'Go ahead.'

'The police never expect to track a hundred percent of assets, they don't need to, they never do. Especially where, for example, foreign banks are involved.'

'Were foreign banks involved?'

Lee ignored the question. 'If I, or anyone else in the company, had 'hidden' assets that had been acquired in a criminal fashion, in the way you suggest, and we knew that, we might have been committing a criminal offence. I hope you're not accusing me of that.'

Kate wondered where this was leading. Lee had contacted her anonymously, out of the blue; he had known that she had reported on the original case, twelve years earlier - that would not have been difficult to discover. She wondered whether he was absolutely committed to going through with whatever he had planned. He must have something to say to her, something worth telling, or there was no reason for meeting. So far, she had heard nothing she did not already know, but she felt she had to go through the routine of teasing it out of him.

'No, I don't have evidence for that. Look, Lee, I'm not trying to entrap you. I don't need an arrest out of this, even if you did do something wrong.'

'Good. Thank you.'

'But you won't deny that some of the cash got 'parked', would you? Where it couldn't easily be found. I'm not saying it was necessarily parked by you, or with your authority, but by someone in the company, more than likely - and definitely on behalf of, and in the interests of, and possibly on the instruction of: Guy Campbell.'

'Now you're getting there. Shall we proceed on the understanding that none of the money concerned has been positively identified as of criminal origin, that every penny of it is innocent, at least until proved otherwise?'

'For the sake of argument, OK.' If that was the only way to make progress…

'Guy authorised everything that was done in the company, sometimes retrospectively, but the fact that he trusted his team and backed us up in all that we did was a positive aspect of working there.'

'Is he still in charge? Does he run the company from prison?'

'It depends on what you mean by 'in charge'. He wasn't technically declared bankrupt, but he's clearly not running MEKANICK, even though it's much smaller, these days, on a day-to-day basis. On the other hand, he's not taken a vow of silence.'

Staving off frustration, Kate said: 'Let me be blunt: is there money that should have been, could have been, accounted for twelve years ago, during the court proceedings which led to Guy Campbell being convicted, but was hidden from the view of the investigators?'

'Hidden? If you mean ill-gotten gains that were deliberately removed from the sight of authorities pursuing a legitimate enquiry, then I wouldn't say that, no.'

Why would they want to hide legitimate funds? she wondered. Where was this taking her? Why could he not just tell her the story? Where was the smoking gun? She tried again.

'So, there was money that, for one reason or another, the authorities didn't see, even if it came from legal sources?'

'Yes.'

At last! She was going to have to respect Lee's request for non-attribution. It was a professional courtesy, at the very least; that last 'yes' would not have been uttered without that assurance.

'Go on…'

'The story I have is not about where the money came from but where it went to. I know where some of it went.'

'Ball Park figure?'

'You must have some idea yourself.'

'I'm guessing twenty, thirty million. Fifty, tops.'

Lee acknowledged that Kate had done her homework; her estimate was close to the total. He raised an eyebrow and gave the slightest of nods, a comment that was genuinely unattributable.

Lee was considering his next words carefully; there was a political element to his strategy, and he needed to check that he was on firm ground. Kate waited patiently.

'This is a story about only some of that money. Your newspaper hasn't been too keen on HM Government recently, has it?' he asked.

'We're a paper with liberal values, we always have been. Is that what you mean?'

'And pro-European.'

'We like to call ourselves internationalist. Were we against Brexit? Yes, we were.'

'Me, too.'

From what she had discovered of Lee, Kate had guessed as much. 'Good.'

'It was a huge mistake. Mistake then, mistake now.'

Kate wondered where this was going and why it was relevant.

'If I give you a name, can you absolutely promise me that you won't ever disclose where you got it from, Kate?'

'Yes, I'm happy to confirm that.'

'I'm talking about only a small proportion of... the funds that you're asking about.'

'Understood.' At least it was something. 'How much?'

'About 750k.' This was peanuts. Kate was disappointed. But it was better than nothing, and just about enough to build a story upon.

'Am I looking for a company or a person?'

Lee smiled. 'Sometimes it's difficult to tell the difference.'

'In this case?'

'A loan to a lawyer, or rather to a law firm. To fund their expansion, ease their move into new offices. In part, at least.'

'You made an investment?'

'You might say that.'

'Twelve years ago?'

'Eleven and a bit. But the company didn't expand. They didn't move to new offices.'

'So what was...' Her train of thought was overtaken by another, on the express line: 'So, any loan made twelve years ago... even at a low rate of interest - that's quite a windfall for you. I mean - for MEKANICK.'

The expression on Lee's face reassured Kate that she had made a pertinent observation.

'So… what did they do with the money?'

'Who?'

'The recipient -'

Lee anticipated the question that was to follow: 'It was entirely up to the recipient, the loanee, as to what they did with the money.'

'And probably better that you, and MEKANICK, didn't know… OK… so, in this case?'

'It was used to finance Parliamentary campaigns.'

Kate put the jigsaw pieces together. This was a former Tory candidate who had been an active member of the Conservative party twelve years previously. He would know people in politics, would have mixed with other candidates, appreciated the need for both well-funded campaigns at election time and, more generally, lobbying. There were strict rules governing expenditure on both, but MEKANICK cash was not renowned for its diligent adherence to rules. Nor did the company actively or publicly support any Party or political agenda, come to that. But if it was Lee that had done the hiding, deliberately loaning out assets in ways that Guy would not know about, had to not know about, in order to legitimise any future denial Guy may ever have to make… Moments earlier she had come close to writing off 750k as not worth pursuing, but now, in this new context of campaign funding, it was a massive amount of money. Furthermore, Lee's pro-European views were mainstream in 2010 but now he was one of yesterday's men in the modern Tory Party. If he was still a member, that is.

'I have a story for you which is part fact, though only part of that can I prove, and part speculation. But I have good reason to believe that my speculation is well founded.'

Kate smiled. 'Go on, but please indicate which is which.'

'For the purposes of this conversation I will stick to fact: MEKANICK made three payments of different sizes, over six months, in 2010-11, to a law firm called Steel & Partners. £750,000 in total.'

'Please can I write this down? The numbers, at least.'

'Yes, go on. But it's still unattributable. Fact: the three records show that two smaller payments were made in respect of legal advice given and there was also a larger sum, all paid into the same account. This larger sum, more than half of the total, was a loan to cover relocation costs and the upgrading of facilities. Those changes never happened.'

'Nor were they intended to…' Kate realised what was happening.

'That's right.'

'And the loan was never repaid.'

'Well, that was the deal - at the time. I'll explain.'

'And was the advice ever given? What was it that was worth that much?'

'Let's say the money was legitimate, that it really did belong to Guy Campbell. Let's assume that 300k's worth of advice was given, it's not an incredible figure, perhaps Guy was prepared to pay a little over the odds for good advice. And I don't know what the advice was supposed to be about. Now look at it the other way round. What if someone asks you for a loan just when you're about to spend five or six years in prison - which is what Guy thought he would get - you don't really need the money that's sitting in your bank until you're out in the fresh air again.'

A pigeon landed on the far end of the bench. Ignored, it flew away again.

'I see… so it was lent for the duration. But it's been nearly twelve years, not five, and - oh! He's probably coming out soon…' A light went on inside Kate's brain. 'And he wants his money back?'

'Technically the loans were interest-free, but recipients would be expected to show their gratitude,' Lee went on.

'Why interest-free?'

'I don't care what you do with it, take risks, support legitimate businesses, whatever, it's up to you. Put it on deposit, generate a return on investment. Buy lottery tickets with it, if you like. But keep it above board and keep the total in the black.'

'Even at a low rate of interest, sitting in a bank account, it would earn a fair bit over 12 years…'

'And if it makes a fortune, feel free to show your appreciation.'

'He can't lose…'

Where was this going? Kate considered the loose ends. The principal was due to be returned on Campbell's liberation day or thereabouts, together with some extra, but Campbell did not really care how much the extra was. Even one percent compound on twenty million over eleven years was worth having, it would encourage the loanees to take good care of the money. Clever. Why had Lee asked about the paper's political stance? And why was he telling her all this now? She had a 'lightbulb' moment.

'You don't think you're getting this money back from those lawyers, do you?'

Lee looked almost inscrutable: 'Kate... I couldn't possibly comment.'

We know what that phrase means, she thought! There was a hint of a smile on Lee's lips.

She thought it through: 'If it's been spent on campaigning then there will be no financial return on the investment...' Another lightbulb: 'And if that campaigning has been on something - or someone - that the funder disapproves of, like... say, Brexit... then he'd be doubly pissed off!'

'You have a vivid imagination, Kate.'

'I'm not wrong, Lee, am I?'

Again, Lee was silent. He stared her directly in the eye and his face again displayed the slightest possible expression of encouragement. She tried a different tack.

'And political campaign funding is subject to its own strict rules...'

She took Lee's slight nod of the head and raised eyebrow as confirmation: she was on the right track.

'So... Steel & Partners, you say. I've never heard of them.' She wrote the name down.

Lee told her the name of the town in the leafy home counties. 'James Steel is a lifelong Tory Party member. He keeps his head below the parapet and his powder dry. If you judge him by the company he keeps, I'd say he's well to the right. But... it wasn't him I was dealing with.'

If Kate expected a name to be mentioned at this point, she was disappointed.

'Then who...?' She prompted.

'You wouldn't want me to spoon feed you, Kate. You've got to do some of the work.'

Was he teasing her now? It almost felt like it.

'So, I guess they have a web site.'

Lee nodded, once.

It was Kate's turn to raise her eyebrows in acknowledgement. She reached for her phone: 'Hey, Siri.'

'Uh, huh?' said an electronic woman.

'Who are the partners at Steel & Partners, solicitors?'

After a moment Siri replied: 'OK, this is what I've found. The partners at Steel & Partners, solicitors, are:'

There was a pause, after which the voice continued 'James Steel senior, Alice Brain, Indira Sharma, Damon Hough.'

Kate felt as though she had been dropped from a great height into a deep, dark chasm filled with ice-cold water; her face paled, her jaw dropped, and her skin crept.

'It can't be...'

'I thought you'd like that,' said Lee, thinking that he was waving the red rag of dark blue politics in front of a ravenous left-wing journalist.

But politics was not what had prompted Kate's electric frisson of needle-sharp apprehension.

'Surely,' she thought, 'he can't know about me and Damon... Can he?'

How Things Were - Kate & Damon: 2000-2002

There was not much more to tell. The justification for the combined 'gift' and loan was a pretence. A hundred percent of the capital was due for return to MEKANICK in the near future, plus a bonus. The Steel loan, in the care of a particularly unpleasant, right-wing Tory MP, was unlikely to be returned in full because he had spent too much of it, illicitly, on campaigning.

There was more to come but Lee was not yet ready to reveal some of his still tentative findings; he promised to contact Kate again as soon as he had something.

The interview over, Kate hurried back to the office. She would normally have taken tea in the afternoon, but today it was espresso - a double. She knew there was a bottle of brandy in a drawer of the temporarily unoccupied desk opposite hers, but she resisted. Greg was an old mate, he would not have begrudged her a slug or two, and he would have understood why she needed it; but she resisted, nonetheless. She had work to do. But first, she let that swell of emotion run through her again; it was prompted by revulsion, she now realised, not intimacy. Or was it a mixture?

Damon Hough. Oh God, please, not Damon Hough.

They had both been eighteen years young. He was studying law and she was reading English. In freshers' week of 2000 he left a lasting impression on her - he was garrulous, outspoken, provocative but also charming, in a very Edwardian sort of way. Even his clothes were New Romantic, not new century. They smiled at each other a couple of times across a bar in the first term - he appeared to wilt in her presence - but their first proper conversation was at a student ball to celebrate the first Saturday of 2001 when students were back after the Christmas break. The event was advertised as the Pedants 'Millennium Ball, as it was genuinely taking place in the first month of the new millennium - whereas most of the population had celebrated the event a year prematurely. In practice, this student body had contrived to enjoy the dawn of the new age twice over.

Whatever type of function it was, this was a brand-new year in their young lives, and everyone had at least two goals to achieve that night: to wear their most outrageous clothes and to get drunk. A fair few, of various genders, were also hoping to get laid for the first time in the new era, or perhaps just for the first time. Damon only wanted to talk.

They found a quiet spot in a corridor where they leant on a bannister broad enough to place their drinks upon; a gin and tonic for her, a double vodka and orange for him. As a gentleman he would not countenance having a lady buy him a drink. Kate wore a skimpy dress in twinkling cobalt blue, more suitable for summer, with a plunging neckline which left little of her athletic figure to the imagination. For reasons of monthly inconvenience, however, pulling was not on her 'to do' list that night.

Damon, the Jekyll and Hyde character who could be so loud with the boys and so meek in her presence, was not preventing himself from viewing her exposed cleavage more openly than a proper gentleman should. But then she already guessed that he was less than a hundred percent gentleman, and that bare female torso at close range was still a novelty for the young man. Nor was he a hundred percent sober.

Indeed, they were both lubricated with alcohol but experienced eighteen-year-old drinkers can develop daunting powers of self-control. It was not the first time she had noted that he was subdued in her presence; she found this unnerving, if slightly flattering. They shared tales of their respective childhoods, but the next morning all Kate could remember of Damon's account was his 'difficult' relationship with his father, a navy man. She could not recall ever having had an intimate conversation with a teenage male who had not said something similar about diplomatic relations on the paternal front.

After the ball was over, well after midnight, they walked together towards the north of the campus, where Kate was living. It was cold but no longer raining and a faux fur coat was all that protected her from the weather. This was poor planning, she realised, but even though it was mild for January, she appreciated it when Damon placed his Barbour jacket - which smelt of the countryside - around her shoulders. At the entrance to her block, he took her hand, kissed it as a Victorian gentleman would and turned to go. She stopped him, said 'thank you' and gave him a brief hug as the Barbour fell to the floor. He picked up the soiled garment, shook it, smiled with tight lips, turned on his heel and walked smartly south.

For the next six months they were regular companions, a status two levels below 'inseparable'. They went to talks together, including once to the theatre, though Damon did not appreciate the subtlety of Brecht - he was more of an Ayckbourn man, he said. Several months later, hearing this explanation of his lack of dramatic discrimination for the third time, she wondered if he knew the work of any playwright other than Scarborough's finest. They rarely spoke of political issues - neither first year was interested in the blinkered world of student politics whilst both were professed humanitarians. Whilst Kate would, occasionally, buy a Guardian at weekends and more often an Observer for the Sunday morning lie-in, the only time she saw Damon with a newspaper, folded into the massive pockets of that old, oiled jacket, it was a Telegraph. 'Family tradition,' he explained, 'for the sport'. Which sport it was that interested him, she never found out.

Returning from the Easter break in 2001 Kate was looking forward to seeing her new friend again. They had chalked up three months of reasonably satisfying friendship by then, but no more than that. Their chaste relationship was the talk of the lewd girls with whom Kate shared a kitchen. It was about time, she thought, that either he stays the night here or I stay at his. If fate decreed 'neither', it might be time to move on.

With the new summer term Damon arrived back on campus with a new toy: an elderly MG Midget, an early present from his parents for his upcoming 19th birthday. Things back home must be on an even keel for once, Kate surmised. They went for a 'spin' in the sunny if chilly countryside where, clad in thick woollen jumpers, they drank a bottle of cava beside a stream. On the way home Kate decided, quite deliberately, to flirt: she caressed the gear stick provocatively, making sure he saw what she was doing, licked her lips and watched his face as the countryside whizzed by. He smiled a mild smile, appreciatively. She judged it premature to think of the vehicle as a 'penis extension', the popular image associated with bright red sports cars, without having seen the genuine Hough equipment for comparison. Nevertheless, she hoped her message had got through.

Back at the residence block she lured him into her room with the promise of coffee, but appeared to immediately forget her pledge, opening a bottle of red wine instead. Booze was one thing to which Damon never said 'no'. Towards the end of their first glass, she peeled off her jumper - she was overheating in her outdoor clothing - but realised that she was wearing a sloppy old grey tee-shirt, faded and worn, beneath it. How embarrassing was that? She hatched a plan.

'Let's have some music - there are some CDs in the corner, Damon, can you lean over and choose one?'

He turned his back and started to rummage; there were not many albums to choose from and she guessed, correctly, that his taste did not match hers. After a few seconds of leeway - he was failing to find one he wanted to hear - she sat down on the bed beside him, there being limited alternative furniture in her cell. Then, carefully (not wanting to waste it) she dripped a drop of red wine onto the old tee-shirt. Damon surfaced from his search, suggesting she make the difficult choice of music as he repositioned himself, clumsily as ever, beside her. She said, playfully, pointing to the stain, 'Oh, look what you've made me do!', leaned over to put her glass on the floor then sat up and started to peel off the tee-shirt in the pretence of needing to soak it.

She had his attention. She looked at him and smiled, challenging. His gaze was once again captured by her breasts, which were even more exposed now, in a lightweight, soft beige bra, than they had been in the cobalt blue. On the positive side Kate was proud of her slim body, it was lean and functional, it had been a friend to her over recent years. She was not a virgin and had enjoyed sharing her flesh with a boy on the couple of occasions so far when that had been appropriate; and even once when it had not. She was in good shape and, this afternoon, she thought she smelled good. Up to this point they had not discussed sex, although she suspected that gentle, sensitive Damon might not yet have 'broken his duck'. Which was true. Up to a point.

On the negative side they were frozen into a tableau: what was going to happen now?

'Can I have a hug?' she said, almost coquettishly.

The hug was clumsy. Damon had been content to look, even ogle, but was ham-fisted when it came to touching. He appeared content to rest his palms on her naked shoulder blades as he at last embraced her, taking care not to spill his glass. However, he appeared wary of approaching her breasts, even chest to chest and through his pullover, and he positively shied away from touching the fabric of the bra. To have done so would indicate wanting to take control; he had no urge to do that, and it was not what he wanted to be seen to be doing. After a moment, she pushed him a few inches away from herself but only to reach out for the hem of his jumper, which she removed by pulling over his head, a move which required a complex balancing act with the wineglass. Then she pushed him backwards, onto the bed, laying her hands on his prostrate chest. The shirt felt soft, expensive.

'What do we have here…?' she said.

Smiling to reassure the child, she started to undo his shirt, one button, two buttons, three. He looked on passively, silent, almost terrified.

This moment had been coming for a whole term, Kate reasoned. If she abandoned the campaign now it would mean abandoning Damon, whose friendship had become as comfortable as a pair of slippers. She had not had sex since an unexpected Auld Lang Syne present from a former boyfriend, back home, and that was not going to be repeated. Perhaps it really was time to consummate this relationship if it was going to continue. Decisions, Kate, decisions.

To have invested so much time in this boy and not have a sexual relationship seemed to be a waste, somehow, at their age, a failure to follow the learning curve that university laid out before young adults. Walking out now would cut her losses. Waiting for him, nudging him to take the initiative threatened to be a wait in vain. There was one other option: take charge.

She had been kneeling next to him on the single bed, in her bra, jeans and socks. He was flat out prone, beside her, fully dressed, his shoes still touching the floor and his shirt partly unbuttoned, partly untucked. Throughout the time that she had been looking at him he had remained silent, occasionally sipping his wine which he had managed not to spill. Kate decided to buy some time. She stood up, stepped back. Putting an album on the CD player would give her a few more seconds to calculate, whilst providing a conveniently noisy backdrop to frustrate prying ears in the students' communal kitchen on the other side of the wall. There was a Pretenders disc already in the machine. To make life even more exciting, she instructed the player to operate a 'random shuffle'. She picked up her own glass of wine, still almost full, and drained it in one.

She topped them both up as 'Brass in Pocket' rang out, it was one of her favourite tracks. It was old - from a time before she was born, the album had belonged to her late father - but it was still definitely cool. Chrissie Hynde was immortal. Damon lay, frozen, silent, though did she detect a thawing at the edges? Or was he just unsettled by the raw alien chords?

She removed his glass from his hand and placed it out of harm's way.

Gonna make you, make you notice, sang Chrissie.

'Stick or twist?' Kate thought.

I gotta have some of your… attention.

Decision made. She unhooked the button of her jeans and wriggled out of them, deftly slipping a thumb inside each sock as she did so, adding to the mounting pile of clothing on the floor.

Give it to me!

Clad only in skimpy pants and bra she climbed back onto the bed and took his face in her hands, kissing him directly on the lips. She felt his face quiver, his arms twitch and then he was holding her…

Gonna use my arms.

She put her arms around him, allowing herself to fall onto the bed by his side, so she was no longer above him but beside him…

Gonna use my legs.

This movement freed up both her hands to return to his shirt buttons which yielded, in short order.

Gonna use my style.

Her hands delved into his shirt, touching flesh - pale, white, hairless, clammy -

Gonna use my sidestep.

He's like a giant bald teddy bear, she thought, and as she fixed his gaze her hand went to his crotch -

Gonna use my fingers.

She kissed him harder, grabbing his - where was it? She paused momentarily, then undid his trouser button with her right hand. Still, he remained passive, though his breathing was laboured and shallow. He had noticed her.

Gonna use my, my, my…

Her hand went into his pants as she pushed her almost bare breasts up, towards his face. There was some response 'downstairs', which was good. Something at last for her to get hold of.

…imagination!

She stopped. Left her hand where it was, moved her body back so he could see her face and breasts, and gave him a lascivious grin.

'Yes?' she asked.

I gotta have some of your… attention.

Damon nodded, timorous but not resisting. She withdrew further, stepped off the bed and started to remove his trousers. Halfway down she stopped and let him finish the job whilst she deftly removed first her bra and then her pants. Christ, she thought, he's wearing Union Jack boxers… and he's keeping them on!

Give it to me!

Nude, she now mounted the bed once more and started the routine again, lying beside him and taking his face in her hands to kiss him on the mouth; he was slightly more relaxed, but only slightly. She became convinced that he had never been on a bed and so intimate with a naked woman before; she vowed to take care. This time when she reached down his member was not only large and hard but was also patently throbbing. A moment later…

Gonna make you notice!

Well, she thought, that was memorable.

…

It did not deter her. A week later, at the second attempt, things were more 'normal'. Thenceforward they would have sex about once a month, never achieving the status of 'frequent', whilst continuing to see each other for social companionship at least twice a week.

Intimacy can take many forms: touching a partner in places no one else touches, being similarly touched; or it may be expressed in words. Intimacy can involve the telling, the sharing, of secrets.

One weekend in June was particularly trying for Kate. She had just returned from ten unscheduled days away, coping with her mother's death after a long battle with cancer. As Eileen's approaching demise became clearer Kate's brother, Nick, was summoned from Japan - though he was never expected to make it home in time to say goodbye. Kate took time out from university to handle everything.

The mother died in her daughter's arms.

It was a moment Kate would never forget, shortly before two in the morning in a side ward of a small hospital. Kate had continued to remind her mother of fond memories and her parent had acknowledged them with a blink, a tiny smile or a nod. They talked for a while, and then only Kate was talking, and soon neither was talking any more. Nothing, only breathing. And then - Kate had no idea how time was progressing, every moment was writ large and glowing in her consciousness - Eileen's breathing became unreliable. Lacking the strength to catch her breath,

Kate's mother stifled shallow coughs; as though clearing her throat during a silent prayer.

Kate laid her down, stood, stepped back, opened the door and peered into the corridor. There was no one around. Later she would challenge herself to wonder: was she seeking help and support or was she checking if the coast was clear?

She re-entered the room, closing the door to re-establish their privacy. There was a button to summon help, but she declined to use it. The older woman's breaths were louder yet still quiet, becoming more laboured and physical. Kate leaned over and kissed her mother on the cheek; the flesh was cold and clammy, the gentle texture of soft, cold dough.

She leaned forward further, took the small, frail shoulders in her hands, pressed her mother to her own bosom. Did she imagine a splutter? She felt a tear well up in her eye but was holding her mother so tightly that she could not relax enough to wipe it away.

Long moments later she released the tension, laid the woman back onto her pillow.

There were no more sounds.

The soft, irregular, aching rumbles from deep in the throat were no more.

'Good-bye, mum,' she said, aloud. 'I love you.'

The 19-year-old coped well with the immediate impact of bereavement. Now an orphan, she finalised the funeral arrangements before Nick joined her to share the burden of the event itself and its associated public grieving. The cremation was on the Friday morning and at 8 that same evening Kate found Damon and his red sports car waiting for her at the drizzling station which served the University. He barely spoke but that felt respectful, proper, the right thing to do.

Damon stayed with Kate from that Friday evening until the Monday morning, the longest time they had ever spent continuously together. Company was all she needed. On the Saturday the mourning that she had hitherto compressed and hidden came flooding out in a wave of catharsis lasting several hours. There were tears, screams and intimate revelations about the woman who was now mere ashes in an urn. Kate so needed to have someone beside her, to touch, but mostly not, to listen, or give the appearance of doing so, to feel what she was feeling. One out of three was good.

At the nadir of the Saturday afternoon, she may have said something like 'I killed my mother'. Or maybe 'I might have…' or simply 'Did I…?' What did it matter? She certainly told again how she clutched Eileen's head tightly, excruciatingly, to her just as the breathing stopped. Stopped for ever. She certainly said something about her feelings to Damon that afternoon though, as the years rolled by, she could never remember exactly what words she had used, nor in what order. Nor did she try to.

Unable to face lunch, and better for both of them, Kate slept from mid-afternoon to early evening on the Saturday. Did she dream that she had confessed murder to Damon? Or did she actually tell him that? Could it be that in clutching her mother she really had 'finished her off', to coin a tasteless phrase? It was a horrible thought, one that once surfaced could never again be forgotten. Never. She could not recall any response he might have made, or whether one had been forthcoming at all, so perhaps she had not said it, after all. She vowed never to speak of it again.

When she awoke, at seven that evening, she could smell the Italian meal that Damon had prepared. It turned out to be freshly delivered pizzas that he had ordered, but they were of her favourite recipe, so that was good. She anticipated, too, the taste of a decent Malbec, their mutually favourite wine, already chambré and more than ready to drink.

And drink. Damon's one insight into her psychology, apart from an innate sense of when to keep quiet, was that at some point that weekend vast amounts of alcohol would be required.

They spent three nights in the same bed, as brother and sister.

On the Sunday morning, after the papers in bed (Damon found reading the Observer quite a novelty) they took the MG to a local beauty spot for a long walk and stopped for lunch in a favourite pub. Things were beginning to return to normal.

They made separate plans for the summer vacation, keeping in touch through brief text messages. Kate was a little surprised to receive a phone call in early September, in which Damon invited her to Dorset for the upcoming weekend. His parents were having a dinner party on the Friday, and she was not only welcome to come but he even invited her to stay over. Drat! Whilst it sounded interesting (what were the Houghs really like?) it clashed with her best friend's hen night, which promised to be the social event of the year, and Kate was pledged…

'I'm sorry, Damon. Another time?'

He did not seem too upset, suggesting that instead she could say hello to his parents by telephone, at 9 a.m. on the Saturday?

After a hen night? Don't be silly. Make it eleven. Deal.

It was only after putting the phone down that it occurred to her how odd his request had been. There was no 'How nice to talk to you!', no 'I do hope you can come', but both oversights were so Damon; she had learned to expect his tone to be dry and emotion-free. Above all, she realised, there was no explanation as to why she was being invited. Was it to be a 'Meet the parents' event? Corny but well, yes, obviously. Would not the phone call be sufficient? It was feeling a bit 'Look, parents, I've got a girlfriend! I'm capable of getting one, after all! Look!' How immature was that? She was sure she was making that bit up. Or was she…?

The least he could have done was to be honest with her.

He called her ten minutes before the scheduled summit; fortunately, she was ready.

'Remember, Kate, my dad's ex-navy, a Commander in the submarines. That's how he runs his family, his crew, it's how he thinks the country should be run, too. With iron discipline,' warned Damon, before reeling off a list of topics for Kate to avoid.

The call took place and Kate was shocked how exactly like Damon his father sounded on the phone. Gerald's voice - 'Call me Gerald, please, none of this 'Mr Hough' business!' - suggested a lifetime of smoking, the sailor's curse; she could hear the smoker's wrinkles, subdivided on every surface of his face, at every angle, almost smell them. Gerald dominated the conversation, with enthusiasm and bonhomie that felt practiced but fabricated; the mother, perched on the sitting room extension, said little. Both parents adopted cocktail party small talk mode and Kate found it easy to play the brand new but serious girlfriend. She did so to perfection, circumscribed only by her conscience's diktat that she should not actually lie. She had always believed that facial expressions could be heard down the phone line, so she smiled until her face ached, saying as many nice things about Damon - the sweetie - as she could conceivably justify. She even found herself believing some of them. Otherwise, less was better. If the Hough seniors were unhappy with this 12-minute encounter they hid it well, but it would probably be beneath them to have revealed any disappointment to her, in any case.

That Christmas Damon gave her a book token, which she considered decidedly unromantic. Although it was a genuine let-down, she found a good use for it. In return she gave him a small box, delicately wrapped, with instructions not to open it until Christmas Day. She supposed that cuff links were routine, too, they were so unimaginative. Nevertheless, she hoped that the pretty, silver, four leafed clovers - a nod to her own Irish ancestry, several generations removed - would bring him luck. She knew that they were not solid silver; she was a student, after all.

During their second spring at university, they continued their relationship as before although Kate reasoned that, had she counted the hours, she was spending less time with Damon than she had in the summer. The sex tailed off - it happened only once during that spring term, an occasion that was eminently, sadly, forgettable. 'It's not you,' he explained, and she believed him.

Damon failed to show up a couple of times when they had arranged to meet and he could not, in Kate's view, even be bothered to construct a decent excuse. He muttered something about how law was so taxing, with constant assessments, though other law students she knew did not complain as much.

Throughout the Easter vacation of 2002 there was silence between them. As term re-started the girls who shared Kate's kitchen also shared their gossip: 'Well, everyone knows, but we didn't like to say anything...' There was a bar on the campus which had grown a reputation as the haunt of the far right in student politics. Kate had become aware that her significant other might tend towards that end of the spectrum but her views on freedom, for example, as a liberal, had sufficient in common with his as a libertarian for them not to waste time on political disagreement. Politics was not high on the agenda for either of them. Damon had become a regular in that bar, the girls reported, mixing with loud and unpleasant types, and had been ejected from it, after hours, more than once. One said that Damon had crashed his lovely MG when drunk, a week earlier, when Kate did not even know that he was back from Swanage. Another said that police had broken up a clandestine dog-fighting syndicate and Damon had been amongst those present cautioned for placing bets. He later denied this, but he was unconvincing.

For these and other reasons she wondered if Damon was lying to her, systematically. They were undoubtedly moving apart, but why could he not tell her the truth? The long gaps, the deceit, the double life; the boring conversation. The sparkle that had undoubtedly been there a year previously had gone, as Kate's emotional pendulum swung towards 'better off without him'. He let his phone ring, unanswered, when she called him. She texted him using her new Nokia on Saturday, 8th May 2002, to say 'Monday, I'll be home all evening. We need to talk. Please come round.' There was no immediate response.

Just before 7 p.m. on that Monday she received a text. She worried that he was upset that she had overlooked his birthday, on the second; how childish that would be. Hers was coming up, a week later, but she ought not to expect a present. It was all going to be over soon. Something inside her was looking forward to that moment, but it had to be handled properly.

The text told her to meet him at a nearby park bench, at 7.15. It was not warm, and it looked like rain; she took a light coat and an unseasonal woollen hat from her wardrobe. She arrived at the appointed place in good time but could see no-one. She texted him and a moment later he called from a different bench, fifty yards away, 'Over here!'

She walked without hurrying; he stood as she approached.

'Hello, Damon.'

'Hello.'

She found herself saying 'Look, I need to tell you something -'

'My father's dead.'

That was not what she had expected to hear. She had only ever met the man once, by phone, for just twelve minutes. She could hardly say that she knew him.

'I'm so sorry to hear that, Damon.'

'Not your fault. Not this time.'

'No,' she thought, 'obviously'. And then: ''Not this time'? What did he mean by that?'

Damon went on 'He killed himself.'

Kate took a sharp intake of breath and brought both hands to her mouth. This was a shock. She had never heard those words before in real life and nor, as far as she was aware, had anyone that she knew.

'Hung himself. From a road bridge.'

'Damon. I am so sorry…' Genuinely upset, she took a pace towards him; he held up a hand defensively and took a step backwards.

'It's fine. Really.'

'Why…?'

'Because he was a sad old, angry old bastard. Fuck him.' That was no way to speak of his father! Even though they clearly had never got on he had never used such language before about his dad. Was Damon drunk? He appeared to be neither inebriated nor in the process of becoming so.

'When?'

'May the second.'

'Your birthday!'

'That wouldn't have meant anything to him. But it meant something else to him. That date always has.'

'What was that?'

He refused to meet her gaze. 'It doesn't matter.'

'I'm so sorry…' She knew she could not go through with what she had intended, with 'finishing' with him. This was not the time. When her mother had died, she had needed someone to be physically close, to help absorb her grief. Although he had provided her with that service then, she sensed that he might not appreciate her reciprocal attention now. But she had to be available, just in case. That's what friends do.

'Kate…'

She hardly ever heard him use her name. He must be about to say something important.

'Yes?'

He still failed to return her gaze.

'I don't want to see you anymore.'

A plethora of words came into her mind, of which 'bastard' predominated. But it did not come out. It stayed inside her. You fucking bastard. I set this meeting up, not you! I was going to say that to you - and you've beaten me to it. She had not anticipated him taking this particular initiative…

After a moment she found herself calmly asking him 'Why not?' though that mood did not reflect what she was thinking.

'Because I don't need you. Thank you, and all that. It was… good. Very helpful.' Sincerity was lacking from his voice and although he still would not look into her eyes, she could not take hers off him.

'Did you say 'helpful'?' She started to find words, which she proceeded to release in a calm, cold and scathing manner: 'What do you think I am, Damon, a bloody tour guide? Well, I hope you enjoyed the fucking ride.' She was amazed at how calmly her voice was behaving, despite her emotion. Physically, she found herself shaking.

'I didn't want this to happen. Not like this,' he said.

She felt an icy chill throughout every muscle: 'Like what, then?' She was losing her equilibrium. 'What the fuck are you trying to say to me, Damon?'

Kate was still wearing her woollen hat. It suddenly felt conspicuous, inappropriate, wrong. She pulled it off and stretched it from hand to hand, even though it was spitting with rain. They were standing ten feet apart, as though social distancing in lockdown.

Kate closed her eyes. 'If you don't tell me I'll only wonder, speculate. ' She opened her eyes again. 'So: tell me now.' Then sarcasm got the better of her: 'If you don't mind.'

This way might help you, too, she thought, rationally. She waited for him to speak; he was gathering his thoughts.

'My father had high hopes for me. He gave up on me becoming a soldier, he knew a long time ago that I was never going to go into the forces, but that's what he really wanted for me. It's a man's occupation, being a soldier. They're 'real men', he used to say. Then he decided that I was going to be a high-flier in business, a corporate lawyer. He never went to university, I was his proxy, and that bit, the university bit, well, at least I could go along with that. I ticked a box for him. And coming here meant that I didn't have to get a job for a few years. Get into business via law school, not business school, that was his advice. Go in at the top. Well, you know what? I hate corporate law. There's too much risk. Too narrow a set of interests, it's not any… it's not any fun. And it's too much hard work. I get vertigo - no, I'm serious. Literally, all his ambition stuff just drives me silly, into a spin.'

Kate had regained some composure. She decided to do him the courtesy of listening even if this self-centred drivel had nothing to do with her or their current situation.

'I'm doing a law degree, I'm over halfway done, I'll see it through. But I won't be going into corporate law. I'm going to be a solicitor. House conveyancing, you can make quick money that way, good margins, seller's market, lots of time for my own - you don't get that as a corporate lawyer, not unless you reach the very top. Where the vertigo's at its worst.'

He looked pathetic. Throughout this monologue his gaze had still not lifted from the floor. Was he hiding his shame? His face was drawn and grey.

'He had other ambitions for me, too. He was against me being active in politics; money was more important, more powerful than 'power', he said. As a military man he learned the importance of doing what you were told. Politics was a dirty business, that was his view, I had to think of the family dignity and keep my distance. And yet... his best friend, my so-called godfather, is a politician! Well, sod that, that's going to change now. And he told me I'd meet the girl that I'd marry at university. God knows where he got that idea from. What does he know about it?'

Kate blanched. Marriage was one subject they had never discussed in over a year of being, more or less, together. She realised that she had never even considered marriage, not to Damon, at least. She held her counsel.

'He kept going on at me, 'Why haven't you got a girlfriend?' Nagging away like an old woman.'

She failed to appreciate the simile. Nor what was coming next.

'Made me fucking sick. Every time I went home, nag, nag. Then you came along, I told him I'd got a girlfriend. A year ago, I told them.'

Against her better judgment, Kate's blood was starting to boil. She finally spoke.

'So - that call, last September - that was to show them that I really existed, was it? The future Mrs Hough? That I was not a figment of your imagination? Look, I was friendly to them, I knew they'd kindly invited me to a party, that was very nice of them, but -'

'An engagement party.'

'And you know I couldn't go because - what? Whose...? Mine? You fucking shit!'

'It was quite a relief when you couldn't come.'

'You shit! That was... eight months ago! They've been thinking that we're engaged for the last eight months?'

Kate was speechless, another shiver of anger ran through her: she really was being used.

'It doesn't matter,' he said.

''It doesn't matter'? Damon, you've used me and it's not fucking nice! What do you mean, 'it doesn't fucking matter'?'

Damon shouted: 'For fuck's sake, Kate, it doesn't matter because the fucker's dead!'

'What?'

'It's got nothing to do with you!'

'Nothing to do...!' She was appalled. What a shit!

'It wasn't you that was living a lie, Kate, it was my father. One thing he did respect was a long engagement, thank Christ, so there was no sodding pressure to name a date. And my bloody mother…'

'What about her?'

'She kept asking to see the ring. Someone on my course got engaged, I told this woman she should keep a photo of the ring in case she ever lost it, and that I would take a picture of it, on her hand, and print it off for her…'

'So you made a copy and sent that to your mother!'

'She was very insistent…'

Kate's anger came out: 'You were the one that was living a lie!'

Damon grasped for words that did not come. Still no eye contact.

'And what about your mother, Damon? She's still alive. Does she think we're engaged?'

'No, I mean yes, she's still alive. But no, the silly cow saw through all my crap ages ago.'

'What?'

'When I was at home at Christmas. She told me she didn't believe that I was engaged. Or even had a girlfriend. But she didn't want to upset my father, she didn't want to be the one who told him that I was a fraud. So, she never did.'

'For fuck's sake, Damon!'

'My father was a submariner.'

'Yes, I know. What the hell has that got to do with anything?'

'There was something about that job that he really detested, though he did it for years.'

'He was claustrophobic, was he? Got seasick? My heart bleeds for him.' She knew she was being disrespectful; she could not help it. She could not care less.

'Please don't mock, no, that's not it. He… he hated gay men.'

Kate paused, suddenly anticipating what was coming next. It would explain a lot. Actually, it explained everything.

She said 'I don't suppose it was exactly rare in the submarines.'

'I could never tell him… that I was gay. I had to hide it from him, hide it from everyone. Even you. Especially you. I got to university, thinking, you know, this is where I find myself. Sexual freedom, and all that… gay liberation.'

You thought you'd hidden it, did you? she said to herself. This explained everything. How could I have been so blind? Damon was continuing:

'It wasn't my intention to deceive my father or go against his wishes. But then I met you, and… I thought I ought to test myself. Could I cope with a straight relationship? Could I… lose my virginity to a woman? I could do so physically…'

'Just about,' thought Kate.

'But in my head, I couldn't. And certainly not in my heart.' He glanced at her, momentarily, possibly for the first time.

There was a silence. They still stood several feet apart. It was starting to rain more steadily but Kate resisted putting her hat back on.

'You should have told me, Damon. We could have talked about this.'

'Yes. I'm sorry. I should. After all, you told me your innermost secrets - do you remember? About killing your mother. But I never told you mine. Your nightmare is in the past but I was living mine every day. And that was going to be the case for the foreseeable future - as long as that bastard was alive!'

Killing my…? Kate was taken aback, then fuming.

'I never said I killed my mother!' There was a powerful, raw venom in her voice: 'I said I held her, as she died -'

Now, at last, he looked at her and spoke adamantly: 'You said you suffocated her, in so many words. At least I never did that!' He spat out the words.

Now he was looking at her, directly, for the first time in the conversation, accusing.

Kate struggled to speak in a calm voice: 'You shit, Damon, you… you little shit!'

There was only one thing to do as the rain took a turn for the worst and a cold wind whipped it up. She held herself back to consider whether to let him have both barrels, to respond to his cruel, heartless - false! - words, to defend herself, her honour, her reputation, her dear mother… but there was no point. There was simply no point in being there, in continuing this conversation further. She would only hurt herself more.

Now it was she that would not engage Damon's gaze. There were suddenly tears in her eyes.

'Goodbye, Damon. And just… fuck off, will you? Just fuck the hell off.'

She deliberately said no more. There were tears in her eyes, real tears.

Before he could respond, Kate turned on her heel and walked determinedly out of the park and back towards her room. As she walked, she pulled that ridiculous hat over her head and ears, a bobble hat in May! She could summon not a single coherent thought on that journey as she juggled a kaleidoscope of thoughts with a metaphorical axe and the rain came on yet more heavily, urged on by the penetrating wind under a leaden sky.

Arriving in her room she slammed the door behind her, kicked off her boots, threw her coat and woolly hat to the floor. She fell onto the bed, still clothed, and began beating hell out of her pillow. And beating it again. And again, until the sobbing exhausted her.

She cried until she fell asleep.

Was she crying for Damon?

Of course not. He was a shit. And you know what? He always had been.

She was crying for the last 16 lost months of her life.

Half of her University career.

…

Damon never tried to contact her again.

In the year that remained of their time at university he determined to hide if ever he saw her approaching on campus, which did not happen often. He avoided the bars and other places where he thought she might be and thanked heavens they were following different courses. He knew he had let her down, but he felt as certain as he could be that his secrets, such as they were, were safe with her. He had told no-one else about the gay stuff but he sensed that he would protect it less diligently from now on. And there was now a balance of terror, in terms of secrets shared. If she did not want to be reminded of what she had said after her mother died, then she should not have said it.

Released from his father's edict Damon became more active in the campus Conservative group. This was ironic, because his father had dropped a hint that if he was ever to be asked to become a freemason he should accept, and it was good to make such contacts when one was young. The Tory Party was as good a way as any to access the masonic realm, though it was not the route his father had anticipated. It might not be so important for the corporate lawyer, Damon reasoned, but the market town solicitor really had to be 'on the level' if he wanted to get on.

Inspired by Damon's new-found enthusiasm for politics his new group of friends took their right wing causes to the student union meetings and debating chambers. Now Damon found himself peddling a new persona - the entertaining, witty, devastating, destructive orator, the upsetter of apple carts. From chamber daises, town centre street corners and even across the odd pub table he would declaim the cause of freedom from tyranny, from socialism, from… government. It was kudos for old rope for the reborn extrovert.

At the same time Damon's social life became dominated by a group of former public school-types who ran a pale imitation of Eton's Bullingdon Club, but without the class. Not of their ilk, the state-school boy worked hard to be accepted and his investment paid off: he enjoyed their male and raucous company. They had exorbitant dinner parties, got very drunk on fine wines and jumped over dining tables, spreading cutlery and crockery asunder. On such occasions (and every other) they would denounce every aspect of the Blair government and drink 'anti-toasts'. Damon's voice came to dominate public proceedings in which the faction was involved. At each dinner the attendees would vote for who had been 'loser of the month', the 'naughtiest boy' - for they were all boys - and who the winner, the most outrageous and daring orator. After the dessert course the victim would stand on a table, drop his trousers and receive a single lash of a leather tawse on his bare arse from the victor. It was only a ritual, a symbolic beating. But unless you had both received and administered the tawse in front of your peers you weren't, in their eyes, a proper man. Damon naturally became a beater fairly often and he contrived just once to be a beaten, for the hell of it, too.

Prior to university Damon was an enthusiast for mutual masturbation with friends and had even kissed a boy once with tongues (they were both 17, drunk and doing it for a bet). But it was not until the day before the winter break began, in his final University year, that Damon popped his cherry for a second time, courtesy of a middle-aged commercial traveller in a hotel room. There was strict, clinical and one-off anonymity.

Such adventures, of which there were soon too many to count, were added to Damon's growing pile of secrets.

This sort of sex was much more fun, thought Damon, the pending graduate, a year on from that rainy evening in the park. It generated a real sense of adventure, daring, courage and power. It was so much more fun than those months of embarrassed fumbling with… goodness!

He could barely remember her name.

Paul's Dilemmas:

Saturday 23rd April 2022

Paul Roe was getting cold feet. In line with the plan that he had announced to Henry he drove to London on the Saturday afternoon, following his morning advice surgery and a long but teetotal pub lunch with the Leader of the Council. The football match on the car radio took his mind off the matters in hand as it would go some way to deciding the outcome of the Premier League. Not that either team in the featured commentary was his favourite; ideally, he wanted them both to lose. He plugged in his electric car in the Parliamentary car park and surfaced from the underground catacomb, just as London started to relax. His overnight bag was bulging with casework but at least it had wheels. He had allocated Sunday to trawling through these files. His flat, off the Kennington Road, was only five stops away from the Commons by bus and it was much easier to park in Parliament than in Lambeth's overcrowded side streets.

As usual, the Palace of Westminster was deserted at the weekend. The empty Gothic pile was eerie with echoes, with occasional police officers the only humans visible to acknowledge. Every MP knew to say hello to every officer: Members never knew when they might need a constable's help. Each officer already knew every MP by name.

Heading for the gate, the exit from New Palace Yard into Parliament Square, Paul remembered with a chill the Westminster terror attack of five years previously. A perpetrator, whose name he had deliberately forgotten, had mowed down 50 pedestrians on the bridge with his car and then knifed a police officer to death before being shot dead himself. As he recalled that day, the MP found himself walking past the very spot where PC Keith Palmer had fallen; Paul himself had been less than a hundred metres away at the time, as the crow flies, and remembered the chaotic aftermath all too well.

The memory would stay with him forever.

Once inside his flat he drew the curtains to shut out the intrusive sunlight. Last night's encounter with Maureen Greatbach was still troubling him. Although his discussion with Henry on managing the case had been helpful, he knew that he had told the young man far too much about his own history. Yes, he could rely on Henry's discretion, that was taken as read, that was not what troubled him. It had always been his secret, his secret alone, and now he had shared it; he found the act of revelation to be of more concern, more exposing than the nature of the tawdry confidence itself. Whilst he was more than confident that he had graduated from his teenage years as a fully qualified heterosexual, a straight, cis man, he had often queried his own ambiguous internal response to Damon's molestation... and found it troublingly disconcerting. It wasn't the physical nature of the - he hesitated to call it an 'attack' - the 'intervention', it was the absence of an emotional context, the lack of tenderness, the uninvited invasion of personal space, all these plus the degree of presumption displayed by the other that worried him more.

There was plenty of dried pasta in the cupboard and half a jar of sauce to go with it, even some exceedingly dry parmesan, followed by a yoghurt and custard cream biscuits for dessert. The biscuits were in an unopened pack but, as Paul observed with prescience, the pack would likely not survive the evening. Nor, for certain, would the bottle of red wine that he now took from his case, where the padding provided by copious case files had kept it safe. It stood, beckoning, on the kitchen table.

Tonight's routine was laid down before him as if by edict: a leisurely supper followed by an hour of reading designed to delay the onset of drinking. Then he would search Netflix for a binge-worthy box set, taking a break from that to watch Match of the Day. The viewing process would be accompanied by the full-bodied budget Cabernet, and, at some point, he would probably fall asleep in front of the TV. If that was during the football, he would watch what he had missed on catch-up in the morning. By eight on a Sunday he would normally be up and have completed his morning routine, which was typified by the mnemonic 'shower, shit, shave and shag'; or perm any three. Breakfast saw him opening a carton of long-life milk to service his cereal whilst brewing a huge mug of English Breakfast tea. Then he would hit the casework and hope to be free by noon.

From what he recalled on the following morning the evening had not disappointed. How many episodes had he watched? At least three. Had he seen Match of the Day through to the end? Did it matter? The last match was usually a tedious nil-nil. Such great questions of life would remain a mystery.

He would delay the dictation relating to the Greatbach case as no other matter, small beer by comparison, would tax his brain as much as that issue did.

His options, as discussed with Henry in the pub, were to name Hough in a debate, ask the Speaker to slap his wrists, seek Law Society advice or some combination of the above. Another alternative - if slightly below the belt - was to call a left-sympathising journalist of his acquaintance and ask them to expose the malpractice; the alleged malpractice, he conceded. That approach would avoid the possibility of either the Speaker or the Law Society telling him 'There's nothing to see here', an outcome that needed to be avoided as it might prevent the resolution that his constituent was expecting him to magic together.

Nevertheless, he thought, as he consulted the address book of journos that he kept in his head, although a story of an MP with his fingers in the till had a tabloid ring, Maureen Greatbach could not be painted a working-class hero. No. Certainly not. She was trying to protect hundreds of thousands of pounds, potentially, if not more - a cause not likely to tug on red-top readers' heartstrings. Even if it could be sculpted to touch the right nerve, splashing such headlines would not only damage Damon but the ordure would inevitably rub off on all MPs equally - 'they're all as bad as each other'. Paul would be fingered and inspected himself - 'let he who is without sin…' - whilst some would regard him as a sneak, a snitch, a teller of tales. He would not want to trigger such a media reaction without talking it over with his Whip, whose advice would probably be 'don't do it'. The broadsheets would be no different, assuming they could translate the dry world of personal finance into something readable. The devil was in the detail, and detail rarely leads the line on journalistic crusades.

There was another problem: getting the media in at this stage would need Mrs Greatbach's consent and he was not certain that she would agree. She was a homely, fulfilled, anxious and careful woman, unused to being in the news. She had a dreadful interview technique. No, the media route was not going to work.

Reluctantly, he concluded that telling all to a journalist would be abrogating his responsibilities. Whatever happened, from the moment his tale was told he would lose control of it, which was only a good thing if it brought a resolution nearer. Would it do that? No, it was a shot in the dark.

How about a frank conversation with Damon, off the record? He was a lawyer, for heaven's sake: surely the man had the capacity to be reasonable, especially when out of the limelight? Well, there was a first time for everything... They had muddled along in their occasional coincidental co-operations over the last seven years, principally those involving footpath legislation. Such contacts had involved issues which, in the grand scheme of things, were uncontroversial, superficial, trivial, issues which lacked any emotional element. Such meetings had never been one-to-one and, through mutual neglect, Damon and Paul had never had a second attempt at socialising in Strangers' Bar. Equally, Damon had never shown Paul respect in the chamber.

Since Friday night and his confession to Henry, Paul was being haunted by the hand down the teenage trousers episode. No, he could not sit down and have a serious conversation with Damon: if the bastard did what he did with those snake charmer's eyes, Paul knew, he would fall to pieces, fragmented by anger.

So, what was he really trying to achieve? The only clear answer was 'justice for my constituent', which is all that any MP seeks to obtain, either individually or collectively. It was not essential to have a public aspect to this 'campaign', publicity would not necessarily assist in achieving a settlement. That conclusion ruled out an adjournment debate, also. What else? Discrediting a Tory MP was rarely the wrong option, but one always had to consider time and place. And Damon had once been a friend.

A friend? He was a cock-grabbing bastard. But no, this had to be kept out of the headlines.

Rationally, if Mrs Smith had signed a legal Power of Attorney in the solicitor's favour, whilst she still had the capacity to do so, then there was probably very little that could be done about that. That it had not been challenged at the time would make justice even harder to obtain. Maureen had told him that she possessed no copy of the original document: why should she have one? She was not a party to it. Nor, from his admittedly limited experience of the process, was it likely that any such document would detail the agreed fees or the solicitor's freedom to alter that charge. It would probably say 'standard terms apply' and 'standard terms' would certainly not put the lawyer at a disadvantage! However, he guessed that, even without such a clause, legitimate changes ought to be possible. It was reasonable to expect a solicitor to levy some charge, however trivial the task... especially when the client was wealthy.

So, to the size of the fee. £100 each month to compile or simply glance at a sheet of figures, which probably changed little over time, sounded a lot, whilst £300 per month sounded like... three times as much. A solicitor's rate of, say, £75 an hour meant that he was charging for 4 hours for a task which probably took 10 minutes, if any time at all.

Inherent in managing the account for the purposes of long-term income was the ability to move funds from one source of interest to another. This brought an element of risk and a need for professional insurance and indemnity into the equation, something else that came with a cost. But that was the role of professional fund managers, not country solicitors! Where did they fit in? Their fees - including due diligence, risk management and professional expertise - would have been met before Hilda Smith even received her money.

Maureen probably had no idea what transactions were being made on Hilda's behalf. It was possible that the funds had been extraordinarily successful, that £300 represented a smaller proportion of the wealth today even than the original £100 had done a few years back. In that case surely Damon would simply say so, portraying Maureen as greedy and ill informed, seeking to cut off her own nose to spite her face. He might even produce a spreadsheet, to prove his point. Whatever happened, she and her brother were going to inherit all of it before too long.

So, the charge was not the main problem. Hilda Smith had been justified in seeking help and the solicitor had been in order in charging a fee. The old lady's offspring had effectively agreed, by default, that they would not provide that help collectively. The circumstances around the decision still did not look good: the next of kin was supposed to have attended the meeting but she had been delayed and missed it, so it had gone ahead without her. Was that acceptable? Although the client was on the edge of dementia, upon which side of that edge had she been, back then? And how could they prove it, after so much time? If only the agreement had been challenged, back then! The only question remaining was whether the rise in fees was allowed or justified. And without knowing the detail of the contract it was impossible to make that judgment.

Already Paul was downgrading the case from a crusade to an enquiry. The fact remained that Damon was an unscrupulous politician with several significant second incomes, and his conduct felt wrong. On top of that, he was giving every indication of cynically manipulating a rich old woman with dementia, in his own interests. It might be legal, but it was odious.

It had to stop; and Paul had to stop it.

This new-found spirit of confidence did not last. By about 11.40 on the Sunday morning Paul reached the Maureen Greatbach file at the bottom of his pile. He spoke to Hazel via his digital dictation machine. Reliable, sensible, helpful Hazel would knock what would be a scrappy letter into shape and have a draft ready for him to revisit by Monday evening. How blessed he was to have someone dedicated, like Hazel, working for him.

'Dear Damon,' he dictated, 'Oh, this is addressed to… Mr Hough at Steel & Partners, not at the Commons. You can still put MP after his name, no need to get up his nose unnecessarily.

'I hope you are well. (No, scrub that. Start again).

'I understand that in your capacity as partner at Steel (with no 'e') (I mean, no final 'e', I mean) and (that's an ampersand, by the way) Partners, (capital P), you act on behalf of Mrs Hilda Smith, a resident of (put the name of the nursing home in here, it's in the case file). Mrs Smith is the mother of my constituent, Mrs Maureen Greatbach, full stop. I believe that you were granted Power of Attorney over Mrs Smith's affairs some three years ago… in the absence of an agreement between her offspring over how best to manage this matter, no, her finances, 'manage her finances'.

'We will probably be able to agree that Mrs Smith's dementia (slash) condition - what's best? …has deteriorated over recent years. My constituent's view is that her mother is no longer capable of making decisions (maybe make that 'financial decisions'?) of her own accord. New paragraph.

'Mrs Greatbach is concerned that the fees paid to you, which her mother had previously agreed, have recently been trebled. As her - Mrs Smith's - next of kin and heir (can I say 'co-heir'?) Mrs Greatbach would have expected to have been consulted on this matter. Make that: 'consulted before such a massive rise was implemented'. (Scrub 'massive', it's a value judgment, lawyers don't like value judgments). Carrying on: Given Mrs Smith's circumstances, Mrs Greatbach fears that the rise may be disproportionate and accordingly unfair on a vulnerable old lady.'

He knew that the letter was not up to his usual standard. It was all over the place.

'May I therefore demand - (asking permission to demand? No, scrub that). May I therefore request that you provide Mrs Smith, through me, with the following information, in writing.

'One: a note on the performance of Mrs Greatbach's mother's financial assets since you took over PoA.

'Two: a justification for the increase in fees.

'Three: a description of the basis upon which you are able to implement such an increase without consultation with her family, given her dementia.

'I would be further grateful if you would elucidate (I do like that word!) the procedure to be followed for the transfer of the PoA to Mrs Smith's next of kin.

'I remain, etc.'

Sod it.

'And then I need a letter to the Law Society not mentioning any names - though it will have our case reference number on it, obviously - but simply saying that earlier on in her dementia my constituent's mother gave her assent to her solicitor to take on Power of Attorney, PoA, over her financial affairs. (Make that 'over what are significant financial affairs') but now her condition has deteriorated and her next of kin, my constituents, are concerned.

'The solicitor is releasing no information about the performance of her mother's assets nor the management of the PoA to my constituent. With no grounds or justification given, he has recently trebled the administration charge for the PoA from £100 a month to £300. It is not at all clear what services he is providing for that money. Please tell me what rights my constituent has in respect of:

'Bullet - Access to information from the solicitor about the performance of her mother's financial assets.

'Bullet - Being consulted, being able to object to or veto such a large rise in fees.

'Bullet - Transferring PoA from the solicitor to the daughter, and

'Bullet - what redress my constituent has should the solicitor decline to discuss these matters with her.

'Yours, etc.'

In a confessional moment he spoke earnestly to his dictation machine.

'Hazel, I'm sorry, this is going to read like crap. Just get me a draft of this up asap, please, don't print off top copies yet. I'll need to edit it again, I'm sure. Thanks.

'It's all a bit of a mess.'

Paul switched off the machine.

A bit of a mess? Had he said that to himself or out loud? Had he said it before he switched off the Dictaphone or afterwards? Could he be bothered to check?

Sod it.

It was noon. It was Sunday.

No more work today... Is that art deco exhibition still on? Are Surrey playing at the Oval, ten minutes' walk away? What's the weather going to be like? It might be a good day to lose myself in a novel. Where's that Hilary Mantel I've been meaning to read?

Maybe I should go for a walk, it looks quite bright out there today. A veritable spring day. Maybe Hazel would like to join me? That would be nice. Perhaps I could go out west to meet her? Maybe Kew Gardens?

No. It's the weekend. Hazel has her son to look after. Best not to disturb her weekend.

Lee Investigates:
Friday 29th April

It was Friday, 29th April 2022, two weeks before Guy Campbell was due to be released from prison. From what Lee Hardman knew of his boss and his associated lifestyle Campbell would probably spend no more than a day in the office before jetting off to the south of France for a month of R&R. Lee had no desire to spend even that single day in Guy's company - that era of his life was over - and he had plans to minimise that risk.

Fortunately for him, none of Guy's 'people' had been studying the accounts which he was overseeing, as expected - but then neither had Lee, over much of the past 12 years: they looked after themselves. The plan was always intended to play out at arm's length.

When the boss had been anticipating a five-year absence, the arrangement was to keep Lee on the MEKANICK payroll for the duration but in 2014, eight years back, that had changed. In acknowledging that Campbell's absence was going to be a prolonged one, Guy had approved Lee's switch from 'staff' to 'consultant'. Although he was thus no longer fully employed by MEKANICK, Lee had been receiving a generous annual retainer from them ever since. Oodles a year for monitoring a few spreadsheets each month and occasionally touching base with a handful of compliant 'clients' was not a bad life; he had no complaints. He visited the office occasionally, to show his face to the remaining staff, express solidarity with them and even advise them from time to time. They were also sitting comfortably: no one in the remains of the Campbell empire had any reason to be fearful or unhappy. This pleasant atmosphere was built, in part, upon the reassuring knowledge that everything they were currently doing appeared to be routine, legal and above board.

Almost everything.

This arm's length arrangement allowed Lee to pursue parallel interests whilst remaining obligated in respect of his MEKANICK responsibilities, right up until the day that Campbell was released. The flaw in the contract was not immediately obvious: it allowed Lee to depart early on resurrection morning, without having to account to Guy in the flesh, and he had decided to make the most of the opportunity.

Lawyer and boss were, nevertheless, on good terms from the start. Way back, Guy had personally agreed to grant Lee a three-month sabbatical, on half pay, to assist him in fighting the 2010 general election. Back then the chickens had not yet come home to roost although both had known that the company was sailing close to the wind on several fronts, and that the authorities were sniffing around and getting very close. Lee's own hands were clean and always had been. Although Guy knew nothing about politics and wanted to know even less, he admired the young man's drive and gave him his head. He judged, naively, that it would do MEKANICK no harm to have their own man inside the corridors of power.

2010 did not, of course, deliver electoral success for Lee, who returned to the grindstone. His 'man of the world' credentials were enhanced by this brush with power and he was rewarded with more responsibility in the company whilst gaining more insight into what was actually going on. He was impressed with Guy's audacity. The set-up was slick and effective, speed of mouse deceiving the eye at almost every turn. The likes of MEKANICK and alternative MEKANICK, the alternative entity which inhabited the dark web, turning shadows into Bitcoin and derivatives into an art form, were pounding away behind the scenes were changing the world just as effectively as the steam engine had done two hundred years previously, if less overtly.

When Campbell's day of reckoning came, late in 2010, it was sudden - but Lee had anticipated it. He had the knowledge and skills to remain insulated from the bad stuff, he was protected and could ride the storm. The firm was able to continue, after licking its wounds and after their leader had been toppled from his chariot, though its dark web activity was virtually shut down as a precaution.

The disappointment of 2010 did not shatter Lee's belief in the Conservative Party and its values: after all, Cameron was now Leader of a Coalition Government and Lee preferred to see a Liberal Democrat tail trying to wag the Tory dog than a hard right one.

Professionally, from 2014, he used the freedom that his retainer gave him to the full. Being released from full time work with MEKANICK the Party's former standard bearer took up a part time role in Conservative Central Office, working on economic policy with a focus on The City. In 2015 he became a part time adviser to an American bank with a small UK operation, a role which lasted until late 2017. When the bankers saw the writing on the Brexit wall and realised that London was no longer their gateway to Europe they walked. Lee, equally horrified at the outcome of the 2016 plebiscite, wished he could do the same - but the terms of Guy's generous contract obliged him to remain a UK resident for the duration.

His most enjoyable period was his attachment to a centre-right think tank in Tufton Street, a stone's throw from Parliament. Here he could almost come and go as he wished, committing himself to projects rather than days. Having recently made a substantial donation to the operation he realised that he was effectively employing himself, which made Lee smile. He laughed again because his donation was tax exempt, as the secretive think tank had charitable status. He wondered why he had been allowed to make his charitable donation anonymously, when the organisation was so close to politics, but did not spend too long fretting about that.

An inheritance allowed Lee to pay off his mortgage in 2016 and he bought a holiday cottage in Ireland. He was comfortable (a euphemism for rich), fulfilled and happy. Single and celibate, by choice, his greatest passion outside spreadsheets, politics and corporate law was the second world war. He was a profound consumer of history books and an aficionado of 'dark tourism', visiting at least one battleground each year. Initially these were in Europe, but he spread his wings over time to take in North Africa, Pearl Harbor and Hiroshima.

Thus, in recent times, history had overtaken politics in Lee's affections. He was disheartened by the Brexit vote, shocked when Cameron gave up the ghost so easily, frustrated that the well-intentioned Mrs May was undermined by her Party's right wing. He saw the Party to which he had always been committed move inexorably away from his political home, the centre ground. When Boris Johnson became Prime Minister, in 2019, Lee retired from all Party activity and even let his membership lapse. He declined to vote in the general election of that year, for the first time in his adult life.

Lee checked occasionally, diplomatically, that each of his 'hosts' was problem-free. The thirty million for which he had responsibility was a relatively small portfolio and its terms, the return of the investment principal, interest-free, plus an unspecified share of the profit, were simple. In other circles it might be known as equity participation or even halal finance. Even a few tens of thousands of 'profit share' from each participant would satisfy Guy that the outsourcing programme had been worthwhile. In the early years everything went to plan with none of the 'investments 'seeming likely to return a deficit, which was reassuring. When he enquired after the balances at the start of 2020 things looked generally good. Lee predicted that some of the 'bonuses' might even reach six figures, presenting him with the facility - should it prove necessary - to offset weaker performances against the bigger successes. Any such adjustment could be made on a single spreadsheet and Guy need never be any the wiser. It was never anticipated, in any of Lee's spreadsheet scenario calculations, that any host might return less than 100 percent of the capital.

Even in his semi-formal review of 2021 every host readily assured him that they were on track - apart from one who did not reply. When Lee enquired further, concerns that had first stirred in his mind in 2017 came home to roost. The reticent host was no longer simply underperforming, he had become a basket case. Although in the grand scheme of things the £750,000 principal involved was of little significance, if the operation collapsed it could put the whole plan in jeopardy.

He should never have trusted that shit, Damon Hough.

Hough needed to be reminded that although only £400,000 of the £750,000 was branded 'loan' in truth all of it was. Lee chased the MP for a statement of account and when he finally received the requested figures, in late January of 2022, the covering personal email contained a litany of excuses. Not only could the MP show no net income - after 12 years! - but he could account for only £600,000 of the principal: £150,000 had disappeared. Over these last few years, the idiot had been lying.

Hough did not try to deny it. 'Unavoidable, essential expenses,' he pleaded in a handwritten note on plain copy paper, leaving no email trail, 'will repay by end 2022'. That was no good to Lee unless the parole board turned unexpectedly harsh. But how to communicate this urgency to Hough?

As some of the money really had been a loan a carefully crafted formal letter could be sent, on the record, emphasising the imperative need for repayment. The missive, of mid-February 2022, received no reply. Lee sent a copy a fortnight later, with a bland email chaser to add emphasis, but once more Damon clammed up.

Lee decided to look deeper into Damon's affairs. Withdrawals from the fund, probably several, must have taken place between 2016 and 2019. Still a politician at heart, Lee could see a possible pattern: the spread of dates included not only a referendum but two general elections, also. Although it took him less than three minutes to find Damon Hough's record on Parliament's Register of Members' Interests, he was none the wiser for doing so. And yet it was patently clear that most of the £150,000 had gone over that three-year period; it had surely been spent on political causes. In this day and age, for an MP not to declare on the public record that he had received such an amount was unthinkable. This was not because the political classes were all so scrupulously honest and pure at heart - though most were - but because they would know that the consequence of being caught was disgrace and political suicide.

Lee accessed Tory Head Office records on the Electoral Commission web site. This search took longer, even when confined to the three six-month periods which constituted the run-up to the polls of 2016, 2017 and 2019. He located nothing that might reflect Damon's 'generosity'. And yet he knew, from his experience of 2010, that after every general election over two thousand people across Britain, the election agents for party candidates, submit their nominations for the Booker Fiction Prize entitled: 'Parliamentary election expenses'. Such was their flimsy effort at storytelling that none ever won a prize - even if few were ever disqualified on the grounds that their work was factual. Again, the returns by Damon Hough's Election Agent of 2017 and 2019 revealed nothing out of the ordinary.

This did not mean that the money had not been spent on campaigning. The 2016, 2017 and 2019 votes had taken place at just a few months' notice. This made the dropping of a newsletter through every letterbox, a week before the election kicked off - pre-empting the most highly scrutinised accounting period - much more difficult than in 2010 or 2015, when the Parliaments had gone full term. But anyone could have spent furiously in advance of the Brexit poll and hidden it in the national melee of spending by both sides. To make matters even worse, Damon had clearly not been backing Lee's favoured 'Remain' team!

Undertaking more detailed analysis Lee noted that in 2017 and 2019 Damon had outperformed the national shift in the Conservative vote - and even his local pro-Brexit vote in 2016 was stronger than the area's demographics suggested it should have been. It could be that he had not outperformed in terms of votes per pound of spending but had simply spent more pounds than had been recorded. The evidence was circumstantial, but the theory would explain the pattern.

Think tanks cultured databases of MPs' media pronouncements. In Tufton Street he accessed digitised paper records and online archives of Damon's cuttings. After three days of trawling, another pattern emerged: cutting a long story short, Damon liked to help people out when they were in trouble. He came across as kind, concerned, hardworking and generous with his voters. Lee had to admit that although he hated the man's politics his record 'on the patch', as a constituency Member, appeared to be exemplary.

MPs know that even a small charitable donation can often help a community organisation put on an event, a disadvantaged student get to university, or a beloved pet receive an operation. Damon not only had an unerring nose for people in distress but also, it seemed, ready access to charitable funds. Posing for photos at every turn was par for the course for MPs; they not only sought them out but set them up. Here he was, donating to a foodbank. Here again, seated on a playgroup's new climbing frame. And there, sponsoring six members of a synchronised swimming team raising funds for charity. These pictures were all taken in a single week, Lee noted, and no gift was more than a few hundred pounds. They all used money from the Entropy Foundation.

This London-based charity, he discovered, provided small gifts of aid to those in need when they needed it. Entropy can be thought of as a measure of chaos; the Foundation's mission was to help bring order to people with chaotic lives, which was all very worthy. According to its website the Foundation operated nationally, its site was glossy and heartrending with several accounts of damaged lives made good. It did not reveal where the unfortunate souls were based, but they all had a white, suburban Britishness about them. A button on the screen allowed anyone to apply for help but when Lee clicked it a message appeared: 'Sorry, we are currently closed for new applications. Please come back later'.

On the Charity Commission website, the Foundation listed its registered number but no current chief executive. Its accounts were a few months out of date and its turnover was measured in thousands of pounds, much less than the tens or hundreds of thousands a charity operating nationally would be expected to need as a minimum. It had tens of thousands in reserves. Unlike the beneficiaries portrayed on the site the charity's board of trustees did tick the diversity box, as was to be expected in 21st century Britain. Three of them were called James Steel, Alice Brain and Indira Sharma. Now, where had Lee heard those names before?

The fourth name came as no surprise, either.

Lee Hardman had always thought of himself as straight, honest, dependable. If that meant he was also reliable and ethical then he was proud, and he would throw in 'responsible' too, which was why he had previously been committed to a highly principled approach to politics. Today he still possessed all those qualities, he would assert - though a couple might require a modicum of qualification.

11 years of overseeing potentially dodgy accounts as a corporate lawyer was a possible stain on his character, though if he was ever guilty of a misdemeanour it would only be a technicality; never more than 'aiding and abetting'. He was ethical, in that he had values and an innate sense of right, though this allowed him to indulge in some flexibility as he protected his employer's legitimate assets. When you added it all up, he calculated, overseeing just £30M-worth of Guy Campbell's quasi-dodgy accounts was only a single aberration, albeit one that was eleven years long. Everyone would be better off when it was all over.

Everyone… except one.

Damon Hough would be destroyed. Lee hated everything the man had come to stand for, and that the MP was the cause of Lee's greatest current headache was only one more reason to finish him. A detailed plan was needed.

Lee's state of the art smartphone told him all he needed to know. He used it to remind him about events, set up video calls, keep tabs on news, share prices and the rest - and he had programmed it to count down the days until Guy Campbell would return. It could even find twelve-year-old press reports of Campbell's trial. But it could not do everything. From his desk he took out an older, less sophisticated phone, a battery and a SIM card and assembled the burner. He hardly ever used it, and by never leaving it with its battery and SIM card in place he made it practically untraceable. He went onto the internet, looked up a number and dialled it.

'Steel and Partners, how may I help you?'

'Good afternoon, I'm calling from the Charity Commission, may I have a brief word with Alice Brain, please?'

'I'm afraid Mrs Brain's out of the office this afternoon, what is it concerning, please?'

'It's about a charity that she… is Indira Sharma available?'

'I think so, hold the line, please.'

Ten seconds felt like ten minutes. It occurred to him that he needed a name. His next-door neighbour, the unknown man whose mail occasionally found its way into his foyer mailbox, was called Norman Barnes.

'Indira Sharma.'

'Ah, Miss Sharma, Norman Barnes here, Charity Commission. It's about the Entropy Foundation, the charity of which you're a trustee, do you have a moment?'

'I will do what I can... Charity Commission, you said? I'm sorry, I'm not a trustee of any charity.'

'Not the Entropy Foundation?'

'No, I'm sorry. I don't think I know it.' Was this confirmation that the Foundation was indeed a front for Damon's money laundering? Lee had to think quickly.

'That is Indira Sharma MBE, is it?'

He could hear his correspondent relax.

'No, I'm sorry, you need a different Indira Sharma! I don't have the MBE.'

'I do apologise, so sorry for bothering you. Goodbye.'

That was all the proof he needed.

Lee Hardman knew how difficult it was to pin MPs down; he might need to pull a few strings. He called the Commons switchboard and asked for Damon Hough's secretary. After five rings there was a female 'Hello?', which sounded unprofessional. He set about playing the old boy network card, in spades, establishing that Damon was out of the office, as expected. Moments later the woman had secured for him half an hour of Damon's time - which was probably 25 minutes longer than he would require - at 10am on Thursday, 5th May, in the Central Lobby of the Houses of Parliament.

It was dirty work, but someone had to do it.

Hazel with Hazel Eyes:

Monday 25th April

There was only one man in Hazel's life. He was tall, slim, good looking and bright, he wore his brown hair in a fundamentally conventional manner but with an idiosyncratic air. She was proud to be associated with him and loved the air of mutual dependence that existed between them, though its nature ebbed and flowed over the years. At almost 13, an emerging teenager, her son, Matthew, was the source of that pride and she was confident that there would be much more of that to come over the years ahead.

Hazel considered herself to be an independent, self-sufficient spirit. Her commitment to her son was total, a deliberate choice. In Matthew's earliest years Hazel had taken a prolonged career break which was made possible, she had to admit, by the earnings of her then husband, an international business consultant with a special interest in Lebanon. Gradually, as a temporary secretary, some ranks below her pre-motherhood role as an up-and-coming office manager, she had tiptoed her way back into work. First, she covered a maternity leave for an employee of a friend who ran a small business in Ealing, then she was a part time receptionist at a Health Club in Hammersmith. She knew that the putting of distance between her and her son was important for them both, now that he was approaching puberty and adolescence, however painful that might be.

Five years ago, separation from her husband completed (why was he in so much of a hurry?) and divorce imminent, living in a supportive middle-class community in Chiswick, her son well established at primary school, she made a decision. Being a receptionist was not a career goal achieved: the role lacked progression, purpose - she wanted to make a difference to the world. Or, at least, to support someone, or some cause, that would do so.

Such musing came to the attention of a neighbour, Jo, who asked 'Have you seen this?' All the email contained was a link to a website called 'Working for an MP'. She was not particularly 'political', but she always voted Labour and knew that she could never commit to working for a Tory.

The first and, as it transpired, only job interview she obtained from that source was with Paul Roe. In all honesty, she had never heard of him; but she did her homework and approved of what she found. Clearly, following her application and subsequent interview, he had thought the same.

As the only member of this MP's staff to be London-based, she was able to work from home much of the time. When she did come into the Commons, she made a point of getting to know her opposite numbers in neighbouring offices. She travelled to the constituency to meet Carol and Henry at an early stage and occasionally thereafter. This team approach was invaluable in coming to terms with the idiosyncrasies of Parliamentary and constituency life. Her natural flair for detail, organisation and hard work - together with a bright and lively mind and a heart which guided her head - meant that she soon became a fully-fledged member of the team. Her fitting in quickly, Paul readily recognised, was very much to the advantage of his constituents. Hazel was a star.

In the early days it was quite common for Hazel and her employer to share a coffee and extend their conversations beyond the immediate demands of administration. One day Paul joked that her jumper matched her hazel eyes though, in reality, her eyes were darker than that, almost sultry, sparkling. During those chats it transpired that both were in the process of recovering, or removing themselves, from significant relationships. More than once, it crossed her mind that there was a gap in her life which someone like Paul might fill: when she was ready. But that was not now, not yet, certainly not at the start of their new professional relationship. For the foreseeable future Matthew would be her number one priority.

That was five years ago. The professional relationship had blossomed: Hazel found that she soon learned to anticipate her boss' response to requests, questions and situations, though she never usurped his authority. On organisational matters, however, he acknowledged her superior skills, and she had all the necessary systems running smoothly.

From year two they spent less time together in an almost deliberate choice not to get under each other's feet, but they still met up at least once, often twice, each week to assess work. Regular hours, predictable situations, never any surprises - in no way did this describe Parliamentary life! Hazel found that she loved the variety almost as much as, she assumed, Paul did.

In the past year the two singles, both now married to their jobs, had drifted into a slightly more casual aspect of friendship. She threw a birthday party in January, inviting Paul and - perhaps subliminally to make it look proper - Henry, too. She was excited to have Paul visit her home, for the first time, and delighted that he made a good impression on Matthew. She briefed key friends - 'Don't have a go at him about politics, this is supposed to be a happy, relaxed party' - in advance. Was she being too protective? she worried.

But it was not politics which the neighbour, Jo, picked up on. The two women were in the kitchen, both nicely relaxed by the occasion, and Hazel was topping up a particularly fiery mulled wine preparation.

'He's fit, isn't he, your boss?' Jo had a reputation for plain, often coarse speaking to live up to, whether she knew it or not.

'What do you mean?'

'Hips. I like slim hips on a man. I haven't seen him from behind yet, but I bet he's got a nice arse.'

'Well,' Hazel found herself smiling, 'Now you mention it…'

'You're sitting there at your desk, eyes at arse level, and he walks in the room… I don't know how you concentrate on your work!'

'Jo, it's not like that! You know that's not me.' Slightly irritated, she was reassured by the confidence that her closest friend was teasing, not serious. Or was she?

'You got that mulled wine ready, hun?'

'Just coming!'

'You've not shagged him yet, have you?'

Hazel's mouth fell open in disbelief. 'Jo, really! I said, it's not like that!'

'Been a while, hasn't it, hun?'

'A while?'

'Since you had it off with anyone. Shagged. Bonked. Yeah? Am I right?' She would not talk like this if she were sober.

'I can't keep secrets from you, Jo. I cannot deny my celibacy…'

'Temporary, I hope!'

'I've taken no vow, if that's what you mean.'

'I bet you would shag him. Given half the chance.'

Hazel was tasting the mulled wine, adding more cinnamon, when she muttered something that might have included the word 'unprofessional'.

'Go on, Haze, say it! He is shaggable, isn't he? It's not just the arse.'

Hazel put down her wooden spoon, turned to face her friend and put on her most serious face. After a moment of thought, during which the red wine, the prospect and the situation combined to cause her face to redden in an involuntary grin of embarrassment. She was a mature woman, for heaven's sake, a responsible mother: she was not supposed to respond to teasing like this! As she spoke Hazel could not hold her friend's gaze: her behaviour over those two seconds appeared to Jo to confirm every lascivious thought that was po-going through her head.

'Yes, Jo, all right, I guess Paul is shaggable. In theory. All right?'

'Hi, Hazel, is there any more mulled wine?' Henry had joined them, unnoticed. How much had he heard?

Aware that he had entered a potentially embarrassing situation, and with Jo convulsing in giggles without spilling a drop, Henry did the English thing: 'I'm sorry, was I interrupting something?'

'Ah! Hi, Henry, this is my friend Jo - I mean, I was saying… in principle. Not that I'm…'

'Don't mind me! I didn't hear… anything. Much.'

Jo adopted an oratorical pose, fist aloft: 'What is said in Chiswick stays in Chiswick! Right, Henry?'

Henry was, for once, lost for words.

'Absolutely,' Hazel reassured the assembled company. 'Party banter, that's all. You're terrible, Jo, you really are! Now… you wanted mulled wine, Henry, I've got a fresh batch ready. Here you go!'

The Candidates' Weekend:

October 2009

Lee recalled his very first encounter with Damon Hough. It was at the Conservative Party Conference of September 2009. Both were debutant Parliamentary candidates, though Damon was set to inherit a workable majority whilst Lee would probably fail, in fact, only if he was very lucky would he save his deposit. He was hopeful but in no way confident of defying the electoral calculus, but he had accepted his lot, with realistic expectations.

Even back then Damon was an extrovert, one who not so much sought attention through his behaviour as demanded it. His views on everything were firm, right wing and loud. Slipping out of Manchester Central conference centre to a small room in a nearby hotel for a private morning training session for first time candidates, Lee heard Damon's commanding, forthright and well-projected delivery for the first time.

The first presentation given by the Party was called 'Meeting the Public' and whilst most of the didactic information delivered - it was that sort of event - was dry and predictable, in Lee's eyes it did contain some nuggets. Never let the candidate stray off alone in public places, always have someone with them. Keep the candidate's phone switched off or have someone else carry it. Maintain positive eye contact in any conversation. The candidate should smile all the time unless there's a very good reason not to do so: it may make you look like you're having a heart attack, but it will do more good than harm in the long run. More about eye contact. Press the flesh whenever you enter the room. And whenever you leave. And in between. Whilst maintaining eye contact.

A question was asked about accepting invitations to debates and the male presenter's reply was understandably equivocal. 'In principle, yes, but it depends on who's inviting you - if it's a church, or the local newspaper, then, of course, you accept. If it's CND or the Stop the War Coalition then it's 'sorry, I've got something else on that night'. Just don't tell them you're washing your hair!' The speaker was almost bald; a polite titter ran around the room.

A few moments later Damon raised his hand and assumed the floor. Previous questioners had remained seated, but he stood. He had a dashing style, this 21st century beau, energetic and forceful. He was sitting four rows from the front, at the side of the room, perfectly positioned to command the attention of all and sundry.

'Damon Hough, Mr Chairman.' A couple of sycophantic acolytes shouted 'Whoop, whoop!' - he already had his cheerleaders in place.

'I say no; I say so-called public debates are a waste of our time, Mr Chairman, and I'll tell you why, if I may. So many of them are set-ups. They're designed to catch us out. You say don't go to a Stop the War event or is it 'Only Stop Some Wars'?' - some of the audience chuckled '- oh, yes, they're happy to support the Russians, all right, or the Taliban, it's our boys they don't want to support' - harrumphs of approval from the audience - 'and of course your advice is, as far as it goes, correct. But you said say 'yes' to churches; let me tell you, colleagues, that the Anglican Church, the Church of England, is no longer the Tory Party at prayer, not as it once was. You go along to some of these places of worship, like the Methodists, they look more like the Charles Manson hippy murder cult!'

This time there was an appreciative laugh. Damon was on a roll.

'Rope shoes, vegetarians, peaceniks, the lot of them. You go to 'meet the people' events and there's two men and a dog there, what's the use of debating with them? You get most sense from the dog!'

More laughter. Even Lee managed a smile.

'Mr Chairman, let me make a serious point. This election is ours to lose. If we do nothing for the next six months, we will walk it in May 2010, winning an election for the first time in eighteen years, and we will form a Conservative government!' He put his hands together in mock prayer. 'Praise the Lord!' More laughter. Serious again: 'What we don't want are custard pie moments. What we don't want is attention being taken away, being diverted from our front bench team - Liam Fox, Chris Grayling, Michael Gove, William Hague, George Osborne and, of course, David Cameron' - the cognoscenti spotted a quick raise of the eyes to the heavens, hardly a ringing endorsement of the Leader - 'it's their job to get our message across to and through the media. The press is, by and large, on our side but we need no hostages to fortune, so let us leave it to the professionals!'

The cheering was tempered with applause; Damon had clearly judged the temperature of the room correctly. Yet, sitting at the back of the room,

Lee briefly sighed; Damon's list of stars to defer to consisted of only middle-aged white men: really? What century was he living in?

'One last word, if I may', Damon went on. 'Let's say there's a debate with all four or five candidates, quite possibly in a church. Four or five journalists sit scribbling in the front row - if you're lucky. A local celebrity is in the chair, there are lights, invitations have gone to all comers. And all do come! Perhaps the meeting is packed to the rafters. How many of these good burghers will change their minds about the way they vote in the next two hours? I'll tell you how many: none! Not one! Some of them have come to clap and cheer their favourite son, but no more than that, and that applies to all the parties. But some have come just to attack, attack, attack! All they want is to land a killer blow and you can bet your bottom dollar that the one most of them have come to attack is the Tory! Oh, yes!' - more cheers - 'It wasn't us that were in power for the last 13 years, it wasn't us who screwed up the economy with the so-called crash! We're not the ones who should be under the most intense spotlight of scrutiny!'

There were yet more cheers. Lee resisted the temptation to argue. As a corporate lawyer in a finance company, he knew very well where the crash had come from, and it hadn't been Number Ten - or even Eleven.

'So, here's what you do: you boycott those debates. You're going to be busy enough anyway, so take the night off. If they've got any decency about them, they'll cancel the debate when they know they haven't got what they like to call a balanced panel - one Tory and three against us! That's what they call balanced, by the way, just like on the BBC!'

The cheers were louder than ever. 'Attacking the BBC?' thought Lee, as his heart sank. 'Whatever next?'

'And you'll be lucky if you get to speak for ten minutes in every hour. No, you stay at home, colleagues. If you can't resist doing something then it's off to the Mothers' Union, the nursing home or the Conservative supper club, to rally the troops. Stay at home, colleagues! Win this election!'

There was a spontaneous standing ovation from select parts of the audience. As the Chairman nodded approvingly Lee looked around, trying in vain to reassure himself that he was not alone in declining to back the paean of cynical disdain for the public that they had just witnessed. The Party authorities would be relieved that such a firebrand, such a forceful, natural orator, was on their side. For now, at least.

The candidates' bonding weekend to which Lee had subscribed took place two weeks after that 2009 conference. Six Parliamentary hopefuls were to gather in a former vicarage in a Derbyshire village. Even though it was known that David Cameron's office had wanted to encourage more Tory candidates to emerge from 'non-traditional' backgrounds - women, black people, out gays - this group was completely male and white. Although they were all relatively young, by Tory standards, on sexuality it was very much 'no questions asked'. Damon Hough and Lee Hardman were both 27 years old and only one member of the group, it transpired, was over 35.

Alasdair Michael-Owen was the older one. He made it known from the off that his surname was both genuine and of Welsh heritage, though he also conceded that he would be dropping the 'Michael' both on the stump and on his election material. This was not so much out of the Welsh rugby fan's limited respect for England's former record-breaking soccer player, more the Party's desire to keep 'divisive' double barrelled names off the Tory candidate lists. James Edwards, a philosophy PhD student inspired by Roger Scruton to stand for Parliament, was the youngest at 25; he never called himself Jimmy, despite knowing that his famous, moustachioed namesake had once been a Conservative candidate. Lee noticed James' large, pock-marked nose and habit of fidgeting - literally, he was never still - right from the off. Philip 'Call me Piggy' Eliot was 32, the shortest and roundest of the team. He had the palest skin, contrasting with a well-groomed full head of tidy, jet-black hair. Piggy was a futures trader with ministerial ambitions. He had a modest but slightly unruly, small, dark moustache which looked as though it was glued at random onto a tubby child's smooth face. The overall impact of the topiary was so disconcerting that, a few weeks later, image consultants would have the 'tash' removed. Then came Tim Stuart, a quiet, nondescript estate agent. Damon and Lee completed the roster.

Those that travelled by train from London had shared a taxi from Sheffield. Lee drove a hire car over from his parents' home on the comfortable edge of Manchester, where he had endured a rare, but polite and uneventful, overnight stay.

The large, detached cottage was on the edge of a village of a hundred homes. A pub and a gift shop (which included a tiny grocery and off licence) provided what appeared to be the only retail services in this

Derbyshire Dales community - apart from the farrier who also sold equine accessories. A middle-aged woman in an apron greeted them at the front door as they all descended upon their destination, coincidentally arriving within minutes of each other, shortly before noon. She was the housekeeper, she explained. Her role was to make sure that their food was available in the dining room, starting with sandwiches and soup at 1.30, then tea at 4. After half an hour of champagne and canapés from 7 p.m. a grand four course dinner would follow. There were no vegetarians, were there? Of course not! Blue blood and red meat were a formidable combination... Overt external input into the candidates' timetable would be minimal, comprising just an hour with a party official, scheduled for immediately before the final event of the weekend, Sunday lunch.

Alasdair, whom Piggy innocently kept calling Michael, was nominally in charge. He reported that their agenda, approved by CCHQ, would commence with a structured icebreaker in the form of an hour's brisk walk around the village boundary right away, before lunch. There would be a session focusing on campaigning during the afternoon and the first of two policy discussions before dinner. For the first of two Sunday morning sessions each man had been asked to give a five-minute presentation on a policy area of their choice and then field questions upon it.

The walk was bracing, and the first hints of autumn colour promised spectacular vistas over coming weeks. It was dry underfoot and Lee liked to hear the crackling of twigs; mostly oak, if he was not mistaken. During the brisk stroll they were to walk in pairs and find out as much as they could about their partner. After half an hour they would change partners and repeat the exercise whilst re-tracing their steps, and then over lunch each would report back on what they had discovered about their two walking companions.

Lee found Piggy, his first partner, to be shallow and privileged. Born in Kenya of colonial stock and educated at Harrow and Cambridge, he had a blue in Greco-Roman wrestling. Alasdair, his partner on the return, was quiet, droll and politically experienced - the deputy leader of the ruling Tory group on his local borough council. Lee's first goal had been successfully achieved: to avoid partnering with the arrogant Hough in the 'getting to know you' process.

By the time dinner was served their food was well earned. The advance briefing had informed them that the meal would be formal, so five of them came down, at 7 p.m. prompt, wearing jackets and ties but not suits.

Piggy, to the amusement of all, wore full evening dress: his dinner jacket had tails, his shoes were patent leather, and he sported a modest white bowtie. 'Isn't this how everyone dresses for supper?' he asked, innocently. Lee wondered if the man was being serious.

There was champagne before dinner and an excellent Cabernet to accompany the meal. And then more wine. They sat around a large rustic table, Lee at one end and Damon at the other, not far from a massive grate which hosted a roaring fire. The food was excellent and copious. When the gentlemen retired, they simply left the table at one end of the large room and moved to easy chairs close to both the fire and the cocktail cabinet at the other. Before she left, the housekeeper cleared the table and briefed Alasdair on matters such as what to do if they ran out of wine or firewood and assured him that the gentlemen did not have to worry about the washing up. That would happen, as if by magic, before breakfast.

The tableau established around the fire could have been a scene from a period drama or an Agatha Christie finale. The image would have been even more marked had everyone been dressed as per Piggy's Edwardian bearing - which he maintained even after most others had shed their jackets and ties. Each had a wine glass in hand and Alasdair, with booming voice and masterly air, sparingly used, made sure that the glasses stayed full - for the first hour. After that it was every man for himself, and God bless the cocktail cabinet. There was a ribald, almost rugby club atmosphere, with coarse and tasteless jokes escaping from the locker from early on.

Lee started to relax. He and Damon had briefly, silently, acknowledged mutual recognition from the Party conference and the six men were settling into a routine. Alasdair was restrained, using his command function selectively - but less and less as the evening wore on. James was quiet but alert, Tim appeared stuck in second gear; Lee made a point of engaging with each. Needless to say, Damon gravitated towards centre stage, but it appeared that he had a rival there: Piggy was also a showman, especially with a few glasses inside him. Lee could imagine the trader standing beside a grand piano, presenting a recital of humorous Victorian monologues set to music each Christmas, with real candles on a full-sized tree imported, especially for the evening, from Norway.

The fire was hot. After an hour Lee was feeling weary, but it was clear that no one wanted to be the first to retire. Every jacket and tie had been removed by ten, bar Piggy's white dicky. Their discussion had dealt with politics and current affairs, and they were now having a bragging match as to the famous people each knew best. James got the round off to a roaring start with his detailed insight into Scruton's private opinion of Tory elders, and Lee could see the boy growing in confidence as his tale progressed. When his own turn came, he spoke with genuine warmth of how he once met Ken Clark on Kings Cross station and travelled with him on the Nottingham train. The others listened in polite deference. Whether or not they were politically sympathetic to Clark, they chuckled approvingly when Lee revealed his punch line: his ticket had only been valid as far as Leicester and the young man's enthusiasm had cost him an excess fare charge.

The last to perform was Damon Hough. It was ten thirty by now and Alasdair had stacked the fire high with logs; wine and spirits both flowed freely. Damon spoke admiringly but briefly about Iain Duncan Smith but then moved his focus onto a demolition of Labour people including the Prime Minister, 'blind' Gordon Brown. It was almost as though he had a prepared stand-up set which he now delivered from centre stage. Alcohol had loosened his tongue and the use of expletives in his polemic was the only thing about it that was liberal.

He joked about lesbians, about disabled people and Asians, truly a Bernard Manning tribute act. Then he started on women and, full circle, to Labour women, milking an impression, a parody of Diane Abbott, for all it was worth. Lee felt that the maestro was running out of steam and guessed that his finale was imminent. Damon set about it: how could Glenda Jackson be a credible MP, let alone minister, when all the world and his dog had seen her bare flat chest on the big screen? There was hilarity when he stood, back to the fire, his almost clenched fists pressed one against each nipple through his shirt, his extended index fingers pointing down towards the floor.

'Look,' he said, 'who's this?'

He moved his hips from side to side, causing his two downwardly perpendicular fingers to oscillate accordingly, like two small pendulums - depicting a woman's small breasts in motion. His audience was puzzled to a man.

'It's Glenda Jackson in *The Music Lovers*.'

There was raucous laughter.

'Now this, who's this?'

Identical posture and motion, but hips and knees even more exaggerated, lips pursed.

'Got it, eh? Glenda Jackson in *Sunday, Bloody Sunday*'.

There was more uproar in which even Lee found himself grinning, against his better judgement.

'Hey, James!' Damon picked on the youngest of the men. 'James, with all these tits around, I can see you've got a hard on.' More laughter. 'Come poke the fire for us, will you?'

James laughed as much as anyone; the joke had worked.

'Give him his due,' thought Lee, 'he can work an audience.'

'So, what about this one?'

The same mime again, this time even more exaggerated and prolonged.

'Glenda Jackson in *Women in Love*.'

James fell off his chair laughing and rolled on the floor clutching his stomach, Alasdair wasn't laughing but had a huge, slightly embarrassed if appreciative grin, Tim was chuckling, and Piggy's giggling face was screwed up like a dishcloth posing as a grimace. Spittle was spraying from his mouth, so hard was he aspirating laughter through clenched jaw and teeth, snorting, his eyes almost hidden, his white shirt and tie still immaculate. Lee could not resist a sense of amusement at the scene.

'You know…,' said Damon, regaining control of the mirth-racked mob. 'Come on, it's not that funny… she can't help it!'

This provoked even more laughter, which was further encouraged by a final wiggle of Damon's, arse, knees and dangling finger tits.

Piggy, barely able to breathe, found his rictus expression causing him to sniff so hard and regularly that his dark moustache threatened to leap up high into his nasal cavities. He clutched a tumbler of neat whisky to his chest with one hand whilst emulating Damon's wriggling hand with the other, creasing himself with ill-suppressed laughter at his own digital wobble.

'Hey, look, everyone - Piggy's wearing nipple tassels under that shirt, I can see them.'

Peals of laughter broke out again as Piggy waggled his finger even harder. Damon took two large paces towards him and tweaked his nipples, which caused Piggy to take a step back, still laughing, giggling, semi-crouching to protect his vulnerable chest - and his whisky.

Damon resumed his position on the imaginary stage.

'Piggy - Piggy. Look. Get it to do - this!'

He had the attention of all. Fist still pressing against his chest, one of Damon's fingers pointed instead to the ceiling. As soon as Piggy copied him Damon dropped his hand and pointed directly at Piggy Eliot:

'Look everyone! Now Piggy's pleased to see me!' he teased, coyly rolling his eyes in faux innocence, index finger provocatively touching his own cleft chin, arse sticking out Marilyn-style, pouting, his pinky finger cocked as though drinking polite tea.

Everyone but Alasdair was laughing. His furrowed brow turned towards Lee. He didn't need to say 'I don't understand' but Lee had picked up his body language.

'He's saying Philip's got a hard on,' Lee explained, discreetly.

'Oh yes,' Alasdair chuckled, 'I see.'

'Seriously, Piggy. Seriously...' said Damon, still in command. It was going to be one of those acts where the 'volunteer' was railroaded into a starring role against their will.

Master of his audience, Damon waited for the room to fall quiet. Lee, already thinking that Damon had taken this quite far enough, now realised that there was more to come: Damon had not yet reached his climax.

'Piggy?' said Damon, with an exaggeratedly serious, almost music-hall air, 'Don't you think that *Women in Love* is Glenda's very best film?'

'A bit before my time, old chap,' the trader with sleeked back, very black hair, protested. 'But yes, it was very good, as I recall. Wizard! Ken Russell, wasn't it?'

'And what was your favourite scene in it, Piggy?'

Damon was centre stage, dominant. Piggy, no shrinking violet, was pinned to the spot.

'As I say, it was a bit before my time... I've read the original Lawrence, of course.'

'David Herbert Lawrence. Phew... Lady Chatterley, eh? Nudge, nudge! Know what I mean?' There were chuckles. 'All that fucking and grinding?' He ground out the words as though rubbing sandpaper sadistically against their skins and generating more laughter. The all-male audience was on the edge of their seats. Where was Damon going to take them next?

'You know, I think it was this wonderful open fire that reminded me of it, of *Women in Love,* I mean. This glorious, roaring fire. Piggy, do you remember the scene with Oliver Reed and Alan Bates, in front of the fire?'

Piggy had no words to reply; his sense of anticipation was working overtime but failing to deliver the appropriate data into his consciousness. Neither did he laugh, nor smile. Only the crackle of the fire and an occasional snigger could be heard. Piggy felt obliged to respond: he raised both his eyebrows and intoned: 'Err...?'

'The wrestling match, Piggy. Do you remember the wrestling match?'

Damon left Piggy hanging for a moment, before Piggy's face lit up in a lightbulb moment.

'Aah!'

Damon turned to the audience, winding down the tension and addressing them directly. 'Now, who remembers Larry Grayson?'

'He wasn't in *Women in Love*, was he?' said James, pseudo-naively, extracting still more laughter from the company.

'He wasn't into women in anything!' added Tim, as the mirth peaked again.

Damon regained control: 'Larry Grayson was once asked what he thought of Alan Bates, as an actor. Do you know what he said?'

With a wonderful sense of timing Damon clasped his hands together in camp Grayson style and projected his voice impressively, albeit more Lady Bracknell than Larry Grayson, hyping it up to eleven out of ten: 'Alan Bates? Alan Bates? What's he ever done... except wrestle naked with Oliver Reed?'

After a brief but pregnant pause, a couple of anticipatory titters preceded the punchline:

'And we've all done that! Ha-ha!'

The group was genuinely entertained, the laughter once more raucous, profound and prolonged.

Damon waited for the hilarity to subside, standing his ground.

'Have you ever done that, Piggy? Have you ever... wrestled naked?'

As he spoke, Damon started unbuttoning his own shirt. Piggy was frozen to the spot.

'Not with Oliver Reed, that's not what I mean, but... Piggy, have you?

Shirt hanging loose, Damon now kicked off his shoes. Silence suddenly descended, punctured only by the reassuring and innocent crackle and spit of the fire.

'What's that, Piggy? What did you say?'

Damon dropped his trousers and kicked them to one side. He was now wearing a white shirt, unbuttoned, black socks, black underpants, tight and sleek.

In the middle of the hearthrug, against the backdrop of the raging fire, Damon started a rhythmic handclap. Tim picked up the beat and joined him, then James followed.

'Pig-gy, Pig-gy, Pig-gy…'

Alasdair motioned as though even he might be clapping one palm onto his seated lap; Lee, sitting furthest from the fire, felt himself to be an observer only - but he could not take his gaze off the cameo being played out before him.

'Pig-gy, Pig-gy…' louder.

Piggy was now red in the face, silent, his jaw firm. He put his whisky glass on the table at his side. He started fiddling with his cufflinks and Damon did the same with his.

Now Piggy started on his shirt buttons and James, emboldened by alcohol and occasion, started to hum a well-known, iconic theme… The Stripper.

The chanting stopped and turned to a cheer. Then it restarted, but this time quieter, more encouraging, more wonder than mockery.

Piggy reached for the top of his shirt front, struggled with the white bowtie before recalling that it was hooked at the back, not tied at the front. Off it came, then the shirt. He was wearing a white, short-sleeved crew neck vest. He turned to a nearby chair and placed one gleaming foot upon it, then leaned down to untie his patent leather shoes. Meanwhile Damon, following the rhythm of James' 'musical' accompaniment, was removing his own shirt. His torso was perfectly white, hairless apart from a few pale stragglers around each nipple and a slim column descending from just beneath his navel; he was not exactly overweight, but his body could not have been described as 'well defined'. Now wearing just his pants and socks, thumbs provocatively resting one on each hip, he stood waiting like a cowboy preparing to draw, his head tossed back, confident. His hair rested where his collar would have been, an urban Tarzan.

Piggy now dropped his trousers: his baggy white shorts were funny in an anachronistic, Laurel and Hardy sort of way, but it was the revelation of the suspenders holding up each sock that prompted the most hilarity.

Damon pointedly restrained his smile. He turned with a knowing look and puckered lips to empathise with his audience like a true, if almost naked, drag queen.

Then he beckoned with his palm and united fingers to indicate to Piggy what to do next -

'Vest off, Piggy' and off it came. If Damon's torso was white, Piggy's was whiter, balder and even less well defined.

Neither man was beefcake, observed Lee. Whatever was coming next?

Piggy, in tethered black socks and baggy white shorts, stepped forward. His gait suggested that he might have some idea what he was doing, fighting-wise; Lee recalled that the public-school boy had wrestled for Cambridge… then realised that Piggy was been paired with Damon during the latter part of the lunchtime walk. Hough must have been privy to the same information about the 'blue' as Piggy had shared with Lee.

Damon bent his knees in a parody of Piggy's stance, as Piggy loomed forward, but Damon then raised his hand to effect a pause, a time out: turning to face his audience, he dropped his underpants then immediately turned back, full frontal, to face his foe who was rooted to the spot. The drunken chant of 'Pig-gy, pig-gy!' resumed.

'Come on then, Piggy' taunted Damon, ready to wrestle and circling the 'ring', nude apart from his socks. 'I'll be Alan… and you can be Oliver - I mean Reed, not Hardy!'

Hilarity burst out: but only briefly. The look on Piggy's face, as he drew himself to his full and furious height, commanded instant anticipatory attention and respect.

Piggy was breathing deeply through his nose, his mouth welded shut. No one was laughing now.

Damon was standing closer to the fire than his adversary and now, tensing every sinew hard, he was the sweatier; the moisture on his body glistened, reflecting the flames. His posed nudity had a sense of glory about it, something Piggy's flaccid physique certainly lacked. Although in a proper wrestling match one would not bet against the experienced Piggy, Lee thought, he suddenly sensed that this imminent bout was not, in fact, going to happen. Piggy's gaze was intense, strained and focused on Damon's face. He sported an element of certainty and purpose, of readiness and deadliness, combined with a dreadful anxiety not to demean himself.

In the absence of combat Damon entertained the crowd of four, performing parodic naturist mimes: first Rodin's Thinker, then a muscle man with imaginary rippling biceps, now Thor, the cartoon character, then the flying Superman, arm outstretched in what at first glance appeared to be a fascist salute, still wearing only his socks. He hopped daintily over to Piggy like an Easter bunny and slapped him on his face, possibly harder than it looked, before mincing back to the other end of the rug and shaking his bare arse in Piggy's direction.

And that was enough.

Piggy turned away. Stone-faced and without a word he picked up his shirt, vest, trousers and shoes and headed for the door, declining to meet the gaze of a single colleague, all of whom were focused only on him. On his silent way out, he collected his jacket and clasped the bundle of clothes to his chest.

Under a fireside chair lay the white dicky bow, forlorn.

Damon applauded his audience who went through the ritual of subdued cheering back to him. His hand reached down and pushed his penis back between his legs, which he crossed to ensure that both it and his balls were out of sight, mimicking the female pubic region; he put his fingers to his nipples and then his fists, repeating the 'small breasts' routine from earlier, but this time naked. His finger-tits wobbled to the music in his head but within moments the crescendo had passed, the curtain had come down and the audience was, metaphorically, heading for the doors.

Alasdair opened another bottle of wine and came around the room to provide top-ups. Damon quietly dressed whilst the remainder broke into quiet conversation, punctuated only by the odd muffled and disbelieving chuckle at what they had witnessed.

The final score was one-nil, to Damon.

Piggy missed breakfast and was absent, too, from the first of the morning's working sessions. No one said anything about last night. Neither did anyone check how Piggy was feeling. After coffee, when the group gathered in the sitting room for their pre-lunch chat with the guest from head office, Piggy was already in his place: he was wearing a brown tweed three-piece suit and a checkered woollen tie. He had his pen and pad laid out in front of him, ready for tuition, the first to be so prepared. He smiled as his colleagues entered the room, as charming and outgoing as ever.

Piggy was clearly a professional: it was as though the previous evening had never happened. Throughout the rest of the day no one, not even Damon, mentioned the 'performance' in any way.

But Piggy had the last laugh, twice over. Firstly, it transpired that whilst the others had been in their first session of the morning, learning policy headlines, he had spent forty minutes in a one to one with the chap from head office, endearing himself significantly with the 'powers that be'.

Secondly, some years later he held a junior post in the foreign office for six years, which was a longer ministerial career than all the rest of them, put together.

Mayo and Ketchup – Kate:
Tuesday 3rd May 2022

On Tuesday, 3rd May, Kate was doing her homework thoroughly. She read every article, every Parliamentary intervention by Damon Hough and every story about him from recent years - of which there were many. Few were complimentary: a Rottweiler, a loose cannon, lazy, 'not ministerial material' were some of the less extreme terms heaped upon him. A Guardian sketch writer had captured him to a tee, a couple of years previously:

'This dandy, this throwback to regency pomp, sprays arrogant superiority with every word that spills from his mouth, of which there are far too many. He might be hanging on his own every word, often giving the impression that he has no idea what he's going to say next, but we are not. Spewing entitlement is obviously his hobby; he practices it diligently. He has to, as it certainly doesn't come naturally to Hough, this middle class oik with a massive chip on his shoulder.'

In some senses the man was a libertarian and that, in the eyes of some, bestowed upon him the epithet 'principled'. He certainly seemed to define 'liberty' as 'not being bound by what the Whips told him to do' when it came to voting in the lobbies. He had a poor attendance record in Parliament, equalled only by the busiest of cabinet members. When she painstakingly checked the record, she found that he did not vote against the government - his own party's government - anything like as often as his hard-won reputation might imply that he did. Instead, he simply absented himself from controversial key votes where, his on-the-record opinions might suggest, he opposed a measure which could be interpreted as restricting 'liberty'.

By adopting this approach Hough had attracted a group of followers on the Tory back benches. A couple of these were new to Parliament, having stood unsuccessfully against sitting pro-European Tories, as pro-Brexit UKIP candidates, as recently as the 2015 election. A couple more were in their eighties, generally regarded by journalists she respected as being well beyond their 'sell-by' dates. They had witnessed Hough's barely challenged perverse behaviour opening doors for them and - after a generation of toeing the line, now felt free to rebel, to vote with their hitherto ill-disguised hearts. The rest of the group, perhaps half a dozen, were younger Tory time servers. This group had worked their apprenticeships in an era which had seen a backlash against political correctness in Conservative ranks, a mood which embodied a disregard for accuracy, 'experts' and (many would say) truth, and which had brought Boris Johnson to power. The group was exclusively white, male and gut-wrenchingly anti-institution (apart from being pro-the Lords, pro-monarchy, pro-armed forces and - at a push - pro the Commons itself). One, once tipped as a future Head of Communications at Tory Central Office, had fallen out with the leadership big time, once he was elected. He was a shadowy figure who barely ever spoke in the chamber, but Kate identified him as the Svengali, the Bannon to Hough's Trump. A former journalist, he had taken on the responsibility of keeping Damon's media profile disproportionately high for one with fewer followers in the chamber than Christ had at the last supper.

The story of Hough, the politician, was interesting, there was much to go on, but it hardly advanced the story she was writing. That concerned financial manipulation, keeping ill-gotten gains away from the prying eyes of the courts: let's call it what it is, she thought: money laundering. Even if only rinsing, there would still be spin involved and someone would eventually be hung out to dry. Holding onto someone else's assets, criminally acquired or otherwise, with the intention of withholding them from the attention of the proper authorities, even if just for a short while, must be a criminal offence, isn't it? Memo to self: check with paper's lawyers.

She considered her own memories of Damon. There was the reluctant clown (in her presence, at least), the right-wing bombast (in the months after their break-up, his final year at university), the shy but potentially caring young man. But there was the duplicitous snake, too, the evil, conniving… All this was twenty years ago. People change. Would she be happy to be judged today on who she was then? So much else had changed, too. But who said journalism had to be fair?

Mayo and ketchup.

Two sauces. 'Mayo and ketchup' was one of the best bits of advice the young journalist had been given at the start of her career: 'make sure every story has at least two sources'. She had before her one very strong central source who was certainly in a position to know if the story was true, but by the tale's secretive nature it was difficult to work out where a second source might be found. Unless she were to confront Damon, face to face? Common sense prevailed: at the very least it was too soon to adopt that approach. She needed more evidence, whilst her own memories brought not insight but frustration and vulnerability to the table.

So, did Damon really have three quarters of a million pounds of someone else's money simply lying around on deposit? The Damon she had once known had been a subdued sort of fellow, but that was in the presence of women. She knew he had changed, she had seen the evidence of her own eyes, read in the Parliamentary gossip columns and elsewhere. Damon's normal mode was to be effusive, boorish - a risk taker. Perhaps evidence for unexplained wealth could be found not just in the hoarding of it but in the spending of it, too. And what might a politician like to spend money on?

It was a difficult challenge because she knew that even backbench MPs were well paid - equal to a deputy head in a medium sized comprehensive school, as a deputy head in a medium sized comprehensive school had once pointed out to her. Most received an additional allowance for maintaining a second home in London, but that was a source not of profit, only of compensation of costs already incurred. She knew that they had an office expenses account, too, largely to pay for staff, and some access to funds for political (though not Party political) work. She also knew that all these things were very closely scrutinised and authorised these days. People also donated to political causes…

The Parliamentary Register of Members' Interests soon revealed its online secrets and within an hour she had scoured Damon's entire Parliamentary career. There was nothing unusual about his footprint, as a few more minutes spent skimming the records of half a dozen Tory backbenchers, for comparison, soon confirmed. But this was only a record of payments in; she needed to look at payments out, too.

Kate did not believe that coincidence necessarily implied meaning or causation, so it was fortuitous that, at that very moment, her phone pinged. The text message from 'Number withheld' read 'Entropy Foundation'. This is from Lee, she reasoned. As she was not the sort of journalist who ran several stories at a time there was no other current source who might be approaching her in such a clandestine fashion.

'Thank you', she typed, and pressed 'send'. Two seconds later she received a 'message not sent' notification; the burner had already been disabled. It must have been Lee.

Lunch first, then Entropy.

There were two obvious sources of information about Entropy: the Charity Commission (assuming that 'Foundation' meant 'charity'), and the organisation's own web site. If they both drew blanks, she would have to think harder but, fortunately, they did not. Unwittingly following the same path Lee Hardman had taken she first found Entropy's web site. There was no point saving a record of it as it consisted mostly of glossy, if oddly anonymous, photographs of smiling children and their doting parents. It appeared to be a charitable foundation, existing 'to help vulnerable children bring some order to the chaos of their daily lives'. That was certainly the theme that accompanied the several stories under the photos. A button was labelled 'Can we help you?' She clicked on it, only to receive a 'Sorry, we are currently closed for new applications. Please come back later' response, which was probably not unique in the charity world.

What else? Registered with the Charity Commission, Entropy was based in London - in the City, she noted, guessing that it was a *post restante* address. She looked up the address on Street View and saw an anonymous building with multiple occupants' plaques by the front door. Entropy's remit allowed it to issue grants 'to alleviate personal and organisational hardship' across the United Kingdom. At the bottom of the web page, it said 'Powered by Wordpress'. The site looked professional, it was certainly adequate in getting the charity's message across, but this label suggested that huge amounts of money had not been spent on it. So why was Lee pointing her here?

To the Charity Commission pages on the Government web site next, a site she had never had cause to visit previously. Charities are warm, cuddly, smiley things, she thought, but the relevant pages were not: they were dry, factual, minimalist. They told no story; or did they? She searched for 'Entropy Foundation' and found that the charity was late filing its accounts. The last available set revealed modest income and even more modest expenditure. There was no information on how or where the money had been spent. Data from previous years showed that the charity had been set up in 2014 with an initial endowment of £50,000 from Steel & Partners, the lawyers where Damon was a partner. At last!

Perhaps they were just an altruistic lot, that philanthropy was embedded in their Corporate Social Responsibility commitments. Or perhaps this was part of Lee's stash. Her initial thought was 'no', that could not be the case as, she recalled from an earlier story, money put into a charity's account cannot be retrieved without discharging a charitable purpose on the way. She saw that the lawyers had made further, smaller donations over the years, too, and whilst the charity's expenditure had been roughly constant over the period it had not been huge.

A button on the Commission site revealed the names of the foundation's trustees: they were James Steel, Alice Brain, Indira Sharma and Damon Hough, the four partners of the law firm. Now that did look suspicious, though being a charity trustee was not in itself a crime.

There was one way to find out the nature and depth of the relationship between Steel & Partners and Entropy. She picked up her phone and picked one of the first three names at random.

'Hello, could I speak to Indira Sharma, please? My name's Kate Mellor, I'm from… well, if possible, it would be just five minutes, max… that would be lovely if she would call back, thank you… No, she doesn't know me. I'm a journalist, but it's not urgent. I wanted to ask about the Entropy Foundation. Entropy, E, N… yes. I'm on… oh, you've got my number, of course. That's great, thank you… Mellor, yes… Bye.'

She put 'Entropy Foundation' into Google again and noted how few results were returned. She was not, however, surprised to see that far from demonstrating national coverage, the charity's beneficence appeared to encompass only a single rural area in the home counties. And she recognised immediately the smiling face of the blond benefactor in several of the accompanying photographs.

Thank you, Lee, she thought. Here is the meat to wrap around the bones of my story. Is this what happened to your money? That Damon used fifty grand to make sure his smiling face appeared in the press more often than it otherwise would?

Kate cut and pasted text from several of the online stories into a document on her computer. She guessed from the evidence of the site that Damon was the proud owner of a large, rigid, plastic cheque on which one could write the name of the beneficiary and the sum, take a photo, then wipe it off and use the cheque again. Some of the donations were small - £50 to replace a potted palm tree stolen from an old people's home, £60 for a boy dying of cancer who wanted to watch a match at his favourite

Premier League football ground. If a picture really was worth a thousand words this was not bad value for money, though wordsmiths like herself had always questioned that formula.

She took a break and went to the office kitchen at three in the afternoon to make a cup of tea. When she got back her phone was vibrating almost silently on her desk. Miraculously, she caught it just as it reached the edge of the desk and threatened to topple, managing to salvage the call.

'Hello?'

'Kate Mellor?'

'Speaking.'

'Indira Sharma.'

'Oh, thank you for returning my call so promptly.'

'Not at all. Look, I don't know anything about this foundation that you're enquiring about.'

'Ah, I thought -'

'Really, I'm only responding out of courtesy and because you're the second person to ask me about it.'

'Oh…'

'But I think the other chap had the wrong Indira Sharma; he was looking for Indira Sharma MBE, and that's not me, unfortunately.'

Wrestling with the phone between her cheek and her collarbone Kate typed 'Indira Sharma MBE' into Google on her laptop. There was no Indira Sharma, MBE to be found. She replied 'No, it's definitely you I'm looking for.'

'Why do you think that?'

'Because it's not just you: all four of the partners in your practice are listed as trustees of the Entropy Foundation: yourself, Ms Bain, sorry, Brain, Mr Steel… and Mr Hough.'

'There's some mistake here, I'm sorry.'

'May I ask - does your firm support local charities?'

'Which news outlet did you say you worked for?'

Kate disclosed the name of her employer.

'I'm doing background for a piece on how businesses support charities,' she lied. 'It's all very… positive, a feelgood story.'

'I see. Well, I know Mr Steel likes to, yes. If a charity come to us for, say, to get a legal document certified then we'll probably do it for free, and we encourage all our clients to think of legacies, leaving money to charities in their wills, of course...'

'I was thinking more along the line of cash donations... CSR, is that what they call it?'

'Oh, yes, yes we do! Sorry, I was thinking... Mr Steel is only part time, these days, he's past retirement age, but he's still active. Mr Hough too, of course, being a Member of Parliament, does a lot of community work. There will be a new partner joining us soon. Mr Steel loves his golf, you know, and we sponsor a charity golf day every summer, that's become a sort of tradition. I don't play myself, but there's a big lunch - I mean lots of people, not lots of food - it's a good way to befriend important clients, isn't it? I believe we gave two thousand pounds last year, from the golf day - children's cancer, I think it was. That's the most we've ever given, since I've been here, anyway. We had a good year. Plus, the lunch, of course, we paid for that. Is that the sort of thing you mean?'

'I guess so... and you do that directly, these charity donations, or through an intermediary?'

'I think it's direct. Maybe we've donated to this Energy - is that it? - Foundation in the past. I don't normally handle the charity stuff. That would probably be Mr Hough.'

It probably would, thought Kate. Indira was talking about hundreds of pounds a year; the lawyers were not Premier League philanthropists. If Indira had known about a 50k donation she would have said so; the firm would have been boasting about it.

'How long have you been with Steel & Partners, Miss Sharma?'

'Five years.'

So, the Campbell deal was done before Sharma had emerged and Entropy had been set up at about the same time as her arrival.

'I don't think I need trouble you anymore, you've been very helpful, Ms Sharma. Thank you so much.'

The idiot! Unearthing evidence that the Entropy Foundation could be a front had been a matter of five minutes work, a schoolgirl could have done it. Using his partners' names was pretty damn foolish, it was inevitable that soon someone like her would come along and ask an innocent question. On the other hand, those names had been buried on the website for up to five years already. without anyone tripping over them...

Central Lobby - Lee & Damon:

Thursday 5th May

The Central Lobby of Parliament is known as such because it is both between and equidistant from the chambers of the Commons and the Lords. It is a grand edifice, part of the design by Charles Barry to rebuild the seat of government, a royal palace, after the devastating fire of 1834. It opened for use in 1841. The area's function then, as now, is to provide an interface between the public and their representatives; creating a degree of accountability unthinkable prior to the Reform Acts of the nineteenth century. Not so long ago the best way to contact your MP personally was to arrive in Central Lobby and ask an usher, a messenger, to go off and search the Palace of Westminster for him and bring him to you, a process that sometimes worked.

Today most such assignations are pre-arranged but Central Lobby remains their locus, being as far into Parliament's inner sanctum as most members of the public are allowed to wander unaccompanied. Under the gaze of statues representing a thousand years of monarchy, this august space witnesses the Speaker's daily procession. The crowd parts to allow Mr Speaker, an elected member chosen by his peers to conduct their business, to stride through the Lobby preceded by the Mace of Office. This constitutional ritual embodies the Whig ideal, the right of commoners to partake in the triad of Britain's constitutional government by monarch, aristocracy and people.

Not since his school days had Lee Hardman witnessed this brief pageant but he knew he could set his clock by it: it was 9.28 in the morning of Thursday, 5th May 2022. He was very early for his 10 a.m. assignation but he would spend the intervening time as a tourist, pondering what might have been, had he been able to take advantage of that one opportunity fate had bestowed upon him, a dozen years earlier, to become a Member of Parliament himself.

It was only the second time he had seen Damon Hough in the flesh since that Derbyshire weekend, more than twelve years previously. After their initial negotiation in the City, they had communicated rarely, mostly by phone and in coded emails. Initially Damon had been understanding, not needing to have details spelled out, co-operative. Assuming total discretion throughout it was difficult to see any downside in the arrangement for the MP. The original agreement was for five years but its extension to ten, then for an unspecified further period, had been routine and went without hitch. Not only did avoiding physical meetings help maintain secrecy but neither man was over-keen to spend time in the company of the other.

Now, however, Lee had only a matter of days to recover the capital. It was more than a week since he had asked for this meeting and yet the person most likely to be disconcerted by the delay, the prevarication, was Damon himself. Distasteful as it was, Lee felt that a face-to-face meeting was the only way to resolve matters in a timely manner.

Hough was all sweetness and charm when he strode into Central Lobby only ten minutes late. Close up, he was greyer around the temples than the TV cameras had led Lee to believe, the skin of his cheeks more colourless than ever, suggesting that he lived in the dark like a bat. When he smiled his welcome, he did so with his mouth, but not his eyes.

'You've not changed a bit, Lee! How are you?' Hough's right hand grasped Lee's own, his left grabbed Lee's right elbow but the gesture ended almost before it began. Lee ignored the question to which, he knew, no reply was expected.

'Hi, Damon.'

'First things first, old chap. Tea? Coffee?'

'Sure…'

Damon turned to lead the way but paused immediately, pointing up to the portrayal of a saint above the archway ahead of them. This was a ritual he had performed a thousand times, a Pavlovian reaction to taking a stranger - as non-Parliamentarians are known within the Palace, often impressionable constituents - for refreshment.

'Can you see, there's a patron saint of the United Kingdom above each entrance to the lobby? Do you know how we remember which is which?'

Without pausing for an answer, he gestured in the direction of the Lords.

'That's where the wisdom comes from, so that's George, the patron saint of the English,' then to the Commons - 'All the hot air comes from over there, so that's David of Wales.' Then up to the archway under which they stood: 'Andrew of Scotland marks the way to the bar, of course,' he smiled, then indicated behind him: 'And Patrick of Ireland is on the way out!' Lee recalled that the Palace was built barely 40 years after the Act of Union had cemented Ireland's place inside the United Kingdom for ever; and just seventy before most of that country achieved its independence. For ever?

Damon gave his guest a brief and satisfied smile; job done. They walked together in silence to the next lobby, passing a security post, and turning right into a tall, dark, oak-lined corridor which ran parallel to the River Thames. Where the carpet changed from Commons' green to Lords' red, they turned left.

In the modest and elegant space of the Pugin Room they found a small, cramped table which had been polished until it shone. Beside the window overlooking the river Lee spied a small showcase, housing Augustus Welby Pugin's very own mallet and chisel. The great man carved some of this profuse and ornate Gothic detail himself when decorating Barry's building to his own design.

The time for sightseeing was over.

'It's quiet here this morning,' mused Lee. Might as well stay polite, do the niceties.

'It's local election day in some parts of the country. There are no votes in the Commons today. They allow the keen ones to go home and wring the electoral mop dry.'

Lee smiled briefly. No more niceties.

'Damon, as I hoped I had made clear, I need your loans returned, pretty soon. Like… within a week.'

The MP proceeded as though needing no explanation.

'As I recall, the deal was…'

'The deal was you could use it for five years, which is how long we thought that Guy Campbell would be out of circulation. You've had it for almost twelve and I hope you've found good use for it. But,' his voice became firmer, more authoritative, but still too quiet to avoid extraneous attention. 'I need the capital back - now.' He wanted to explain to Damon that if he had agreed to meet promptly, as Lee had requested, ten days previously, he would have had more than double the time to comply; but there was nothing to be gained from reminding him.

'I understand. OK, Lee, that's fine.'

'Really?' thought Lee. He didn't believe it. 'I do mean the whole seven fifty.'

'Well… perhaps not all at once.' That was more like it.

Lee adopted a conciliatory tone.

'The deal was also that if you've made anything as a result of sweating the principal you can say 'thank you' to Guy in an appropriate manner. But given that you're in deficit, I understand, and the short notice, I'm willing to set any 'thank you bonus' to one side for the moment. But I do need the capital.'

'Well, thank you, Lee,' but it didn't sound especially grateful.

'That's all I have to say on the matter, Damon. It's over to you now.'

'Look, er... five I can do. No problem.'

Lee assumed that 'five' meant '500,000'. 'Good. Well, that's a start.' Lee produced a blank white card from his pocket, the size of a business card. He turned it over to reveal a handwritten set of numbers. 'You can transfer it into this account.'

Damon took the card and, without looking, slipped it into his breast pocket.

Lee went on: 'You have to read the numbers backwards, sort code and then account number. And the account will be closed five days from today. It will disappear without trace at midnight on Tuesday, 10th. Put five in there today, by all means, but however you do it have seven fifty in it by Tuesday. Please.'

'I will certainly do what I can, Lee.'

They paused as a waiter in a silver waistcoat, white shirt and black bowtie, deposited a fully equipped tea tray on their table.

'If you find it difficult, then I'm sure Mr Steel can help you out. Or when people have financial problems, Damon, you know that sometimes they go to a charity for help.'

Damon froze. 'What do you mean, a charity?'

'Perhaps you can get a grant from the Entropy Foundation.'

There was no point asking Lee how he knew about Entropy; the question would trigger no reply and Damon, too, wanted to reveal nothing. Few had ever seen him so lost for words.

The exchange was witnessed by an ornate silver tea pot, two delicate china cups with matching saucers, a silver sugar bowl containing a dozen cubes, two delicate teaspoons and a pair of silver sugar tongs. The entourage lay untouched on the table.

The silence was inordinately protracted, perhaps as long as eight seconds. Damon was clearly disorientated by the mention of Entropy, Lee observed.

'I have another problem, Damon. Thankfully it's not quite so serious, but it is more immediate. I don't think I'm allowed to see myself out, am I? Don't you have to accompany me back to the lobby?'

There was no reply. Damon appeared to be scrutinising the sugar bowl. Rather than move from seated to standing Lee relaxed in his chair and surveyed the decor of the Pugin Room.

'Such a great artist, Pugin, wasn't he? A magnificent style, such opulence. Didn't he design this amazing wallpaper, too?'

Again, there was no response.

'It's magnificent. It really is.'

Damon had the look of a humiliated schoolboy awaiting punishment.

'He mostly designed churches, didn't he, Damon? Lots and lots of them.'

Still no response.

'Pugin achieved so much, in such little time. He died at the age of 40, did you know that? The same age as you and I are now…'

Damon was clearly fuming, but silently. His lips were tight, his brow firm and set, his pale blue eyes fixed on Lee Hardman.

'Well, look, Damon, it's been an absolute pleasure. So good to see you again.'

Lee stood, only half expecting his host to do likewise. 'Shall we go?' he asked. 'I wouldn't want to break the rules by retracing my steps alone. We have to stick to the rules, Damon, don't we?'

Sod the rules. Hough remained frozen to the spot.

'No? OK, then. Enjoy your tea, Damon.'

Lee smiled and stood. He knew his way out, of course: it was not difficult. Solo, he was back in Central Lobby within twenty seconds, having successfully avoided both suspicion from and apprehension by the authorities.

He hoped that was an omen.

Chilli sin Carne - Paul & Damon:

Thursday 5th May

The much-edited letter to Damon Hough was eventually sent, via a Parliamentary envelope and second-class post. Paul Roe thought he should be able to relax for a few days but, if anything, the air of anticipation of Hough's reply started to build the moment that Hazel placed it, along with a hundred others, into the Portcullis House post box. It would stand out in the solicitors' in-tray; envelopes printed with 'House of Commons' and an embossed portcullis always do.

Paul remembered being invited into the front room of an elderly lady on a council estate when canvassing, about three years into his first term. On her mantelpiece a House of Commons envelope was wedged behind the clock. To break the ice, Paul pointed to it and said, 'I see you have my letter.'

'That's from my MP,' she said, with pride. 'He signed it himself!'

Paul's ego was dented. Who did she think that he was, sitting on her sofa? Back in the office he discovered that the letter had been sent two years previously. Relating the story to an old hand in the Commons tearoom he was told that this almost sentimental attachment to 'official' letters was not unusual.

He hoped that his current epistle, to Damon Hough, Esq., MP, of Steel & Partners, solicitors and commissioners of oaths, might receive the same degree of respect; somehow, he doubted it.

On Thursday, 5th May, Paul was eating lunch in the Portcullis House cafeteria, The Debate. The daily 'special' was a vegetarian chilli sin carne with rice, with a chunk of crusty bread and a pat of soft, nice, salty butter, in accord with his flexitarian diet. He was eating whilst catching up with committee papers. By mid-afternoon he would be wending his way back to the constituency to be seen by the Party faithful; he planned to join them to drum out electors to vote that evening.

A shadow loomed over his table.

He raised his head from his reading to see Damon Hough: a smile on the face of the tiger.

'Paul, how are you? No, don't get up.' A hand placed on his shoulder deterred such a response even if he had desired it. His mouth was full of chillied kidney beans, soya and rice - he needed to swallow before he could speak.

'And I'm fine too, thank you,' Damon went on, pretending that he had heard a response. 'I got your letter, thanks. Look, you needn't have bothered: you could have had a little word with me in the division lobby, you know - I mean, I know we're not often in the same lobby, perish the thought, but then perhaps there's a reason for that.'

'Yes, Damon, look, about the letter…' Another manicured hand gently landed beside Paul's plate. Paul was apprehensive.

'I don't understand why it needed a formal letter, Paul. I mean, we're pals, aren't we? We were, anyway. Once. Do you remember?'

Paul remembered, all right. His wince was prolonged. Where was this going?

'Or just a note in the internal mail, an email, perhaps. Why stretch the Post Office? The poor taxpayers had to pay for that letter to go fifty miles when it could have gone 50 yards for next to nothing!'

'The point is, Damon -'

'The point is, Paul, that I'm disappointed.' The choirboy expression, the butter wouldn't melt in his mouth, oh, so reasonable tone, the ominous whiff of threat. But at least he now removed his hand from Paul's clavicle. 'You know, this isn't the way Honourable Members relate to each other, really it isn't. Full and frank, face to face, or any other effing way. But not a fucking formal letter, Paul. Particularly when we're friends.'

'My constituent -'

'What about my client?' Damon spoke rapidly but quietly through almost clenched teeth, his lips barely moving: 'Look, I should point out that Mrs Smith is the proud possessor of something called a postcode, and that postcode confers upon her the absolute, unique privilege of being one of someone else's constituents and not. One. Of. Yours! I won't be writing to you about any of your constituents, Paul, so - hands off my clients, OK?'

'So, should Mrs Greatbach approach you directly?'

'Who?'

'The daughter.'

'Your constituent.' The standing man moved his face closer to the seated one's: 'That's… the one I'm not going to write to you about, isn't it? Because she's your constituent, and not mine. Do you follow?'

'So how does Mrs Greatbach raise an issue like this? Look, it wouldn't happen if you weren't conflicted!'

'Conflicted?'

Still smarting from his confrontation with Lee Hardman a few hours earlier, Damon was on the edge of losing what little remaining patience he had brought to the table. He was now leaning with both sets of knuckles on the edge of Paul's dining table, taking his weight on his fists. Paul, still sitting, felt that this arrangement put him at a tactical disadvantage: there was no room for him to stand up without either contorting his body in an unseemly manner or pushing Damon away. To make matters worse, he had a paper serviette tucked into his shirtfront. Rose had never liked it when he pushed a serviette between shirt buttons, she used to say it looked silly. He repositioned the serviette to his lap to retrieve a modicum of decorum.

'I'm not conflicted, Paul. People have called me many things over the years -' they certainly had, thought Paul, and I'm thinking a few of them now '- but 'conflicted' has never been one of them. I know exactly what I'm doing, thank you.'

'So why did you treble the fee?'

Damon smiled unconvincingly and relaxed. 'Look. Up to now I've been talking to you as a Member of Parliament, a colleague, a friend, an equal. Now I'm going to speak to you as a lawyer, as Mrs Smith's solicitor. And I'm going to give you some very helpful advice, Paul, so listen very, very carefully. Are you ready? There are two things I'm going to say, and I'm only going to say them once each.' He raised two fingers in a very un-Churchillian 'V', directly in front of Paul's face and pushed one of them, the index finger, forward: 'One of them is: lawyer client privilege.'

Paul waited for the second point.

'And the second one is:'

The middle finger came forward to join its partner: here it came: *sotto voce* without losing an ounce of threat.

'Fuck off.'

Hough turned on his heel and left the cafeteria brusquely. An intern, who had been loitering in the doorway, waiting to catch the great man's attention, trotted after him like a small dog.

Paul was seething but could not, must not, show the world what he was thinking... This was just too much. He felt angry, even close to tears.

Basil Cheney had been in Parliament for forty-three years. He never missed an opportunity to tell all and sundry how much everything had changed, and how very little of it was for the better. He had a halo of snow-white hair and a pencil thin, matching, moustache. As an 'old school' loyal Tory, Basil was renowned for speaking his mind - which was frequently indiscreet and often in a manner not very complimentary of his colleagues. The first time Paul had ever spoken to Basil was on a Parliamentary delegation to Australia on Commons business a few years earlier, where they had got to know each other on the long flight. It had been Paul's first official trip abroad and he had found the unflappable One Nation Tory more than agreeable company.

Paul Roe picked at the remains of his food disinterestedly, suffering from the irrational belief that the whole world had just witnessed him being undermined and insulted by Damon Hough. The humiliated MP did not notice Basil approaching. When once again a hand rested upon his shoulder a shock ran throughout his body - had his tormentor returned? Immediately he relaxed as the reassuring presence of a diminutive political fixture materialised, apparently from thin air, before seating itself at Paul's table. Cheney always looked as though he suffered from shrinkage caused by over-washing: the man, not the clothes. A Commons wag, observing Cheney sliding into the lobby, once remarked that he had to take three steps to every one taken by his suit.

Paul looked up and smiled, wistfully: 'Hello, Basil.'

The older man composed himself: Paul sensed the imminent arrival of one of Basil's gems of wisdom, the delivery of which appeared to be the doyen's major occupation, these days.

'You know, dear boy, there are a lot of shits in politics. Your party has many shits in it. My party has many shits in it. But my party has more shits than yours.'

Paul smiled again. Auto-deprecation was the patrician way of saying 'There, there.'

'Well, that's because there are more of you lot… unfortunately.' Basil took the riposte in good humour and smiled, as Paul had hoped he would. 'You saw all that, just now?'

Cheney nodded, before sagely continuing where he had left off: 'But none of them is as big a shit as Damon Hough.'

Paul smiled, more in relief than gratitude. 'Thank you, Basil.'

'I've been in this place a long time…' Paul settled back in his seat, preparing to listen to a choice reminiscence, Basil's trademark repartee. Fortunately, the older man was concise on this occasion, his quiet, sonorous and perfectly articulated tones oozing reassurance.

'I can honestly say that he is the very worst I've come across. And I've been here forty-three years… as I may have mentioned.'

'Once or twice!'

'It's a sign of changing times, dear boy, lower standards, he's interested only in himself. I can't understand why he came into politics in the first place. He didn't want to change the world, he wanted to milk it.'

'Thank you. Yes, I could've done without that confrontation.'

Basil nodded, using his tongue to adjust his dentures, which also gave the impression of being too large for him. 'Oh, congratulations by the way, on your front bench position… DWP, is it?'

'It is. Thank you.'

'Well, good luck. Haven't seen you for a while to say so. Settled in now, I assume?'

'Indeed, yes, I have, thank you.'

'You know, people think I'm a bit of an ornament around here,' he went on, adjusting a green, hand-tied bowtie with white spots. 'Forty-three years on the back bench, but it's not true.'

'You mean you're not an ornament, Basil?' Paul could feel his good humour returning slightly.

'I mean, people forget I wasn't always lobby fodder. No, once upon a time I organised the lobby fodder. I was in the Whip's office for several years, you know, back in the late eighties, early nineties, long before your time. Long before. Even before I took the select committee chair.' Paul wryly wondered if there had ever been a time before Basil had taken the select committee chair. 'And once a whip, you know, always a whip. One knows where the bodies are buried and one doesn't forget, and one knows what to look for in a chap. Or a chap-ess, of course, these days.'

Paul was interested. This did not feel like one of Basil's usual, star-studded, name-dropping stories. They could be entertaining on long flights, but he rarely had the time to listen to them here in the House. Not even Basil would spill Whips' Office secrets, let alone Tory Whips ' Office secrets, to an Opposition front bencher, surely?

'Go on.'

'Of course, this was long before young fellow-me-lad came into the House, but the basics don't change. And… one stays in touch.'

Paul recalled, from somewhere in the deep recesses of his mind, that Basil was brother-in-law to Charles Mallory, the Government Chief Whip. No doubt staying in touch included, though was not confined to, the occasional relaxed Sunday lunch with the family.

'He's gay, you know, Hough', said Basil. 'But it's not public. He's not 'out', which is damn silly of him. One avoids so much fuss by putting all one's cards on the table, don't you think? Especially the Queens… sorry, that's my little joke. Not very PC, I'm afraid.'

Paul agreed. 'But I know what you mean.'

Paul knew exactly what Basil meant. He prayed that Basil didn't know that one of Damon's little secrets was one of his own hidden truths, too.

'Just so much easier to manage, when they're out. Makes it much more… normal.'

'I don't think Damon's sexuality is one of the world's best kept secrets.'

'Possibly not, possibly not. But I've heard… rent boys.'

Basil tapped the side of his nose, knowingly.

Paul's eyes opened wide: 'Really?'

'They think paying for it is a way of keeping it secret, the bigger tip you pay the deeper the silence you buy. Utter nonsense, of course, sheer bunkum; rent boys squeal like pigs under a gate. They always did. Nothing's changed since the days of Jeremy Thorpe. We almost overlapped, you know, Thorpe and I. I came into Parliament in '79, which is when he departed, after all that… fiddle-de-dee…'

Paul wanted not to appear over keen but did want to hear more - though not about Jeremy Thorpe.

'Hough's father committed suicide, you know.' Paul did not know. He barely remembered his childhood friend's authoritarian father, who was so often 'away at sea'. 'Charles Mallory was very close to the dad. They say he died of shame. So often the case with hanging.'

'So, Charles Mallory has known Damon a long time…'

'Hung himself from a motorway bridge. 2002.'

'Ashamed of what?'

'I'd like to think he was ashamed of his shit of a son, but I don't suppose so. Damon would only have been, what? Twenty, then, still at university. He was in the forces, was the pa. Lots of people in the forces have something to feel guilty about, especially if they've seen active service. Hough Senior saw his in the Falklands.'

'Really? Damon's the same age as me, almost exactly.'

Basil's tongue adjusted his palette again and then retrieved a small piece of spittle from his loose lower lip. He appeared to be thinking intently.

'I have this theory… you know, we've had a few suicides over the years that the Whips offices, of all parties, have had to deal with. It's not just Members but their families, too, you know.'

'A theory?' This part of a Whip's responsibilities was new to Paul.

'The more public they make it the more shame is involved. Shame isn't the only motive for suicide, but it's a pretty potent one.' His tone was measured, discreet, almost soporific - were it not for the content. 'If you feel that you have no other option the final choice that you must make is whether to go with a bang or with a whimper. If you want to make a statement, a protest, to clear the air, get something off your chest, then you do it in public, make a statement to the world, defy God's plans for your three score and ten, where everyone can see you. You pop off a bridge, or in front of a train, whatever.

'But if you really just want the whole thing to be over,' he went on, 'to accept the blame for whatever it was, then it's, I don't know, pills in the bathroom, with a chair lodged under the door handle to stop anyone getting in.'

Paul made a face to portray distaste: 'You are really cheering me up, Basil!'

'I say, you're not going to use any of this, are you?'

'Use? I'm assuming you're telling me all this in confidence'.

'So far, yes. Just passing the time with a pal.'

Paul quite liked the idea of being Basil's pal.

'But here's another: fingers in the till. So rumour has it. I imagine rent boys can get to be expensive, especially if they become a habit. Only rumours, but I believe in quality, not quantity. I only listen to well informed rumours, Paul, as you will appreciate. I can say no more.'

'Financial misconduct, really?' That rang a bell. 'Because that's what I'm accusing him of, more or less, but I'm struggling to find a way to take it further…'

Over the next five minutes Paul outlined what had happened, how Damon had continued to practice as a solicitor whilst being an MP, how he had - was 'tricked' too strong a word? - bamboozled Paul's constituent's mother into giving him her Power of Attorney. How he had charged a fee for the service, and how, after her dementia became worse, he had trebled the fee without consulting the family. And how now he was evidently refusing to surrender the PoA to the daughter.

'I'll be honest with you, Basil, I don't know how to handle this. What you saw just now was Damon laying out a policy of non-co-operation on all fronts, telling me to keep my nose out. And doing so in a way which leaves no record, no witness. Apart from you!'

Basil smiled sympathetically. 'I saw the… sign language.'

'I don't know how to handle it as a constituency Member; how do I take this forward? What does an MP do when a colleague's being a shit? I thought of having a word with Mr Speaker, but…'

'Tricky. Yes, I can see it's tricky.'

'Any advice would be welcome.'

'Mr Speaker will want the simple life. He's very much in favour of sweetness and light in all things' - Basil raised his eyes briefly to the heavens and tutted in mock despair - 'He won't turn the screw, not even on Damon.'

Basil reached out and put his hand on Paul's sleeve.

'Leave it with me. We'll talk again.'

Cheney disappeared without a ripple, almost as supernaturally as he had arrived. One thing was for certain: Charles Mallory would know of what Paul was accusing Hough of doing before the day was out. And that could only be helpful to Paul.

Paul's mug of tea had gone cold. He cleared his table, bought another brew, in a paper cup, and headed back up to his office. Yet another pile of casework would take his mind off Damon for the next hour or more.

At Home with Kate & Mark:

Thursday 5th May

Professor Mark Shield enjoyed sharing a glass of wine with his wife - warm, generous, supportive Kate - over their evening meal, and what was even nicer was when they could relax with a further bottle afterwards. They each sat on their favourite easy chair, on either side of their Victorian fireplace. In the grate a gas fire, faux flames designed to make it look like blazing logs, gently warmed the whole room. Sophie was watching an online show in the den with Poops, who was waiting for Helen to collect her.

Mark had started his day's work on the Minotaur book at 6am and had adjourned, after a successful day, to prepare tonight's roast chicken and trimmings, his favourite meal to cook. His only other break, apart from calls of nature, had been the mid-morning stroll to the polling station. In line with tradition, he had cast his vote for Labour in the borough elections, just like everyone else he knew here in north London - though some did so more reluctantly than others, these days. Kate was supposed to have done her democratic duty after walking Sophie and Poops to school on her way to the office, early that morning.

He had timed the meal preparation so that when she got home Kate could cap it off by making the gravy, a task of which he had never got the hang. Indeed, he had concluded, years ago, that he was cursed to make gravy badly as inevitably as Ancient Greek sailors were lured by sirens to their watery graves. After a few glasses of wine at a dinner party it was not unknown for Kate to recount the tale of when Mark had been left in charge of the process. He knew to add a teaspoon of cornflour and to stir the jus well with a wooden spoon, but lumps formed which refused to break up. His masculine initiative and intelligence were demonstrated by using a sieve to rescue his creation, but he omitted to catch the flavoursome liquid and watched it slide down the drain, whilst preserving the lumps in the sieve.

Kate would smile, ending the story with 'Men, eh?' She would often follow this with a good line she had picked up from the radio: 'You can't live with 'em and… well, that's it, really.'

Fortunately, Mark found the story almost as funny as their guests did. Every time.

There was a Schubert Quartet playing, one of Mark's favourites. He had completed a productive day's work, cooked a lovely meal and was now relaxing over a decent Chianti with his gorgeous wife, who also happened to be his best friend. Could life get any better? He put the newspaper down and glanced across. Kate was sitting up in her chair, eyes closed, feet in fluffy slippers perched on a stool. Was she about to drop the (thankfully empty) wine glass from her hand? Mark stood, collected the bottle and walked over to her.

'Top up?'

She awoke with a start. 'Please, yes, lovely. Thank you. Sorry, I was… lots of brain work today. It's exhausting!'

'So, this is your big story, then?'

'Maybe… you know who Damon Hough is, don't you?'

'The Tory MP? I've heard of him. That reminds me, did you vote today?'

Her look said 'of course'.

'So, Hough: Brexit supporter, was he not? Bit of a prat, by all accounts.'

Mark was not aware of Kate's intimate knowledge of Damon. Both as a professor and a former student, he knew very well what went on at universities, but the couple had a tacit agreement, in force since day one, that tales of youthful conquests involving either loins or emotions, prior to 25 years of age, were for ever off their agenda.

'That's the one.'

'He's your target?'

Kate knew that nothing she said to Mark about her work would ever leave the room. That clause did not apply the other way round; unwittingly Mark had often provided material for her 'family life' column. Even the hilarious gravy story had featured in one of her weekly musings.

Even so, she was not yet ready to share all the details - insofar as she knew them - of the MEKANICK tale. She had the mayo on that one, but the ketchup was still to be confirmed. MEKANICK was bad. Entropy was bad. Although Damon linked the two stories, she was far from proving that MEKANICK money was funding Entropy.

'He appears to be using a charity front to boost his profile. And his ego, no doubt.'

'How do you mean?'

'He's MP for the constituency next door to where he has a rural solicitor's practice. All the firm's partners are trustees of a so-called national charity. The practice is a major, if not the major, funder of the charity. It's supported dozens of good causes over the last six or seven years - people who've taken a knock or needed a door opening, by and large.'

'Sounds like the charity's doing its job.'

'That's what he'd like you to think. The problem is -' she counted the issues off on her fingers '- one, the partners don't know they're trustees, the one I spoke to had never heard of Entropy. Two, they've no track record of making big charity donations - we're talking five digits here - and three, this national charity only seems to fund good causes in Hough's constituency. And only then, when there's a camera about.'

'I see what you mean… five figures?'

'I've got to find some way of confirming what happened. There was an initial donation to set the charity up, five or six years ago, of £50,000, and there have been a few top ups since then. All apparently from the solicitors.'

'And all its grant payments have been to his constituency?'

'Either that or the beneficiaries are incredibly shy, everywhere in the country except in his patch!'

'And you've spoken to one of the partners?'

'She knows absolutely nothing, and the biggest donation happened before she came on board. I dare say the idea that all this money had gone from the partners to this 'good cause' over the years would appal her.'

Mark had his sceptical face on. 'But it probably hasn't.'

'What do you mean?'

'It doesn't have to have come from the partners, Kate. It could have come from a client account.'

'Explain.'

'If I'm in a house chain, the money I get from my sale doesn't come to me, it goes to my solicitor. Maybe on the same day, maybe there's a gap, but it's my solicitor who then transfers the cash to my vendor's solicitor. They make sure it all happens in a coordinated way, it's not down to me to organise that. The arrangement ensures that the solicitor can complete the sale on the correct day and that the chain won't be impeded. But that money doesn't belong to the solicitor, to the partner - it's still mine. It goes into a client account so that it doesn't get mixed up with the partnership's own money. If it stays there for any period of time it will even earn interest - minimal, probably - just as it would if I'd been holding on to it in my bank savings account. And that interest is eventually paid to me, less any fees which the solicitor might charge.'

'Of course!'

'Even a small solicitors' practice, doing the conveyancing for just a handful of houses each month would see millions pass through their client accounts every year. When the transfer from me to the person I'm buying from happens the bank will record it as from one solicitor to another, but in fact it was my money all along.'

'Sometimes a bit of mansplaining of an evening can be quite helpful, Mark, thank you!'

She blew him a kiss. He smiled.

'But I don't suppose that every client account contains the proceeds of house sales,' she added.

'No, that's right. They would be used to manage any financial transaction that a solicitor carries out on a client's behalf.'

Kate speculated further: 'And when a partner is overseeing a client account it's possible that the other partners wouldn't know what's going on inside that account…'

'Almost certainly possible, I guess, yes. I mean, why would they? Sure.'

'Mark, have you heard of sequestration?'

'Is that when a court seizes assets pending further action? Like proceeds of crime, grabbing them before the criminal magics them away?' A light turned on inside the Professor's head: 'Oh, the Miners' strike! In the 1980s. That's where I've heard the word. The union thought it was going to be fined and it wasn't keen on paying, but the courts came in and took the money from them anyway. They sequestered it. So the union got wise and hived off funds into individual people's accounts - for a few years. They hid it from the sequestrator until the heat went off.'

'Really?' This was exactly what she thought was happening to the MEKANICK money.

'Sure. I read a book about it. Ages ago.' His gaze wandered along the book-laden shelves which dominated the room, but the title did not spring to his attention.

'That's it! So, there's another part of this story.' She had gone too far, too deep into the tale to retreat now. It was necessary to relate the MEKANICK story to complete her picture of Damon's dodgy dealings.

'Are you sitting comfortably?'

Mark smiled his acquiescence.

'Right. A man called Guy Campbell went to prison eleven years ago. Fraud, money laundering, that sort of stuff, stuff he was doing about the time of the Crash.'

'It was a free-for-all back then! Those financiers were getting away with murder.'

'Yup. I covered the story. The authorities had enough strong evidence to convict him and the court put him away for twenty years, on several counts. That was far longer than anyone expected him to get, but that's life, it's by the by.'

'It sounds like he must have pleaded not guilty,' Mark went on.

'Uh-huh,' Kate confirmed. 'Supremely confident sort of chap.'

'He missed a chance to conduct a bit of plea bargaining.'

'I guess so. Anyway, with parole and so on he's due out imminently,' she went on. 'Maybe as early as a week or so. The point is, they didn't pursue cases where the evidence was weak, of course not. They had enough on him to achieve what they wanted, which was to put him away big time. There was quite a lot of cash in those 'grey' categories - cash that Campbell's people wanted to hide - so they mixed it up with legitimate money and farmed it out as loans to a host of outsiders to look after. They did this to protect it from being sequestered - is that the word? Sequestrated? Anyway, I think - I'm still looking for evidence on this - I think that some of that money landed in the Entropy Foundation, via Steel's solicitors. On loan, as it were, until Campbell came out.'

'And it went there via a client account over which Hough had control?'

'That's exactly what it looks like.' Kate had completed her story. All it needed now was an ending.

'So the charity's a front. And now Campbell's coming out he wants his cash back?'

'I think that's it! He's about to be released and he wants to get back to the world he knows - and the profits he makes from it. And, you know what? I think Hough can't account for all his loan. I think he's in trouble… big trouble.'

Mark was impressed: 'Wow!'

'It gets worse. The fifty thousand that went initially to Entropy is only part of the amount he was babysitting; there was more, a lot more. What if some of it was spent on political campaigns…?'

'Around which there are some pretty tight spending rules…'

'…about declaration, openness, and so on, yes, there are. But perhaps they aren't watertight. As I say, I still need evidence. Everything I've got so far is either circumstantial or hearsay. But it all fits.'

'Well done, Kate. It would be electoral suicide for Hough if this was all true! It couldn't happen to a nicer person…'

'Absolutely. The authorities would be down on him like a ton of clichés. You know, I'm sure most MPs genuinely want to make the world a better place, by their own, quirky definitions. But just occasionally you get one who can't see beyond his own poisoned ego. And I say 'his' advisedly…'

'If you can prove either of these stories, Campbell or the charity, he'd be finished in politics… better still, both! Do be careful, Kate.'

Kate smiled. 'I will. I've got a few more days to work on it so I've no need to cut corners. And I've got a good feeling that it's all going to come together.'

'And I think you've got a scoop, my love!'

Mark raised his glass and proposed a toast to his wife.

'Cheers!' she responded. Never had a glass of red wine felt more deserved: full bodied, fruity, with a spicy edge.

Next time, when the story broke, they would have champagne.

Adolfo Seeks Advice:

Wednesday 11th May

Adolfo Bocca plucked up his courage and entered Charing Cross Police Station.

It was busy. This part of London, close to Soho, attracted more pickpockets and fraudsters, illegal gambling and assaults connected with the sex trade than anywhere else in the country, let alone the capital.

He was of medium height and exceptionally slim. His full head of thick black hair was severely cropped over his whole scalp, and he was clean shaven apart from bold sideburns. A small cross was tattooed on the large lobe of each ear, one of which also sported a modest silver cross hanging from a piercing. His expensive shirt was tailored to that slim body, hinting at a hirsute, tanned torso beneath, whilst a blue suit of fine wool, accentuating snake-like hips, completed his outfit. The elegant lines of the 32-year old's sleek attire were disfigured only by a folded copy of a newspaper protruding from the inside pocket of his jacket.

He had deliberately chosen to call on a weekday morning, Wednesday 11th May 2022, thinking that he would be seen quickly - although he still had to wait twenty minutes. This was disappointing.

There was something about police stations that made him nervous, even repulsed him, but when needs must… he was no faint heart. Adolfo was sure that he could find what he needed to know - confirmation of a theory he was developing - without divulging too much of the reason for his needing the advice.

'Can I help you, sir?' The constable behind the desk was young, tired and approaching the end of his shift.

'*Si*, yes, please.'

'And how might that be?'

'This, er… newspaper?' He took the paper from his jacket and spread it on the table.

'That would be the Evening Standard, sir, if I'm not mistaken. Er… Monday night's.'

'*Si*.' Adolfo was turning the pages, looking for something. He found it on page 8.

'This man… how I… I need ask question. Er, me ask question him.'

'Let's have a look, now, sir.'

Adolfo was pointing at a photograph, his finger pressing down so hard that the officer had to use the finger as a pivot to swivel the paper around in order to read the story.

The constable recognised the man in the photograph. The caption read 'MP dies in bridge fall' and beneath it were four paragraphs of story; it looked as though the man had fallen to his death from a disused former railway bridge in Derbyshire. The police had not ruled out foul play but equally were 'not looking for anyone else in connection with the incident'. Apparently, the man left no living relatives. There was a statement from the Government Chief Whip, Charles Mallory: 'Damon was an exciting Member of Parliament who had his own unique and energetic approach to politics. He will be much missed.'

From the little that the constable knew of the reputation of the man in the picture even he doubted whether the last sentiment was universally true. There was no speculation in the story as to the recent state of the MP's mind.

'So, you need to speak to Mr Hough?'

'*Si*.'

'Well, as the story says, sir, the gentlemen is deceased, dead, caput, so you're not going to be able to speak to him, I'm afraid.'

'*Si*, yes, I know. So, who I to speak?'

'May I ask why you need to speak to him, sir? Is that something you can tell me?'

Adolfo pursed his lips, giving the matter some consideration. There was not very much about his quest that he felt at liberty to disclose to the officer. All he wanted was to be put in touch with whoever had access to Hough's money…

Adolfo Bocca replied with a fiction: 'My name Adolfo. No PH, with 'f'… Soares. Me Adolfo Soares.'

'And where are you from, sir?'

'I live here. London.'

'Would I be right in guessing that you're Spanish sir, are you from Spain?'

'No, no.' The proud Argentine suppressed his natural urge to proudly declare his nationality and opted for a vague response: 'South America.'

'South America? We don't get many South Americans in here.'

'*Si*. I know.'

The constable had an idea: 'You don't want to make a complaint against the gentleman, by any chance, sir?'

Adolfo thought about this one and scratched his head.

'No, no complain. I no want, er... police. Just me and him. I want, who to I talk.'

'I see. Well, as I say, you can't speak to the gentleman himself, sir, for obvious reasons.'

'*Si*. I know.' Both men were extending the natural limit of their patience.

The officer was starting to think that it was not worth initiating the necessary paperwork.

'And it says here, he's left no family.'

'*Si*.'

'So, you can't speak to them. It's not that you just want to leave your condolences, is it sir? Was he a friend of yours?'

Adolfo was puzzled. 'Cond... o...'

'I mean, telling his family that you're sorry that he's died, sympathy. But he has no family.'

'Ah! *Sympatia*. No, me no sorry! Me no do thing make sorry,' Adolfo gave a little laugh.

'No, I didn't mean, er... you had anything to be... sorry about. Maybe, er, do you owe him money or something?'

Adolfo said nothing.

'Or he owes you?'

The Argentine smiled and shrugged his shoulders. Sometimes it helped to be ignorant.

The constable had heard enough. He considered possible exit strategies. On the blank page in front of him he had written 'Adolfo Soares, South America'. That piece of paper would be in the waste bin in the next thirty seconds if his plan worked.

'I'll tell you what, sir. This man here...' He turned the newspaper back so that Adolfo could read it and pointed at the name. 'Charles Mallory. Why don't you go and have a word with him? That's probably for the best. He's - how shall I put this? He's like... your friend's boss. His employer... sort of. He would know the answers to your questions.'

He tapped the paper, picked it up, folded it so the article remained visible and handed it back to Adolfo.

'And I'll tell you what, sir - this gentleman only works ten minutes' walk down the road from here. In the House of Commons, do you know where that is? House of Commons. Parliament. You can walk from here, ten minutes. Fifteen max. Or take any bus that goes down Whitehall. Two stops.'

He paused, to think hard about the directions he was giving.

'Maybe three.'

Adolfo had a question on his face. The officer continued: 'Trafalgar Square, you know Trafalgar Square?' He pointed. 'Just 200 metres from here, that way.' He pointed through the window. 'Then down Whitehall, then there it is.' Was his arm indicating that he should walk the full length of Whitehall or was the officer directing traffic in his mind? 'Houses of Parliament, that's where you'll find him. Parliament.'

'Parliament.'

'You ask for Charles Mallory.'

'Charles Mallory, *si*. Oh, Parliament! Big Ben?'

'Yes, *si*, that's right! Charles Mallory. Big Ben. Go to Big Ben and ask for Mr Mallory.'

'Thank you, sir, thank you!'

'My pleasure, Mr Soares.'

Adolfo held out his hand. The officer took it and they shook hands.

Adolfo smiled as he left, job done. He had confirmation of who he had to see, and the police officer would remember him even though he had made no official record. If things did not go quite to plan that could be useful.

The officer looked at his hand and stretched his palm out, twice, then wiggled his fingers. He had never felt such a loose, limp and clammy handshake in his life.

Deception? Alison & Ruth:

Wednesday 11ᵗʰ May

Wednesday. Over recent days Alison and Ruth had been distracted with other police business whilst they awaited forensic evidence analysis, but today their desks were clear and they returned to the suicide, once more taking over the desk in the incident room. The working assumption was still that it was, indeed, a suicide…

'So,' said Alison, 'what makes us think it's self-inflicted? Then we'll consider what doesn't fit.'

'Well, a jump is consistent with so much of the evidence - where his car was, where the body landed, the nature of the injuries. We shouldn't need to look any further, Boss.'

'Death by a third party?'

'Scuffed shoe came off close to the departure point on the bridge, ditto the cufflink and phone. I suppose that might indicate there'd been a struggle, a fight.'

'Extraneous or ambiguous evidence that looks interesting, but we can't say why?'

'Oh, lots of that. Not just the three business cards but…' Ruth wondered: 'Is it odd that he carried no other paperwork, ID and so on?'

'He had his phone with him. You can use your phone to pay for stuff, so what more did he need to carry?'

'True… house keys?'

'Hmm. You found the car key by accident; it was probably thrown. You weren't looking for keys so perhaps his house keys are still out there somewhere. It'll be God's own fuss to find them, we just don't have the manpower to search that area. And finding them wouldn't tell us much.'

'And not finding them would tell us nothing at all.'

Alison's laptop informed her of an incoming email. 'Ah, we've got the post-mortem, at last… oh, and the phone analysis, too. Goodness, it must be Christmas.'

'The fight could have been a set-up - the shoe, the cufflink, arranged to make it look as though someone had attacked him - but if there was a real fight it must likely have been with someone who knew him.'

'Why?' Alison asked, distracted by her screen.

'Because the bridge is a dead end. You can only get up onto it from the far end, the east, and when you get to the end where he fell the only direction you can go is back where you just came from. Or off the top, like he did. Why would a second person walk all the way to the broken end of the bridge while Hough was there if he didn't know him?'

Alison considered the case. She had prints of the photographs she had taken of the bridge laid out across the desk. Ruth was right, there was no way someone in a suit and brogues - without ropes and crampons - could have got up to the top of the bridge from the business end.

'So why did he jump from this end and not somewhere else along its length?'

'Oh, that's easy, Boss. I had to walk the full length of the bridge, remember? Everywhere else you might jump you might land on soil or scrub, apart from where there's a narrow stream. This end is the only place where you're guaranteed to land on bare rocks or on roadway.'

'Which suggests a planned suicide. Or a coincidence.'

'Which makes the business cards red herrings.'

'Not quite, Ruth. They could be pointers. Perhaps he's saying, 'these people made me do this'.'

'But that doesn't make them guilty. And… the car key must be a red herring, too.'

'How do you mean?' Alison encouraged the younger woman to expound.

'It wasn't on or near the body. I found it totally by chance, yards away from the body. Either the deceased threw it from the bridge - making it likely it wouldn't be found, and that would make us think the assailant had made off with it -'

'- which would have been odd, as the car itself was still there.'

'Or the assailant threw it… which, by the same logic…'

'Means that the assailant wanted us to know that there was an assailant.'

'Which is also a bit odd.'

'So, Hough threw the key. Whether he was attacked or not. All part of a plan to muddy the waters.'

'So I was right, Boss?'

'In that…?'

'The car key doesn't help us. It's a red herring.'

'Hmm... Let's take a look at these reports...' Alison clicked her mouse on her screen Mail. 'Have you got the SOCO report from Sunday?'

'I'll check.' She found the SOCO email easily. It was not marked urgent, and it had been sent only to herself, not copied to Alison. She had paid it little attention initially, but the attendant delay was of no significance.

As she forwarded it to share with the Inspector, Ruth said 'They say they got there on Sunday midday but it had been raining heavily overnight. We'd already removed the shoe, the cufflink and the phone and they found nothing else of interest on top of the bridge... or near the impact point.'

'No surprise there. I've had the autopsy report, too...'

'Any surprises, Boss?'

'Severe trauma to the head, frontal lobe, crushed skull. Surprise, surprise. Death would have been instantaneous. Neck broken, too.'

'Not guaranteed, though?'

'If you mean he couldn't be sure he'd land on his head, that's true. And if he fell as the result of a fight, or if it was an accidental fall, then he'd have had even less control of where or how he landed.'

'Drunks are more likely to survive a fall from height than sober folk, their muscles are more relaxed.'

'That's not much help when they land head first.'

'True.'

'Let's see...' Alison gave the autopsy email her full attention. 'There wasn't much alcohol in him, a little bit but probably from the night before, he wasn't drunk. Or drugs. You wouldn't catch me with an alcohol-free Saturday. Unless, of course, I'm sitting on a farm track in the middle of nowhere with a dead politician. Now, that rings a bell...'

Ruth smiled. 'Alcohol aside, I think death from that fall was by no means guaranteed. He could so easily have just... crippled himself.'

'You mean like breaking his neck?'

'Or his back. What do they call it when you're fine from the neck upwards but can't move any limbs?'

'Paralytic. I know the feeling...'

'No, tetra...'

Alison interrupted, inspired: 'Paraplegic, that's the word. You're saying he was lucky not to just be crippled?'

'If dying was what he wanted then he was lucky it was instantaneous, yes.'

The two women dedicated a common moment to musing.

'Let's have a look at this phone.' Alison scanned the relevant email before reporting back. There was little of apparent significance to report, except…

'Well, well, well. Both Kate Mellor and Paul Roe are in his phone log during the last week of his life. Plus, there were several incoming calls that Saturday morning from a number that they were unable to identify. I'm willing to bet they're from a single source. Whoever that caller was, they left no messages.'

'A burner?'

'Could be.'

'Who uses a burner?' Ruth's thought was barely expressed aloud.

'Bad guys.'

'Guess so. What about emails?'

'On his Parliamentary account, nothing special. Someone has obviously managed that account since the death. We ought to have a word.'

'It'll be his Parliamentary staff. I'm on it, Boss.'

'Thanks, Ruth. But it doesn't look as though there's anything there that's suspicious.'

'Personal account?'

'Not a lot of activity apart from circulars, lots of those… different political causes and so on. Mostly circulars. Can you take a detailed look?'

'Sure. He's very lucky having so little spam!'

'You keep saying how lucky he is, Ruth, but he's dead!' They both laughed. Alison continued: 'So, back to our three musketeers with the business cards: Roe, Mellor, Hardman.'

They both now had the same email open on their screens. After a moment, Ruth summarised what they were seeing. 'According to the log, Roe rang him but he rang Mellor, both on the Thursday evening. After the connection was made each call only lasted for a second or two. There was clearly no conversation with either of them.'

'That's doesn't feel like blackmail, does it? What sort of threat can you deliver in two seconds?'

'There are no other calls involving those two, I've put them in order of senders and the list goes back over several weeks. The Thursday night calls were both one-offs. Where does that leave us, Boss?'

Alison quite liked being called 'boss'. It was better than 'ma'am' and it made her feel like The Sweeney. 'We're going to have to talk to them.'

'I've got his text messages up. All pretty boring... not many of them.'

'The surveillance society, eh, Boss? I know how they feel.'

'But these texts don't say anything significant. Maybe take a closer look later…'

'So we look into all three? Roe, Mellor, Hardman?'

'Hardman isn't on the phone log. Let's see… nothing on the emails, either. Maybe Hough's staff know him. Let's start with Roe and Mellor.'

'Right you are, Boss.'

'I'd hoped that we wouldn't need to. But something about this death just doesn't feel right. It's neither fish nor fowl.'

'Eh?'

'It's not a slam dunk suicide, it feels like a complex set up. Maybe he did design it to confuse us. But is that because he was having a laugh, or does it mean something? Is he pointing at one of these three? Did one of them drive him to it?'

'Or all of them?'

'A committee? No, that only happens in Agatha Christie, Ruth! So, motive, means, opportunity. Three suspects, for want of a better word, by three criteria. That's nine squares, nine empty squares. This is getting complicated. And if they really were all in it together…'

It was a daunting thought.

…

Darren Ogenga was a fastidious sort of cop. Aged 30, a detective constable with the City of London police, he was ambitious, competent and smart. But he was still only a DC.

Much of the work of the City police focused on financial crime, which appealed to the young man's analytical brain: he had joined the force as a graduate with a degree in mathematics. Single, if not by choice, he had always found his police conscience came first; several attempts to find the right woman had fallen at the first fence. The lifestyle did not generally support romance, he had concluded; but he could wait. Having a female officer as a partner would be ideal, amongst other criteria, but the City force, being overwhelmingly male, presented few opportunities... as he had recently explained to his father.

Sidney Ogenga was 70, also single, a loud voice in Hackney's Nigerian community. He was proud of his three sons, fathered by three different mothers, none of whom had remained in the family for more than a few years. All the boys had found themselves in secure, not to say security, jobs. Darren was the youngest; Philbert was a security guard in a government building in Westminster and Jason, the oldest, a civilian working for South Yorkshire police. Jason lived with his wife, Janey, in a market town in Derbyshire from where it was only a short commute to work. Sidney did not see Jason very often - which was perhaps just as well, as he could never understand a word that Janey, the Barnsley Tyke, said - but Darren kept in touch with his brother on the family's behalf, so that was all right.

Darren was the only one of the three with a white mother, so when he was with his favourite brother, Jason, the family connection was not immediately obvious. His recent few days of sibling bonding in Derbyshire had included a couple of nights out and a chance encounter with a gorgeous young woman. He was now finding that he could not keep her out of his thoughts, though he spared her from his most lustful imagination.

She was blonde and petite, a writhely, lively dancer with a red dress that hugged every one of her slick and fascinating contours. She had energy, zest and a smile to die for. If he had been ten years younger, he might have said that he was experiencing love at first sight at this moment, but now that he was thirty - probably closer to the mysterious Ruth's age than twenty was - he knew better. Nevertheless...

They had talked as freely as the night club music allowed, which was not much. He had given her his business card which she had barely scanned before slipping it into her tiny handbag. He had bought her a drink (with a tap water chaser) and, needing to leave the club early, she had apologised for not reciprocating. 'Next time', he said. Smiling coyly, she had not disabused him of the prospect.

Darren could not recall if he had told Ruth that he was Jason's sibling, but he noted that when she was leaving the club, she'd given each of Jason and Janey a peck on the cheek. He hoped that this meant that Jason had Ruth's number. He'd lost count of the number of times he'd given his card to women, never to hear from them again; did the phrase 'detective constable' scare them off? Not Ruth, surely! He had, at least, established that she and he were members of the same profession.

Next morning Jason smiled as he read out the number. Darren sent her a text and was thrilled, some hours later, to receive an acknowledgement. It was only 'Hi Darren' but that was so much more scintillating than 'Who is this?' or nothing at all. When they at last had a telephone conversation, a protracted one on the Wednesday evening, he felt very much at home talking with her. She, too, was relaxed and informal. Next time, perhaps they would use Zoom or FaceTime, another step on the road to intimacy! From the hour's chat he felt that he had learned only a little about Ruth Gaunt. He'd talked about social life, she about police procedure. He had talked about his family; she'd described her boss in some detail. He had talked about coming up to Derbyshire again (to see Jason, of course), and she had talked about the case that was prepossessing her - at some length.

In the City of London, it was inevitable that financial crime took up a disproportionate amount of police time. Darren had helped to solve more than a few such cases - but he brought minnows, not sharks, to book. Nevertheless, he knew how such investigations worked and was more than familiar with the type of person who would try to deceive the authorities about their assets; he hoped she would find his insights useful - and that they could find an opportunity to share them.

On the Thursday morning, May 12th, Darren came into work early, creating time to look up the Guy Campbell fraud case. It would be presumptuous of him to assume that anything he might find had a bearing on the Damon Hough suicide, but you never know. It did not take him long to identify the lawyer that Ruth must have had in mind: Lee Hardman. She had not disclosed his name but had mentioned that he worked for MEKANICK, had provided a witness defence statement and had once been a Conservative election candidate. It had to be Hardman! There was a bold portrait photo on file: a smiling, confident, almost arrogant Lee peered out from the screen. The man who had not yet been invited for interview.

It was 9am before he knew it and time to start work proper. Just occasionally his role was super-mundane, and this morning was one such occasion: at eight that morning a patrol car had dropped off his Chief Superintendent at the Leonardo Royal Hotel near Tower Bridge to address a business meeting; at 10am it would be Darren's responsibility to pick her up, in an unmarked car, and drive her a few minutes up the river to a meeting at New Scotland Yard.

He was early. He parked in the drop off bay outside the hotel entrance and prepared to wait. Within minutes, a commissionaire sidled over, no doubt to draw his attention to the 'no parking' sign. The commissionaire stood beside his vehicle with eyebrows raised. Darren wound down the window and engaged his stare. The commissioner pursed his lips; Darren produced his warrant card. The commissionaire relaxed, nodded, said 'Ten minutes' and returned to his foyer.

Out of habit, Darren scrutinised every person who entered and left the hotel. A Hassidic Jew entered, dressed in black including his homburg, white shirt untucked, ringlets and white scarf procuring from under his jacket, bottle-glass spectacles, flustered and anxious. Coming the other way was a large, well dressed and successful black businessman with two small men running to keep up with him, probably foreign. An overdressed, over-preserved woman with a small dog of indeterminate breed. Then a pause. The commissionaire was nowhere to be seen. From out of the hotel then came a tall, white man with pale skin and rimless glasses, doing up his coat whilst clumsily trying to adjust his scarf at the same time - it was not that cold, was it? Darren looked away but then immediately transferred his gaze back to the man who was now standing still, looking at his phone. Was he calculating a route, perhaps? He was not six feet away from where Darren sat.

The man was undoubtedly Lee Hardman.

Damn. The superintendent was due out of the building at any moment and there was no way the DC could abandon his duty. Hardman, who carried no bag or any other burden, turned and walked away, probably heading towards the Tower Hill underground station. Darren thought quickly: he got out of the car, locked it, and entered the hotel. When the commissionaire spotted him, he said, secretively: 'Just need a leak - won't be a mo, then I'm gone.' The commissionaire nodded.

But instead of heading for the toilets Darren made for the reception desk which was, fortunately, quiet. It took a moment - and another flash of the warrant card - to ascertain that yes, that was indeed Mr Hardman, and that he was planning to check out tomorrow.

A man who lived in London was staying at a hotel.

But not for long.

Darren turned and almost knocked over the Chief Superintendent, who had spotted him at the desk.

'Sorry, Ma'am,' he said apologetically.

'Shall we go, Constable?'

'Of course, Ma'am.'

They left.

Taking Stock – Paul:

Wednesday 11th May

The good news was that Henry had enjoyed his first week as a local councillor, and he spent half an hour on FaceTime that Wednesday, 11th May, telling Paul all about it. It was the first time that a suitably long 'window' for this disgorgement was available, and tonight Paul relished the distraction. Unfortunately, it would not last for ever.

Paul was supposed to be writing a speech and working on casework in his London flat that evening, as there were no more Commons votes scheduled, but one matter preyed on his mind which did not allow him to concentrate on any of his other priorities. He turned the problem over in his head: did Damon's death make it easier to resolve the Power of Attorney problem or harder? Easier, because no one could be as obstructive, devious or unhelpful as he had been, or harder because the other partners at the law firm would be coming cold into the situation and would need to get up to speed? What if they supported what Damon had done? In either case a respectable period had to be allowed to lapse before he approached Steel & Partners, but how long was 'respectable'? A couple of days? A week? Leave it too long and his pleas would look less urgent. He vowed to think about the matter again in a day or two…

He dictated a holding letter to Maureen Greatbach: due to Mr Hough's untimely death… inevitable delay… still confident of a positive outcome…

His own letter to Damon and the covering note to Maureen were the only written records of this case apart from the notes that his assistant, Carol, had made at Maureen's interview and the copy of Damon's original letter to Maureen. Paul had withdrawn the letter to the Law Society without posting it; he wanted to think through exactly what he needed to know again before sending it, perhaps talk to a lawyer off the record, and that had not yet happened. Plenty of Labour MPs were lawyers, it would not be difficult to get some pro bono input on this. It was just that… he had never been so hesitant about anything in his life, and he did not like the feeling. Then again, surely the law firm Partners would have something in their risk register about this situation, contingency plans for one of them passing away before his time? What if, in temper or simply out of spite, Damon had destroyed his copy of my letter? The partners would have no knowledge of any issue here. But they would have a record of the contract with Hilda Smith on file... would they not?

A thought came to him which he had not previously considered: who were Damon's next of kin? He had no surviving close relatives but - what if the PoA deal had not legally been with Steel & Partners, but with Damon himself? If the 'agreement' Hough had made with Hilda Smith was with the firm - three years earlier - it might not lapse just because a partner had died. However, if the money was being paid into Damon's personal account, whose job was it to find that out, to inform Mrs Smith's bank and to get future payments stopped? This was why it was important to identify the next of kin and the executor.

There must be a way of finding out.

He still did not know whether £300 a month was a significant sum to Hilda, or whether she herself - or Maureen, as her daughter - even knew how rich Hilda was. Maureen had said that the dementia had got worse in recent years, so it was possible that her mother could not read a bank statement anymore. Did that add further urgency to the case? Whatever: he was up against a brick wall.

He started to write a list of questions that either he or Maureen had to answer.

First, did her mother keep her paper bank statements? If she did, presumably Maureen could get access to them. But if she received them electronically - being realistic, if they simply accumulated in a folder within her bank account's web page that she never saw, then they were as inaccessible as the account itself, without Hilda's or the PoA's permission. Was she capable of giving permission? What if only Damon could access the records?

Second, does Maureen have online access to any of her mother's accounts? Unlikely: she would have said.

Third, there must have been a witness to the original agreement, apparently the proprietor of the care home. But the job of a witness is only to verify that the person in question is the person signing their name. They do not witness the content of the contract... Finding out who the witness was would take him no further forward. Forget that one.

He decided to scrap the note to Maureen and call her, instead. Now. It was 7pm, normally a good time to catch someone. The mobile was answered after about six rings.

'Hello, Mrs Greatbach, it's Paul Roe here, the MP. How are you?'

'Oh, Mr Roe, it's you… thank you for calling. This isn't really a good time.'

'I just wanted to assure you that Damon Hough being no longer with us may actually make it easier to resolve your mother's case. I need to ask you, very quickly… are you OK?'

There was a pause. 'What did you need to ask me?'

Was it poor reception or was the voice faint?

'Do you have access to your mother's bank statements, by any chance?'

There was silence at the other end of the line.

'Mrs Greatbach?'

He thought that he could hear a woman sobbing.

'Maureen?'

'My mum's had a fall, Mr Roe. We're at the hospital with her now.'

'I'm so sorry to hear that. Is she going to be OK?'

'How can they tell? She can't even tell them where it hurts, but we know she hit her head. I mean you can see… She's in and out of consciousness… there was a lot of blood…' More sobbing. 'It was everywhere…'

'Mrs Greatbach, we'll leave it there. You obviously need to be with your mum right now… I'll be in touch in a few days. My very best to your mum, and to you. And your husband. Goodnight, Maureen.'

He hated himself for his next thought, which was truly beneath him. If Hilda Smith died this frustrating case, with all his associated, difficult, childhood memories, would die with her. It would all be over.

He was still admonishing himself when his phone pinged: it was a text from Hazel, his Westminster aide. 'Pls ack text sent @ 5pm', it said. Hazel did not trust predictive text but after all this time he could understand her code. The 5pm text, which he had indeed missed, read 'Pls call re I/v w police tmrw 9am zoom'.

A call from the police about a constituent's case or another local issue was unusual, but not unheard of. Paul assumed the worst: this was something to do with Damon. He did as he was told and selected a number on speed dial.

'Hi, Paul. Tomorrow at 9 I've put in your diary a video call with the police officer investigating Damon Hough's death. I suggest you do it from the Westminster office because you've got committee at ten. The link's in your calendar. Is that OK?'

It was good to hear her reassuring tones, though he had been with her only a few hours earlier, in the office.

'Yes, sure... thank you, Hazel.' His initial thought was that the broadband connection was better from the office than from his flat, but only then did he wonder why they needed to speak to him. Surely suicides got sorted in under - what was it? Four days so far?

'They called just as I was leaving the office. I texted you just now to make sure you'd seen it.'

'Thank you. I was in the chamber.'

'Of course. They rang while the first vote was on.'

'Thank you, Hazel.' She was good to him. 'Who will I be speaking to?'

'Hey, get this for a name! It's Inspector Alison with an 'i', Allyson with a 'y'. Alison Allyson. East Midlands Police.'

'Very droll. East Midlands, you said?' He sounded puzzled.

'He died in Derbyshire.'

'Of course.'

'She said it was nothing to get worried about, but she knows you had some recent contact with him. I thought, they're being very thorough - it was only the one letter, wasn't it?' Hazel did not know about the lunchtime encounter. 'We've not had a reply, by the way. Public figure and everything, of course the police would take an interest in a suicide. Anyway, I asked, it was suicide, wasn't it, and she said yes, they're not looking for anyone else, just tidying up loose ends. So it's just a formality, I guess.'

'I guess so.'

'I suppose they're trying to find a reason for him... doing what he did.'

'Yes, I imagine that's it...'

'They need to satisfy themselves that it really wasn't... you know.'

'Sure...'

'Helping the family get closure.'

Paul's mind was racing: did the police know that he had accused Damon of scamming a defenceless woman with dementia? They couldn't possibly know about the teenage stuff, could they? Surely not. Did they know about Damon's behaviour in the cafeteria? Had Basil Cheney told them something? Unlikely. He was sure that Basil was the soul of discretion - when it mattered.

'Are you still there, Paul?'

'Sure…'

'Are you OK?'

'Sorry, Hazel. Yes. Thanks for that. No problem.'

'Is there anything else I can do for you?' she asked. She could sense his discomfort. He smiled, despite his rising panic. It *was* good to hear her voice. She obviously cared. He did not need to go through all this crap alone. For his part, he was tempted to say something profound, but he resisted.

'No, I'm fine, thank you. Look, I'll see you tomorrow - after the interview, in the office.'

'I'll be there, Paul,' she reassured him. 'About quarter to ten.'

'Thanks. This is all going to blow over, I'm sure.'

Or would it? What did the police really want from him?

The Interview (Paul):

Thursday 12th May

    Ruth spoke at some length on the phone to both of Damon's staff, his Parliamentary assistant and his constituency office secretary. It was Wednesday, two days since the MP's employees had heard the news and they had, of course, been shocked. They both worked full time, though the constituency secretary said it was normal for her to go a fortnight without seeing the MP. As the Parliamentary assistant worked from home, she only saw Hough in the flesh every couple of months. She had been working for him for less than a year. Ruth concluded that neither woman could claim to know the man behind the mask terribly well, though both were coping with their loss.
    Had he been behaving oddly in recent weeks? Not that they had seen, but for something to be 'odd 'in Damon's life it had to cross a fairly high threshold. Had anyone been pestering him? Not that they knew of. Has anyone ever threatened him? Not especially, though the constituency secretary had reported a constituent to the police for harassment (with Damon's knowledge and approval) about six months earlier. A police sergeant had been sent to have a 'quiet word' with the gentleman in question and they had seen neither hide nor hair of him again since. But that was harassment of the constituency secretary, not of the MP. The degree of similarity between the women's answers convinced Ruth that their convergence was genuine. The older woman, Edith, who had dealt with correspondence from voters not just since 2010 but for Damon's predecessor, too, let one thing slip: she was of the view it was no surprise that the MP had killed himself, if that was what he had done. Yet an accident was credible too, she said. He'd been very fond of the countryside. He lived life a little close to the edge, she said, but declined to be drawn on how she had reached that conclusion.
    'I wouldn't want to speak ill of the dead,' she said, conceding 'it's probably only fancy on my part.' She agreed to send over a copy of Damon's diary, though Ruth sensed that this had not gone straight to the top of the aide's 'to do' list. The women's greatest concerns were that mail should continue to be processed efficiently and, of secondary but not

insignificant importance, whether either or both might be out of a job before too long.

Alison had also been speaking to someone on the Parliamentary estate, a pleasant and efficient, accommodating woman called Hazel, who worked for Paul Roe. Whilst Ruth was interrogating Damon's staff Alison was setting up a video interview with Paul, for the following morning. Alison tried to probe: what did Hazel think of Damon Hough? Had Paul had any contact with him lately? Ever professional, the loyal Hazel gave nothing away, but in the nicest possible manner. Later, Alison snared Kate Mellor in her diary too, their interview being scheduled towards the end of Thursday afternoon.

Lee Hardman was proving more difficult to track down, but he was not their priority. His work mobile number rang without going to voice mail, so an email was sent and a message left with the receptionist at MEKANICK. Their only link between him and Damon - apart from the business card - was twelve years old and tenuous, the links to the others felt potentially stronger. The MP and the journalist were their top priorities.

…

Thursday morning arrived. Police Headquarters had invested in new technology back in the first covid lockdown and Alison was accustomed to carrying out video interviews over the internet. She was wary of using the medium when a suspect was under caution, especially when an arrest might be on the cards, and the protocols for authorising distant witness statements was complex, long winded and tiresome. At least she felt it unlikely that she would be warning either the MP or the journalist that 'You do not have to say anything, but it may harm your defence…' today! On the positive side large, modern, high-resolution screens allowed every tic of body language to be noted, recorded and later analysed. Then there was the time saved, on this occasion, by not having to travel to London and back, or once in the capital needing to fill the vacuum between meetings. That bonus was very gratefully received. The conscientious Alison appreciated the low carbon footprint of the communications technology when compared to the travel, too: the screen used less electricity than a light bulb from her childhood, apparently.

Right now, the agenda was simple: they were going to have a chat.

Paul Roe was in his office on the third floor of Portcullis House. It overlooked both the Thames and the former County Hall, the Edwardian

Neo-Baroque monster which dominated the South Bank of the Thames. From all that Alison could see, however, he could be anywhere on the planet. In Derbyshire, Inspector Allyson's large screen sat across the table from her, making the life size MP appear as though he was there with her in the room: it was like talking to a hologram. Behind the MP the Inspector observed modern, robust cupboard doors, beech perhaps, or light oak, virtually filling the screen from floor to ceiling. The MP wore a suit, neither light nor dark, a brunette sort of grey suit, accompanied by a pale green shirt and a striped tie of pastel hues.

The shadow minister certainly looked the part. He was clean shaven, his brown hair trim, face relaxed, countenance confident. This was a man accustomed to appearing on television. The thought 'I could vote for him' passed through Alison's mind before they had even exchanged a word.

Ruth had asked if she could sit in, and Alison thought this was a good idea. Ruth could take notes: even though the meeting was being routinely recorded it was good to jot down its main points as they went along. They thought at first that Ruth should sit out of shot but, on reflection, opted for openness. The younger woman sat behind Alison, to one side, appearing in the corner of Paul's screen. As well as the notebook on her knee she had a pack of yellow sticky post-it notes, ready to pass ideas over to her boss mid-flow. She hoped that whoever had invented these things, with their non-sticky sticky backs, had won an award.

By default, each conversant dominated the other's screen. Alison was not keen on her larger-than-life image appearing on a big screen, on anybody's screen, but then nobody liked such exaggerated images of themselves, did they? Not only was every flaw magnified - she really did not need that, at her age - but people are so used to seeing their reflection in a mirror. Having the person that others see as you revealed is always slightly disturbing. There was a philosophical lesson here, no doubt. A small, mirrored image of Alison and Ruth appeared in a corner of the screen so that they could be aware of what Paul could see; a video compromise.

After the opening pleasantries Alison set out the terms of reference.

'As you know, Mr Roe, last Saturday the body of Mr Damon Hough was found in a manner that suggests that he died by falling from a disused railway bridge. The line of enquiry that we are currently pursuing is that he might have taken his own life, by jumping from it.'

'Yes, I understand. I was very sorry to hear about... The unexpected death of a colleague, indeed any unnecessary death, is always a matter of great sadness.' He sounded sincere, of course he did. That was his job.

'Indeed.' She paused to see if he had finished. He had.

'Of all Mr Hough's 657 colleagues in Parliament you're no doubt wondering why we're talking to you and not - at the moment, at least - to any other MP.'

With the slightest of nods the MP acknowledged, rather than confirmed, her point. Inside, the realisation that he was the only one being put on the spot, and him not even a fellow Tory, was disconcerting.

'You've been in Parliament, what, seven years, and he's been around a bit longer. How well did you know him?'

After a momentary hesitation Paul said 'Not particularly well', with no qualification.

She let the answer settle.

'Mr Hough didn't have many possessions on his person when he died, indeed we weren't immediately able to identify him...' she didn't add that the face was mangled almost beyond recognition '...but amongst the few things that he did have in his pockets was a small number of business cards. One of them was yours, Mr Roe. Can you think why he might have had your business card on him?'

Paul Roe raised his eyebrows then crunched them, pursed his lips, almost a parody of befuddled innocence, though again it seemed sincere - and his own surprise was also genuine. It was a good question: why on earth would Damon have been carrying his card? This was a moment of decision for Paul: should he tell them that Damon had been scamming an old lady or let it rest? There was no reason to believe that the MPs' recent correspondence was linked to Damon's death, the case was simply a matter of routine. Not even the business card could tie Damon to the Greatbach story, so why should he add conjecture?

'I've no idea, I'm sorry. I've had thousands of business cards printed over the years, as you can imagine. I don't keep track of them, rather we tend to scatter them like confetti.'

'So there's no particular reason why - I mean, he had no other MP's card in his pocket.'

Paul had no explanation and, once more judged that speculation would be unhelpful. He selected a typical MP's response, of almost Pavlovian proportions:

'You know, people think that MPs are at each other's throats all the time in this place, especially Labour versus Tory, but the fact is that Westminster has a very collegiate atmosphere -'

'Oh, come on, you're not on television now, Mr Roe!' As she spoke Alison realised that this was an odd thing to say to a man through the medium of a large screen. 'Why do you think that Damon Hough had *your* card in his pocket? I'm not asking for *the* explanation, but *an* explanation, possibly a choice of explanations. Why *might* he, not why *did* he, have your card?'

'Well, as I was just about to say, MPs do talk to each other, across party lines, and we often work alongside each other on different issues.'

'You would normally see him on a regular basis?'

'Well, literally 'see', yes, several times a week, probably. Be in the same room as, less often, through All Party groups, bill committees, and so on… speak to? Hardly ever.'

'When did you last talk to Damon Hough?'

'Just a few days ago, as it happens, for the first time in a long time. A week ago, to be exact,' he looked at his watch, 'almost to the minute.' This had the advantage of being true, though Paul had been trying hard to forget it. His judgment was that although there was no reason to disclose the details of the meeting, denying it had happened was pointless; there had been witnesses.

'Did you give your card to him on that occasion?'

'No, I had no reason to.'

'Is your mobile number on your business card?'

'No, I don't think it is.'

'You keep that private.'

'Yes.'

'Of course. So, your card would have your London office number?'

'The House of Commons number, yes.'

'And your constituency office number?'

'Do you know, I can't just picture it…'

Like a stage magician he reached into his outer breast pocket and pulled out a card. He examined it. 'Yes, it does.'

'And your email?'

'Yes.'

'Two numbers and the email, yes.' Now it was Alison's turn for the card trick: 'This is the actual card from Mr Hough's pocket.' She held it up towards the camera mounted above the screen, which exaggerated both the card and her fingers into a gross image of disproportionality which, under other circumstances, might have been mildly amusing. The card was almost identical to the one in Paul's hand.

'Inspector, that's an older version of my card, I've not been using those for, oh, three or four months. My new one has 'Spokesperson on Poverty' after where it says 'Labour MP'.' He reciprocated the holding-the-card-up-to-the-screen routine.

'So it does. The email address… Does that follow a formula?'

'Yes… a Parliamentary formula, if you like.'

'And if an MP wanted to contact you he'd call your office in Parliament, which he could do through the Commons switchboard, so he wouldn't need to know your extension number. Or they would use your email address, which they could work out from the formula.'

'Yes, I suppose that's right.'

'Or your constituency office number, which he could find on your website; or your mobile number which is not on the card anyway. Which means that if he had your mobile number, it was possibly because you had given it to him, separately.'

'Are you saying that he did have my mobile number?' Paul was puzzled. But the possibility rang a very distant bell.

Alison parked the question - she would come back to it.

'I can absolutely understand why the card is useful to give to a member of the public, to a voter, whatever. I can't for the life of me see what an MP gains from having another MP's card in his possession.'

'Yes, I see what you're saying. He must have had his reasons.' Paul speculated silently that perhaps Damon had been sticking pins into it, like a voodoo doll.

'He had nothing in his pockets, nothing at all, except for three business cards. On a Saturday evening. In the middle of nowhere. It's almost as though he was trying to send us a message. Do you see what I'm getting at?'

'From beyond the grave!' thought Ruth, but she said nothing. She was impressed with the boss' performance to the extent that she had not yet felt the urge to pass her a post-it note, fascinating though its technology was.

'Obviously, I can't comment on that, Inspector. That would only be speculation.'

'Can I ask you where you were on Saturday afternoon and evening? That's last Saturday, 7th May.'

'Goodness, do I need an alibi? Inspector, really!' Paul chuckled, dismissively.

'We're just having a conversation, Mr Roe.' She was tempted to say 'We're off the record', as might have been the case in the old days of more basic technology, but a small red light in the top left corner of the screen reminded them both that this was not the case.

Paul was genuine in needing a few seconds to collect his thoughts. He had been in London on quite a few recent Saturdays… 'We're talking about last Saturday, for Christ's sake', he reminded himself, 'don't let her get the impression that you can't remember or that you don't want to say!'

'I was at my London flat. I came back to London in the afternoon; I often do that if I've nothing in my constituency diary on the Saturday evening or the Sunday. It's only an hour or so away, with the weekend traffic in London being so much less than it is on weekdays.'

'Is there anyone who -'

'Do I need a witness as well, now? No, I was there by myself. I don't have a witness for the time you're asking about.'

'What time am I asking about?' Old habits die hard.

'You said afternoon and evening. I was in London all evening, I got here about five.'

'On Saturday evening I was examining the body of someone I didn't recognise. That's not because I know nothing about politics, it's because the face was literally mashed to a pulp. He'd just fallen 20 metres and landed on his head.'

Paul felt a shiver run down his spine. 'It must have been horrible.'

'It was. DC Gaunt was there, too. What did you think, Ruth?'

'It was horrible, Boss. A right mess.'

'I thought, straight away, this is suicide. No doubt. If that was what he wanted to do then he chose the best place on that viaduct from which to jump. There was no sign of a third party. There was no indication of any motive anyone might have for - though I gather he wasn't the most popular MP, was he?'

'No,' Paul conceded, thoughtfully. 'No, he wasn't. He was… quite unpopular. He had a small group of friends, followers, some might say 'acolytes', but generally he was regarded as a bit of a thug. That's by all sides, by the way, even his fellow Tories. I think it's fair to say that he could be a pain in the neck for the government whips. He wasn't regarded as very... trustworthy.'

'Tell me more.'

'Damon was quite an arrogant man, intolerant, right wing. Got up people's noses, even the noses of colleagues on his own benches.'

'Ruth, can you write that down, please - I think that's significant. Damon Hough wasn't popular even on his own side. That swings the pendulum further towards a verdict of suicide, don't you think, Ruth?'

'Yes, Boss.'

'What did you talk about, Mr Roe? When you met - bumped into, which was it? When you were with Mr Hough the other day. A week ago, you say?'

'Thursday 5th, it was local election day, that's why I remember the date. A week ago.'

'So - the meeting?'

'Our meeting was neither planned nor expected. But Parliament's a small place. I was having my lunch and he came over to talk.'

Paul stopped the explanation at that point, but Alison was not ready to move on.

'And you talked about...'

'I have a constituent who has an issue... with a company based in Mr Hough's constituency. He was aware of the matter and... it's a very small thing. I've sent a letter to the company involved, to clear the air, and I'm sure that will resolve things.'

'And Mr Hough's contribution to the conversation was...? What did he say to you?'

'He... just wanted to let me know that he was aware of my approach to... and, er... to... he hoped it would all be, you know... sorted. Look, there are issues here of constituent confidentiality. Talking to your MP is a bit like talking to your lawyer, or a priest. People don't expect their MP to go bandying their name... and it's not just names, I mean, describing circumstances can identify a constituent and it's not fair to... can we leave that issue there? After all, you are recording this, aren't you? I don't want to...'

'Of course. I'm sure there's no need to go into detail.'

Ruth was staring at the MP, whose gaze was fixed on Alison. Was this man really the rising star of the Opposition front bench? A future Cabinet minister? He wasn't showing great confidence or grasp right now, she thought. In fact, he was rambling.

'Was that when you gave him your card?'

'No.' A light bulb went on in Paul's mind: 'If I had, it would have been one of these newer ones.' He waved the card that was still in his hand, for emphasis, unnecessarily. 'But there was no reason to, for exactly the reasons you said a moment or two ago.'

'Would you be surprised to know that Mr Hough did actually have your mobile number?'

'Really?' A genuine emotion: Paul was surprised.

'Really, yes. In his phone. How do you think it got there…?'

'I don't recall him ringing me about anything… ever.' This was true.

'No, he didn't. But you rang him. Last Thursday, a week ago, the same day you met with him. Didn't you?'

'I don't think so…' Then Paul remembered. It had been a moment of madness, literally the briefest moment. Unfortunately, what the Inspector was saying must be both true and undeniable. Shit. 'Oh, er… yes, yes I did. That's right. It was about this constituent, the one I was telling you…I just wanted to check a local… a local detail, and I thought he'd be able to help. I rang him late in the evening, but he didn't pick up and didn't call me back, either.'

The last sentence had the advantage of being true. What had happened was that in an angry moment, slightly the worse for alcohol, Paul had toyed with the idea of calling Damon and screaming at him down the phone. He found his number in his own phone's contact list from way, way back - Aha! That explained it! - but common sense had come to the fore, and he had abandoned the idea. Unfortunately, he spotted immediately, this was not before pressing the button to make the call, which he thought he had immediately cancelled. During that intervening second, he had clutched back his judgement, if not his sobriety. At the time he had assumed that this briefest of calls had not even rung, let alone registered on the system as a call. Obviously, however, it had.

'You didn't leave a message?'

'No.'

'Or try him again, later?'

'No.'

'It was a very brief call.'

'Yes. I remember now. I realised what time it was - it was quite late - and I had second thoughts, I knew I shouldn't be ringing a... a colleague at that time of night. And it was election night, too, so my call really wasn't appropriate. So, I... I cancelled the call. Straight away. Next day it became clear that the question that I was going to ask him was... unnecessary, so I didn't call him again.'

'OK... You see... his phone knew that it was you that was calling. It listed your name, not just your number. That means you were already in his phone's memory.'

Paul raised his eyebrows in a moment of genuine bemusement. But he knew now what was coming.

'And how did you have Damon Hough's mobile number? Is it on his card? Do you have his card?'

'His card? No... I don't.'

There was a moment of silence, but then Paul was inspired with a reply which was both accurate and convenient:

'Right... I'll tell you exactly how that must have happened!' A true recollection was now fully formed in his mind, so true it boosted his confidence. 'I'd been an MP for a couple of years when about six of us went on a cross-party delegation to South Africa, looking at skills training, as I recall. Damon was on that trip and, for one reason or another, I can't remember, we decided between us that it was a good idea for each of the delegation - there were only five of us, maybe six, from different parties - to have each other's numbers. In case of emergency, in case we got unintentionally separated. South Africa, especially parts of Johannesburg, where we were, was not a good place to get lost around that time. You wouldn't want to be on the streets alone, especially after dark. I don't think I ever did use his number, or any of the others. I never actually called him, but that was how his number got to be in my phone. And mine would have been in his, too, by the same token. Plus, the numbers of those other three or four MPs, too.'

'So, there were no emergencies on the trip?'

'No, it all went like clockwork.'

'You have never actually tried to speak to Mr Hough on the telephone previously.'

'No, that's right.'

'Until a few days ago.'

'As we've established.'

'Just before he killed himself.'

Paul hesitated. 'Apparently.'

Alison paused, briefly, as though marking the end of a paragraph.

'So… when MPs go on these delegations: do they get to know each other, socially?'

'I guess so.'

'There were six of you -'

'Maybe five? Maybe six. And an organiser, too, though whether he - or she - was in the six or additional, I can't recall.'

'Six of you in the delegation. Six or so. You'll have had dinner together, no doubt.' Paul nodded. 'Breakfast.' He continued to nod. 'Been in meetings?'

'Yes. That sort of…'

'Been in the bar together. Do you like a drink, Mr Roe?'

'Yes…'

'You're a social drinker?'

'I would say so.'

'Was Mr Hough a social drinker?'

'Oh yes! He was never out of Strangers' Bar, here in the Commons, pontificating! Usually in a very loud voice. That was his reputation, but I don't spend a lot of time in Strangers' myself.' And that's the reason why, he did not add.

'On that trip? Did you do social drinking together on that trip?'

'Along with the others, I suppose, yes, we did. In the hotel, in the evenings. A nightcap, perhaps.'

'Of course. So, you socialised together, Mr Hough and yourself.'

'In that sense, yes.'

'And since?'

'I don't remember.'

'Would you say never?'

'Perhaps not never.'

'Never in the Strangers' Bar? That's the one down by the river, isn't it?'

'Next to the Terrace, yes. It's the bar where MPs can take visitors. 'Strangers', indeed, as we rather dismissively call them.'

'Have you ever had a drink, or a chat, with Mr Hough, in the Strangers' Bar or on the Terrace?'

'Yes, actually. On the Terrace.'

'I'm so glad we've jogged your memory! I know you're trying to be helpful, Mr Roe. Tell me about your socialising with Mr Hough on the Terrace.'

'Well, it was just once, back when I was first elected, a long time ago…'

'I think he became an MP at the election before you did.'

'Yes, in 2010. I came in at the 2015 election.'

'And he invited you for a drink on the Terrace, he invited the new boy. It would help you settle in, feel at home. Would that be it?'

'Something like that.'

'Why you? Why would a right-wing Tory MP not known for cross-party collaboration invite a progressive Labour MP - I think you've descried yourself as 'progressive' - for a social drink? It doesn't sound to be in his character.'

Paul mumbled a reply.

Alison asked Ruth 'Did you catch that?' Ruth shook her head: 'No.'

Alison smiled, her manner on the generous side of condescending. 'Mr Roe, I did say we're recording this, didn't I? It's just that we didn't pick that up. Could you repeat your answer? For the record.'

'I said yes, we… er, we knew each other before I became an MP.'

'Well?'

'Well, what?'

'Did you know each other well? Before you came an MP?'

'It depends on what you mean by -'

'Were you at school together?'

For the first time, Paul showed signs of being annoyed. 'Why are we playing this game?'

The Inspector took a punt: 'I might ask why you didn't answer my very first question by saying yes, I've known him all my life.'

'Because I haven't. I mean… that wouldn't be an accurate way of describing it.'

'What would be an accurate way of describing it?'

'What makes you think we were at the same school?'

'Well… you're both in Who's Who. You're both in the Parliamentary yearbook. And you're both on Wikipedia. It's fascinating, Wikipedia, do you ever get the time to look at it?'

211

'I've looked at my own page a couple of times, had a couple of libellous statements removed. It's not always the most definitive source of information.'

'It says which primary school you went to, and which secondary. And if you've checked your page then presumably you would have corrected it, had it been wrong. On Mr Hough's page - it had his death up there within hours of the announcement, I don't know who monitors such things, someone obviously does - that's very impressive, don't you think? It only mentions his secondary school, but it's the same one as yours. It was a comprehensive back then, it's an academy nowadays. And you're almost twins… You're not only in the same school year but you're both 40 this month. Happy birthday, by the way.' She smiled.

'Thank you. That doesn't mean we knew each other.'

'I could ask the school. I mean, it's probably been reorganised once or twice since then, but the police can find records when we need to.'

'Why would you need to do that? What are you trying to prove?'

'I'm not trying to prove anything!' Alison was smiling, almost grinning, but it was an expression of incredulity rather than humour. Ruth's brow was furrowed in amazement at how intricate the answer to a simple question had become. 'Mr Roe,' Alison went on, 'I want to know why a successful MP like Mr Hough - I know he wasn't a minister or anything, but most people would regard MPs as being successful *per se*, because he'd won an election. Or, in his case, four. I want to know why he killed himself. And you've known him a long time; longer than most. Maybe longer than anyone, since he left no family members.' She left Charles Mallory out of that equation.

Paul fixed Alison's gaze as well as he could across a video link: 'I don't know why he killed himself. I have absolutely no idea. Look… yes, OK. Our paths crossed at school, but we weren't particularly close. And people move away, and people move apart. I heard nothing about him for years, but I didn't go round thinking 'oh, I wonder what happened to Damon'. No way. After he won in 2010… well, it was probably 2012 before I even put two and two together and thought hey, that was the guy I was at - the guy who was at my school at the same time as me. But people change, Inspector. And it was clear that, once he became an MP, he wanted to build up a public image based on doing what one would expect of a complete prat! A complete prat with an inauthentic posh background, in fact. He came from lower middle-class stock, not that you'd think so from his... I don't know. I guess I was not keen to rekindle...'

The sentence drained away.

Alison raised an eyebrow. Ruth sat open-mouthed. The gestures caused Paul to mentally prepare for worse.

'Rekindle... that's an odd word to describe a relationship with someone you barely knew.'

Paul had no option but to get onto the front foot: 'Really, Inspector, he was an appalling man! Ask anyone. When I came to this place I would not - did not - want him as a friend. Ask around on the Tory benches, they'll say the same. Yes, he might have been short of friends, but he knew exactly what he was doing. He had some sycophantic followers including a few in Parliament, a handful of right-wing, libertarian types. He built up a massive following on Twitter, but Twitter followers are not the same thing as friends! That's not 'real', is it? I think he was probably a very inadequate human being. A pathetic man.'

'Twitter followers were pretty real when they marched on Washington in 2021...'

She had a point. Goodness, what if Damon had chosen to organise a revolt, an insurrection? Surely not. Surely that was too much like hard work.

'Fair enough, Inspector, yes, but he wasn't mobilising his people. He wasn't organising them, there was no structure behind him. I don't think so, anyway... he would just pontificate, throw provocative words into the air and watch how they fell. He was completely irresponsible in much of what he did, if you ask me. He abused his position. And he was a bigot.'

Ruth thought, sarcastically: 'Get off the fence, why don't you?' but Alison, sensing the anger in Paul's words, handled her response better than that.

'Well... thank you for being so honest, Mr Roe. That didn't hurt, did it? You've gone from barely remembering him to talking like you were his counsellor in just five minutes. So, do you think that he did kill himself?'

Paul had already forced himself to calm down. 'I don't know. How would I know? I guess he probably did. I really don't know anything about his personal life, or anything like that: and I have never been part of it. But I know what he's like in the House, in public, in the corridors of this place, and in the media, too: he was a disruptive element, not to be trusted. A loner. And yes, I would hazard a guess that he really wasn't very happy. And when people aren't very happy and can't see a way to handle that, then, especially if they're in the public eye…'

He did not relate that some of these insights derived from the reliable source of Basil Cheney. There was no point in getting Basil involved.

The first yellow post-it note arrived on Alison's desk. It read 'Bulls eye!'

'Thank you, Mr Roe. I think you're probably right.'

In Portcullis House, Westminster, even though the conversation had been private, Paul's humiliation felt very public. But at least his secrets were safe, and they remained hidden.

The Interview (Kate):
Thursday 12th May

Later that day, as the next video link opened it was clear that Kate Mellor was not quite ready to start a conversation. In the background behind the journalist Alison could see part of an open plan office, separated from Kate by a window which stretched the full height of the room. All she could see of the woman herself was a shoulder in a blue jumper, moving as she rummaged with something at her feet. From what can be gleaned from half a torso bobbing up and down behind a table edge Alison judged Kate to be slim and athletic, a taller version of Ruth but with longer, less garishly blonde, hair. 'Slim' and 'athletic' were both aspirations long since abandoned by the senior police officer herself. When Kate emerged after an age, possibly no more than six seconds, she was tying her hair back. It was darker than the ash blonde in the photographs that Alison had seen, and on top of the hair perched a pair of glasses with thick blue rims, as seen on none of the photos.

'Miss Mellor.'

'Hi, yes, I'm here now.' She leant down again, however, hauling an overlarge, overfull, over worn leather handbag up onto the desk where it sat, just in shot, for the duration. Kate caught her breath as Alison introduced herself. She was flying solo: Ruth was busy elsewhere and not involved.

'Sorry. Right. Ready. What can I do for you, inspector?'

Alison realised that Kate was using a stand-alone camera which sat an inch or two to the side of the screen upon which Alison herself appeared. This gave the impression that the journalist was looking at an invisible person sitting beside Alison, rather than at the Inspector herself, throughout the interview, when, in fact, she was looking directly at Alison's image on her screen. This was a slightly disconcerting arrangement and Alison wondered if Kate was experiencing the same disconnect. Probably not, or she would have done something about it.

'You're Kate, that's Kathryn, Mellor?'

'Yes.'

'I'm conducting an enquiry into the death of Damon Hough; it really shouldn't take very much of your time. The interview is being recorded but... well, you're not under caution or anything like that.'

'I should hope not!' It was a throwaway line, a tease, not an accusation.

'I take it you know who Damon Hough is, Miss Mellor? Or was?'

'I do, yes. Please, call me Kate.'

'...and his apparent suicide last weekend.'

'Apparent? Is there some doubt?'

'Well, it looks like suicide, we're just tying up some loose ends. Trying to understand a bit more about the circumstances.'

'I see. It's very sad, what a horrible way to go.' In the pause that followed it was Kate, not Alison, who wrote something down.

This added to Kate's air of distraction, which was accentuated further as her gaze flitted regularly into and out of the line of the off-centre camera. She was busy but the professional woman was more than capable of multitasking. She was handsome and not obviously made-up; tidy but not quite elegant; she was present, after a fashion, but not, so far, involved in the discussion. She had not yet smiled. She was a journalist, so Alison had to be wary of the interview being turned round - she did not want to allow Kate to interview her about the case.

'Indeed. Can you tell me a bit about your job?'

'My job?' This got her attention.

'Please.'

There was a 'ping' and Kate reached for her mobile phone out of habit, then realised her *faux pas*.

'Oh, I'm sorry. Look, I'll just switch this onto silent... there.' She placed the phone into the mammoth handbag.

'You were saying,' Alison prompted.

'Yes... I'm a journalist, I work in a newsroom -' she indicated the area beyond the window '- on a Sunday paper, where I write a regular, weekly, column and the occasional feature. Sometimes I do a bit of subediting. Why do you need to know that?'

'So you don't do news reporting?'

'I used to. Before I came here. I've been in journalism nearly twenty years, I've had different roles from time to time.'

'Did you know Damon Hough?'

A microscopic pause. 'Not in a professional capacity.'

Kate had been practising how to answer that inevitable question. It was too early to disclose news of her scoop, though Damon's death had given the story potential topicality. Indeed, it had caused her deadline to be brought forward to the upcoming weekend; the Damon Dossier remained incomplete, and her master plan dictated that it should not be exposed any earlier than currently scheduled. Even to the police. The story of Guy Campbell's hidden money, and the Entropy exposé, would remain outwith the remit of today's conversation as far as Kate was concerned.

'In what capacity, then? Were you friends?'

'We were at University together.'

'Ah. Yes, you're the same age, aren't you?'

'Same year. Different courses.'

'Almost exactly the same age.'

Kate's brow wrinkled as she recalled, then immediately unfurrowed. 'A couple of weeks apart, I think.'

'Is anyone on your paper writing anything about him this weekend?'

This was the question for which Kate had practiced her reply. She smiled: 'I'm not the editor, Inspector.'

'No one's asked you for your reminiscence of him?'

'No. Why would they? I don't suppose anyone knows that I knew him. It was a very long time ago.'

Kate bit her tongue. She had been about to say 'I have nothing to say about him' but that would have extended her prevarication to the edge of falsehood, which was not a good place to be.

'I see.' Alison considered where to go next. What would the editor say, a week hence, when she found out that one of her reporters had a key historic angle on a dead celebrity? 'What was he like, back when you knew him?'

There was no flicker of emotion on Kate's face. She turned her head away by twenty degrees and thought for two seconds.

'He could be charming - and he could be a boor.'

'I'm sorry, the English language can be ambiguous, as you will know better than most, Miss Mellor. Do you mean he could be boring or… bad mannered?'

'Damon has never been boring.'

'So, bad mannered?'

Again, no flicker on Kate's face. 'He achieved that reputation.'

'How well did you know him?'

'I haven't spoken to him for years. Literally. Not since University.'

'How well did you know him back then? I'm trying to get a deeper insight into his character. Did you spend much time together?'

'When you say 'together' do you mean -'

'Whatever you want it to mean. Another quirk of the English language.'

Again, Kate thought. It was pointless denying that they had spent time together. From what she knew of his subsequent life their relationship was not a typical one for Damon.

'We were close… for a short time. A few months.'

One and a half wasted bloody years, Kate thought.

Alison tested Charles Mallory's story: 'Were you an 'item', then?'

'I suppose so… Sort of. I don't think that commitment was a big word in Damon's dictionary. I wouldn't be surprised if he'd never had a long-term partner, you know?'

There was a lump in her throat that really did not ought to have been there. It was that word 'commitment' that had caused it to arise. At best theirs had been a part time relationship, at worst a meaningless one. One and a half wasted bloody years, in fact.

'We… don't think he was in a relationship when he died. We've seen nothing to suggest that he'd ever had a 'significant other', if that's a term we can use, as you say, though we've not delved very deep, as yet. You, Kate, might therefore have insights that others could not have, and I'm sure that hearing about them would be very helpful to us.'

Kate smiled and Alison felt slightly patronised. 'It really was eons ago, Inspector. Ancient history. A lot of water has flowed under the bridge since then.'

Here's a (presumably) well paid journalist using one of the dullest, most common clichés in the language, thought Alison. What is the media coming to?

'Maybe you can help me out, then, Kate; to the best of your knowledge has he ever had a 'significant other' at any time? A partner?'

'Not that I'm aware of, no. But I really wouldn't know.'

'So, you didn't stay in touch after University? For a short while, you know, people say they will, they meet up once or twice, but it doesn't quite work out. Maybe the odd Christmas card, a reunion after twenty years…'

'Nothing like that. No Christmas cards, no reunion. Whatever we had was well over by the time we left University - and, of course, social media, Facebook and all that, wasn't anything like as freely available as it is now.'

'When you say 'Whatever we had', you mean…?'

'Our… friendship.'

Alison guessed that ambiguities around Damon's sexuality had played a role in their breakup and his behaviour, but she was wary of raising the issue. It was usually as well, in her experience, not to tell a journalist something important that they might not have known already; she could not assume that the whole world knew Parliament's worst kept secret. Nevertheless, she was interested in Kate's thoughts on the matter, and would return to the theme if she could weave it in.

'You've said he could be charming but he was also a boor. You're saying that he was a Jekyll and Hyde character?'

If you can use clichés then so can I, thought the police officer.

'He was always - almost always - charming, with me. Deferential, polite. Attentive. He could be very quiet, you'll be surprised to hear. Occasionally, very quiet indeed. I'm sure there were other qualities that got hidden by his public persona in later life. To be honest, I sometimes wondered whether the Damon you see in the media, in politics, was all an act.'

'Why would he put on an act for you?'

'No, not for me. All this pantomime villain stuff. Yes, he loves the sound of his own voice - he did back then, too. He's obviously been trying to push the envelope on Parliamentary behaviour, and getting away with murder… I didn't mean! Not real murder.'

'Of course not.' That was the trouble with clichés. Kate went on:

'He always had a manipulative side to him. He just seems to have turned that from a strategy into an art form, performance art, if you like. In public.'

'But you didn't see that, back then, at least in private. You saw his sensitive side.'

'Yes, I suppose so.'

'You were close; he behaved with you in ways that… he didn't with anyone else?'

'I guess.'

'How close?'

Kate thought again. Talk of Damon as a twenty-year-old was safer than talking of him in the present day, given the dynamite that she had been stacking underneath him just before he - unfortunately for himself, herself and her editor - had died.

She smiled, at last. 'Look, this is a crazy thing for me, of all people, to say; but I don't want any of this to get into the press. You know what I'm saying?' Having an alternative Damon story run in another medium a day or two before her scoop would not be good news.

Now it was Alison's turn to chuckle. 'It won't come from me. Or my office. There's absolutely no reason why it should.'

'Thank you. We were... close, to use your word, for over a year. Yes, we were lovers. He wasn't... he wasn't enthusiastic about, you know, the 'physical aspect'. He was happiest when we went for a walk in the countryside...'

'But you did have sex?'

'Jesus, Inspector!' Kate averted her gaze from the camera and gave an embarrassed smile as she briefly exhaled; ironically, appearing to look directly at Alison as she did. She resumed immediately: 'Yes, we did! But it was twenty years ago, and that's what students did back then! I guess they still do. Look, I haven't clapped eyes on him since we left University. We shagged maybe six, maybe eight times, over - I don't know - a year? About a year.'

'Do you think it's possible... I'm just surmising, here – that you're the only woman who could say that? Not necessarily that you had sex with Damon, but that you had an ongoing sexual relationship with him?'

'Twenty years ago!'

'Nevertheless...'

Kate thought hard, scratched behind her right ear. Unwittingly she left a strand of hair sticking up into the air, a hint of unkemptness.

'I think that's possible, yes, quite conceivable. At University, at least, I'm pretty certain that was the case. I would have been the only one, yes.'

Alison said nothing, but watched her prey kindly.

'And yes, in answer to your next question, I think he was probably gay back then. In fact, I know he was. He said so, when we...'

'Broke up?'

'Broke up.'

Out in the open, on the record. Corroboration of Mallory's story. Alison wrote 'Gay' on the pad in front of her; not that it was necessary, but it created a gap into which Kate might pour more information.

Kate was looking down, making virtual eye contact even more difficult than before. Alison was surprised to see that the reporter had had a tear in her eye. She wiped it away with a finger: now it had never existed.

'You know something, Inspector, he used me. I don't mean that he exploited me, I'm certainly not saying that he treated me unfairly or badly. I said 'used', but I wouldn't call it 'abused'. As I say, he could be a gentleman. The nights we spent together when we didn't... have sex - we never lived together, he probably stayed at mine, once or twice a week - I think he enjoyed the nights we spent together when we didn't have sex, when we just cuddled under the duvet, more than those when we did... 'make love'. He used me to work out an important part of his identity. His sexuality. I was his experiment, I guess. And, you know what? That's absolutely fine. We all do it. Don't we?'

Alison supposed we did. She remembered her career as a WPC before she became a detective. She'd scored more coppers in her first ten years in the force than she'd had hot dinners... another cliché jackpot! When she became a detective, she moved to a new part of the country and started afresh. In the next nick they called her the Mother Superior, such was the reputation she gained for being straight-laced, untouchable. And then Eric had come along. Bloody Eric. She'd gone from polyamorous to abstinent to monogamous. A sort of monogamous, at least. Monogamous in principle.

Kate said, largely to herself, 'I just wish he'd found himself a bit quicker'.

'So... he talked about being gay to you? I don't think it's something he's ever spoken about on the public record.'

Kate thought about her response carefully. 'He couldn't admit it in public, certainly not whilst his father was alive. It was when his father died that he felt able to tell me... and to justify ending our... friendship. He'd just got so used to hiding his sexuality that he never came to terms with it, either when he couldn't reveal it or later, when he could. I mean could, in theory. After his father died.'

Alison let the words sink in. Kate was describing a conflicted psychology that had lasted a lifetime, of a type that had, she had no doubt, prompted many suicides over the years.

The journalist was talking again, the epitome of calm, her tones relaxed and thoughtful.

'I've sometimes wondered if Damon was slightly… on the spectrum? The autistic spectrum? He really didn't judge emotional messaging very well and I think that might explain his solitary existence, his lack of deep relationships. I've been reading about him, as you can gather. General interest, I'm a journalist, after all… but, I admit, there was a touch of nostalgia, too. I'm assuming that he had a lack of, you know, emotional intelligence. Either that or maybe his parents, especially his father, made his life hell. It makes you wonder… Let me give you an example.'

'Please.' More quietly, Alison added: 'This is fascinating.'

'It was Christmas of our second year at university. You're right about our ages, we're almost twins, we had our birthdays just after the Easter break, very close to each other. Actually, it was his birthday last week, mine next week… Do you know what he bought for me, for Christmas that year? A bloody book token…' her 'bloody' was spoken wistfully, without anger. 'A book token. Five pounds. Nothing says romance like a cheap book token, don't you agree, Inspector?'

'Alison'. The Inspector felt the need to identify with the woman before her.

'Yes, Inspector Allyson, I know.'

'No, I'm… Alison. Alison Allyson. With an 'i' and then with a 'y'.'

'Really? Wow…' Kate smiled, then adopted her serious face once more. 'So… he gave me a bloody book token, when I'd given him some lovely silver cufflinks.'

'Cufflinks?'

'Yes… Christmas 2001, it must have been.'

'Can you describe them?'

'Gosh, well, if you think it'll help…! They were silver… clover leaf design - they might have been four-leaf clovers. For good luck.'

'Kate, you're not in a hurry, are you?' Alison was thinking twenty to the dozen.

'Me? Not particularly. My work is flexible' (though I'm not telling you what I'm working on, she failed to add) 'and I'll have to go home to a hungry daughter before too long…'

'Can you wait here just a minute?'

'Of course.'

'I'll be back very soon.'

Alison pressed a button and a 'pause' symbol appeared on the screen as the video picture froze. Kate had forgotten they were being recorded but the icon now reminded her. So far, so good, she thought, she had succeeded in keeping the Inspector's attention away from Damon's finances. She would talk about anything, even what passed for the intimate secrets of her youth, to avoid mentioning the Campbell connection.

Kate was feeling a sense of relief... it had never occurred to her that talking to a police officer would feel so liberating. It was as though two decades of pent-up anxiety were being permitted to break into the open air at last. Where had that feeling come from? That her relationship with Damon had not 'worked', whatever that meant, was palpably true, but she had never rationalised her experience with Damon in quite this way before.

But if the experience had helped him discover his true self then maybe the pain she experienced at the time was worthwhile, in the great scheme of things. Perhaps it had even helped her, too, to become the complete person she felt that she was today... Kate had never wondered what the word 'fulfilled' meant. However, if the concept included a good job, regular intellectual stimulation and being loved by the two people she adored the most, Mark and Sophie, in their comfortable home, then the Kate of 2022 was exactly that: fulfilled. And whatever had happened to Kate, vintage 2002, Kate at the dawn of adulthood, it must have contributed to that outcome in some way.

She took a deep breath, exhaling slowly. This was more interesting than she had expected. It was almost therapy.

Her relationship with Damon had always been destined to end, of course, and even back then she thought she had let it go on too long. If only it had not ended in that thoroughly humiliating way...

The screen was suddenly live again. A second police officer, a young woman, half the size of the inspector, was sitting at Alison's side. She had short, straight blonde hair and a hint of a cheeky disposition.

'Kate, this is DC Ruth Gaunt.'

'Hi!' Ruth waved a waggly fingered wave and smiled. This was not how police interviews were supposed to be conducted! thought Kate. There was something disarmingly innocent about the younger woman. She smiled back: 'Hi'.

'I've asked Ruth to show you something, then she's going to tell you something that I want your word you won't pass on. And I say that, knowing that you're a journalist.'

This was quite a call, but she would take the risk that whether the outcome was useful to the police or not, it would not be pertinent to her own secret - still secret - story. 'OK.'

'I'd like you to take a look at this, please, Kate. Ruth?'

Ruth leaned forward and held her clenched left fist up to the camera, in a non-aggressive style. She opened her palm to reveal its contents.

Kate gasped and put her hand to her mouth. She did not believe what she was seeing! Nevertheless, it took no more than a moment to confirm the identification.

'That's them! That's the pair I bought for his birthday, twenty years ago!'

The delicate four-leaf clover motif was clear.

'Interesting…' said Alison, though she had not intended to say it aloud. 'I've news for you, Kate - you said they were silver, but they're not.'

'No?'

'EPNS, silver plated. You can see where the surface has worn away.' She pointed to the pivoted bar designed to hold the decoration in place, perched still on Ruth's palm. 'Silver doesn't do that. He obviously had good use out of them, he must have worn them a lot.'

'Well, that explains the price. To be honest, they weren't that expensive and that's a consideration when you're a student.'

Ruth lowered her hand.

'Even so, they cost more than a five-pound book token! Skinflint.' Kate smiled briefly, then reminded the Inspector 'Was that the secret you were going to tell me?'

Alison had one last consideration of whether Ruth's suggestion of how to handle the cufflinks was wise. But Kate had earned it.

'Ruth…'

'Right. When Inspector Allyson and I attended the scene, we found Mr Hough's body where we would have expected to find it, if he'd jumped or fallen from the bridge. I was tasked to examine the location at the top of the aforementioned bridge, which was very high, about 20 metres above us.'

Kate winced. That was quite a fall.

'To get up to the top of the bridge I had to walk quite some way, go to the far end of the viaduct and scramble up a bank, and from there walk back along its full length. When I reached the spot from where he must have fallen, I found one of the cufflinks.'

Alison added: 'He was still wearing the other.'

Kate realised the implications of what she was being told. 'Does that mean… are you saying there was a fight? A struggle?'

The officers had agreed not to mention the shoes.

Alison continued 'Perhaps he wanted us to think there'd been a struggle.'

'Goodness…' Kate did not know what to think. He might be a pain but surely no-one would want Damon dead, not even Guy Campbell. Certainly not Campbell and Lee Hardman - a living Damon was a better bet than a dead one in terms of getting their money back. According to Lee, the financier did not know that the MP was at risk of defaulting on the repayment of the loan; was he even aware that Damon was one of Lee's 'flock'? No, it was impossible. Campbell was not due out of jail until… goodness. Tomorrow morning. Time flies.

'We've reached no final conclusions,' said Alison. 'There is one more thing…'

'And I have one more thing for you. I wasn't going to mention it because I find it slightly embarrassing, frankly. But it fits with your story.'

'Go on. Please.'

'When we broke up, Damon and me, it was just after his father had died. I never met his parents, not in the flesh. Video technology wasn't around in 2002, not for students, anyway. Damon invited me to go for the weekend - to stay with him and his parents, in Dorset - but I had a diary clash and really felt I couldn't go. So, he set up a telephone call, for me to meet his parents. He wanted to give them the impression that we were… more of a couple than we really were. I think he wanted them - certainly his father - to be… reassured about him? Reassured that we were heterosexual, no, no, that *he* was heterosexual. Anyway, that's by the by. We broke up - or rather, he broke up with me a few months later, within days of his father dying.'

Kate wondered why she was saying all this: it was more difficult than she had thought it was going to be. She could feel tears welling up, but she was still in control. And would remain so. She went on:

'It was May, birthday time, a few months after I'd given him those cufflinks. 2002. It really seemed as though his father's death had released him from a spell! He didn't have to pretend to be straight anymore. I don't think he had a good relationship with his father on any level, so the man's passing was really a release for Damon, as I said earlier. That's when he told me he was gay, and that our relationship, such as it was, was over. After that, I don't think I ever saw him with anyone, man or woman. Not a partner man, if you get my drift. And I certainly never saw him with another woman. He was always in men's company, though, and by the end of the third year you could see that he'd, what shall I say? He'd cultivated, literally, cultivated! He'd acquired an almost cultish following from right wing students, an exclusively male cohort... a bit like the group he gathered around him in Parliament, years later, it seems to me.'

There was a natural pause. Kate was breathing deeply, looking drawn. Ruth had not heard the earlier exchange and was quite taken aback by the woman's emotion.

'Thank you,' said Alison, 'telling us all this can't be easy. I'm guessing you've not told that story before.'

'I... knew I'd have to confront it some time, but I've always found it rather uncomfortable. Easy to postpone. I guess you shouldn't hide these feelings for ever.'

'No... I've got just two more questions. When I searched his body, I found some business cards in the breast pocket of his jacket: one of them was yours.'

'Mine? Really?' Kate was genuinely incredulous.

'Do you know how it got there?'

'I have absolutely no idea!' The astonishment seemed sincere.

Kate felt the floor give way underneath her. How Damon got the card was not the question, the issue was *why* did he have it? And why was it in his breast pocket? Why did he wear those cufflinks, those 'good luck' cufflinks, her cufflinks, on the day that he was intending to kill himself? Why did he then - maybe - use the cufflinks to leave a false trail which led from the top of the bridge to the rocks below? Did he go to his death with her name deliberately close to his heart?

Her mouth fell open. The officers waited patiently for the emotional surge to pass. It took a few moments as Kate fought back a torrent of emotions and questions.

The bastard. How long had he planned this? Did he know about her investigation? Had he known - yes, he must have known, he did know - that Guy Campbell wanted his money back and that Lee Hardman was hot on his trail. If he had not already known that by the morning of Thursday, the fifth, then Lee would have left him in no doubt when they met on that day. But he can't have known of my involvement in that, could he? Lee would not have told him. Lee definitely would not have told him about her and the story, and Lee did not know about her past acquaintance with Damon, she had made sure of that. Surely, Lee keeping Damon in the dark about his dalliance with the press was an absolutely essential element of the plan? If Damon had known about their investigation, then not only would the story have never worked but it would have jeopardised Lee's recovery of the money, too...

Was this then a final, planned set-up, designed by Damon to upset and humiliate her? Was it vengeance for what had happened 20 years ago, when he may have thought that she, in league with his father, had been standing between him and his true identity? Or had he known what she was up to now, and was thumbing his nose at her investigation from beyond the grave?

Her memories of those last few minutes with Damon, in the park, came flooding back.

She had never hated anyone as much as she did at that moment when he accused her of killing her mother.

Her strained fists were now pressing down on the desk.

Kate's eyes were closed, her teeth gritted, her breathing tense and deep.

The breathing helped, as she took back control.

After a few moments more she realised that Alison was talking.

'And a few days before he died, he tried to call you. What was that about?'

'What? No... oh, no!' Still reeling from the earlier revelation Kate found herself again on the verge of not being able to cope. With a massive effort she pulled herself together: 'That's not true! It can't be true! I would have known. I never spoke to him, believe me!'

'He rang your mobile. No, you didn't answer the call, that's right. But it's in his call log: 5th May, two days before he died. In the evening.'

Ruth interpreted the expression on Kate's face as sheer horror; she'd watched enough films of the genre to recognise terror when she saw it.

Under normal circumstances such a response would have been inexplicable but, to be fair, they had clearly put this innocent woman through quite an emotional roller coaster over the last few minutes.

Kate was suddenly convinced that Damon had known about her story, that the knowledge had contributed to his suicide. Why else would he have wanted to speak to her, only hours after his scheduled meeting with Lee? But how could he have known? Again, she was convinced that Lee would not have given the game away. She tried to catch her breath, compose herself. How much of her emotional turmoil was she exhibiting? She glanced at her small portrait in the corner of the screen. Hand over her mouth, she might just have got away with hiding the depth of the confusion she now felt.

'Would you mind checking your call log? On your phone?'

Kate had nothing to hide - or had she? Yes, she had. All those brief calls and texts to and from an unidentified number, concentrated over recent days, to and from the anonymous Lee and his burner phone, both leading up to and since Damon's death. They would stand out like a sore... of course, they would not accuse her of a conspiracy, but... what if there really was a call there from Damon, one that she had genuinely missed? What did he want? Oh, God, he must have known what she was doing, he must!

This looked bad. She thought of buying time by saying that she had left her phone at home, then realised that Alison had seen the device at the start of the interview - when it had pinged, and she had switched it to 'silent'. Slowly, reluctantly, she pulled the handbag towards her and started to rummage. She found the phone immediately but continued her search for a few seconds more in order to buy time to think. She had nothing illegal to hide, after all... but the story of Damon and the money would add a new dimension to the police case, and she really did not want that to happen.

It was Ruth who rescued her. The younger woman realised that the dead man's phone record had identified the number he had fruitlessly rung two days before he died as Kate's, and the name tallied with the business card. The number would not have been displayed on the phone if the phone thought that it could match it with the name, only the name would show. But the police had not cross-checked the number in the phone against the one on the card - or against Kate's own call log (which they could have accessed, had they really needed to do so). It was an oversight. Ruth consulted her notes, and after flicking over several pages, found what she was seeking. She looked down at the business card on the table and realised their error. She whispered to Alison 'Can I speak?'

'Go ahead.'

'Kate, does your number begin 07931…?'

'No. No, it's, er…'

'It doesn't matter. I'm sorry, we appear to have crossed wires here -'

'But that did used to be my number, 07931. Back when I was at University. Then six, double five, something. It was a very long time ago. I had a Nokia. A state-of-the-art Nokia.'

07931 was the number Damon had called. It was no wonder that Kate did not know that he had tried to reach her. He had dialled a number that was out-of-date by twenty years.

Ruth was busy dialling on her own phone. She held up the screen for Alison to see as the device peeped at her. 'There you go! Number not available.'

'So that's why he didn't get through to you, Kate,' intoned Alison, 'and also why he couldn't leave a message.'

A profound if brief wave of relief permeated the journalist's body. It immediately curdled: I still don't know why he was trying to call me! Did he know about her story? Or did he want to talk about his imminent suicide? Which was worse?

That was a thought she really did not want to consider.

Alison looked at the journalist, who was staring into the middle distance, although still not in exactly the direction of the camera. Her emotional response to the interrogation - the conversation - clearly ran deeper than Kate had expected, and Alison was not minded to push her any further.

'Thank you, Kate,' she said. 'I'm sorry if this conversation has upset you. We'll leave it there for now. Thank you.'

For a full half minute after Alison broke the video connection Kate remained frozen to her seat, her breathing shallow. She knew she was innocent, and they now knew that she had not lied about not receiving Damon's call. Why had bloody Damon tried to call her in the first place, and why now, after all these years? She realised that if the conversation with the police had lasted another five minutes, at that pace, she might well have cracked - and told them all about MEKANICK, Entropy, Lee and Campbell.

But she hadn't. Her story was safe.

She needed to pull herself out of this trance: she took a very deep breath and blinked twice. She held her face in her hands, little fingers touching her lips, the others splayed up to both her cheek bones, her thumbs on her neck where she could sense a strong and urgent pulse. She held the pose for perhaps eight seconds, then forced herself to snap out of the becalmed torpor.

Then she headed for the still vacant desk which belonged to her office neighbour, Greg. Where was his bloody brandy when she really needed it?

…

Alison and Ruth were aware that they had come close to making a major error. If Damon had used Kate's current number, she would have had some explaining to do. But he did have it! Kate's current mobile number was on the business card.

'Think it through, Ruth. Why go to the trouble of dialling a number - bringing up the keypad on your screen, pressing ten digits and then the 'call' button, when you believe that the number is already in your phone's memory? Saying 'Hey Thingy, call Kate Mellor' was all that he needed to do. All we know is that Damon had wanted to ring Kate and I'm pretty certain that she doesn't know why.'

'From the way she reacted, yes. She was really shaken.'

'If I'd found out that someone from my past had tried to call me out of the blue, 48 hours before killing themselves, I'd be shaken, too. Anyway. I don't think we'll get any more from Kate Mellor.'

'So why did he have her card in the first place?' asked Ruth.

'He might have been upset about something. It was late when he made that call, he might have been the worse for wear. It wouldn't have occurred to him that there were two different numbers: people keep the same number for life these days, don't they? It was less so back then, you're more likely to change your bank account than your phone number these days, but not then. You're too young to remember, Ruth.'

The DC smiled indulgently.

Alison continued 'As for how, why, when he got hold of her card, it's the same answer as for Paul Roe, I'll bet. Journalists must give them out ten a penny, she probably didn't know he had it. He could have picked it up years ago.'

'So… it's unlikely he got it directly from her.'

'Indeed.' They exchanged weary smiles.

The Inspector continued her analysis: 'I think Damon was in an emotional state last Thursday night, two days before things got so bad for him that he killed himself. He needed reassurance, wanted to hear a friendly, familiar voice. The present was letting him down, so he tried to summon his past, calling a number he'd last used twenty years ago, in the hope of finding some sympathy from someone who once meant something to him.'

Ruth nodded. 'I reckon so.' Then: 'Shall we call it a day, Boss?'

After a moment of consideration, Alison replied 'Let's do that.'

Ruth put the cufflinks back into their evidence bag. They collected their papers, removed any evidence that they had ever been in the video conference room and left. As they walked down the corridor and towards their office each discovered that the other was planning to eat supper in the canteen. After pausing briefly in the office to close the operation down for the day they headed there, together.

As they entered the dining area Alison's own mobile phone rang.

'Inspector Allyson. Hello?'

'Inspector Allyson?'

'Yes, speaking.'

'It's Jen Graham here.'

'Sorry? Who?'

'Jen… Sister Graham. From the hospital.'

'Ah, yes, of course. Hi. Sorry, I was miles away. I wasn't expecting to speak to you until next week, I guess. What can I do for you?'

'I'm sorry to have to -'

'Not a problem.'

'Well, it is, actually. It's about your husband…'

…

Alison placed the phone in her pocket and promptly disappeared, almost as quickly, mused Ruth, as a pantomime fairy… though she was somewhat overweight by pantomime fairy standards. The Inspector glanced across at Ruth just once, her face drained white, and said 'I've got to go.'

Ruth had thus dined alone before heading straight home.

Following the text message she had received on the Sunday, another had arrived on Monday - 'I meant it!', accompanied by a black smiley face emoji. Later, she had sent a three-word acknowledgement, texting

'Yeah me too'. Then there was yet another on Wednesday: 'Can we talk some time? Would be nice'. This was healthy, she thought, his behaviour was serious whilst remaining well short of obsessive. Now, 24 hours later, there had been no further reply. Was the whole thing a false alarm? There was only one way to find out.

She made a cup of cocoa, curled up in front of the television, turned the volume low and looked again at her phone. 'Why not?' she thought, and dialled Darren's number. They spoke for an hour, as she was surprised to discover, after saying goodbye. Time flew. When she finally cut off the call, she realised that she had talked mostly about the Hough case. She trusted her new friend to be discreet, hoping that he had not been disappointed with her work-focused repartee.

He was a copper, too, he would understand.

And there could always be a next time.

Lee Plans his Escape:

Friday 13th May

Lee Hardman had spent most of the past 48 hours hesitating, close to his laptop and phone. No message arrived from his former employer, no word that Guy Campbell had now been released from the open prison, no advice from Jacob Singh, no reassurance that things were going according to plan. It was just possible, Lee reasoned, that he might not be the first person on the money man's 'to do' list; finding himself in that prominent position might have portended trouble. He could live with that small dent to his ego. Thus, he rationalised, 'no news' must be good news, there being no suggestion that anything had gone wrong on the Campbell front.

Today, Friday, was Guy's, and therefore Lee's, first day of freedom. Being no longer tied by a contract to MEKANICK Lee felt a growing sense of uneasy release, even if it marked the end of the most highly lucrative passage of his career.

And it felt good. Each added hour brought no more news and a fraction less tension.

As agreed, Lee's sign-off report had been on Guy's desk - to be accurate, in Jacob Singh's inbox - on the twelfth, yesterday. Singh had confirmed receipt, as requested. Last night Lee had placed his work phone in a padded envelope and dropped it through the MEKANICK letterbox, with a note to the receptionist. Almost £30 million, the money that Lee had been overseeing, was back in accounts that were accessible to Guy, including almost two million in bonus. There would have been even more if one element of the capital had not gone missing. The whole of the lost £750,000, the money that had been lent to the incompetent Damon Hough, was delicately handled in the anonymised report and barely stood out at all. Together, all the other loans, those which had found more amenable, dependable foster homes, had more than covered the loss. And why should they not have been amenable? They had been promised five years of interest free loan and received nearly twelve! These partners were not just amenable, they were grateful, happy - and rich.

All except one. And he was dead.

The prospect of presenting Campbell with less money than he started with posed all sorts of problems; right up to the last minute Lee believed that he would have to confront Steel urgently to get the money back, in order to reach his target. The well-deserved dressing down that Lee would have received from Guy, had he failed, would have included meeting the shortfall from his own pocket - as stipulated in the contract. How much did Steel know about the money in his company's client account? Probably not much, hopefully nothing. How keen would Steel be to return the cash? Would he make a fuss? It was impossible to tell, he had never met the man. As it was in a client account it should have been obvious to him that it did not properly belong to his law firm.

By a stroke of fate on the Tuesday morning, three days earlier, a massive transfer had arrived from a grateful confederate in Spain. At over four million pounds-worth of Euros it was considerably more than Lee had expected. Boosted by a favourable exchange rate the overall target had been achieved without him needing to turn the screw on the bereaved elderly solicitor. Lee could relax, write off the Hough episode and deliver the desired outcome too. Guy would not be expecting detail; the high levels of secrecy were there to protect him as much as anyone else. It would be better to approach Steel once the dust had settled, after Kate Mellor's story had run its course. Maybe Lee could keep some of the money for himself, perhaps all that he could recover, if Guy really did not realise that any was missing... In any event, Guy would not be suffering with his return on investment. Even if Lee had to write off the whole three quarters of a million, that would be a small price to pay. If Guy ever found out what had happened, then, by rights, he should be impressed that only one of the many ventures in Lee's portfolio had failed, but it was best not to test that theorem.

Guy's over-riding priority at this point would be to take MEKANICK out of semi-suspended animation and resume his work on both its legitimate and discreetly semi-legitimate elements. He would carry on where he had left off, twelve years previously. Lee suspected that a change of name for the company would be on the cards - there was no point reminding everyone of MEKANICK's past at every turn, was there?

After their meeting in Parliament on the fifth, Lee had expected Damon to deposit £500,000 promptly, in line with the MP's own assessment of what was possible. That would have reduced the deficit to only £250,000, which would have been even easier to manage. Lee had given the MP a five-day window before the Isle of Man account ceased to exist and that should have been plenty, assuming the man was as good as his word.

But he was not, having died before returning any of the cash.

The proverbial was due to hit the fan with the publication of Kate Mellor's story, but it should land well and truly in Damon's late lap, not Lee's, he reasoned. The piece was due to go live on Sunday, the fifteenth, though its impact would be much reduced now that its subject was no more. With Damon gone there was a risk that the media spotlight would fall closer to Guy, but that was manageable, and the financier's people would have anticipated it. Although anyone with a past fraud conviction could expect some media attention once back in circulation, it would be as nothing compared to that which a dodgy MP in the present tense would have got. Singh's people did not yet know about Kate's story, but Lee was confident that they could handle it and that his own hands would appear clean.

Publication was now less than 48 hours away, but Lee did not know how Kate's editor was going to respond to the new circumstances. This was yet another reason why Lee had decided to put distance between himself and Campbell - immediately.

Lee had done well for himself over the past twelve years. Setting aside these few minor travails he felt at ease with the world. He was relieved that he had evaded the clutches of Parliament, that his bank account and investment portfolios were overflowing and that several lifetime ambitions had been fulfilled. He had sold his London flat, liquidising some silly money, and for the past few weeks had been living in a hotel near the Tower of London. Three years earlier he had purchased a cottage in a remote part of Kerry. All those possessions that had previously been in his flat were already in storage, or in Ireland, or had otherwise been disposed of. None of his associates knew where he was going; his parents knew that a 'holiday home' existed but not precisely where. The cottage had been ridiculously cheap but had undergone a major makeover; its fibre Wi-Fi was state of the art. Lee's contacts file was bulging with possible names for remote but legitimate consultancy, but they could wait until after a long break communing with the majestic Atlantic coast. A handful of opportunities was already lined up, but Lee was in no hurry to relaunch his career. Life was going to be lonely, but Lee was used to lonely. He liked it.

Remote... the word had a magical ring to it.

He had a new phone, a new number and a new life ahead of him.

He relaxed and smiled, for the first time in weeks, as he left the hotel that morning, a solitary suitcase in hand, and headed to the waiting Uber that would now carry him directly to Luton airport.

Suddenly there was an obstacle between himself and the car. The obstacle, the same height as himself, was significantly heavier than he - no doubt the body of a rugby player - and it was not going anywhere. The well-tanned man with a small amount of dark black hair held up what could only be a warrant card close to Lee's face. Thinking fast, he paused to effect reading it: Detective Constable Darren Ogenga, City of London Police. These were the people who had done for Guy Campbell, twelve years earlier. Lee's brain told his body not to panic but he could sense that his hormones were telling it otherwise.

'Will you excuse, me, please, I have a...' Plane to catch? That might ring alarm bells. 'An appointment.'

'Mr Hardman. Lee. It is Mr Hardman, isn't it?'

'You are well informed, constable.' It was a bit worrying that he'd been identified but expressing concern in that direction could only result in him talking himself into a hole.

'It's my job to be well informed, sir. It's nothing serious, I'm sure, but...'

'In that case, perhaps you could stand aside and let -'

'Your appointment, sir? Yes, of course. In just a moment.'

Darren had never actually considered what might happen if his stab in the dark, his return to the Leonardo Royal Hotel on the off chance that he might see Hardman, came off. He had no authority to be there, was on no formal mission, and yet had 'come up trumps', within literally two minutes of arrival. Here he was, talking to Lee Hardman, the missing man from Ruth's investigation! How impressed would she be if he could hand over her prize?

'Are you aware that East Midlands constabulary are hoping to have a chat with you, sir?'

Lee thought quickly: no, he was not aware, but nor was he surprised. What was unclear was why: because his name was in in Damon Hough's diary or because his money was in Damon Hough's account? He prayed to God it was only the former. If it was the latter then his conversation with the constable, on behalf of the City authorities, risked becoming prolonged.

He adopted an innocent expression. 'Are they? In connection with…?'

Darren paused. It was perfectly feasible that the man's ignorance was genuine, legitimate. Or had Hardman already put two and two together? Had he expected to be apprehended?

'A suicide case, I believe -'

'Oh, of course! That would be poor Mr Hough! Do you know, I only spoke to him last week, for the first time in, oh, years and years - and only for five minutes. How terribly sad, oh, that is upsetting. But you are not from - East Midlands, did you say?'

'No sir.'

'And the City of London police are waiting for me outside my hotel because…?'

'Because we're on the spot, sir, in a spirit of co-operation with our Derbyshire colleagues.'

'Of course.' Lee sensed that after his first moment of surprise he was now gaining the upper hand.

For his own part, Darren was suddenly feeling uncertain. He was not supposed to be there, not authorised to approach Hardman and certainly not in a position to disclose that he knew that Hardman was staying at the hotel; still less that Lee was due to check out today. To disclose that information would alert and possibly alarm the man more than necessary - and that would be as nothing to what his DCI, whose back it did not pay to go behind, might say. He would call it 'taking the law into your own hands' and he would not like it. Why was the man staying in the hotel? Why was he leaving, and why now? This serendipitous encounter had left Darren with no time to create a strategy.

Lee continued 'So, yes, I understand why they may want to see me. I guess they want to know whether the balance of Mr Hough's mind was disturbed when I saw him, which…' Lee paused as he genuinely calculated… 'was barely forty-eight hours before he must have died, according to the papers. Oh, my goodness! Do you know what, officer? Now I think about it, I'd say yes, he did have something on his mind last Thursday. He definitely had something important on his mind, but I have no idea what it was. Is that the sort of thing they want to know?'

'Erm… I guess…'

'No idea at all what it was that was bothering him. How could I possibly have known? We had a five-minute chat in the House of Commons, that was all. The Pugin Room. It was good to catch up with him, I think he was relieved to see me; I mean that my presence must have brought some respite from whatever it was that was preying on his mind, that would be my analysis.'

Darren was in danger of finding himself out of his depth.

Lee continued 'Do you think that is that the sort of thing they would want to know?'

'Yes, I would think so. I think they would be very grateful if you gave them a call.'

Gave them a call? That was interesting. Not 'come along with me to make a statement'? This was fishy. Why on earth did it require valuable police hours to brief the City constabulary, have them lie in wait, then intercept him, if all they wanted was an innocent chat? No doubt it was to 'rule out certain avenues from our enquiry'. But it all seemed a bit over the top.

'Maybe you could tell them for me. Look, I am in a bit of a hurry, so if you don't mind…'

The young DC could think of nothing more to say: he was on very dodgy ground.

'Er…'

'Look, officer, I do want to be helpful. I'll tell you what: I will go now to my appointment - I am already a little late, you do understand, my cab's waiting, and as soon as it's over I will give them a call. How's that? Is that all right? I do want to be helpful if I possibly can.'

Darren was about to thank the man and suggest he contact DC Ruth Gaunt. Suddenly he felt discretion was the better route; he was out of order, and it was best if his contribution - and Ruth's name - did not come to light. It was probably too late: someone was bound to say 'Oh, so Hardman was stopped in the street by a big, bronze Adonis built like a shit house who works for the City Constabulary and who knows all about the Hough case, I wonder who that could have been?' Adding 'who knows Ruth' to the description would only dig the hole that he was already in deeper.

'I'm sure that would be fine, sir. It was just that they hadn't been able to locate you, sir, that's all. This is a chance encounter… I was passing and I happened to recognise you.'

'My arse was it a chance encounter' was the thought that went through both minds, simultaneously and independently. In Lee's mind he was curious to know how the young man had come to recognise him, but he bit his tongue. Darren, meanwhile, was sincerely hoping that his unusual surname would hinder Hardman's future recognition of it. Both also concluded that the sooner this conversation was over, the better.

'Then that is what I shall do!' Lee confirmed, with a rare smile. 'I shall give them a call before the day is out; you have my word.'

'Thank you, sir,' said Darren - but for some reason there was little gratitude in his heart and little confidence in his mind.

'Then I shall wish you good day, officer.'

Lee and his suitcase took the five or six strides towards the impatient Uber, which immediately moved off and out of Darren's life for ever.

The young man had the distinct impression that Ruth would never hear from Hardman, which meant that she would never know how he had tried to help her. Telling her what he had done and then failing to deliver the desired outcome would look bad. Two shame-tinged thoughts passed through his mind: one, that he had been patronising towards Ruth and over-stepped the mark, probably ensuring that she never would hear from the man; and two, that in that brief conversation in the street just now he had been well and truly kippered. Two minutes later the same hotel receptionist, remembering Darren from the previous day, confirmed that Hardman had indeed checked out, as expected, leaving no forwarding address.

'An appointment,' indeed! Why was Darren not surprised? That was the last he - let alone Ruth Gaunt - would ever see of Mr Hardman. The question was: was that suspicious?

Hazel to the Rescue:

Friday 13th May

Paul's secret was safe.

He chastised himself for this recurring, self-centred thought. It had been his first reaction upon hearing, back on Monday, that Damon Hough was dead. No one would ever know about that summer afternoon on a track near the playing fields, almost 26 years earlier… apart from Henry, and he was sound, reliable. Everyone has their secrets, thought Paul. Don't they?

He had already dictated a letter to James Steel, pitching it as reasonably as possible; it would have gone in yesterday's post. He pleaded that the Greatbach family had initially misunderstood the nature of the arrangement for overseeing their mother's financial affairs and now wanted to terminate it, along with Steel's late colleague's Power of Attorney. He was proposing a clean break with no recriminations, no consequences. No reasonable person could refuse such a suggestion. It would cost the lawyers £300 each month, money they should not have been getting in the first place, though he did not accuse Steel of that. Did Steel even know about Damon's little business side-line?

Friday was when most of the week's constituency engagements got squeezed into an MP's schedule and this week the distraction of a 14-hour working day was more than usually appreciated. He had finished his morning's schedule, which had started with a 'question time' with sixth form students at the other end of the constituency, continued with a photo-call at an engineering company to launch a new product (the technology of which, he admitted, baffled him), and it had ended with a meeting with the Council's housing committee chair to plan a joint lobby of government. The afternoon would be equally busy. A shadow environment minister would arrive late in the day and Paul would be his host for a tree planting ceremony, a private briefing with local Labour leaders and then the constituency Party dinner. Henry would have briefed the front bencher's office on what would go down well with local Party members whilst all Paul had to do was host the event with a smile, introduce the guest and administer the raffle draw. These dinners were normally enjoyable (and profitable) although the 'posh clothes, three courses and a disco' format felt more anachronistic every year. Paul would only get away before ten on the pretext of escorting his visitor to the station to catch the last train.

Lunch was therefore necessarily brief. Carol had bought him a shop-made pasta salad, which he ate at his desk whilst reading a briefing on the housing issue prepared by Henry. Paul's 'inner sanctum' was separate from the busy general office, which was Carol's domain. There was a knock on his door and Carol entered.

'Sorry to bother you, Paul -'

'No problem.'

'I've had Mrs Greatbach on the phone.'

Paul felt his spirits fall.

'Her mother's died.'

'Oh…' Paul searched for a word: 'Dear. Poor her. Is she still…?'

'No, she left you a message, there's no need to call back. Died last night.'

'From the fall?'

'Yes, she never really got fully conscious. She just said: please don't pursue her case anymore. Her brother's lawyer will do the will, the inheritance, and all that. She said thank you for all your help, but she wants to call it a day.'

'Fine… I mean… there wasn't a lot more I could do…'

He recused himself from expressing the feelings of immense relief that were washing over him, even to Carol.

'I gave her your condolences.'

'Thank you. Of course, you met her at the surgery… Perhaps we can send her a card.'

'Sure, I'll arrange that. Look, you're busy, I'll let you finish your lunch. I don't envy your timetable today!'

'That's Henry's doing for you… thanks, Carol.'

It felt like the end of an era. Though the era was measured only in days, so much had happened.

Paul returned to London on the morning of Saturday, 14th, for a scheduled speaking engagement in the afternoon. As a junior shadow minister, he was to deliver a keynote speech on tackling poverty to a big Fabian event. Having arrived back at his London flat mid-morning he was perfecting his script, getting completely on top of his policy game, honing to perfection his descriptions of some interesting initiatives he had in mind. Henry had already drafted a press release, which Paul would modify in due course to reflect what he had said in his speech. He would ping it out to the usual suspects himself - probably on Sunday morning.

On the Thursday afternoon Paul had caught up with Hazel in the London office, following his unsettling police interview and before his mad dash back to the constituency for Friday's gallimaufry of appointments. After the business chat she told her boss that he looked like a man under pressure. They got coffees in Portcullis House, and he told her a bowdlerised version of the Hough story. Hazel, familiar with the Greatbach file, was sympathetic. Had he heard about Mrs Smith's passing 24 hours earlier Paul might have avoided a lot of stress; but he was glad that his discomfort had created an excuse to sit down and be sociable with Hazel. It was good office management practice, after all.

When he first knew her, Hazel had appeared happily married to a business consultant who spent far too much time in the Middle East, but they had separated five years ago. For months Hazel, and her then eight-year-old son, lived like hermits before she started to relax. One day she brought young Matthew into the office, as the boy's school was closed for a teacher training day, which both the boy and the MP appeared to enjoy.

Earlier this year, on a chilly February evening, Hazel had invited Paul to join Matthew and herself on a tourist 'Ghost Walk' around Westminster which proved a relaxing and enjoyable distraction. Afterwards Paul had returned to the House for a ten o'clock vote and Hazel took the boy home. That evening felt good: there had been someone at his side who wanted to be there, understood his politics, shared his values, humour and sense of duty; someone who smiled a lot. Hazel was 'easy on the eye', whilst being in no respect a clone of his previous partner, 'The English Rose'. Above all, she was not ashamed to be seen with an MP in public. During the ghost walk, which passed just yards from his place of work, the company of strangers in the darkness had rendered the three of them anonymous. That had definitely been part of the fun.

Hazel never volunteered unnecessary information or concerns about her marriage or the divorce; Paul had never presumed to ask.

Only once had Paul ever visited his PA's home in Chiswick, a place that Paul had hitherto only known as the start of the M4. Hazel had invited both Paul and Henry to her most recent birthday party, on a

January Friday a few weeks before the Ghost Walk. Paul had enjoyed meeting her friends, who took him at face value: they included a writer, a chef, an actor who had once appeared in 'Casualty' and several local mums. Either they were genuinely nice people, or they had been expertly briefed by Hazel, but Paul did not feel as awkward as he had feared he might. He always tried not to brag about being an MP but neither did he feel that he had to hide this key part of his identity.

It was on the occasion of the party that Henry had overheard Hazel tell a girlfriend in the kitchen that she 'wouldn't say no to shagging Paul, given half a chance', though nothing had ever happened, then or subsequently, to translate the words into action. Hazel, tongue no doubt loosened by wine, would surely have forgotten ever speaking in such terms by now. Perhaps Henry been deliberately exposed to the words, to wind him up, tease him? In the pub, that night of the advice session at which the Greatbach story had come to light, the young man had, for a third or fourth time, ragged his employer in turn by dropping his lascivious recollection into the conversation.

By now, of course, the exercise had become just a routine tease. It was not intended as anything more than that.

Nevertheless, Paul had to admit that it might be nice to spend some time with Hazel. He must not pursue her, abusing his position as her employer. 'Office romances' were notorious for negative consequences, but it was not as if they were under each other's feet. They were mature people, not fliberty-gibbets who could not cope with grown up affection. He was fond of her, certainly, and, he had to admit, he was lonely. Maybe she was, too? She had never spoken about a boyfriend - apart from Matthew, of course.

This was all speculation and imagination; 'What if?' never helped anyone. The last thing he wanted to do was damage a friendship or disrupt a successful working relationship.

That afternoon, he would remind his Fabian audience that 'Possibility without opportunity is sterile', urging them to focus on victory at all costs. The phrase seemed suddenly apposite.

He left the flat and headed for the conference, a journey of around thirty minutes by public transport. That was when his phone beeped.

The style of the text message immediately identified the author: 'P ICUR in London this w/e. dinner 2nite?'

He smiled. It would be presumptuous to respond straight away. He left it ten minutes before texting from the bus: 'Sounds good. Thank you. Where/what time?' He was tempted to end the message with 'x' but decided against it.

Immediately: 'Mine @ 7. want try new French on High Rd. Sound gd?'

It might be that no one else was involved, which was interesting. This time he responded with a smiley face emoji before checking that her home address was indeed in his contacts app. Of course it was.

Another text arrived from Hazel: 'Isnt yr bday nxt wk. We must [party emoji].'

And then, before he had time to respond: 'Matthew sleepover @ friends.'

Why did she need to tell him that? Best not to read anything into it.

Kate's Story:

Friday 13th May

Damon's death had obliged Kate to completely re-write her story, but it would still run this coming weekend. Whilst retaining the 'Probe' banner the story was now slated for page 10, which was disappointing, and the proposed flag on the front page, designed to draw attention to it, was probably going to be dropped. Then again, it was her first solo investigative piece for some years so, rationally, she ought not be too disappointed. She had suggesting rewriting the focus, onto Guy Campbell, but the paper's legal department had poured cold water on that. As he had just served 12 years, they said, they should try to avoid any idea that he was being subjected to double jeopardy, even if the second time was only trial by media. Re-focusing on evidence pertinent to a trial of a dozen years ago, in which Campbell had been found guilty and well punished, would neither serve the truth nor attract new readers. It could also go badly wrong.

Whilst it was fair to hint that Damon's money was related to Guy's money, in a story focusing on the rogue MP, there was not much to that relationship to report. Guy and Damon had neither met nor communicated directly, as far as Kate knew. Lee Hardman was the go-between, and she was pledged not to mention him. Kate's final version of the story was thus vague on where Hough had got the Entropy money from - but deadly on how he used it.

In fact, Kate realised, that was the point. Guy had said to Lee 'hide this money until I come back' and there was no proof that these particular pounds, the ones that headed for the Steel client account, were corruptly acquired. The instruction was that it should be hidden where even Guy himself could not reveal its whereabouts, so that he could not disclose it himself under potentially hostile questioning. Even Lee's connection to Damon was old, dating back to a time shortly after the trial. Lee had chosen Damon because the MP was both not averse to sailing close to the wind and could keep secrets. And that was all; it was a low bar.

What Damon was not capable of doing, however, was keeping his hands off a potential resource. He was a solicitor and an MP, not a businessman, and handling money on that scale did not come naturally. Asking someone with an ego the size of Damon's to leave the cash untouched was asking the impossible: as Lee surely ought to have recognised.

This was where the story got interesting, from an editorial point of view. It was no longer about how Damon got the money but what he did with it. Since he was dead, and there would be a by-election, the money could no longer influence the politics. Damon had severed his last connection with the Conservative Party by taking his own life, insulating his former colleagues from any fallout from any financial scandal.

Two paragraphs in the story described Damon, the man. Without revealing the nature of her insight Kate described his shy side, contrasted it with the popular image of overt, robust and camp showmanship. Dusting off old stories from Fleet Street's collective memory of unpublished gossip she hinted at a passion for right wing memorabilia and possible sadistic tendencies (still utilising the mayo and ketchup principle). She considered outing him as gay, privately wondering why he had never admitted in public what he had told her in private but judged that the story did not need that element. It was a distraction, and her paper was not a purveyor of tittle-tattle. She knew not what Charles Mallory, Basil Cheney or even Adolfo Bocca knew; Mallory had refused to talk to her and the others were not even on her 'to see' list.

She told, too, of Damon's limited ambition, a man who had gone as far as he was ever going to go in politics, having spurned any possibility of ministerial preferment. He must have resented the fact that whichever way he departed the peak of a political foothill he would have to descend. She concluded that Damon's brand of right-wing populism, the fabricated facade behind which he hid, was a cruel drug, a personal crusade that would ultimately fail and destroy its proponents. Perhaps, after all, the political lessons of Damon Hough's life were more important than the sordid finances.

Why? Because his way of operating united people around what they were against and that was no basis for building a policy, strategy or country. Trump had been against immigrants, Muslims, scientists and Democrats, but what was he for? The Brexit hordes had been united in what they were against. Their *bêtes noires* included foreigners and 'experts', but once they had won the 2016 referendum their passionate opposition to the European Union failed to create a consensus on what it was that they wanted instead, beyond shallow, undeliverable and contradictory slogans. The seeds of inevitable chaos could be seen, for precisely this reason, in the governments of Brazil, Turkey, Hungary and elsewhere over recent years. Populism was a destructive force in politics and Damon Hough one of its leading proponents. But that story was over; she speculated that 'Houghism' would not survive, post-Hough.

Earlier in the week Kate had emailed and then spoken to a leading person at the Charity Commission: in her story she speculated that the suspension of Entropy's charitable status was imminent. This meant nothing, though there was a slight risk that three people who did not know that they were charity trustees might ultimately find themselves barred from serving in that capacity in future. The money that Entropy had spent on creating photo opportunities to serve a Member of Parliament, who supported every good cause in his constituency, was lost forever and could never be returned. It would be months before the authorities could confirm that the charity was genuinely a 'front'.

A living MP benefitting to the tune of tens of thousands of pounds siphoned deliberately into his election campaigns, over and above the level allowed by law, was a scandal. But if the MP was dead, even if the backbencher's body was still politically warm, then the story had already become nothing more than folklore. What was it they used to say? Tomorrow's chip wrappers. Hough was, ultimately, a politician of little consequence. With the loan, the charity and the unregistered and thus illegal donations to his own electoral campaigns, there was only one villain in this story, a villain who would now never be punished.

Were there lessons to be learned? Yes. Stick to the rules. Or else.

Some lesson.

There were so many reasons why Damon's death had pushed the story from the front page to page 10, not least the warmongering in eastern Europe. Had he still been alive, it could have damaged him badly - but to what end? A solitary backbencher with no experience of high office might have been obliged by his Party to retire at the next election. His seat would be safe for the Tories, whatever happened, and the incoming Member's commitment to meaningful and positive change for his constituents, built upon a clean slate, could hardly be less than that of the previous incumbent. A lawyer forced out of office and obliged to make a living as… a lawyer. My heart bleeds for him, Kate thought, sarcastically.

The final element was the return of the loan. Kate was adamant that Lee Hardman would not appear in the story and her lips would remain sealed about her sources. What Lee had done in 'lending' the money to Damon was not illegal, as far as she could tell, as long as the origins of the cash were legitimate. She gave him the benefit of the doubt on that, in the absence of any evidence to the contrary, though she suspected the trust was misplaced. Some of Campbell's gains were more ill-gotten than others and he had already been punished for conduct relating to the illest-gotten of those. The purpose of hiding this money was to 'protect' apparently legitimate assets from a heavy handed and overarching sequestrator, for the duration, she reasoned. This was not the same thing as laundering stolen cash or creating poisonous financial 'derivatives'.

Lee had been expecting the money back from Damon before Campbell left jail and since earlier this morning Campbell had been a free man. She had received a text message from Lee, anonymously, back on 5th May when he had written: 'Just seen our friend. No joy yet'. During the course of this week, she had texted Lee three times with variants of 'Have you had £ returned?' but each time her phone reported that the number was not in use. Today a bland email to Lee's work address had evinced an autoreply: 'Please note: I no longer work at MEKANICK'. Had Damon returned the money? She thought it unlikely; Lee would have told her.

Kate paused at her desk, puffed out her cheeks then protractedly exhaled through the small aperture created by firm lips, and reflected.

Damon had disappeared from her life the day she left university, twenty years ago, if not before. It was not that she had never thought about him, nor read about his antics in the political columns, but she had not followed his progress assiduously. She could never relate to him again in the way that she had tried to, in the early to middle phase of their student relationship, nor in the way that he had pretended she did, to his parents, towards the end. He had clearly undergone a Damascene moment, with the explosive energy of a cork being released from a shaken bottle, when his overbearing father had died, releasing him from the need to feign straight 'normality' on the sexual (and every other) front. Not only had the paternal passing allowed him to admit, in her presence, that he was gay, but it had fired his enthusiasm for right wing activism, also. This had come about from a heady mixture of philosophical libertarianism, which they had discussed together superficially on occasion, and a massive dose of ill-focused resentment of 'normality'.

One thing was clear: any form of relationship with Damon was one of which Kate was, there was absolutely no doubt, better off out.

It was Friday afternoon. None of her personal connections to Damon, nor any personal insight which may reflect upon herself, featured in the story. Within an hour it would be too late to make further amendments. Kate Mellor herself played no part in the story of Damon's life, of that she was adamant. It was a ridiculous idea.

Or did she? Why and how had Damon got hold of her business card? She most certainly had not given it to him, nor sent it; they had literally never been in the same room, the same building for twenty years, as far as she knew. Her work took her to Parliament occasionally, perhaps once or twice a year, but she had never spotted him - seven thousand people worked there, so that was no surprise. And why did he have her card with him when he died? Who were the other cards from, were they connected to her? Was Lee, perhaps, one? Why had Damon called her? If he had a message for her, why did he not try other ways to contact her when phoning failed? Maybe he was trying to frame her, tie her in to his inadequacies. He had tried to call after his meeting with Lee, which she knew had taken place - was that significant? What had Lee said to him? Damon's death occurred just two days later… surely Lee had not told Damon about her involvement? Did Lee give her card to Damon? No, it would have given Lee's game away, it was not in his interests to reveal that any journalist was involved, least of all her. Her card had her current mobile number on it, so why did Damon ring the old number, impotently stored in his phone for all those years? Was he in full possession of his senses at the time? Had his attempt to call her had a direct bearing on his decision to die?

Was he trying to talk to his past…?

Thank God Damon would never read her article; he could have made her life thereafter hell.

Kate noticed that an email had arrived from Ruth Gaunt. Ruth who? Oh, the police. She decided not to respond to the request to call back until it was too late to change the story. She would then have a good reason to tell the girl that the copy had gone to press. However, if she timed her response exactly right, and there was something juicy on offer, it may not be too late to change something, after all.

Back to her reverie.

The cufflinks... those fucking cufflinks. Tying them to the death scene must be some sort of message from Damon! But what? What was he trying to say?

Does he blame me for all this? she asked herself. Twenty years ago, did I screw up his life so much that he became a vicious, foul mouthed, nasty, exploitative, right-wing thug?

Was he right to blame me? Had he set up clues to focus police attention on me? Why would he do that?

An image came into her mind: her eyes welled up as she saw her mother, frail, shrunken, clutched in her arms. She was lifting the woman's shoulders up from the bed and pressing the woman's face tightly against her own chest. She could feel the fabric of the sweater, the touch of her mother's cheek; she could smell the hospital and taste the salty tears as her mother passed away once more.

In her mind she turned to Damon again and screamed 'I did not kill my mother!'

Then she started to weep.

The Chief Whip Negotiates:

Friday 13th May

Charles Mallory ended the meeting, dismissed his team for the weekend and looked at his phone. There were no messages, which was unusual. It was half past twelve on Friday afternoon and he was ready to go home, to shut politics out of his life; the weekend could not come soon enough. At least this devil of a week was now finished, done, over. Private members' business would be completed in a couple of hours - there were only a few dozen Members on the premises that day - and then, like everyone else, he would absent himself immediately. Ever since that idiot had topped himself things had been… upside down. Thank heavens Hough's parents had not been around to witness such goings on.

48 hours earlier, on the Wednesday, he had thought that they - the government, the Tory Party, Mallory himself - had been on top of things. They had posted the press release about the suicide, answered some low-key questions from the media and published a soul-less 'in memoriam' that might just pass as a eulogy to someone who, most who knew him considered, was better off dead.

And then Wednesday afternoon had happened. That Spanish-speaking chap had turned up out of the blue, if you please, wanting to talk about Damon.

It was preposterous. If Mallory had not been Damon's 'godfather', if any other backbencher had died - there were literally hundreds of the useless sods - then he would have ignored the outrageous approach and most certainly not succumbed to the man's demands. But the ties ran too deep: Mallory's loyalty to the memory of that dear, dear man, Gerald Hough, was profound. At least, now that this most distasteful of episodes was over, the matter had finally been despatched. It was Friday the bloody thirteenth, nearly time to go home and shut out the world.

Mallory had not liked the look of his visitor from the word 'go'. As soon as he clapped eyes on him, in the Central Lobby late on Wednesday afternoon, he had taken the skinny man in the blue suit to be a sleazy dago, as indeed the scoundrel had turned out to be… should that be dago, or wop? Mallory had never really known the difference. Mediterranean, that was enough. He could sense that his patience was about to be tested.

'Mister Mallory, sir,' said the Central Lobby attendant behind the desk that they called the pulpit, for obvious reasons. 'There's a gentleman to see you, sir. The chap in the blue suit, sitting in front of the post office. He may be Spanish, a Mr Soares. It's about Mr Hough, I believe. Sad business, sir.'

'Indeed, it is. Very sad. Thank you.'

They sat at the edge of the open space of the Lobby, which was unusually quiet. After introductions Mallory immediately pressed upon Adolfo how fortunate he was to have been granted an audience.

'Normally, of course, one would make an appointment to see one's own Member of Parliament, but on this occasion, with Mr Hough... permanently indisposed, I've agreed to meet you. Now, what is it that you want?'

'I business partner Mr Hough,' said Adolfo Bocca, who had once more adopted the name 'Soares'.

'Business partner? What sort of business partner?'

'I set up club.'

'A club?'

'Night club. Small. Select. Discreet. I think you understand.'

Mallory could imagine. The need for discretion around Damon's extramural activities was usually paramount.

'Go on.'

'He promise invest. I make plan. He say he invest twenty thousand pounds, this week, I agree meet him today, but before he pay me money he... he no can give now.'

'Twenty thousand pounds... I honestly don't know how I can help -' Mallory clearly possessed a limited imagination.

Soares was serious, looked Mallory straight in the eye: 'He owe me this money, sir! How I get it, now he dead?'

'Well, I...'

Adolfo took the newspaper from his pocket as he had in the police station a couple of hours earlier; it was still folded to highlight the story of Damon's death. He pointed to Mallory's name in the story.

'This say you person I talk to.'

'Well, I'm his Chief Whip, and I... I do know the family.'

'Policeman he say, yes, you...'

'Police?' Mallory was alarmed. 'Surely - I mean, it's not really…'

'Who else I talk? It busy - no, not busy - urgent? Urgent. Who I see?'

'No one' was probably the best answer, thought Mallory, better still 'absolutely no one at all'. This did not feel good.

'Well, yes, I suppose you could talk to me.'

On reflection, that would be marginally better than talking to anyone else.

Adolfo smiled. He was keeping a low profile, not raising his voice, and felt that he had made a breakthrough. It would be downhill from here, surely? 'We comprehend each other, you, me, Mr Mallory.'

'This club… this 'discreet' club. What sort of club are we talking about?'

Bocca had made up the story as he walked down Whitehall, his pretence not restricted to the fake surname. Using his own name would have added a risk too far. Damon did really owe him six thousand pounds, which had a complicated and dishonourable explanation, best avoided. In order to make the risk worth his while, therefore, he had upped the sum to ten thousand, which he justified by creating the slight fiction of the club. Now he thought of it, he had lost a couple of thousand, accidentally, at the weekend so covering that, too, would be helpful. Adolfo then gave the attendant the same false name that he had used with the police, earlier that afternoon: Soares was a more common name than Bocca, so he was hiding in plain sight. Sitting there in Central Lobby - with its extravagant statues, ornamental splendour and palatial design - he considered the possibility of raising his target to twenty. The moment he saw the tall, confident, elegant, immaculately groomed, elderly man walking towards him in an expensive three-piece suit, white handkerchief poking from his breast pocket, he knew. Twenty thousand was the right call and Mallory was the man to deliver it.

Contrary to the ignorant impression he had given to the young policeman, Adolfo knew very well what the Chief Whip's job was: not least because Damon had described the role to him at great length one drunken night, with an additional, sadistic, jokey interpretation of 'whipping'. 'Drunken' applied to only Damon, but as ever he bore the status with some dignity and professionalism. Adolfo knew from experience that losing control of your faculties when managing a ring of boy prostitutes was not good for trade. He had thus been teetotal for four years.

'I think you know Mr Hough, how he is. In privado.'

Chief Whips develop a nose for deciphering code. 'Ye-e-es. I think I understand you.'

Charles had heard the same quiet rumours to which Basil Cheney was party. Some emanated from sources more reliable than others, but they had a disturbing consistency. He did not disbelieve anything that Adolfo might be hinting because it was in accord with the intelligence, the rusty, spasmodic intelligence, available. And nothing he might hear about the late Damon Hough could possibly surprise him.

'It club where men come see dancers.'

That was almost a relief, even if the man was talking about lap dancers. But was he?

'There are many such clubs in London. Or so I am led to believe.'

'Boy dancers.'

'Ah.'

'Intima... intimate.'

After a perfunctory eyebrow raise, which lowered again as he realised the inevitability of the proposition that was heading his way, Mallory sighed the words 'Boy dancers...'

They let the words rest in the air.

'Mr Soares, did you have a contract with Damon Hough? I suppose I can find out who's handling his estate, then I can let you know, and you can make a claim.'

'No contract.'

'In that case, I really don't know...' Mallory was muttering. He felt defeated. 'I can let you have... the solicitor, all the more reason, really, and you can... take it up with him. Is that all right?' He knew his suggestion was hopeless. 'I say, perhaps you have a card?'

Mallory assumed that Steel would do the legal stuff on Damon's estate, but he would need much preparation and briefing on this case and would have to be the absolute soul of discretion.

'I think better if... no paper.'

'Do you mean there's more to this story?'

'Mr Hough he, you know, he do sex with boys.'

'I, erm, yes, I... I think I know about that.'

'Boy dancers. Maybe the boys, they are very young. Maybe boys remember. Maybe Mr Hough meet them to other...' Adolfo waved his hand in the air, revolving his wrist in a circular motion to indicate the whole of the Parliamentary estate around them.

'Other MPs? Oh, my God.' Suddenly the sympathetic friend of the Hough family was plummeting back into the seedy world of which the Chief Whip sometimes has to learn. The swarthy, slight and skinny man in the blue suit was staring directly at him again.

'I think, Mr Mallory, maybe we do this no with lawyer.' The emphasis was on the 'no'. 'Better that way.'

Adolfo smiled benignly.

Charles Mallory was starting to agree that omitting the lawyer might indeed be a good idea. No paperwork. No record. No third party. Cash. But twenty thousand pounds? Finding it might not be a problem but if he started off down this route, where would it all end? But then what was the alternative, how secure was that? How much would it take to stop this chap from spilling the beans? If I say no, Soares could easily find a reporter within five minutes of where we're sitting, and…

Adolfo started to describe some graphic encounters, overlooking his own role in facilitating them, allowing Mallory to believe that he spoke with authority. In truth, only some of what he planned to describe had actually involved Damon, but it would not harm Adolfo's cause for Mallory to believe that they all could have done. Especially the more graphic ones. '*Si solo mi inglés fuera mejor, más expresivo,*' thought Adolfo. Mallory's biggest worry at that moment was that in the very public Central Lobby someone might overhear these graphic descriptions, albeit in broken English. The Chief screwed up his face in anguish at the stories, as though his contortion could protect his ears from defilement. Fortunately, no passer-by came close, and Adolfo kept his voice low. Within as little as a minute Mallory had heard all he needed to hear.

The conversation staggered along for a few more seconds. Increasingly twitchy, Mallory had allowed himself to be convinced that the debt could be legitimate - the whole thing sounded so typically Damon. The fool, the stupid, stupid, damn fool. He was not worthy to be called Hough.

What was being described was a whorehouse populated by adolescent, maybe even prepubescent, boys of dubious heritage, with lascivious and inadequate older men.

'Stop now, please,' Mallory cautioned in a whisper, 'I've heard enough. Thank you.' More than enough.

'I think if you no help me, maybe -' he waved his newspaper gently in the air '- newspaper pay me so I get money that way. You think, yes?'

Adolfo's expression was perfect in its naive innocence.

The thought that any of this might enter the public domain was beyond the pale, literally outrageous. Unthinkable. If other MPs really were involved, living ones, then Bocca - or Soares, as Mallory knew him - was revealing no names. Yet. Mallory suspected that even Damon had boundaries, that even Damon would not be so foolish as to expose himself - an unfortunate term - to the gaze of Parliamentary colleagues in this way.

The Chief cast his mind back: he had been interviewing Piggy Eliot with a view to the PM appointing him as a junior minister back in 2014. He had asked him the standard internal interview question: 'Are there any skeletons in your cupboard that we should know about?'

Piggy had immediately said 'no' but then paused as the colour drained from his cheeks. 'Perhaps there's just one incident you should know about... I mean, you never know... it was totally innocent, I can assure you.' He paused. 'On my part.'

Piggy told the story. Of the six candidates on the Derbyshire training weekend only Eliot and Hough had made it into the Commons, hence the story had not previously come to the Chief's attention. Upon first hearing of Damon's naked and challenging public grandstanding Mallory had been prepared to dismiss it as a drunken lark, horseplay, boys being boys... But over the years his bank of covert intelligence had grown. Now, with Soares' revelations, Mallory saw that the expression of graphic sexual challenge, domination and humiliation was part of an ominous and disturbing pattern.

Adolfo returned to the subject of money. He gently insisted that a gentlemen's agreement existed which obligated Damon's estate to meet its debts, correctly judging that the Victorian concept carried more currency with the likes of Charles Mallory than it might with many others.

What if all this were to go public? Mallory did not put it past Damon to take revenge from beyond the grave. Revenge for what? Revenge for Mallory's friendship with Hough's father, revenge for what Damon would construe as him, Mallory, siding with Gerald against his son? Only Mallory himself knew exactly how deep his relationship with both of Damon's parents went, the bonds that united all three, a story which would never, ever, see the light of day. The current Mrs Mallory was living in blissful ignorance, and he wanted to keep it that way.

Was Soares' story more likely to become public if Mallory paid Damon's debt, or if he did not? If he did not, obviously. Either way, it could be front page news within days.

A judgment had to be made, now.

There were no other claims on the estate, as far as Mallory knew. In one respect the dago had it right: in the absence of family, of parents, he had come to plead his case to the right person, if more by luck than judgement. Soares could not have known his good fortune in identifying Mallory from the Evening Standard. The rogue had even revealed that he had sought advice from a police officer at Charing Cross police station, helping to further establish the legitimacy of his claim. If the man was bright enough to set up a sting then, the Chief had to admit, letting the police know he was seeking Mallory out was a sound tactic. But did the man have his wits about him to that extent?

'Soares' told Mallory that he was from South America but had resided in London for ten years and had known Damon for about five. He admitted neither his real name nor his job description: pimp.

Ten minutes into the conversation Mallory was prepared to believe that the request was both genuine and urgent. Whilst its legitimacy was not proven beyond doubt any attempt to delve further could open a can of very unpleasant worms, so he had to take the man on trust. He appreciated why Soares found the prospect of anonymity as attractive as he did. Equally, if it all blew up then the man would face arrest, and not just for extortion. It was better that Mallory did not know details, such as whether any of the boys were underage. If it all came out later that he had paid the man for his silence then the damage to himself, to the Tory party that he served and to the institution of Parliament would be immense, though ignorance might afford some mitigation. Finally, he reasoned optimistically, if there were other such claims on the Hough estate they should have surfaced by now.

Although twenty thousand was a lot of money, more than he could access at short notice, he was relieved that the figure was not even bigger than it was. Perhaps paying Damon's debt promptly would help all concerned to get off lightly. The sooner this gruesome matter was resolved, the better.

Mallory made a decision.

'I say, would you excuse me for a moment? I need to make a call, to make sure I can get the money for you. It's Wednesday afternoon and I need to talk to my bank… you know how difficult it is to get anything out of bankers after lunch…'

Adolfo thought quickly; he needed a commitment before he let the man out of his sight.

'I see you; you no go away.'

It was Mallory's turn to calculate.

'Jolly good.'

He stood, took out his mobile and dialled a number from its memory. It was answered immediately.

'Dicky, is that you? Charles Mallory. One moment.'

Mallory stood, motioned to Adolfo to remain seated, strode determinedly about five yards, stood facing the wall and conducted a conversation in hushed tones.

For Bocca this was crunch time. He was indeed sincere: getting this money would buy his silence, for ever. He took Mallory at his word that the call was only about how and when the money would be delivered, though he expected that he might yet need to bargain. He judged that Mallory shared his view that the sooner this was over, the better.

Mallory was concise. He put his phone back in his pocket and flashed a weak smile momentarily in Adolfo's direction. He followed it back to the seat.

'In the absence of a contract, or of evidence of the size of Damon's debt, I'm not sure I can, or indeed want to, get my hands on twenty thousand pounds. As far as I know you have made that figure up…' Adolfo put on a resentful expression, offended, but Mallory raised a calming hand. 'But your story is, nevertheless, credible, in principle. And I do want to resolve it, believe me. I can therefore have twelve thousand pounds for you, on Friday at 11 in the morning.'

Adolfo raised one eyebrow. He had heard the expression 'a bird in the hand…'; although he knew of no equivalent in Argentina, it now made sense. He gave the impression of considering the offer. Mallory continued 'But don't come in here, not into the Palace; there are cameras all over the place, as I'm sure you're aware.' He pointedly did not indicate where they were but smiled seraphically, in order to convey to any hidden watchers that nothing was amiss. 'Meet me in Victoria Tower Gardens, it's just south of the House of Lords, it's freely open to the public. Be there on

Friday morning at eleven. Do you know the Buxton Memorial Fountain? It's at the Lambeth Bridge end of the gardens, near the children's play area. I will be nearby. The cash will be in a brown envelope in used, large denomination notes. If I can get more than twelve then there will be more than twelve.'

This sounded suitably sincere, but Mallory had no intention of providing more. It was the only bit of hard bargaining he calculated that he might win.

'Please understand, Mr Soares,' if that was the man's name, he wondered, 'this is a one-off, a once and for all payment, do you understand? The matter will be over, and you will accept whatever I bring, be it twelve thousand or be it more.'

It was time for Adolfo to decide and to commit.

'*Si*. Vittoria Tower Garden, by river, two hundred metre. The statue?'

'That's the place. The Buxton Memorial Fountain, it's not exactly a statue. It's an outrageous piece of Gothic… from 1843. It commemorates the role of Parliamentarians such as Mr Buxton in the emancipation of slaves.'

In order to be certain, Mallory took out his phone again. He typed 'Buxton fountain Victoria gardens' into its search engine and then showed Adolfo a picture.

'That's it. 11 a.m. on Friday.'

'*Si. Entiendo*. I understand.' He repeated the details back.

Mallory spelt out his final words, slowly and firmly annunciating 'There will be no more.' Smiling again for the cameras, but with teeth clenched, he added, in a voice trained from years of pressing reluctant backbenchers into submission: 'Is that understood?'

A big smile grew across Adolfo's face, which Mallory was relieved to see. It looked in order, it did not appear to be that of a plotter, a manipulator, as these swarthy types were wont to sometimes be.

Adolfo put out his hand. A tremor of uncertainty ran down Mallory's spine, but only momentarily.

'How you say? 'Don'.'

The peremptory handshake was enough, for both men. An Englishman's word was his bond, thought Mallory, and when in Rome the Spaniard… South American… whatever… it jolly well ought to be enough for him, too.

259

Adolfo rose to his feet. He then marched out of the Palace and out of Mallory's life for ever - apart from a brief moment on Friday at eleven, two days hence.

The smile drained from Mallory's face. The hand he had shaken was cold, clammy, weak. He hoped to God that he would never see it again after Friday. The bastard had added another worry to his list and another weekend had been ruined. That was how Mrs Mallory would see it. Charles 'more optimistic take was that this could be twelve thousand well spent.

Adolfo did not for one moment believe that there would be a penny more than twelve thousand pounds in the envelope. And twelve thousand was not twenty thousand. But it was still double what Damon owed him – and it covered his weekend losses, too, so Bocca considered it a good day's work.

At 11.01 a.m. on Friday both parties would draw a line under the matter.

And now, 90 further minutes after that meeting, Mallory was sitting behind his desk in the Chief Whip's Parliamentary office. Its surface was almost clear, which was how he liked to leave it each weekend. He sat motionless, rarely blinking, his chest barely rising with each breath, his mind full of horror, disgust, shame - and relief. Oh, the relief.

On the desk was a glass of decent Scotch, untouched, though he did not normally take his regular medication before the sun fell below the yardarm. He remembered the happy day he had become Chief Whip, when a civil servant in Number Twelve had asked him about his favourite tipple. When he replied: 'a decent Scotch', the civil servant smiled assent and asked 'And what would you like with that, minister?' He meant ice, soda, water or... surely nothing else was conceivable.

'Another one!' the gloriously joyous Mallory had replied.

How different he felt now.

But the deed had been done. It had gone without hitch or delay, precisely at eleven, without a word spoken. Twelve thousand pounds was a small price to pay for peace of mind.

Mallory downed the Scotch in one. He sincerely believed that the way was now clear for that worthless piece of garbage, Damon Hough, to get out of his life for ever.

Ruth Ploughs On:

Friday 13th May

It was Friday, six days into the investigation, and her pile of 'to do's' was at last under control. That Ruth Gaunt was snowed under was not because there was so much to process on the Hough case - there was not - but because not only had other issues pushed it off the top of her agenda in recent days but she was working on the case by herself. Today was the day she was determined to crack it.

So, spread across the desk were photographs: of business cards, cufflinks, shoes (two), a car and a car key, several of a pile of clothes, including a bloodied shirt and jacket, which could once have contained a body. On the display boards were more photographs: a living Damon Hough, proud, posing, chin up, doing it for England; Ruth could imagine a Union Jack fluttering behind him. There was Paul Roe, equally glossy but more casual and relaxed, oozing confidence and authority. Kate Mellor's was probably from her driving licence, a staring rabbit in headlights, unflattering. Lee Hardman was there too, one of a group of Tory candidates from 2010, blown up and encircled by a superimposed red loop, a grown-up Harry Potter. Also there, almost unrecognisable when expanded, were her own photographs from on top of the viaduct. These were two views of the shoe to capture its exact location and scuff marks in the dust - or were they? Printed out and blown up, the evidence for a struggle was less convincing than she had first thought - and then the Sunday morning SOCO team had failed to confirm her theory. Another was of the phone. And a cufflink, in situ, half buried in dust.

Ruth had been busy with other things for most of Friday but by mid-afternoon she had cleared her own desk and decamped onto the incident table, which she and Inspector Allyson had claimed for the duration. In a folder on her laptop, she had the autopsy report, confirming that massive trauma to the front and top of the skull was the cause of death, consistent with falling from a great height onto a hard, rough surface. There was no evidence of recent alcohol or drug use although the liver was not in perfect condition, suggesting habitual intoxication of one form or another. There was a PDF of Hough's digital address book, a week's worth of email titles, his most recent bank statement (showing him comfortably solvent), his health record (generally very good), and even a confidential end of term whips' report, which revealed very little about his state of mind.

There was a folder of press cuttings too, with every move, word, fart and belch Hough had made in the past year preserved for the record. She had access to his Twitter feed, too. Did this guy model himself on Trump?

CCTV from the M1's junction 1 showed Hough's vehicle and its lone occupant departing from London. Another feed confirmed that it left the motorway at junction 23A, for Donington Services, 110 miles away, an hour and a half later. It was likely that he had broken the speed limit significantly on the motorway but an average speed of 74mph was probably about right for a Saturday. The Porsche was powerful and the calculation somewhat academic.

From three that Friday afternoon Ruth had speed-read the information yet again, for the umpteenth time, yet it still felt incomplete.

She had heard nothing from Alison for 24 hours. Late on the Thursday evening she had sent her a text - 'U OK?' - which prompted no reply. Experience told her that pestering her boss was not a good move, so she had not tried a second time. If the older woman wanted to do a Garbo that was up to her. The reasons why Alison had left so abruptly last evening, with barely a word, surely had nothing to do with the case.

Ruth paused and thought. Alison never spoke about Eric, her husband. Ruth knew that things were difficult between them, that he had been in hospital ever since his stroke, but little more than that. A crisis involving Eric was the obvious explanation for the Inspector's behaviour. 'If she'd answered my text, I'd know,' thought Ruth. But then she heard Alison's voice in her head: 'You've got a job to do, Ruth, get on with it!'

There was nothing to suggest that Damon Hough's death was anything but suicide. In the absence of new and overwhelming evidence emerging to the contrary in the next couple of hours, a suicide it would remain. The aim had always been to make a determination by today, but it was literally above Ruth's pay grade to presume to make that call by herself. In Alison's absence the decision might have to wait until Monday; if she was still missing then Ruth would take the matter upstairs. At least there were no anxious relatives baying for the body to be released for burial.

However, the scene still posed unanswered questions:

Why and how had the shoes become separated? One was still on his foot, one was twenty metres above it, on top of the incomplete bridge. That shoe was slightly scuffed, but when did the scuff happen? What did it tell us? Oxidation suggested that it was probably inflicted less than a day before he was found, thought the lab, but to be significant it would have had to be in the moments before he fell, and that could not be confirmed.

How had the cufflinks become separated? Had he been intending to remove his shirt for some reason, for which discarding not one but both links was a precondition, or had the link come off during a struggle? He was still wearing his jacket: the idea that he was removing his shirt in some Houdini tribute was absurd. Or had he deliberately planted the cufflink, in the same way that he must have deliberately chosen to keep four cards - only four - in his pocket?

There was no definitive evidence of a fight. Even the circumstantial evidence, the scuffed-up dirt and grass, required a degree of imagination to make it fit the scenario. Overnight weather had put paid to delicate new detail coming to light. A struggle would have required a foe: was there any evidence of a second person being present? No. None.

If only rural beauty spots had CCTV, she mused.

Ruth reasoned: the cufflinks had been a birthday present from Kate Mellor, twenty years previously. Her business card was in Hough's possession when he died but we know not how or when he had acquired it. He had tried to call her on the Thursday before he died (why?) but had used a number that was way out of date. She had not spoken to him since leaving University and certainly did not give him her card herself. Maybe his intention to call her on Thursday was an emotional precursor to suicide... was Thursday the day Damon had made the decision to kill himself? Had he reached out to share his thoughts with the only person with whom he had ever had an intense, emotional, intimate, sexual relationship? The conversation had never happened: we would never know.

Ruth had the recording of Alison's interview with Kate to hand. She skipped to the bit where Alison asked Kate if anyone on the paper was writing a retrospective story about the dead MP. The reply had been 'I'm not the editor', not 'no', or 'not as far as I know'. Had Alison missed a trick? If an MP who is sufficiently charismatic to merit a few column inches on the following Sunday dies, and you're a journalist, and you have some gossip about him, don't you want to help your paper get ahead of the pack?

Ruth made a decision. She typed an email to Kate Mellor: 'Please call me on my mobile for a two-minute follow-up about the case we discussed.' Her number was in the email footer.

Paul Roe's card had also been in the jacket pocket. He and Damon had known each other in childhood and, whilst aware of each other's presence in Parliament, they were on opposite sides. There was no love lost between them, though professional courtesies were, no doubt, observed. A constituent of Roe's had a gripe against someone in Hough's patch, which raised tension between the MPs, but that was no reason to wish Hough dead! Such minor conflicts must happen all the time. Murder was hardly Parliamentary behaviour, though she recalled from history lessons that there was an era when MPs risked death on a regular basis. Did not Canning, a future Prime Minister, get himself into a duel? Was not another PM, Perceval, shot dead inside Parliament itself? Surely those days were gone, though that chap from Southend who got stabbed rather suggested they weren't. Roe and Hough had last spoken barely 48 hours before the latter's death, but it had been brief; Hough had likely been the more aggressive, Roe the more pliant. Roe had tried abortively to call Hough a few hours later; was that standard practice with an inter-constituency case? Possibly. Again, the attempted call had not resulted in a conversation because Roe had changed his mind about making it.

Ruth had used Alison's name to call in a favour from the motorway CCTV people, whose evidence confirmed Roe's story. His car had indeed been on a motorway that day, but it was the M4, not the M1, and he had been heading into London and not out of it. Judging by the time he had entered the capital he could not have been in Derbyshire during the window. Once in London the car had not left the city. Neither Kate nor Lee owned cars, though they would have needed one to get to the site and back. Examining hire car records was well beyond the detective capacity available to this case…

The name on the third printed card was MEKANICK's Lee Hardman. A low priority, he had proved impossible to track down, after a belated start. At 4.30 she rang his work number, only to be told that he no longer worked there.

'That's not what I was told earlier the other day! I was told he was out of the office.'

'Oh, he's usually out of the office; his contract doesn't require him to be on site much. But his contract expired, yesterday.'

'Yesterday? Why is he leaving so suddenly?'

'It's not sudden. His contract was tied to certain events, we've known for a while that it was going to end yesterday. I'm not sure I can…'

'How long has he known that he would be leaving this week?'

'Well, I've known for a few weeks. It's really not that sudden, officer.'

'Thank you. I have his mobile number -'

'And I have his mobile,' said the receptionist. 'Here in front of me. He surrendered it when he left.'

'Do you have another number for him? A home number, a personal mobile?'

'Let me see… no, neither. Sorry.'

'An address?'

'I believe he sold his flat, I think he might have been living in a hotel for the last few weeks. I'm not sure which one. We don't keep tabs… and I don't speak to him very often.'

'Which one? Which hotel?'

'Are you trying to speak to him for a reason? Is it anything we should know about?'

'Not if he's out of contract, no.'

'Of course. No. Wait a moment, officer.'

There was a brief pause before the receptionist spoke again.

'I've checked: I'm sorry, I don't know which hotel he was staying in.'

Ruth ended the call, picked up the blown-up photo of Lee's business card and typed the printed mobile number into her phone. It was answered after just one ring: 'I just told you, detective. I have his phone on my desk.'

Damn the man. Leaving his job was clearly coincidence, but leaving his flat, too? Maybe she could ask Darren to investigate some hotels in the City area, he was bound to know a few… and it was an opportunity to be in touch. She had not heard from her new friend, Jason's brother, since their hour-long chat on Wednesday; she hoped that she'd not frightened him off. He would not have been the first. Had her conversation - too much shop - proved too boring? If he was still interested, however… she smiled and dreamed of the London Eye, the Shard, the Tate Modern and other places they might go together for a day out in that there London… maybe his flat? No, it would be unprofessional to involve Darren in the case, and she didn't have the authority to ask him. It would probably be a wild goose chase, too.

In any case, she wanted him to herself and not to have to talk about work. She had done too much of that on Wednesday.

So: Lee was a missing link. Neither of the other two knew why their cards were in Hough's pocket and she guessed Lee would say the same. There was no reason to justify spending more time trying to track him down, no reason to believe that Lee Hardman had been on that bridge in Derbyshire last Saturday afternoon.

Kate had not yet called her back and she wondered whether the email had been the right thing to do. Was 'You didn't tell us if your paper was covering Hough's death' a strong enough reason to be back in touch? Could there be a better question? Yes, there could… how about 'Do you know Paul Roe?' Better still 'Do you know where we can find the elusive Lee Hardman?' They had not disclosed the names on the other two cards to anyone outside the investigation. Hardman was a Tory and a lawyer but so were many other people; the facts did not constitute a strong link to Hough. Roe and Mellor both had a past which featured Damon - did Hardman have one too, other than them being candidates together in the same election, twelve years previously?

It was a long shot. Hough's office had sent her a printout of Damon's diary for the last three months, but she had barely glanced at it. Perhaps… Shit. There it was: 10 a.m., Thursday 5th May, Central Lobby. Lee Hardman. Two days before Damon died. Why had she not looked at this before? She guessed it was unlikely that Lee was Damon's constituent, though not impossible, so what was the connection?

On impulse she rang the House of Commons and asked to speak to Damon's secretary. This time the brusque woman answered promptly, explaining that she was on her way out of the door for the weekend, so it had to be quick. Ruth asked what the meeting had been about: in less than ninety seconds she confirmed that there was nothing about it on file.

'Probably a personal matter,' the secretary ventured. 'They often are. But I must go now, sorry…'

Another dead end. Like the railway bridge.

Why was Hough on the bridge in the first place? Literally, she had no clue, unless it was with the specific intention of jumping; he had not been dressed for rambling. She parked the question and turned to the fourth card with its 14 handwritten digits, etched on an otherwise blank card.

This time she looked at the card itself, more carefully, closely… she still thought it had to be a bank account. It would normally be written with three pairs of digits as a sort code and an 8-digit account number but the spacing might just suggest that the number might have been arranged the other way round, account number first. But she had already tested that theory, finding that no such bank existed, no such account. But the six:eight split still might mean something.

The other way round? Read the number backwards! On a scrap of paper, she transposed the digits, three pairs starting from the end and then 8 more. She went back to the web site she had used previously and discovered that a sort code with those numbers did exist, a private bank in the Isle of Man. Although there was no such account number that did not mean that the account had never existed… though Manx accounts were notoriously difficult to interrogate. Park that idea, it could be coincidence - or unconnected with the case. Back to the bridge - and the car.

Damon's journey from London to Donington Park was verified but what did he do once he arrived at the service station? He might not have gone straight to the bridge; it was too early. Had they been pursuing a murderer Alison would have asked for permission to access the service station's CCTV, but everything had a cost and Ruth did not believe that the authorities would grant her permission. For a start, the case belonged to Alison. She hoped the boss was all right: Ruth's mind wandered back to the call Alison had received. Had Eric come out of his coma, perhaps? Had he died? Had she found cause to rekindle her feelings for him? Who knows…?

There were very few traffic cameras between Donington Park and the old quarry where Damon's car had been left at some point on the Saturday afternoon, and little to be gained by interrogating them. The inside of the car was in immaculate condition, recent valeting having left practically no evidence that anyone had ever sat inside it - even the driver! Would someone contemplating suicide make sure their car was pristine before they did the deed? Not really… but then again, why not? If they were being completely rational, they would probably not be contemplating taking their own life in the first place. The question of what prompted the suicide once more raised its ugly head.

Ruth had been fortunate in finding the car key, by chance, in the dusk, on the floor of the valley. It had either been dropped by someone walking at ground level or, more dramatically, thrown from the top of the bridge.

Why might Damon have done that? What was he trying to achieve? Such a random finding, which made no sense, tipped the pendulum once again towards the balance of his mind being disturbed, again consistent with suicide.

She calculated: it would take 20 minutes to walk from the car park to the bridge along the track, but the period between his arrival at Donington and the estimated time of death was a lot longer than that. He could have had lunch at Donington - CCTV could certainly confirm that - though that might only account for half an hour. She checked the autopsy: he had certainly had lunch - chicken sandwiches - somewhere. Was lunch a priority for someone anticipating imminent suicide? Then she realised that Damon could not have walked directly to the bridge; being on top of it, at the west end, he could only have accessed the top from the east end. She knew that it took some minutes to reach the top at the east end and then traverse the bridge. The gaps in the timeline were starting to fill. Perhaps…

She pulled up an ordinance survey map on her screen. From the car park it was a five-minute walk north along the track to a junction; the track continued north to meet the deformed western end of the bridge but there was a lesser, narrower path that rambled off eastwards. It crossed the valley floor, parallel with the viaduct. It spanned the stream via a small bridge and once established on the east flank it meandered left and right, up and down contours until it reached the leviathan. Not only was this a longer route than the direct track but it must be slower, too. A northbound walker would have to pass under the eastern arch and turn back on themselves to clamber up the slope to the top. From what she had seen on the Saturday evening someone in brogues, Damon, might have found the going more difficult on that east side than would have been the case when following the better-defined western track. From that north easterly point of the route, it was easy to mount the bridge, as she had discovered. The internet confirmed that the viaduct was originally 290 metres long, now 250 without that final arch. Earlier in the week she had browsed a learned book on the pathways of Derbyshire, online. Although she could only see a few pages without committing to buy the publication, the bridge and associated footpath were displayed in all their glory. The viaduct had been formally closed in 1962 after its use had been temporarily suspended after a long, cold winter had rendered its western arch unsafe. The authorities anticipated Beeching and deemed the train line vulnerable, so why would they spend money strengthening it? It was abandoned and left to decay. In 1978, another bitterly cold winter, the first major collapse had occurred, and the bridge became disconnected from the valley's western side.

Did Damon know that the bridge was incomplete when he embarked upon his last journey? How could he not have done?

There was a beautiful, stunning view from the top of the bridge, making it well worth the climb. But why then go all the way to the far end? Because it was the only spot where he could guarantee a hard landing. Even for a mild May Saturday, Damon was not dressed for rambling, yet he was a rambler! He had been an officer of the All-Party Parliamentary Group on Rambling; he would have known the importance of proper footwear. Perhaps his ill-preparedness again reflected the balance of his mind being disturbed...

The detective constable was wondering what to do next when her phone rang.

'DC Gaunt.'

'Kate Mellor. You wanted a word.'

'Ah, yes... thank you for calling back.'

'Have you made progress?'

'We're still in the process... I think you'd need to speak to Inspector Allyson about that.' The woman was a journalist, and it was not Ruth's job to disclose anything without authority. 'I just wanted to ask... do you know Paul Roe?'

'The MP? I know who he is, I've never met him. Wasn't he recently promoted?'

'You're sure you've never met him...?'

'We may have been at the same Parliamentary function some time, but I'm sure I've never spoken to him.'

'OK, thanks. What about... a chap called Lee Hardman?'

Kate realised that her pause was going on for far too long. What the Hell, her story in Sunday's paper had already been set and had already gone for printing. It was too late to stop it now. That was the one advantage of being hidden on page ten.

'Lee Hardman? Where would I know that name from?'

Here was another answer which lacked the clarity of 'yes' or 'no', thought Ruth. 'He works for a finance company called MEKANICK.'

Kate was worried. It would not take the police long to establish that she had reported on the original MEKANICK case, many years ago. Lee had already started working for the company then, but she was certain they had not met at that time. Would the police believe her?

'Is he something to do with Damon?'

Another prevarication.

'They may have had contact in the days before the suicide.' It occurred to Ruth that although the meeting had been in Damon's diary for the Thursday morning his office could not confirm that it had actually taken place.

'I see.' She also 'saw' that Lee was no longer contactable, would have left MEKANICK and gone abroad by now, though she knew no more than that. Does Lee have something to do with Damon's death, after all? She felt obliged to reveal that her story would appear on Sunday and that it had a MEKANICK connection.

'By the way, Ruth - can I call you Ruth? I wouldn't want to mislead you, but about something I said the other day. Yes, there will be a story about Damon in our paper on Sunday. That's normal, you know, when a high-profile MP dies.'

'What does it say?'

'The usual thing... expenses. We believe that he was making hidden political and strategic charitable donations for reasons of political advancement using money, the source of which was not declared.'

'I see.'

'It's not a massive story, very much inside page, Westminster Village stuff, you know. Not life and death.'

Both women immediately regretted Kate's use of the unfortunate phrase. Kate tried to hide her *faux pas*, finding herself continuing: 'And we believe that some of that money may have come from MEKANICK.'

Ruth felt angry but controlled her tongue: 'Why didn't you tell us this before? It wasn't 'the other day' we spoke, it was yesterday.'

'Well... you didn't ask!' Her laugh was brief, ineffective and strangled. 'The story has nothing to do with my past with Damon, they asked me to do it because I'd covered the MEKANICK case in the first place, twelve years ago, and there's no suggestion that this was dirty money -'

'So you do know Lee Hardman?'

'I didn't meet him when I covered the story.' Kate was pleased with that response, and she was fairly sure it was true, too. The standard 'I can't disclose my sources' would have pointed straight to him.

Ruth took a deep breath.

'Did Mr Hough know about the story?'

'No. Certainly not from me, no, I'm pretty certain that he knew nothing about it.'

'It could explain why he tried to call you -'

'- but not why he didn't persist. I've been thinking about that. If Damon thought that there was a story about him breaking on my paper, and especially if he thought I was involved, he would have found a way of talking to me, even if the number he had in his phone was out of date. Like you said, he had my card with the correct number on it. And he didn't try to contact anyone else at the paper, I'd have known if he had. And he didn't try again on the Thursday night, nor any time on the Friday, nor on the Saturday right up until…'

There was a pause.

'Right up until he died.'

And even if he did know, thought Ruth, this was further evidence for suicide and not for unlawful killing. Motive. Opportunity. Means. Still nothing pointed towards murder.

The two women tiptoed around each other for a few seconds longer until the conversation petered out.

Ruth took a break. There was a strong coffee somewhere with her name on it. Most of the police station staff had gone home by now and the coffee area looked like it had been ransacked by baboons; she reflected that this was how the cleaners must find it at the end of every day, yet it would be pristine by next morning.

Back at the incident desk, she made a note on the file of her conversation with Kate Mellor for Alison's perusal. She read again Charles Mallory's email which introduced the attached pages from the whips' report. In their writing he and his colleagues were careful not to give hostages to fortune; he had been more explicit verbally with Alison than he was in writing. He had made it clear that had the black sheep of his flock still been alive then even the police would not have been allowed sight of this document. Ruth recalled a controversy when police had been prevented from enforcing search warrants on Parliamentary premises, so she felt a slight sense of privilege to be reading it. Even if it was not very helpful.

No doubt the list of alleged offences and other tribulations were important in the world of politics, but there was nothing here for her investigation; notably, 'fingers in the till' was not mentioned. Damon may be a flouter of the rules but he did so consistently, habitually, often marginally, and with consequences which appeared modest to the outsider. No doubt, in the great scheme of things, the allegations that Kate Mellor's paper was about to unleash would be water off a dead duck's back.

Then there was the wallet. She knew that many people, including many of her friends, travelled cashless these days so it was no surprise that Damon's pockets - and car - had been devoid of notes or coins. The phone had been recovered - but why had it not been in his pocket? It had not been in use at the time it was dropped. The phone itself could be used to pay for goods, as hers could. But people still normally travelled with a credit card, did they not? There was no driving licence either, no supermarket loyalty card, no membership cards, no coffee tallies to earn the imbiber an eighth or tenth cup free. Where were they? The wallet was not in the car - she had checked the footwells herself to make sure it had not fallen to the floor.

On the Tuesday two Metropolitan Police officers had entered Damon's London flat, a routine procedure after a suicide where there was no known next of kin. They had spent less than an hour there, so the report in front of Ruth was cursory: when she spoke to a searching officer the following day, she reported finding Damon's passport, Parliamentary pass and other key documents. A pair of walking boots was standing in the middle of the floor, as though left behind; a wind cheater screwed up on the bed supported that impression. The flat was untidy but not exceptionally so, for a single man. A small plastic bag was found, containing a small quantity of white powder (of which there were traces in the carpet beside the bed, too). They presumed it to be cocaine in the bag but that in the carpet might equally be talc. There was not enough to write home about, probably not even worth testing, and no cocaine in his body when he died. They found no credit card, no wallet.

It was more than an hour since Ruth had last looked at her phone; most sensible people would have gone home by now on the TGIF principle. She had been busy, neglecting to take it with her when she had gone to make coffee. Accordingly, she had missed both an email and a text message.

The email was crucial and serendipitous, another word she had recently added to her grown up vocabulary. It informed Ruth that earlier that day a police officer had parked his car in the old quarry car park. He had not been investigating anything special but - reading between the lines - had simply gone there for a break. No doubt he was there to relax, undo his top button, sip tea from his flask and maybe even close his eyes for a few moments, whilst monitoring the police wavelengths. She knew what went on! She imagined him just dropping off into a well-deserved nap when there was a knock on the side window. Two elderly ladies, in anoraks, over-trousers and walking boots, carrying ski sticks, were standing patiently awaiting his attention. PC Dyer lowered his window.

'Yes, me ducks?'

'We've just found this!'

The smaller woman proffered a brown, fold-over, man's wallet.

'Where d'you find that, then, duck?'

'Just by the gate into the field, over there.' The other one volunteered 'We made a little pile of stones where we found it -'

'A cairn,' added the other.

'Thank you, Sylvia, I don't think the officer needs to know that. Yes, we made a cairn, so that we can show you exactly where it was found.'

'I'm just trying to be helpful, Janet.'

The wallet was soft leather, expensive, well worn. It had been exposed to the elements, but from its condition and the recent weather Dyer guessed that it had been lying in the open for days rather than weeks. It contained no money, but the leather felt loose, not tight; it would normally have contained several notes. There was a full set of credit and other cards in the name of Mr D Hough. The officer was aware of Saturday's incident, and the MP's name, although a week earlier he would have had no idea who Damon was. Ruth looked again at the OS map. The wallet was found ten minutes' walk from the bridge, so it had not been thrown from the top as the key possibly had. Emptying the wallet of cash and disposing of it quickly was a typical MO for a pickpocket. Did that mean they now had an additional offence to investigate? Had someone found the freshly dead body and helped themselves? Did she need to speak to that innocent-looking man with the gorgeous, equally innocent-looking spaniel, Kipper, again?

Or had Damon planted it there before mounting the bridge, in the same way that he had likely planted the key, shoe, cufflink, business cards, even his own body? Such a pattern of behaviour was designed to confuse and misdirect. When did Hough know that his days in Parliament were numbered? It certainly looked as though Charles Mallory had been going to make sure that Damon was not selected as a candidate to stand for the Party again, and Ruth had the impression that when Mallory took such a decision it stayed took. If Kate Mellor's evidence was true - and there was no reason to believe it was not - Damon must have known if he had broken the law on political funding and yet she still could not prove where the money had come from. It could be anything from winning the lottery to money laundering on behalf of a convicted criminal! If the source had been MEKANICK, then at whose instigation was he given the cash? If Hardman was absenting himself to distance himself from Damon, why had he waited five days to do so? Was the money 'hot' or legit? Did the company know the purpose for which Hough intended to use it? Did they approve? So many questions…

In more mundane mode the MP had just passed the big four-oh, a watershed age, and seen his life prospects changing - and not for the better.

Everything pointed to Damon Hough's death having been suicide, but something did not feel right. Why had so many red herrings been placed in their way? At long last there was some direct evidence that another person was possibly involved, the one who had first taken and then disposed of the wallet. Possibly. Might this new evidence justify keeping this case open?

The self-imposed deadline of Friday afternoon was over, the building was quiet. Ruth picked up her phone again and opened the text message that she had missed. It had arrived over an hour previously:

'Eric's dead. Coming in. Let's wrap this up. See you soon. A.'

Eric was dead… Ruth tried to remember whether she had ever met the man; she thought not, she knew him only by repute. The boss had rarely spoken of him and when she did her words were not overbrimming with compliments. But dead? Alison had not handled emotion too well previously, which was why she had needed so much time off in recent months. It was also why she had returned to work on a regime of - allegedly - 'light duties', which now included sorting the wheat from the chaff in the suspected suicide of a Member of Parliament.

Things were going to be different for Ruth from now on. Would the newly liberated Alison Allyson throw herself into the job with even more energy than usual or would she crack again under the strain?

The door opened and a familiar shape and voice entered the room.

'Hi Ruth. So, it's suicide, yes? Well done. Let's close the book.'

It was as though nothing unusual had happened.

'But first - let's go to the pub.'

'Boss, are you -'

'And we'll get pissed. Is that OK with you?'

The pub? Ruth thought for a moment. The person before her looked like her boss, though she had never heard such words from her before! But she was right. Any alternative to suicide as an explanation was just a theory, very light on evidence of motive, means or opportunity. It was clear that a large quantity of alcohol was what Alison needed and when a friend was in such need it would be churlish not to support them...

'Good to have you back, Boss. Condolences. Yes, let's do that.'

...

It was 6pm on Friday and Darren Ogenga looked at his phone. There was nothing from Ruth, but that was not surprising. He had told her he was working lates for the rest of the week; she would not want to disturb him. Plus, it was understood that as the electronic communication had been his initiative it was his responsibility to keep it going. All the same, it would have been nice to have seen her name, possibly with an 'x' beside it, on a text or a WhatsApp message, however brief. He could call her - as he had been anticipating doing this evening, but... how could he explain what had happened today?

In trying to help her he had made a fool of himself. He had behaved unprofessionally by doing the freelance thing and he could get in real trouble, especially if Lee Hardman made a complaint. The only consolation was that this was not very likely. Not likely at all, in fact. What was much more likely was that no one would ever hear of Mr Hardman, he of the apparently credible explanation for his meeting with Hough, ever again. The explanation would thus go unheard, for ever.

But the real quandary was not what might happen if Hardman complained, nor if Darren's superiors discovered that he had usurped the authority of his warrant card. It was what Ruth would think of him if she found out that he had scared her witness away. OK, it was a near certainty that Hough had killed himself, but what if it that was not the case? What if Hardman turned out to be a material witness or even, God forbid, the perp? Darren's actions would have screwed it up for Ruth and everybody else.

He could not claim that he knew Ruth well, but he so wanted to get to know her. Very much. He already had the sense that he was incapable of lying to her, of obscuring the truth or creating a fiction. Yes, he could try, but with one flash of that smile - it was the way her eyes smiled, not just her small and delicate mouth - he knew he would have to confess everything to her.

Confess how he had let her down. How he had dishonoured his professional code. How he might have wrecked her case.

He was not sure he could face that.

Not now. Not ever.

Alcohol Stimulates the Brain:

Friday 13th May

Alison's first drink, a large Malbec, barely touched the sides of her throat so Ruth was barely halfway through her own glass of Chardonnay when she found herself buying the second round. The conversation that did take place focused initially on trivia. Try as she might, Ruth could not tempt her boss - her friend - to talk about her home situation. She knew that Eric had been in a bad way in hospital - goodness, he must have been there over a year - and that Alison didn't visit him as often as she might. During much of the second drink they sat in silence. By the time it was Alison's turn to visit the bar again, Ruth's assessment was that the older woman was more relaxed than she had seen her for a while. Was that a release, a perverse response to bereavement, or a mirage? Could it simply be attributed to two glasses of Malbec? Who could tell?

Alison placed two fresh glasses on the table, one red and one white, along with two packets of crisps which they demolished in short order.

'Right. So, what's been happening with you, Ruth?'

The word 'Right' had been delivered in such a categorial manner that Ruth knew that no detail of the domestic circumstances of Alison Allyson, née Birkett, newly elevated to widowhood, was going to be forthcoming. The DC did as she was told and related every detail of what had transpired, concisely and logically, and what she had been thinking, being sure to distinguish between the two. She included the late additions of Kate's story, which would be in the paper on Sunday, the wallet discovered in the countryside and the possible evidence of cocaine in Damon's London flat. Alison listened politely and without interruption.

'Which means that a third party could have been involved: the person who took the wallet,' Ruth concluded.

Alison challenged her: 'Does it? How did it get where they found it?'

'Well, someone took the wallet, emptied it and abandoned it, whilst getting away from the scene as quickly as possible.'

'When did they do that?'

'Perhaps they took the wallet from the body.'

'So… after he was dead.'

Ruth hesitated. 'Or before.'

Alison considered the situation. 'I think that Hough has set out to build a scenario, to create a plot, a narrative. I think that's quite clear. The four cards are a set-up; like any good magician the manipulation of the cards is all about misdirection. The cards belong to - one - a man who may have supplied him over a period with money which might be related to criminal activities, given MEKANICK's previous, but we've no idea if it is or not. No one is alleging that it's definitely criminal, not even Kate Mellor. We can't find Hardman, but you've established that he no longer works for Campbell. That sounds legitimate, his contract has finished and it's not as if he rushed off the day after Hough died. Now, I would have thought, if I wanted to get some money back that I'd lent to someone, especially if it's ever so slightly dodgy, it's probably best that the person I lent it to stays alive. There have been no excessive or unusual transactions on Hough's bank account recently. If Hardman is running away, why did he not run earlier? Why is he going now? It's almost a week since the death.'

Ruth nodded. Alison continued.

'Another card is that of a fellow MP who knew him in their youth but there's nothing, as far as we can see, in the present day - except for a tad of political rivalry and a constituency turf war.' She glanced up at the ceiling briefly to dismiss the 'spat' between Roe and Hough. 'It's just fate that has them working in the same building.'

'Thousands of people work there.'

'As I say, fate. And then - thirdly - a woman who's not involved in his life today, or wasn't until she wrote a story about him, but that's only happening after his death. A woman with whom he had a relationship twenty years ago, which ended in tears. Didn't all relationships end that way, back then? Don't they all now?'

Ruth blanched. She hoped not everyone's emotional lives were like Alison's. She lived in hope, on that front. She vowed not to tell Alison yet about meeting Darren, and how much she liked him, until… until there was something to tell. Meanwhile: no comment.

'And that's it, Ruth. There's nothing else in his pockets. It's like we're acting on an almost empty stage.'

'And there's a reference to a bank account on the otherwise blank card.'

'But is it? We don't know that. You say that if you read the last six digits backwards it indicates the sort code of a bank in the Isle of Man, but they said the same about the Beatles' Abbey Road album cover.'

'Sorry?'

Alison smiled. 'Before your time. So, it indicates an account that doesn't exist. The sort code could be coincidence.'

'It could… but it's not unknown for naughty money to end up in tax havens.'

'…and when you give someone an account number it's for them to pay money into, not take money out of. If that's what it is, then someone wanted their money back.'

'Sure, but it doesn't tell us any more about Hough. Maybe he was going to give that card to someone.'

Alison gave a peremptory sigh and carried on. 'Perhaps. So, the wallet: it was found somewhere between the car and the scene. Hough could have left it there himself as yet another misdirection, deliberately emptied of cash, whilst making his way to the bridge. This adds to the mystery. This idea, that it's part of a set-up, would be consistent with you finding the car key where you did, which was lucky, and the - almost literally incredible - juxtaposition of the two cufflinks and the two shoes.'

'I suppose…'

'There's no evidence of a third party being present on the bridge.'

Ruth thought for a moment. 'No, you're right. There isn't,' she conceded. She smiled, after several moments of thinking hard. 'We've no reason to believe that Roe did Hough in over their tiff - or had him done in.'

'No, I agree. Of the three people associated with the business cards he's the one we know, for sure, was not in Derbyshire at the time.'

'We don't even know whether any of the three on the cards know each other,' Ruth added, 'though Mellor doesn't admit to knowing either of the men.'

'The evidence suggests that they don't.'

'But I think she's hiding something, boss. She's too bright to lie outright, it's what she didn't say that gives her away. What if Hardman was the one feeding her the story about the money?'

'What if he was, Ruth? Motive, Opportunity, Means. They're all missing, aren't they?'

'I guess so. They would all have needed Hough alive.'

'We have here a very troubled boy… he's got money troubles. Sex troubles, even identity troubles. Political troubles. The end of his career is looming.'

'We do.'

'Each one of those is a good enough reason for topping himself. Archetypal.'

'Yes…'

'Put them all together…'

'Yes, I see what you're saying, Boss.'

'Add a touch of moondust up the nostril every now and then… And the balance of his mind was disturbed, as they say.'

That phrase again.

'I guess so,' Ruth admitted.

'And someone is to blame for each of those problems, at least in Hough's eyes: the money is Lee Hardman, presumably, the politics, Paul Roe. Or Charles Mallory. Or both. The sex is complex. He's gay but he's not out, the only long-term relationship - longish - he's ever had is with a woman, but that was ages ago. He chooses to hire rent boys these days. In the set-up, sex is represented by Kate Mellor but she's not indicative of his current issues, nor is she involved with him today, or for the last twenty years. He blames each of these three for a different aspect of his quandary - but that doesn't mean any of them killed him. Unless they formed a committee.'

'We're missing someone, Boss.'

'Who?'

'His father. Sex again. He hated his father, who was homophobic. He killed himself almost on the anniversary of his father doing the same.'

'His father wasn't a member of that committee, that we do know!'

'No, of course. But Damon was deeply troubled by his relationship with his father, both Mallory and Mellor said that. Classic frustrated gay suicide stuff, isn't it?'

'Hmm, Mallory…' Alison considered the Chief Whip. 'The first thing he said to me was that he didn't know if Damon's parents were still alive or not; then suddenly remembered that one killed himself and the other died of cancer.'

'And he's Damon's godfather!'

Alison smiled dismissively. 'Rum lot, politicians… but I don't buy Mallory building up the psychological pressure on Hough to force him into suicide. Do you?'

'No…' Ruth had to admit she knew little about the world of Chief Whips. 'Damon can't have felt very fulfilled by his sex life, can he?' Fulfilling sex was important to Ruth, but it could only come about with the right person, was her view, after a limited amount of research. She wondered if that person would prove to be Darren… But more to the point Ruth wondered if 'fulfilled sex lives' was an appropriate thing to talk about with Alison, given her recent loss of an apparently unfulfilling partner? She had said it now, she had to continue. 'I mean, young boys? Immature human beings, a different one every… every time? I just don't know how someone can do that. It must be desperately sad.'

Alison did not appear to be upset by the raising of the subject. 'There were many reasons for Damon to feel inadequate, a failure. Mallory as good as told me Hough had no prospects, with a good chance of being de-selected - not being allowed to stand as a Tory candidate - at the next election.'

There followed the silence that comes with three glasses of wine and a need to contemplate.

'So, we think it was suicide,' Ruth concluded.

Alison sort of nodded.

Her junior mused 'But why Derbyshire? Why go all that way?'

'I don't know. My guess is that he's been to the bridge before, our boy's a bit of a walker, a rambler. It's such a… unique landscape, a stage for a spectacular finale, almost in private, at that time of day, which draws some parallels with his father's suicide.'

'Father's was different, it was very public - hanging from a bridge over a main road.'

Alison shook her head. 'But he wouldn't have wanted it exactly like his father's. Father and son had a lifetime of mistrust, a very poor relationship.'

'Twenty years ago. I was at primary school…!'

'Yes, a long time ago. But you know what, Ruth? We haven't answered everything.'

'You mean like, why did he have the car valeted?'

'No, not an issue. MPs don't use their cars a lot during the week, his vehicle stayed in the Parliament car park most of the time. He didn't go to his constituency that often. The valeting may not have happened in the last few days, maybe he had it done before he decided to make his exit. It looked freshly done, but it didn't smell like it.'

'That's true. So why did he make it so difficult to retrieve the car by throwing the key away?'

'Why not? It adds to the intrigue. He wasn't planning to use it again. I don't have a categorical answer to that, but I don't think we need one. Even so, after all that, there's still something that's bothering me...'

'What's that, Boss?'

'I've been thinking.'

Their glasses were empty again, so Ruth bit her tongue to hold back a witty response: 'Don't you mean drinking?' They should have bought their wine by the bottle; it would have worked out cheaper. Instead, she simply said 'What about?'

'Blood and dust.'

'Is that by EM Forster? I did him for 'A' level. Or is it a western?'

Alison smiled. 'I spoke to the laboratory this morning.'

'Oh?'

'I hadn't spotted it before, and I didn't put two and two together... The dust could be part of the set up, but the blood...'

'Sorry, I don't understand.'

The empty glasses were forgotten.

'Ruth, you thought that the ground on top of the bridge might be showing signs of a struggle. That was your judgment, but proof was very difficult. It was dusty after a long spell of dry weather but overnight it rained, so finding that sort of evidence on the following day was never going to be possible. There were scuff marks on the shoe that was left behind, there was a cufflink lost and he left his phone up top, too. Those things could all have resulted from a struggle. Throwing the key over the side might also indicate that there had been an argument.'

Ruth took over: 'But equally, they could all be signs of this elaborate set up.'

'Yes, they could. And so could the dust.'

Ruth did not follow. 'Explain about the dust, please?'

'There was limestone dust on his suit -'

'He fell onto rubble and stones, it was a dry day, so of course there was dust.'

'That would explain the dust on his back, as a result of the fall. Or on his front, depending on which way he fell after, as we know, he landed on his head.' With her right hand Alison mimed the descent of a body, head first, impacting upon the table and crumpling before toppling, adding sound effects. 'But there was dust on both his front and his back, and on his shoulders and elsewhere too. As though he'd been rolling over and over in it.'

'Couldn't that also be part of the set up?'

'If so, he's really thought this through, hasn't he? You didn't spot any marks that could have been blood up on top, did you?'

Ruth hesitated for a moment. 'No. No, I didn't. And then the rain overnight…'

'Sure. SOCO didn't find any, either.'

'If I had found blood up top, then… he would have been bleeding before he fell.'

'Precisely! And there was blood on both of his hands. A lot. I remember seeing it, and you can see it on the photos, too. I didn't understand the significance at first, it only came to me yesterday, out of the blue. So, I asked the lab: was it Damon Hough's own blood that was on his hands? And they said yes, it was.'

Ruth joined in: 'If it had been someone else's blood, then we'd have a definite second person - and a way of identifying them.'

'I didn't think it would be. And it wasn't. Then I asked if there were any wounds on his hands, where the blood could have come from; and they said no.'

'I don't recall that there was a lot of blood, but… didn't he land with one hand underneath him?'

'Yes! And we didn't spot it!'

'The hand,' Ruth went on, 'that was underneath him - his left hand, wasn't it? - was against his tummy. It was a long way from his face, from where he was bleeding.'

'Exactly, Ruth! You made the same point, exactly, about the shoe! You said it couldn't be underneath him because that would mean it had fallen before he had! Think, Ruth! How could a bloody hand - I mean, a hand covered with blood - be underneath him, underneath his belly, no less, if the only wound inflicted was by the impact, which was focused on his head?'

'Well… it couldn't…'

'So, I asked the lab again - were there any defensive wounds anywhere on the body?'

'And?'

'There were none.'

'The pendulum swings again, Boss. An absence of evidence of an attack.'

'The only wound he had was the massive trauma to the head.'

Ruth recalled what she had seen, the spaniel, pulling on his lead, desperate to lick at the blood. 'And what a wound that was... instant death.'

'Exactly. The hands - certainly, the one underneath him - could not have come into contact with his face and head after he had fallen. He had no other wounds. He must have been bleeding, quite profusely, from somewhere on his head, before he fell off the bridge. There had to be two wounds to the head: one before the fall, which discharged enough blood to mess up both of his hands, and the other, the big one, caused by the fall, so massive that it obliterated any trace of the first wound.'

'And that sounds like chance. It doesn't sound like part of a set-up.'

'Exactly, Ruth.' The older woman was not excited in any normal sense of the word, but she was alert, thinking, stimulated by the narrative.

'So the blood that was on his hands... had to have come from his head. Could it have been self-inflicted?'

The Inspector raised an eyebrow in a manner that said 'Who knows?'. A short period of silence ensued.

'Boss, what do we do now?' asked Ruth.

'We've been on this for a week. Do we have a case that we can take to the CPS?'

'No.'

'No.' The Inspector counted off on her fingers: 'Motive, opportunity, means. There are no clear motives, not enough opportunities and any evidence pertaining to the means is hidden by the consequence of the impact of the fall on his head. There's no evidence that points to anything but suicide.'

Ruth smiled ruefully. 'I was all ready to say 'let's close the case', a definite suicide. But the bloody hands…'

Again, Alison said nothing. Then Ruth had a thought: suddenly she said 'Nosebleed!'

Alison stood immediately, putting down her empty glass and moving round the table to her junior's side. Suddenly sober, she said: 'Put your head back, let me pinch the bridge of your nose!'

A surprised Ruth raised her hands in a defensive posture and Alison ceased her approach: 'No, not me, Boss! Damon Hough! He stuck a fingernail up his nose. He bashed himself in the face, whatever. When you get a nosebleed you can get a lot of blood - some people produce a hell of a lot - and it still leaves them capable of jumping off the bridge!'

'There's no evidence of a nosebleed.'

'There's precious little evidence of a nose, Boss.'

'Well, that's true…'

'Where was the blood spatter on his shirt?'

'I don't remember, and I didn't ask the lab.'

Alison resumed her seat and there was another sharing of silence. Would another glass be taking things too far?

'Boss?'

'Yes?'

What happened next would determine whether the operation would be put to bed or scaled up. If they scaled it up it would become very public indeed, an investigation into the murder of a Member of Parliament.

The silence was becoming both prolonged and profound, hiding much rapid thinking of surprising clarity, given the quantity of alcohol already consumed.

Ruth broke the silence: 'You know what? It was suicide.'

Alison thought for a further moment. 'Suicide. Agreed.' Then 'Ruth?'

'Yes?'

'Another one?'

'Why not? Same again. Please, boss.'

Action Replay:
Saturday 7th May 2022

Damon's phone was ringing incessantly. Whoever was trying to get hold of him, Heaven knows how many times over the last hour, was certainly insistent.

He could hear it ringing but it was early on a Saturday morning, and they could fucking wait. Last night he'd been on a bender involving red wine, whisky and just a single tab of ecstasy, then the boys had come back to his flat in Pimlico. The earlier part of the evening had followed a familiar pattern, with familiar faces: starting at the Spanish bar, where he matched the boys drink for drink. In a private booth at the second club he had kissed the Mexican boy, but the Mexican boy had to leave to fulfil a booking at a Mayfair hotel at midnight. After that the two younger ones came back to his flat for whisky and cocaine.

The cocaine was a magnet; contrary to the reputation he had earned amongst this circle, Damon was not a big user. Bizarrely, he preferred reality. He did enjoy watching the boys snorting, drinking, stripping and touching each other. Only occasionally did he join in, though no-one ever asked why he held back; when he did engage with them physically, he was urgent, dominant, with no frills and no nonsense. But not last night.

He knew that the odds were against this sort of lifestyle remaining secret in a public figure for ever but, so far, master luck had been on his side. And when you're on a lucky streak…

Damon recalled the family breakfast table, on a morning that must have been in 1994. His father was reading the Telegraph, as ever, when he suddenly became agitated, gripped by a story on an inside page. Apoplectic, he threw the paper to the floor and spat out a bad word. This most unusual behaviour earned pa one of ma's withering 'not at the table' looks. His father muttered 'Disgusting pervert', retrieved the periodical shamefacedly and ensured that the breakfast moved on in silence. Once the ritual of the meal was over, the intrigued 12-year-old looked up 'pervert' in a dictionary; his imagination stimulated, he retrieved the paper from the bin. It took but a few moments to locate the story which had upset the man of the house. From that day on, Damon was both haunted and fascinated by his imagined vision of the naked body of a Member of Parliament dangling by the neck from a beam. The man wore only a pair of women's stockings, he had a black bin liner over his head and a complete orange clenched between his teeth. He was a victim of fatal autoerotic asphyxiation (more words that Damon had to look up). He was determined never, ever, to be caught in such a cameo.

With the emphasis on 'caught'.

He had kicked the boys out early, shortly after two. Still fully clothed, Damon instructed the naked youths to dress which they did with impressively well-rehearsed speed. Then he followed them into the street, hailed a taxi for them and paid the driver in advance, in cash, from the wad in his wallet. It was always best to have a supply of used notes for weekends. He was in bed and asleep well before three. Friday nights could be a hell of a lot worse than this. Come to think, much of Thursday night (drinking until the early hours) and Friday (sleeping throughout the morning, walking in Hyde Park to clear his head in the afternoon) had been lost, but Friday night would not be.

Where had his appetite for parties gone? Damon was planning to spend another whole morning in bed but now the bloody phone was ringing once more. He ignored it again: who did they think they were? Who was daring to call him at this ungodly hour?

He looked at the clock; it was approaching 7.30. He had slept for little more than four hours. That was not good enough, for a Saturday, not good enough at all. He rolled over, plumped his pillow, pulled the duvet around him and curled up, closing his eyes.

His life was falling apart. It was not just that the sex parties were no longer as exciting, as fulfilling, as they used to be, but politics was not doing it for him anymore, either. The thrill had gone; as with drugs, with politics (he had found) repeated over-stimulation wears away the sensors and the senses.

He had succeeded in his goal of creating a group of ruthless populists on the Tory back benches, modelled on the early Bannon/Trump era but without the same mistakes - but without achieving the same degree of influence. This anarchic sump of rebellion had, predictably, prompted a hostile reaction within the Party from the few remaining pathetic wets on the moderate wing, and the bloody Whips were seriously organising against him, too. Some of the more politically vulnerable Members on the fringe of Damon's pack had been subjected to deliberate and sustained undermining from the powers that be for months - and it was working. Damon's core support on the back benches had been ebbing away for some time, leaving fewer than a dozen in the cabal. They were, unfortunately, not the dozen he would have chosen as his disciples.

He knew who was behind his undermining. It was his own damn father, coming back to haunt him through the person of Charles Mallory, his alleged godfather, the Chief Whip. It was twenty years since Damon, then a student, had discovered that this bloody fool, then merely an obscure Tory backbencher, had been the guest of honour at the funeral of the late and detested Gerald Hough. Mallory had sat in the place that should have been reserved for Damon himself, the son and heir, on the front pew of the village church in Dorset. Damon's desire, however, was not to say 'farewell' to his father but 'go to Hell'. In deference to his mother, he had therefore diplomatically absented himself from the departure ceremony. Having taken the place of the distant, disgraced and disgraceful son on that occasion, was Mallory attempting to move seamlessly into the role of surrogate parent and his mother's secret companion? Like hell! That was not going to happen.

When Damon returned to the family home that evening the wake at which Mallory had deputised for the funereal host was long over. 'Charles has been a true friend to your father,' said the furious widow, recently diagnosed with cancer, through clenched teeth. There was malice in her eyes, an evil that he had never seen from her before as she spat out: 'Which is more than can ever be said of you!'

Two years later she died, after months of suffering and hospitalisation, a period during which her only child was largely absent. He was determined not to miss her, her slavish support of her evil husband having earned her no credit in Damon's eyes, nor her proximity to Mallory. At least the boy did attend her funeral, by contrast a small, family affair. Mallory arrived late, notably red-eyed and subdued. He sat at the rear of the church and declined to come back to the house afterwards.

Only upon reflection during her period of dying had Damon finally put several twos together: 'Uncle Charles' was not his uncle, not his surrogate father, nor the widow's official post-bereavement companion: nevertheless, he had probably been screwing her for years. It must have started before she was diagnosed with cancer, which meant… he was screwing her before Gerald had died. Did Gerald know? Maybe he did; maybe the three of them…? Mallory was an evil bastard, who clearly did not always play by the rules… respect! Was that why Gerald had killed himself? Had he found out what was going on? Had he been party to it, but fallen out with Mallory? Was that why he killed himself when he did, without waiting for the cancer to take his wife first, the route a loving husband would surely have taken?

At the time of his mother's death the graduate was in the process of learning the practice of law as a very junior member of a big law firm. Here he felt, for the first and only time in his life, out of his depth.

Another ally of Damon's late father was a solicitor, James Steel, a more benign and laid-back character than Mallory. He was not as close to the family as the MP, not close enough to merit a round trip of over two hundred miles to attend Gerald's funeral. The undemonstrative Steel only came to the forefront of Damon's field of vision in 2007.

Steel was much less judgmental about the boy than others in the family circle. Though he was on occasional speaking terms with Mallory, by default the bland Steel kept his distance from the more driven politician. The lawyer took the young man under his professional wing, easing his passage from the big hive in the metropolis to a small-town practice by creating a position for him within his own firm. Steel called his profession 'soliciting', his idea of a slightly smutty joke, one which became less funny with each re-telling. 'Soliciting 101', according to Steel, went as follows: choose the right community, play golf with the right people, support the right charities - oh, and be a diligent legal practitioner who avoids cockups. Follow that course and you will go far in the law. Talent was of secondary importance, he would joke, in an oft-told self-deprecating quip. Settling into the elderly lawyer's nest Damon did as he was told, the first and only phase in his adult life where he was content to learn second fiddle at the master's knee. That situation pertained only for a while as the young man had by then vowed that politics, not the law, was to be his chosen career. He bided his time and readied himself to take the opportunity when it came.

A year before Damon came on the scene the elderly and largely inactive Mr Grey retired from the law firm. Steel, as the only remaining partner now that both Grey brothers had gone, decided to add to the numbers. Thus 'Grey & Steel' became 'Steel & Partners'. The first incomer thus recruited was Alice Brain, a bouncy, northern lass. Her husband was starting a new job in The City, so she was looking for work much closer to home, here in the commuter belt. As the office was situated five minutes' walk from her baby-making production line (three delivered successfully so far) Steel & Partners ticked every box for Alice. Her speciality was conveyancing, the business' bread and butter. She could manage property transfers with her eyes shut and hands tied behind her back. If the two men fell under the same bus Alice's contribution to the practice alone would keep it viable; it was based in a town of owner occupiers with a home counties premium on house prices to cushion them. Steel felt nervously proud of recruiting 'a lady solicitor' to the team, as he never stopped mentioning at social gatherings ('We have a lady solicitor now, you know'). Some years later, to fill the space that Damon's elevation to MP had partly vacated, Steel went even further into the field labelled 'progress'. He plucked up courage and recruited, erm… the petite Indian woman whose name he could never remember. He knew that there had been an Indian cricketer with the same surname, but he could not recall which one it was; it wasn't Tendulkar, that was for sure. Nevertheless, she fitted in, too. The two females were industrious, conscientious and generally quiet; Steel had chosen well.

Steel, now over 60, led the practice from the front. When Damon declared his desire to try for selection for the Parliamentary seat that was coming available in the next constituency, the head of the partnership supported him without question. Steel was thrilled by Damon's commitment to the Conservative cause but channelled his enthusiasm (a rare emotion in the Steel household) into supporting his young proxy. He must not overdo it, risk blunting the hunger that the young man needed to win, even in a seat regarded as a natural Tory hegemony. The candidate selection would be competitive, and he would not clip Hough's wings. In his youth Steel had toyed with the idea of representing the Party himself at the highest level, but a natural shyness had held him back. Such reticence departed him only later in life, when he became a partner at Grey & Steel. (In the 1980s they had resisted forcibly the advice, offered for free by an image consultant working for the Party, to change the firm's name to the more dynamic 'Steel Grey'. The name was about as ridiculous as the oversized shoulder pads that the consultant insisted upon wearing).

Damon realised that he was becoming the son Steel had never had and was doubly grateful: once for the indulgence, the latitude that the old man allowed him, and secondly that the boring old fart wasn't trying to over-parent him as his surrogate father. No one could take the place in the son's esteem that was held by that... bastard.

So: Steel pulled strings, arranged meetings, dragged an appreciative ward around Tory coffee mornings, had him photographed next to the right people, the works. Damon's selection as Conservative candidate in late 2008 progressed like a well-oiled machine, as did his subsequent election to Parliament in May 2010, aged just 28.

The older man continued to indulge the younger over the years that followed. Although he did not need to pay the newly elected MP a retainer from the practice he chose to do so, desirous of both registering his support in a tangible way and encouraging the young man to keep one foot on the ground in the firm. Should Damon ever need a professional bolt hole in future, somewhere safe and profitable to retreat into, it would be there for him. Heaven forbid, perhaps one day in the distant future the Tories might lose an election... Steel also had to consider that he would not lead the practice for ever, but could not bring himself to regard either of the women as his heir.

When Damon eventually arrived in Parliament 'Uncle Charles', formerly of the family circle and already a junior Whip, greeted him politely if formally, eight years after the unfortunate funeral. Was it a guilty welcome? Damon determined that he would never raise the matter of what happened between his mother's bedsheets - it would be the secret that they would never acknowledge, the silent power that he believed he held over Charles Mallory. There was a tacit agreement not to mention any of the bonds that bound Mallory to the Hough family; thus, Damon's carnality theory was never tested.

Without showing overt preference Mallory had eased the novice into his new role on the back benches and spoken to him paternally about building ambition upon the need to do things properly. It soon became clear that 'doing things properly' was not Damon's forte but for a while, at least, his excesses did not break the unwritten code - by too much.

Steel allowed the MP to come and go as he wished from the practice from May 2010, the only condition being that he put fifty billable hours each year for the firm's clients, enabling Steel's accountant to tick some box on a tax form. From Damon's point of view, it became necessary, after a few years, to be seen to have a second income from the law in case he was ever required to explain his lavish lifestyle, his generous charity donations and his pleasant riverside cottage in the constituency. In practice he rarely used the facility, realising both that it was not the private and secluded haven that he thought it would be and that his 'friends' preferred the rush of the metropolis to the rustic peace of the countryside. The rent (which was paid to a party donor friend of Steel's) was not cheap but at least he could reclaim it from the Parliamentary authorities. He much preferred the anonymity of Pimlico, where he had wisely bought a flat at the start of his post-University career. He also enjoyed rental income from two apartments in Eastbourne, inherited from a childless uncle shortly after his mother had died.

Steel neither cared nor asked about Damon's private life, making it clear to the young man that he did not want to know about anything that was not 'mainstream' and reaffirming his belief in the eleventh commandment: 'don't get caught'. Although Damon's 'patch' was next door to the one where the law practice was based, he declined to accept cases from his own constituents. Avoiding potential conflicts of interest was smart and Indira Sharma tended to pick up such referrals. This caused Indira to occasionally indulge in strategic sighing in meetings, hinting that, in her view, Damon was not earning his salt. Once, she even raised her eyes significantly towards the ceiling at the mention of his name. On such occasions Steel would put more work her way, from his own portfolio rather than Damon's already light one, to keep her busy.

Over recent years Damon had managed to generate some side income. Each of his four elderly 'targets', ladies with incipient dementia, netted him a grand or so a year through monthly retainers, and when their disease inevitably went full blown he found he could boost that income. It was like taking candy… until the mischievous Paul Roe came along, making trouble. Fortunately, there was nothing the Labour MP could do about it. Mrs Smith's granting of her Power of Attorney to Damon was legally watertight and although he could easily ditch her if things got bumpy, he would not be falling at the first fence. That would be against his principles. His income from Hilda Smith had trebled but her capital was growing in a very healthy manner, despite the rising cost of the care home. It was a perfectly sustainable, win-win, arrangement, before Roe threatened to derail it. £300 a month for a couple of hours work a year? The old woman could afford it.

Damon never believed in justifying himself to anybody. In the Smith case he could demonstrate that since he had been 'overseeing' her portfolio it had grown, though in reality he had barely touched it. Why should he have to explain his actions? The grasping daughter would get her share when the grim reaper called, inheriting more than she would have got if the PoA had been signed over to her (or so he would claim), so what did she have to worry about? If pushed, he would report that the rise in charges, to a comfortable £3,600 a year, had taken place after a 'general reassessment of the partnership's fee structure'. Such a process had indeed taken place; over a period of five long minutes when sitting in his comfortable Porsche in a rural traffic jam at a road works where the traffic lights had failed. When he presented the outcome of the review to the head of the firm as a *fait accompli* Steel had acquiesced without demur.

Paul Roe, however, clearly had a conscience - a potentially dangerous thing. His bleeding heart jeopardised Damon's success. The money did not motivate Roe - how could it, as neither Roe nor the daughter knew how much Hilda was really worth, how affordable Damon's fee was or, thus, what excellent value the solicitor was providing to his client. It would be the way the PoA was obtained that had caught his imagination. 'I'd be asking questions if it were me, for sure,' Damon conceded to himself, 'but everything I did was above board. I blame the snow. It can be terrible, the weather around here…'

The phone rang again. For Christ's sake. Reverie broken, he dragged himself out of bed.

By the time he located his phone and picked it up the ringing had stopped. Shit. The call had come from a withheld number, the previous ones likewise. He threw it onto the bed. Time for coffee. As a concession to the world, the daylight and the whole human race, which was apparently awake, alert and queuing up to contact him this morning, he would make himself a strong Dutch brew.

Roe was not going to let go, Damon could see that. The Labour man was a shadow minister now, with a reputation of being personally nice, devastatingly reasonable and smoothly effective: a real pain in the arse. However, it had been a mistake to threaten him, Damon conceded. That lunchtime, two days previously, he had been angry following his meeting with Lee Hardman. His symbolic burning of Roe's letter in a drunken rage on that same Thursday evening, local election day, was also an error. He had barely read the epistle before igniting it so could not be certain what his former friend was accusing him of doing. However, his guess that he was being asked to surrender the PoA, and thus his income, was correct.

Go take a walk, Roe.

Damon thought back to the day of the cross-country race: sweet, innocent, Paul Roe, 14 years old, so anxious to be liked that it was sickening. Taking advantage of that smooth faced, skinny boy was like taking candy from a diabetic baby: it was doing him a favour. He supposed they probably had been friends - otherwise why had Paul allowed Damon to touch him? To hug him and kiss his neck? To let him put his hand down inside someone else's trousers, for the very first time… of so many! And to keep it there, gently groping, for… thirty seconds? So much can be achieved in thirty seconds. Although Paul allowed Damon to get so very close that day, he never came near to him again. Oh, well. You win some, some can just piss off. Paul had been a skinny bag of bones, a skeleton marionette. Damon would discover, as his teenage experiences became deeper and more varied, that he preferred a little more meat on the bone, something he could get his teeth into. Metaphorically. The deletion of young Paul Roe from Damon's friendship circle, Roe's response to that summer's day, had been no great loss; if anything, it provided a springboard. Putting it another way, later life with no genuine friends at all had not worked out too badly for Damon Hough.

Shaking off his reverie again, Damon took his coffee back to bed, piling his pillows high. He retrieved the phone from the duvet and placed it on the bedside table, noting that there were now a total of seven missed calls. Could he really have slept through seven in the course of this morning? It looked as though none had left a message.

No, he had not missed seven: two originated not from last night but from late on Thursday. He must have been so out of it throughout Friday that he had not checked his phone. One said it was from Paul Roe - he would ignore that one - whilst the other had been identified by his phone as from Kate Mellor. Who was that? Kate is a common name, so is Mellor. No matter. He put the phone back down on the bedside table.

Kate Mellor!

Of course, there was a Kate Mellor in his contacts list, but it was a name from prehistory, a rave, as it were, from the grave… People change their phones often, perhaps every two years or so, but they always keep the same number, surely? How long had that number been in his phone? It must be 20 years… Surely this was a mistake. Not an error in his phone, of course, you do not pay that sort of money for a device that makes things up. It was her mistake. If she was in his list, then he was likely still in hers. Howard. Horton. Hollinsclough. There were any number of names she might have wanted to call but she must have pressed Hough in error.

Her mistake. Again. No, her mistake had been to love him in the first place, if indeed she had. Did she? There was no message, it had clearly been a mistake. That call was her mistake. Spending so much time with Kate was a mistake, trying to be, pretending to be someone other than who he was, someone he would never be, was a mistake. He had been pretending for the sake of his fucking parents; now that was a big mistake! So many mistakes. Kate was a mistake.

End of story.

Except... it was not Kate's mistake.

He looked again at his smartphone. The list combined calls made with those received. At 10pm on Thursday night, election night, the night before last, it was he who had tried to call her! Thank shit she had not picked up... Almost disbelieving, he checked his contacts app and there she was, twenty years after he had last spoken to her. Twenty years since he had last thought of her; no, that was not quite true. Sometimes when he fastened those cheap, crappy cufflinks onto his shirt, the ones with the scabby clover leaves, she appeared in his thoughts for a nanosecond - but never in his conscience. He was aware that she had become a journalist and, a few years later, a columnist. He had found that out by osmosis, it was not that he cared about her or her poxy career, not that he was the slightest bit interested...

Damon had developed an annoying tendency to lose cufflinks over the years. It was a professional hazard. He had lost good ones, expensive ones, unique ones, cufflinks with important memories attached. A brightly coloured pair from Nepal and a pair with deep blue stones from Cambodia were particularly regrettable losses. As with socks and gloves, however, he would never lose a complete pair - over the years he had accumulated a cornucopia of solo cufflinks, which he kept in a drawer in his sideboard. Losing cufflinks happened far too easily when you found yourself tearing off your shirt and getting ready for action at short notice as often as Damon did, which is why he had taken to wearing the ones with clover leaves so often. That way, he calculated, he would not care if he lost one; they meant nothing to him. But clover is associated with luck and, sure enough, once he started to wear them regularly, he never lost one again. This was truly Sod's law in action.

He thought back to Thursday, local election day. Bloody Lee Hardman had got the day off to a crap start, which upset Damon for the whole day. He'd remained in London instead of going back to the patch for election evening, but they could manage without him. That evening he had got himself very drunk, so drunk that he had no memory of getting home to his flat; no memory of trying to make that call to Kate Mellor, certainly no memory of any reason for doing so. Given the mood he had been in, after what Hardman had done, it was just as well he had not spoken to a journalist that day…

And then there was Guy Campbell. He had never met the man, but back in 2010 he had no reason not to trust the recommendation of their mutual colleague, Lee Hardman. Five years you can have the money for, Lee had said, at least five years, no questions asked, an interest free loan. Fine by me, thought Damon, and made the necessary arrangements. He told Steel that a significant amount of money would be coming into a client account and hanging around there for a while, earning interest. Steel asked no questions, he wanted Damon to believe that he was a man of the world who trusted his apprentice. Three quarters of a million duly came his way, tied to three meaningless contracts, and looking after it was easy-peasy. Take care of it, share any profit, give the capital back in five years or whenever the heat had gone, whichever was later. That was Guy's deal, as brokered by Lee. Things had worked out differently, over a longer timescale, but they had worked to Damon's advantage. Until now.

Within the firm only Damon and Steel knew about the money, the women were in blissful ignorance. One tranche was designated as a loan to help the partnership expand and move to new premises, though there was never any intention of doing either. This morning Damon could not remember the alleged logic behind the other two. Something about paying for advice, maybe? The cash had started to bear fruit quite quickly, even those pounds that were in a simple deposit account earned interest. However base rate, at around five percent before the crash, started to fall and showed no signs of recovering. Damon soon considered that something more clever, useful, practical, was needed. Over the years interest rates tumbled further, but so long as they were positive, and the remaining duration of the loan was long, things would work out OK…

After Campbell's tough sentence the term of the loan was extended to ten years, and it had since passed eleven. It was Christmas Day every day. Gross compound interest over that period at, say, 4 percent, would create a profit of £460,000. Not that it was easy to get 4 percent alongside flexibility of withdrawal, but there were ways.

The only problem was... politics was Damon's passion and politicians are much better at spending money than conserving it.

The timing of the loan was perfect: Damon was able to 'release' tranches of money to support his election campaigns in 2015, 2017 and 2019 and the pro-Brexit campaign in the 2016 referendum. Election spending rules are frustrating because they limit opportunities to oil the system's cogs without being seen to be doing so; it was crucial to strike before each election period started, before the watchdogs arose from their slumbers. In 2010 the Coalition Government had pledged to serve a full five years, so Damon allocated a budget calibrated to boost his profile from late 2014, before the formal reporting period started. The referendum was a different matter; even though only a few months' notice of the poll was given it was easy to pour several relatively modest thousands into a variety of pro-Brexit, pro-Leave organisations. The money flowed like cheap wine at a sponsored charity reception.

The idea of creating a charity to serve his constituents' needs had come from something a Tory colleague had said over dinner at a spontaneous informal gathering of MPs in the Members' Dining Room one night. A moderate Conservative, whom Damon categorised as 'sanctimonious', had been telling colleagues about constituents who lived chaotic lives. Another, who happened to have a physics degree, was prompted to mention 'entropy', describing it as a measure of the chaos within a physical system. He threatened to demonstrate his point using a plate bearing the House of Commons crest:

'If I drop this plate, which is made up of an orderly collection of particles, not just grains of porcelain but molecules and, indeed, atoms, there's an energy transfer when it hits the ground. The noise you hear indicates this, and the chances are that you'll see it break into thousands of pieces,' explained the scientist.

'Damon's a sceptic, he'll want to count them!' said a wag, to laughter.

'But if I took those thousand pieces of plate and dropped them, what are the chances that upon collision with the floor they would recombine to recreate the original plate?'

'Zero', they agreed, 'Even smaller pieces,' said another, who understood.

'That's not just because some of the kinetic energy in the fall was converted to the noise energy you hear upon impact, but some was lost as heat at that point, too. Entropy is that lost heat energy, if you like, it explains why ultimately everything tends towards chaos - unless order, powered by energy from an external source, is applied to it.'

'Everything tends towards chaos, eh? Leave the last Labour Government out of this!' somebody chipped in, to great hilarity.

The plate was saved from chaos and Damon had learnt a new word, a powerful force of nature. The Entropy Foundation was born and registered as a charity.

Even better, whenever Damon transferred what appeared to be his own money into the charity the gift was tax deductible. And whenever money was taken out of the charity's account there was Damon alongside a smiling recipient, close to someone with a camera and, frequently, a large, plastic, reusable Entropy cheque, commissioned for that very purpose.

Temptation eventually overwhelmed Damon as £40,000 of Guy's money found its way to a sympathetic car dealer in exchange for a Porsche Macan, his pride and joy. When challenged that the vehicle was not British made, he laughed it off: 'Well, that's the free market at work - but the dealer was English!' He was indeed. In fact, he was a member of the English Defence League who offered very generous discounts to handpicked senior Conservatives across three counties.

Damon opened his eyes and reached for the breakfast coffee, which had cooled more than he had anticipated; this was entropy at work once more. Perhaps he had dozed. At 40 years and five days he was getting too old for constant partying; that must explain both his failure to sleep properly this morning and his inability to shake it off and get up. But the caffeine, even cool, was starting to do its job, stimulating his nerve cells.

'Fuck Charles Mallory,' he said aloud, then 'Fuck Lee Hardman.' Then, to himself: 'Who do they think they are, making this week a misery? Fuck Paul Roe, if it comes to that. Insolent sod. How I conduct my affairs is none of his fucking business.'

Someone from the Whips' Office had phoned him early on the Thursday afternoon, the fifth, summoning him to meet the Chief Whip at close of play. Damon had thought immediately that this was odd: the Chief would not know about his morning's duel with Lee, nor the spat with Roe at lunchtime, would he? The way Damon led his backbench followers down their populist road was a standing point of conflict between him and Mallory, but there was nothing urgent about that. The group opposed some government policy on principle - the principle being that it was government policy. Another principle that Hough's 'gang' lived by was 'we can annoy the leadership, so we will'.

So, what was there to talk about?

The men in Damon's group - they were all men - operated a concerted social media presence through which they objected to multiculturalism, demanded that England be given the same rights to self-determination as the Scots and opposed any (and all) big government spending projects. They believed that small government was a proper if rare tenet of 'true Conservatism'. They had called for the legalisation of heroin in a Westminster Hall debate, arguing that Britain used to profit from selling opium to China, so why not profit from the equivalent contemporary trade? It was a philosophy more in tune with George III's Tories than those of the present day. Such stand-offs sparked social media interest that regularly proved embarrassing to the Government. On occasion ministers even had to defend their policies on Newsnight, not against the official opposition but in a debate with a 'Houghian' - a Hough ruffian - the group's unofficial but favoured description. Members of the group, which had once peaked at almost twenty, spoke at events in each other's constituencies, praised each other's stances on topical issues, generally seemed to be enjoying themselves. They were 'political surfers', according to one pundit, riding any right-wing wave they could find. Meanwhile they often defied the Whip with impunity just, it seemed, for the hell of it. The Government's majority was rarely in danger and Mallory was prepared to tolerate a bit of mischief; he understood that Damon was leading the group because it was a laugh, not because he was about to organise a coup. But now, with an election on the horizon, it was time to draw stumps on the revellers, a confrontation Mallory was not anticipating with any degree of pleasure. Up to now his plan was to undermine the Hough faction with subtle and sustained action; he had already persuaded several on the fringe of Houghianism to pull back from the brink.

A week earlier, Damon had been to the Commons' hair salon for a trim (a necessity) and a shave (an indulgence). Preened and pleased and peppered with eau de Cologne, the peacock left Fabio, the proprietor, a generous tip and departed from the basement enterprise satisfied. Fabio reached for a long-handled brush but, before sweeping away the Hough offcuts, he bent down on his haunches and, with a tissue, selected a pinch of pale blonde hair. He took a small, plain envelope from behind a mirror and placed the tissue and its contents into it. Fabio invited the next customer to sit but, before serving him, picked up the internal telephone and dialled.

'Chief Whip's office.'

'This is Fabio, from... Yes. It's ready to collect. Thank you.'

On Thursday the gloves had come off in a battle which was part of an ongoing war. When Damon arrived in the Chief's Commons suite shortly after six the secretarial staff had left for the day. Mallory's door was closed and there was no way to tell if he was already occupied. Damon knocked once and walked straight in.

Mallory rose to his feet immediately, recognised the intruder and yelled angrily 'I'm busy!'

A white-haired, balding man sat with his back to the door. The small figure turned to face the source of the interruption and stared straight at Damon: it was Basil Cheney, known within Damon's group as the Poison Dwarf. As they say amongst Houghians, 'once a Whip, never to be trusted'.

Damon stood his ground: though only a moment's hesitation, such bravado demonstrated that his recently consumed whisky had taken the upper hand.

Basil rose, exchanged a nod with Mallory, said 'Don't worry, Charles, I'll be off now, old chap. Cheerio,' waved and headed for the door. He muttered a toneless 'Damon', as he passed the younger man, without engaging eye contact.

'Basil', responded Hough, quietly, in time honoured fashion. Cheney left and closed the door behind him.

'Sit down, Damon.' The three short words conveyed ample impatience.

Damon did as he was told. The Chief sat in the Throne of Power behind a desk which must once have witnessed Empire at its finest. Damon sat opposite.

'You're not back on the patch tonight, harvesting the vote for the local elections?' It was routine banter, someone had to start the conversation. Mallory clearly had little interest in the response. Damon considered responding with 'Neither are you,' but thought the better of it. He went with the more positive 'They weigh the Tory votes in my neck of the woods, Charles, you know that.'

Lassitude could always find a justification. One of Mallory's theories about the Hough approach to politics was that being a minister was hard work. For this reason, if no other, the young man had studiously avoided promotion to the front bench.

'Damon, you can't go on like this.' It was the 'more in sorrow than in anger' approach.

'Like what? Sorry, Charles, you've lost me.' Damon's bemusement was almost genuine. Was the Chief talking about the latest backbench rebellion or the Campbell money? The charity scam? How would he know about that? Was it Paul Roe's complaint? Why would he want to interfere in that?

'Look, you and I have a good relationship, Damon -' Bollocks. It was so good you can give me a complete roasting and I won't hit the roof, thought the recalcitrant child, but I'll still ignore you. 'I can tell you this to your face: the parties. They've got to stop.'

'Parties?'

'You know what I mean. This is just a friendly warning, but I do expect you to take note.'

He couldn't help it. The Pavlovian 'I don't know what you mean' was Hough's response.

As far as detail was concerned, Mallory was also in the dark.

'I know what goes on,' he bluffed. 'I'm not worried about the booze, as long as it's measured in public, controlled in private. Or even the drugs, for heaven's sake, in moderate and discreet proportions. If you had a boyfriend, a partner, then... 'people' would understand. You know they would. These days. But the parties...'

Damon could imagine the speech marks either side of 'people'. Mallory had Conservative voters in mind, leader writers on Conservative newspapers, the social media influencers with whom Damon and the official Tory Party vied for attention. Power to the 'people'.

Mallory went on 'Parties involving young boys, as I understand it, groups of young boys.'

Damon thought quickly. He knew that the intelligence networks that fed into the Whips' offices were second to none. Further denial was pointless, but to what extent clarification would be helpful was open to discussion.

As Mallory spoke his right knee bounced up and down in a frenzy. Above the waterline, behind the desk, he appeared to be in swan-like repose but below the surface that right knee could not stay still. It may only be a few millimetres up and down, up and down, but it was incessant, not indicative of confidence. At least the sturdy old desk hid the limb from Damon's view.

'Look, Chief, they're not -'

'I'm not asking if they're underage, Damon. I expect even you to know where to stop.'

'Charles, you don't know what -'

'I've been told. By someone who knows.'

There was no point asking who that might be. Whips famously never divulge their sources, even under torture. No obvious Judas entered Damon's mind but, he would be the first to admit, he was not currently at his most lucid.

'Jesus, you're as bad as my father,' Damon let the bile spill out.

'Keep your father out of this!' Now angry, Mallory stood up behind his desk, 'He was a decent, honest, loyal, hardworking man. A true servant of our nation.'

It was only just past six in the evening, but Damon had consumed two double whiskies in the Strangers' Bar on his way to the rendezvous. The alcohol loosened his lips: 'He was a bastard, Charles, and you know it. He treated me like shit.'

'Damon, I will not -'

'Listen, will you, for…' - he stammered, fighting back an expletive - 'Hear me out! Look, if I have a problem with my sexuality, which I don't, by the way, but sometimes, in the past, it might have come close, then it's all down to him. He was a repressed, anally retentcitative' - he struggled with the word - 'retentive, homophobic bully. He was so up his own arse he could watch himself swallow!'

'Damon, please!'

'I was glad when he died.' Still seated, Damon raised an admonishing finger and, thinking the better of it, brought it down upon the edge of the desk. 'That meant he was no longer in my face, and I could forget him! And that's the end of it.'

More quietly, Mallory rose to take back control: 'That man fought for his country -'

'And it's my fault that I didn't?' Camping it up, he stood to face Mallory and taunted him, clasping palms together as though a choirboy in sibilant prayer: 'Ooh, I'd have so loved to have been in the army, Charles! With all those sweet, sweet soldier boys!'

'Damon, sit down!' The master was more firm, more confident if also redder in the face: 'Don't be stupid.'

After a moment of stand-off Damon sat, leaving Mallory standing.

'I don't care if you are a homosexual, Damon, I really don't, some of my - you know what I mean. You're hardly the only one, in this place. But secrets are dangerous things! They are the most potent weapons a politician can possess, but they're liable to explode at any moment - especially when one is least prepared. Self-inflicted wounds, you know what I'm saying? For heaven's sake, man, if you can be 'out' about it, then why aren't you? And if you're doing things that you cannot be 'out' about then you must ask yourself why you are in the public eye; and you must decide what really matters to you - the service or the secrets? You cannot live both lives, Damon!'

Hough wanted to ask, facetiously, 'So how does the secret service manage?' But he bit his tongue just in time. He dropped his gaze to the floor, shook his head slowly from side to side and tutted three times, dismissively, despairingly. 'Same old, same old...'

Seated again, Mallory continued 'I don't know what else you're up to, and I don't want to know. You've been a pain in the neck to me over the last few years, a disruptive element on the back benches. You have consistently let the side down and undermined your colleagues. I had high hopes of you, Damon, I thought you could be a real asset to this Party, this government, but instead...'

Mallory considered several trite phrases and rejected them. Saying it like it was became the best feasible option.

'... I've reached the conclusion that we would be better off without you.'

Damon at last understood the phrase 'taken aback'. The thesis could not be denied. So what? It was just a game. Politics. Just a game.

'Charles, consideration of how my behaviour impacts upon you personally does not really figure very highly either in my priorities or my motivations. I'm very sorry about that,' though his expression told a different story. 'Either way, though, to be fair, just so that you know, I am not setting out to deliberately annoy you, just for the hell of it.' He went on to mutter, letting the whisky speak 'Business before pleasure…'

The Chief Whip found his *sang* no longer *froid*: 'Well, you're bloody well succeeding!'

Mallory was breathing heavily. In ten years as a Whip, climbing the ranks to become Chief, he had never lost control of his emotions. He wasn't going to let this little shit get the better of him now.

'Look, Damon, this is a formal warning. Watch yourself, in everything you do. In here, out there. Every damn thing, do you hear me? In the Chamber, in town, in the constituency, on social media. Wherever! I have eyes and I have ears, Damon, and I suspect that what I'm hearing is the tip of a very nasty iceberg, one that could do the Conservative Party an awful lot of damage. An awful lot!'

Damon found it difficult to disagree with that conclusion, but did he care? He recalled a television documentary which had showed that icebergs could indeed be heard. They creaked, scraped, scratched, edged towards destruction. He inflated his cheeks and blew out like a bellows, trying to make a noise like an iceberg. If this was supposed to be a way to recover sobriety, it didn't work. He was slipping backwards again.

Accordingly, there was a silence of four or five seconds. Mallory resumed, magisterial.

'Damon. Listen to me. Consider this your first formal warning. An official reprimand. You know what happens on two.'

He did. This was a Yellow Card. Next time, he would be stripped of the whip and barred from standing as an official Tory candidate at the next election.

'My final word, Damon: I am your Chief Whip. I am responsible for all matters of Party discipline in the House, all of them. It is my job to keep the government afloat and sailing through the choppy waters between now and the next election, with all hands safe and on board.'

The naval analogies. Hough could sense what was coming.

'But if, to save the others, Damon, we have to jettison -'

'Yes, yes, I know. Save your breath.'

'You must -'

'Walk the plank? Leave it out, Charles.'

Mallory had veins standing out all over his face and appeared to be on the verge of explosion: he spoke through gritted teeth.

'As your Chief Whip I assure you that I will be scrupulously fair to you, as I would to any colleague.' What he meant was 'If you find yourself before an internal Party disciplinary tribunal you can bet your bottom dollar I will win.'

Now came the piece that Mallory did not want to have to report. All the rest, including the expletives, he had been mulling over for weeks, preparing not for if but for when he would deploy the words. He had hoped that these few seconds of silence might take the tension out of the air.

More quietly, intimately, Mallory said 'Damon, there's something else I have to tell you -'

'Oh, here we go!'

'Your father -'

'Yeah, yeah, war hero, man of the fucking people!'

'Your father is not -'

'Not here! He's gone! He's rotting in the ground and his soul has gone to Hell! Please don't tell me any more about my father!'

'It's important.'

Damon put his hands over his ears, said 'Don't tell me!' and made a siren noise.

'Damon, this is important. Not for the Party, but... oh, for Heaven's sake!'

It was no good. Mallory could not go through with it. The results of the DNA test would have to stay in the Chief's large box of unshared secrets for now. It was just too painful to try again.

There was another silence, in which Damon sensed that the world was spinning.

'Damon, everything I have said to you in an official capacity in this meeting will go on your record, as will the gist of your responses -'

'You're recording this?'

'No, no recordings. You have my word.'

At last Damon appeared to be listening.

'But let me go off the record and tell you this, also: as someone who loved your father as a brother, that man who served us all, as a loyal and respected member of Her Majesty's Navy, who served diligently, passionately, with honour and principle at our time of great need, just give me one more excuse, Damon. One more excuse is all... I... need.'

He paused for dramatic effect and to weigh his words:

'And I will see you returned as a Conservative Member of this Parliament at the next election - over my dead body!'

Damon was tired and the whisky was doing what whisky does, creating a state of torpor. All he could manage in responding to the provocation was a silent, dismissive sneer.

Again, there was silence; this time Damon allowed what he had heard to sink in.

'There's no more to be said, then, Charles. Look, I've had a couple of drinks and I think it's properly - probably - bubbly - best if we, you know. Another time.'

Was there an air of defeatism about Hough? For the first time ever?

'I'm going to go now, Charles,' Damon stood uncertainly.

'I think that's probably for the best, Damon.'

Hough walked slowly towards the door, opened it and left, leaving the door open. Then he returned.

'What do you mean, 'my father isn't'? What the fuck does that mean?'

'Your father.'

'Eh?' Muttering 'Fucking ridiculous,' over and again Damon left the office for a second and final time.

And then there was Lee. Five days to get all that money back to him? No way. Campbell would understand and Lee really should not be throwing his weight about like this. That was all there was to it.

There was money in the charity, money he could not get at in a form that he could return to Campbell. This minor administrative problem was a function of charitable status which he had overlooked: in effect, once money has been donated to a charity the donor cannot get it back. There probably were ways of doing it, but he was sure that they could not be implemented discreetly within the five days - including a weekend - available. That was a pity, because most of the £50,000 he had transferred to the charity to support his constituency work had yet to be touched.

The remaining balance in the client account was over half a million, though Lee had made clear that 'most' was not enough. Or had he? Perhaps he would take half a million for now. Damon really could not remember exactly what Hardman had said, but he knew that he was not disposed to be helpful to his tormentor.

And Lee was certainly not going to get the car! Damon was determined to take his beloved Porsche with him to the grave. Metaphorically, of course.

It was going to work out all right. It had to. Lee Hardman was the least of Damon's problems. It was only fucking money, after all.

Guy Campbell would understand. Not that Damon had ever met him, nor had any connection to the man's company - Meccano? No, that was wrong. Guy was bound to be a patient person, anyone who factored an eleven-year prison stretch into his business plan must have learned patience. No doubt Campbell was a man after Damon's own heart. He would get five hundred thousand, which was most of the three quarters of a million, back on time. But Campbell was still in prison. Hough had done his homework and decided that the man he needed to speak to was Jacob Singh, who appeared to be the organ grinder's current monkey. But could he be arsed to explain? Probably not. Though if he did, he could probably drop Hardman in the shit, so that was definitely worth considering.

So he would probably authorise the transfer of five hundred k - make it four, that was still more than half - on Monday, that would be a good day for it. It was Saturday morning now and there was nothing he could do in the meantime, even if he wanted to. Monday was both within Lee's time scale - that bit of what Lee said had surfaced in Damon's mind - and yet would still keep the bastard waiting, so that was 'win-win', wasn't it? The rest of the money, Lee would get… well, 'in due course'.

'In the fullness of time'.

'As circumstances allow'.

Or 'according to our stated priorities' and all of the other euphemisms that civil servants use instead of saying 'Fuck knows when'.

Damon had dozed off once more. It was ten a.m. when his phone rang, yet again. This time he picked up effectively, despite sending the half cup of cold coffee spinning - fortunately, it regained its composure without toppling over.

'Hi, who's that? … hello?'

'Is me. You come get me.'

'What?'

'I no can come London; you fetch me now.'

'What the fuck -'

'Damon. Donington Service, M1. I wait you here.'

'Shit. Really?'

He wanted to say that he was busy today but for once he could not bring himself to lie. What the hell, it would be good to take the Porsche for a piss up the motorway, which would be relatively quiet and uncongested on a Saturday; he had not done that for a while. He needed the speed, having been confined to the metropolis for two whole weeks. Damon yawned, the reflex involving every muscle in the top half of his prone body for what seemed like an age.

Adolfo Bocca's words were sinking in.

'Why can't you get back?'

'I no money. I no want hitchhike.'

'Why have you got no money? You're loaded.'

'I lose wallet. In Sheffield. Hitchhike to here but no more. I no like.'

'What the fuck were you doing in Sheffield? Why ever would you want to go there? Don't answer that, it's a shit hole. All right. But I can't leave for a couple of hours. You on the southbound side?'

'There only one service here.'

That rang a bell. Donington Park services was where he turned off whenever he was going to Derbyshire to walk in the White or Dark Peaks, it was right next to East Midlands airport. Derbyshire: the rolling hills, not just the peaks but the dales, too. He peered out of the window. From what he could see from his bed there was bright spring weather outside, it could turn into a nice day. He could do with a walk.

'You in a hurry, Adolfo?'

'Me hurry? No. Today some time is good. But soon please.'

He never is in a hurry. Damon knew no one as laid back as Adolfo, certainly not during the hours of daylight. Even though he owed the Argentinian money he was not being hassled to pay it back. God...! Mallory talked about parties but what did he really know? He would not believe Adolfo's 'party parties'! Just telling Mallory the shit about those little beauties would bring on a heart attack! Perhaps he should have told the bastard, to test that theory. Adolfo organised them perfectly. There were rarely more than three guests, not counting the boys who provided the floor show. There would be at least two boys for every guest, who generally agreed that the entrance fee of two thousand pounds (less a discount for making successful introductions) was well spent. The fee included boys, poppers, drinks, chauffeurs, the odd tab of ecstasy for those so inclined - along with total privacy and discretion. It was the latter that made them expensive.

Damon had been to ten of Adolfo's parties over several years, more than one a year. At one of the early ones, he had encountered a Liberal Democrat peer - the two men experienced a moment's frisson, mutual panic fused with silent terror - though neither was surprised to see the other there. Nor did either of them ever speak about their meeting to anyone, even to Adolfo. And, most definitely, not to each other. That was five years ago; the bond of silence had held steadfast.

About three parties back Damon had been annoyed when a boy he had seen once before had said something out of turn. He could not recall now what it was, but it had clearly been directed at himself. Adolfo agreed that the boy had misbehaved and promised that he would not be at any future party at which Damon was present. He waived Damon's fee for that party in recompense. Despite this, the MP was now three payments behind schedule, as Adolfo had taken to gently reminding him. 'Next time you come party-party you pay, how you say, up front,' he'd said. He was referring to the back payments: it would cost Damon six thousand pounds before he could come through the door, plus two more for the next party.

Damon had been holding the cash back as a matter of pique, a test of Adolfo's loyalty. This was a high stakes gambit because Adolfo had the power to bring him down, but that was also what gave the situation an edge, a psychological thrill which was better than taking drugs! Of course he would pay his debt, in due course, it was not as though he had no cash at all. He would rather his trusted old friend Adolfo had his six thousand than give it to bloody Lee school boy Hardman. But meanwhile, until the very last minute, he would continue to play the South American like a fish on a line.

Just for fun.

'Listen, I'll meet you there at two. Donington Park services, by the main entrance to the building. Make it half past. I'll call you if I'm delayed. Then we'll go for a walk, OK? Not far from where you are. I'd like to breathe in the crystal air of the beautiful Derbyshire countryside, are you up for that?'

'*Si*, OK, if you want. But -'

'You'll get your money, Adolfo.' He had enough battles to fight, he could do without waging this one, too. It was time to land the fish.

For Adolfo it was the first time he had heard Damon volunteer such words: had he just heard him make a promise? He was grateful. Why not go for a countryside walk? He had nothing better to do that day, the weather was mild, and he quite liked Damon's company. Occasionally. In small doses. And he only had four hours to wait.

The deadline did not require Damon to take immediate action. It gave him time to shower, find some breakfast and get over to Parliament where the Porsche was in the underground car park. Fresh air, he thought, was exactly what he needed.

Marginally before eleven thirty Damon was fed and dressed - jeans, walking boots, outdoor jacket, the proper kit for a spring trek - but just as he was leaving the flat he stopped himself. Something did not feel right. He went back inside the flat and over to his desk, where he took a small cardboard box from a drawer. Originally it had contained business cards, hundreds of them, identical, freshly printed with their distinctive smell, though both cards and odour had long since been dispersed. Now it contained other people's business cards, many dozens that he had accumulated, from many sources, over many years. He had a good look through them, selecting three which he laid out on the table.

He went into the bedroom and changed out of his outdoor clothing and into a dark suit, one he would often wear for work, accompanied by a plain white shirt and his new brown brogues. On his dressing table was a small but manly jewellery box; it reminded him of the abortive call that he appeared to have made on Thursday night. The clover cufflinks, the present from Kate, were there. Four-leafed clovers. Perhaps they would bring him luck, after all.

Leaving the flat for a second time he pushed the three cards into his breast pocket and was surprised to find two already there. As the double decker bus took him towards Parliament, a few minutes later, he took the cards out and examined them. One was his own business card; it was unusual to find a solitary one - they normally hunted in packs. On the other, otherwise blank, was 14-digit hand-written number. It was the card Lee had given him on Thursday, identifying the bank account where he was supposed to deposit the money, its digits reversed for security, within the next few days. No chance, Lee, no chance.

He put all five cards back in his pocket. They felt as though they were a set, a poker hand of unknown merit, though why he wanted to take them with him to Derbyshire not even Damon could imagine. It felt like the right thing to do. He anticipated the feel, the thrill of the Porsche's motor powering him up the motorway before he even left London.

As he drove, he considered charging Adolfo five hundred pounds for the taxi service! Get him to knock it off his bill. Could he be bothered with the fuss? No.

Damon's love of the open countryside was genuine and profound, hence his involvement in the all-party group on rambling. Today they would make their way to that splendid old railway viaduct: the first time he had ever seen it was from a distance, on that Sunday afternoon, on leaving the Tory candidates' bonding weekend at the former vicarage. Although it was only thirteen years ago it felt as though a generation had passed. He had revisited the county several times: there was no better countryside for walking. He knew a well-trodden and stimulating route close by the viaduct; it left the car park, crossed to the eastern side of the valley and then more or less followed the contour north. Upon reaching the bridge the itinerary threaded west, weaving through the arches of the broken viaduct, then back down the farm track and returning to the car park. Hopefully the steppingstones in the stream would not be submerged, as they could occasionally be; the last couple of months had been dry so the prospect was good. The hike, 80 or 90 minutes long, would take them past where the viaduct was still connected to the valley wall; if they had time, perhaps a spare twenty minutes, it might be fun to walk along the top to the disconnected far end and survey the valley from there. He knew that this was do-able but had not previously witnessed the acclaimed remarkable vista, from a height of around twenty metres, for himself.

It was nearly three when Damon found Adolfo at Donington Park services and he made the Argentine wait whilst he bought and consumed a sandwich. It took more than half an hour to reach their destination during which time he impressed Adolfo by touching a ton on the A50 dual carriageway. There was no need to plot the route by sat nav as Damon knew exactly where to find the small car park, tucked away amid limestone outcrops; he had parked there once before. It was dry and sunny, with wispy spring cloud, perfect conditions for walking. As the Porsche turned off the main road and onto the minor one it kicked up grit from the side of the carriageway. The dust shower represented power, the aftermath of an explosion; Damon loved this car.

Adolfo told him what had happened in Sheffield and Damon was sympathetic. Someone had known that he was carrying two thousand pounds in cash, the profit from a trade that he had conducted the night before, but Damon knew better than to ask for details. Still less was it appropriate to enquire why - from what the MP was aware of Adolfo's profession - he was conducting his business on another operator's manor. Perhaps there was a franchise system, or this was holiday cover? Neither was likely. Whatever the basis, such a profit from one evening's work obviously justified Adolfo bothering to venture into the alien realm north of Watford.

Shortly after leaving his hotel and heading for to Sheffield station at 7 that morning, Adolfo found himself surrounded by three men. They corralled him into an entry under an old building, a passage which was dark, chillingly cold and almost totally hidden from both prying and casual eyes. Silently, two of the assailants pinned him to the wall - Adolfo was skinny, slight, unarmed, not physically strong; he did not need to be told that resistance was futile. The third thug patted him down, found both his wallet and a reassuringly bulky envelope and pocketed both. One man ran back the way they had come whilst the other two, wallet and envelope, disappeared into unknown territory. This left the Argentine shaken but unbloodied and unbruised, thanks to his principled lack of resistance.

Neither man was surprised how well planned the attack had been. It was not the first time that Adolfo had been set up like this, like some Aunt Sally (a phrase that Damon had to explain). Bocca knew that collecting dues on foreign turf and then getting mugged was par for the course, though thankfully such indignities did not happen that often. In any other field he could have dismissed the experience as a tax loss, Damon mused. 'No,' said Adolfo, with a rare smile. 'For do this I must pay the tax.' The only part of him that had been injured was his pride. He had managed to keep his phone; even sophisticated devices were of little interest to the modern highwaymen, who had correctly judged that their prey was unlikely to call the police as soon as their backs were turned. They had, inadvertently, left him with a couple of notes and some small change, but not enough cash to get home. Buying a train ticket in advance was not Adolfo's way of working: avoiding traceable journeys was second nature to him. A phone app calculated that he should take a bus from the station to the southwest for a few miles, then hitchhike down the M1 to the metropolis. That was the way to go.

However, Damon Hough owed him a favour and now was the time to call it in. Adolfo made his first call at 7.10 a.m., his number, as ever, withheld. And again at 7.20. When he realised that Damon had probably not been asleep too long, he decided to wait a while before trying again. Adolfo was not a man to get angry or frustrated; he assessed his situation philosophically. It made sense to kill time by starting his journey now and arranging to meet his chauffeur at a motorway service station.

A bus took him to the edge of city from where he soon got a lift from a haulier. The driver's thick northern accent and the roar of the engine made it difficult for the Argentine to understand him. The man barely stopped talking at first but was not comfortable with Adolfo's silence and lapsed into an awkward one himself for much of the journey. Adolfo took his leave at Donington and spent five pounds, half of his remaining resources, on breakfast at the service station. He tried calling Damon again, but his erstwhile client was still clearly dead to the world.

Much of the journey from Donington to the Derbyshire beauty spot was given to the telling of Adolfo's tale, in broken English and with much fatalistic equanimity.

They left the car in the designated car park, a former quarry. Just two of its limited vehicle spaces were occupied. Immediately, they could sense the calming warmth of the afternoon, not too hot, not too cold. Bees were flitting between small flowers on the limestone soil. They set out on foot and after a hundred metres Damon indicated that they should take a small path off to their right, crossing the valley. As this path was rougher than the track, the men with their city shoes found its navigation taxing, though progress was by no means impossible or unpleasant. Within a few minutes they could see the distant railway viaduct, spanning a valley almost a quarter of a mile wide.

Pointing to it, Damon explained to the foreigner that trains between Manchester and London, with important passengers, would have powered across that mighty bridge, a wonder of civil engineering, almost two hundred years ago. They were truly iron horses, paid for by private investors, ordinary folk, pioneers of nascent capitalism.

Adolfo was not the most scintillating company; Much of their trek was in silence and Damon felt as though he was being followed by a small dog which resented the rugged terrain. The drive had taken longer than expected and the walk was slow. It was almost five o'clock when they climbed the steep, rough path to join the bed of the former railway line on top of the structure. Both the climb and the view took Damon's breath away.

'Wow… isn't it great up here, Adolfo?' Damon drank in the fresh air, the cool breeze.

'*Si. Bello.*' The Argentine was wearing a long leather coat which accentuated his slim frame but looked out of place in the countryside. For a man who had been mugged and lost so much money that very day he appeared very calm, but 'enjoying himself' would be overstating it.

The bridge must have been magnificent in those early days of steam. It was over 20 metres high across much of the flat-bottomed valley, where Damon imagined a broad river had once powered by. Today the watercourse was barely a stream, a dribble. The iron tracks had long disappeared from their bed and even the stone parapets along either edge showed signs of decay. Along one side - the right as they proceeded from east to west - little remained of a once proud iron railing. Some of the uprights had disappeared, others leant at rakish angles; most of the horizontal rods had gone, too, though one or two lay on the ground nearby. It must be rare for a walker to traverse this High Line structure; the reason it had not been colonised by more than a few bushes and other plants was its arid, well-draining substrate. There was dust but little soil and many stones.

'Let's go right to the other end!' Damon encouraged his non-plussed but compliant guest who had nothing to lose.

As they approached the far end of the viaduct Adolfo spotted the chasm ahead. He had not appreciated that the trail stopped in mid-air - Damon had failed to convey that this was exactly what they had come to see. At some point, sixty years since a train last crossed, the sturdy Victorian bridge had failed, collapsed, disappointed. This felt symbolic of something: capitalism again? Damon chose not to extend the analogy. Adolfo peered carefully over the broken edge; a mound of hostile rocks lay below.

'We no can go, we must back...', he pointed back along the viaduct.

Damon ignored him. He stood, hands in trouser pockets, silent and stony still, more at peace than he had felt in a long time.

After a moment he said 'Indulge me, my friend. Let's stay here for a short while. We're in no hurry.'

Adolfo respected his wishes and the two men stood: Damon with his eyes closed, feeling the soothing spring breeze play with his jacket, his skin. Adolfo mostly looked at the floor, raising his eyes occasionally to see what Damon was doing.

He was doing nothing.

There was no one else in sight. Indeed, there was hardly a sign of human habitation bar the bridge itself - and the farm track beneath where the final, missing arch once stood.

Damon spoke quietly.

'I have some problems, Adolfo.'

The Argentine said nothing but moved slightly closer, the better to hear the soft tones.

'Lots of problems. I don't think I can solve them all.'

The scene was static.

'The list includes you, Adolfo, you're one of my problems.'

No explanation, no reminder about the money, was necessary.

'But I have bigger problems than you, my friend. Much bigger problems.'

Damon took two steps towards the other, whilst reaching into the outer breast pocket of his jacket. He took out some cards, looked at them and put one back. He held out the other four, face down.

'Pick a card, Adolfo. Any card.'

Adolfo considered: he might as well play along, get this thing over with. He took one.

'I look?'

'Yes. Show me.'

Adolfo held out the business card. It had an expensive feel to it.

'Let's see… Lee Hardman. I owe him money - you know the feeling, I owe you money, too! But I owe him real money. Damon owes everybody money! But he's different. He wants £750,000.'

Adolfo looked puzzled. Damon repeated the number: 'Seven hundred… and fifty… thousand… pounds.'

Adolfo blew air from his mouth, impressed.

'You know what they say, Adolfo? No, you probably don't. They say that if I owe you a thousand pounds, or even six thousand, as in your case, then I have a problem; but if I owe you £750,000 then it's you that's got the problem, not me.' He smiled at the aphorism. 'Do they say that in Argentina? Same sort of thing, maybe? Not in pounds, obviously. Do you have lira, is that your money?'

Adolfo shrugged, muttered 'peso' to no one in particular, remained expressionless.

'Anyway, it's his money, Lee's money, there's no denying it… or rather there is, because it's his boss's money, really. And I can give him most of it, so that's not a problem. But he's not satisfied with most of it, he wants it all. And more! I've been looking after it for him. I've not managed it very well, and I've been... Oh, I've been greedy, Adolfo. I was looking after it, that's all, I looked after it for much longer than I'd expected, but instead of protecting it I used it to look after myself.'

He looked directly at Adolfo. 'Did you like my car?'

'Car?'

'The car that brought us here. It's a Macan, a Porsche Macan.'

'*Si*. Nice car. Powerful car.'

'I bought the car with his money. Forty thousand pounds of his money.'

After a moment, Adolfo asked: 'What happen if you no pay?'

Damon laughed, thought about it and laughed again. 'I have absolutely no fucking idea!'

'So what you do?'

Damon's smile was short-lived. 'I wait, see what happens. I don't know what can happen. I've said he can have some of it on Monday, but... It's naughty money, Adolfo.' He waggled his finger in admonishment in the Argentine's direction. 'He can't go telling people about my debt, because he - or his boss - will get caught. I don't know the details, but that's my theory. Best not to know too much about these things, don't you agree?'

Adolfo stood still, watching him.

'I can give him 500k this week... except: you know what? I can't be arsed. I just... The bastard doesn't deserve it.'

He inhaled, exhaled, slowly, enjoying the odours of the countryside.

'I've just realised.' He paused. 'Goodness, yes, it was here, in Derbyshire, not far from here, that I first got to know this man, this man who wants the money. He's called Lee Hardman, he knows stuff about me which could be slightly embarrassing if it got out into the public domain, but in this day and age, well... naked men wrestling certainly isn't career-ending, these days, is it? It's not exactly killer information. You should know that better than anyone, Adolfo!'

Adolfo acknowledged by raising his eyebrows, briefly, nodding once.

'How many naked boys have you seen fighting?'

Adolfo shrugged. Countless. What was the point of this discourse?

'Twelve years ago. No, coming on thirteen, blimey. It was a candidates' training weekend, before I became an MP. In those days everyone wanted to be a Tory Member of Parliament, everyone, even the fucking liberal Lee Hardman thought he was going to become a Tory MP! He didn't manage it, of course. Went frigging native after that, did young Lee... I call him young, he's the same age as me. Just looks like a fucking juvenile. Anyway... we had a wrestling match.'

'You fight with this man?'

'No, the wrestle was with... Piggy Eliot. Do you know who I mean, Piggy Eliot? No? Philip Eliot? Became a Foreign Office minister. A junior Foreign Office minister,' he added, 'with the emphasis on 'junior'.'

'So, you fight?'

'No, actually, we didn't. I challenged him to a fight, you know, wrestling, but he refused to fulfil the conditions. He would not strip. He would not fight naked, in front of the others. He was not a man of honour... in all his glory, not like me.'

Damon extended his arms, Messiah-like, nodding - first to his left, to the centre, then to the right - to acknowledge the non-existent crowd, smiling seraphically.

'You naked for fighting?'

'As the day I was born!' Damon declaimed, then 'No, wait, I kept my socks on. It's how the Olympians used to do it, without the socks, but that's the precedent. If that story got out... not about the socks.' He laughed. 'No one cares about the socks. But nobody would be surprised to hear that I was involved, because I'm a rogue!' The pantomime villain was enjoying the label, the status, the infamy. 'That's what I am! I'm a rogue! A rascal! A scallywag!' he shouted. Then more quietly: 'But what about Piggy? It would have been a story if it had been more recently; or if he'd taken his bloody undies off. Anyway, young Lee witnessed all this, he saw it happen. The non-fight. No, there's nothing there for Lee. There's nothing for Lee there. Too long ago. It's just not a story.'

'But... plenty money.'

'Oh, yes. The amount I owe to you is just peanuts, isn't it?'

He smiled, softly at first.

'You understand, 'peanuts?''

Adolfo shrugged but joined in the joke: 'You owe me, you pay me, you no even notice it gone!' Adolfo's smile was not entirely humorous; perhaps 'rueful' best described it. Damon responded in like mode but with a stupid grin.

Back to business.

'Give me the card back. Now take another.'

He did.

'Katty Mellor. Who she?'

'Kate. A journalist. I can't remember why or how I got her card, I found it in my little box earlier today, it must have been there years... I tried to call her this week. Coincidence or what? Do you think it was my subconscious? You only instigate talking to a journalist when you want to tip them off about something, or you need to find something out, and it's not normally something very nice. Maybe I wanted to wish her happy birthday? It was my birthday on the second, it must be hers soon...'

An image suddenly flashed into Damon's mind, and it took him a moment to place it. It was a scene from about three years earlier.

He had encountered a colleague, an experienced and bucolic gent, on the broad stone staircase in Westminster Hall, on the wide landing adjacent to the old St Stephen's entrance to Parliament. On his way to meet someone in the Jubilee Cafe, Damon had allowed himself to get diverted to chat with the ruddy-faced landowner and fellow traveller. As he listened to what his acquaintance had to say their discourse was punctuated by a woman's laughter, a loud, happy, innocent laugh. Echoing around the chamber, it was a laugh which rang a bell in one of the deeper recesses of his mind.

He could not recall what the man's story was about, but it was certainly going on, and on. Damon glanced towards the foot of the stairs below where he saw yet another Tory MP, a neophyte, talking to a handsome woman in a shapeless overcoat; she must be the one who had laughed. On cue, she guffawed again, but briefly. Now she was reaching into a large leather handbag, rummaging, trying to find something. She had wispy, shoulder-length brown hair, a pair of spectacles pushed up on top of her head. He watched her take out a business card from a card holder retrieved from the depths of her bag and the phrase 'Aladdin's Cave' came into his head. He recalled telling someone once that it described the contents of her handbag. The woman handed a card to the young MP to whom she was speaking, smiled, shook his hand, turned and walked purposefully away. She headed directly towards the public exit at the far end of Westminster Hall, with its massive doors, without ever looking back.

A moment later, the first colleague had finished his tale and was taking his leave whilst the second was climbing the steps towards him. 'Good to see you, George,' Damon said, then hailed the second man: 'Oh, Simon?'

Sightly wary - make that petrified - of being seen talking to the rebellious Hough, the young Member paused hesitantly. 'Yes, Damon?' He was an arch-loyalist, not one of Damon's friends, and this was the first time he had ever spoken to the rebel. The younger MP was inexperienced, wary of the quasi-satanic presence addressing him.

'Sorry, Simon, I couldn't help noticing… who was that you were talking to down there? I thought I recognised her.'

'Oh, just a journo. Look, she gave me her card. Here you go, you can have it. I know where to find her. So - see you around, Damon.' The young man scampered away, considering himself getting off lightly.

The name on the card sounded a distant echo but Damon did not immediately place it. Later that day, queuing in the voting lobby, he took the card from his pocket, examined it again and it finally fell into place. 'Goodness me,' he said to himself, with uncharacteristic restraint, 'small world.' A few days later he took the card from his pocket again and placed it into the small box. There it had remained, untouched, ignored, unnoticed, until this morning.

'Who she?' asked Alfonso. 'Why you have card?'

'I don't know why I have it. Fate, I guess. We have… some history.'

'A woman? You have history with woman?' He chuckled, understandably incredulous.

'Oh, it was a very long time ago,' Damon reassured him, dismissively. 'Twenty years.'

'I go school!' Alfonso smiled. 'Why you have card now?'

Damon spoke quietly. 'I don't know. We were… friends. And then we weren't. She reminds me of the time that my father died.'

'You say me one time, you no like you father. No, you say me many time.'

'It's true. He was a bastard.'

'It happen.'

'That's when Kate and I stopped being friends. The day my father died I knew I could allow myself to be myself, at last, so the first thing I did was to ditch Kate.'

'Dish? What is dish?'

'Like I said, we... stopped being friends. I ended our friendship. I ditched her. Ditched. Threw her in the ditch. Not really, but... you know.'

'You want talk her for that?' Adolfo didn't believe what he was saying. 'Twenty year later?'

'No, no, absolutely not... why should I? But she's a journalist now, so she's dangerous. Maybe she has a story about me, maybe, I don't know, maybe I just received a psychic message from her or something.'

Adolfo raised a sceptical eyebrow.

'No, I don't believe that, either. But what if she does have a story? What if she has a story from Roe, or Hardman? Shit... If I were Paul Roe, I'd seek to undermine me, put me on the back foot, get at me through the press.'

'Poor Roe?'

'It's not his turn. We'll come to him. Or maybe it's Mallory. I think she's sharpening her knife. She's coming for me, Adolfo, I can feel it. And not in a nice way. Especially if she's talked to Roe. Or Hardman. Or fucking Mallory.'

The Argentine went through the motions of appearing to think of an explanation. Damon saved him the bother.

'I just don't trust her, Adolfo. It's not good.'

The two men contemplated Damon's quandary for a moment.

'Who is Mallory?'

'Mallory? I've told you about him before. The Chief Whip, he who must be obeyed!' Damon stood to attention and saluted: 'All hail the head honcho! The Parliamentary Secretary to Her Majesty's Treasury! The Right Honourable Mr Charles Mallory, Esquire, MP, the Head of Discipline!'

The salute ended. At ease, men.

'I've known him all my life, Adolfo. All my fucking life.' Then, under his breath, 'Bastard'.

Adolfo absorbed the information. Charles Mallory. It was good to be reminded who to complain to about Damon. Just in case he kept forgetting to repay the six thousand.

'Give me that card back, that's Kate Mellor done. Take the next one.'

Adolfo performed the exchange.

'It say Paul Roe. MP. This same Paul Roe?'

'He's a shit. He's a shit! I showed him up in public the other day. I embarrassed him in the House of Commons, in front of people. He'd written me a letter to tell me to stop hassling the mother of one of his constituents, who also happens to be my client, as a solicitor.' Damon was rattling the story out, twenty words to the dozen, as though heading down a steep hill with no brakes. 'She was an old woman whose mother is - a very old woman. But the older old woman signed a Power of Attorney perfectly legally, long before... no one will say it wasn't, before she got the dementia, before she got, you know? Then I increased the fee - which I was entitled to do, in pursuance of a clause in which... you're not following this, Adolfo, are you?'

Damon had been speaking with much energy and Adolfo was bemused.

'No. I no understand.'

'Paul has been messing with my head,' Damon tapped his temple for emphasis. 'Pinko -' he repeated the word, aspirating the 'p' more strongly '- Pinko has been messing with my head since we were fourteen years old!'

'You know him?'

'We were at school together, for a while.' Then Damon screamed, punching his own temple 'He's messing with my head!'

The valley's acoustics acknowledged the force of his passion, but the deep resonation lasted barely a second. A skylark flitted by.

There was silence.

Adolfo looked at the card again. 'Card say he Labour. I think you no Labour?' He shook his head.

'That's right. Well done. He sits on the other side of the chamber to me, and I have to pretend he's not there, but he can see me, and he watches me and he knows... and he's been there seven years, and he's going to be a minister in the next government.'

'You no minister?'

'No, I'm not! And he's straight and I'm... I'm not, I don't know what I am, Adolfo.'

The sentence dissolved away. Was he close to tears?

Adolfo still stood, but his patience was starting to wear thin. There was nothing he could say, nor should. He would continue to play along because Damon had told him that he would be getting his money, so there was no point in antagonising him. Adolfo was a stoic. He had a pretty good idea what 'straight' meant and knew that Damon was not 'straight': he had been providing him with young male companions for several years. He trusted Damon with exclusive membership of his party parties. Damon had even, once or twice, brought him new trade. Adolfo realised that he had to be patient for a while longer, not least - and this was his immediate consideration - because he needed that lift back to London.

'Oh, shit... Adolfo, do you think Paul Roe is talking to Kate Mellor? Are they planning a story about me, is that what it is?'

Adolfo shrugged in a 'how would I know?' way.

'Give me the card back.'

Damon now had all three cards in one hand, the last remaining one in the other.

'Here. Take it.'

Adolfo looked at it, puzzled, as Damon slipped the others back into his pocket.

'This you. It your card.'

'Yes. Damon Hough, MP. Member of Purgatory. Purge a Tory, what?' He laughed aloud for a moment; Adolfo could not see the joke. 'But for how much longer? I have a Chief Whip - my boss - fucking Charles Mallory - who wants me out. He doesn't like the parties... I don't mean the Conservative Party; I mean our sort of parties. Your sort, party parties. The sort of parties that you organise, my friend.'

He pointed at the smaller man, then relaxed.

'My good friend.'

Adolfo was worried: 'my good friend' was what people sometimes called him when they were drunk. And that screaming, a moment ago... fortunately there was no-one to hear it. But he had been with Damon for three hours - the man had not been drinking, had not taken anything - had he? Was he fit to drive?

'You are my very good friend... Adolfo.'

The accusatory finger subsided.

Adolfo furrowed his brow. 'How he knows party parties?'

'I don't know. I... I don't think he does know, I think he's guessing. He didn't hear anything from me, I can assure you. But a Chief Whip with a theory is a very dangerous man.'

'You on same side, no?'

'In theory. He doesn't like my politics, my views are more robust than his middle of the road, lily-livered, wanking.... He wouldn't like my money troubles if he knew about them, Adolfo, he'd go up the wall. But above all he doesn't like what I say about my dad.'

'You father?' Adolfo was bemused again.

'My father, yes. He was friends with my fucking father, he says my dad was a war hero.' There was an unpleasant, sardonic tone to his voice.

Adolfo toyed with the words in his mind, dissecting them until they made sense.

'War hero?' he repeated.

'Yes, he was in the navy. He killed a lot of the enemy.'

Adolfo was thinking, calculating. This was news to him. 'What war he fight?'

There was a pause as Damon also appeared to be doing his sums. He knew the answer very well. 'Oh, shit.' Damon realised that he may be opening a Pandora's box.

'Yes, Adolfo, it was the Falklands. Las - what do they call it? Malvinas.'

The Argentine looked more interested.

'Oh, you're really going to hate this, my friend. My father was on the Conqueror, HMS Conqueror, the submarine that sank the General Belgrano.'

The smaller man felt a chill run down his spine. 'Belgrano? That was… terrible war crime.'

'Look, it wasn't me, right? It was my father - Gerald Hough, evil bastard. I hated him.' There were tears in Damon's eyes. 'For other reasons, too, many other reasons.' It was clear to Damon that the Argentine, looking puzzled, needed more of an explanation. 'The Belgrano was sunk, 40 years ago, this week. Everyone knows it was a fucking illegal act. It happened on the very day that I was born, Adolfo. As I was coming into this world my father's fucking boat was firing three torpedoes that took the Belgrano and hundreds of men out of it. The ship was travelling away from the theatre of action - everyone knows that; it should have been protected by the rules of the conduct of war. My father was… a mass murderer.'

Now Adolfo raised his voice as though addressing a wider audience: 'Every man from Argentina he know story Belgrano, Malvinas. We no forgive.' He shook his head. 'We never forgive Thatcher,' though he pronounced the name 'Tatcher'.

Quietly and thoughtfully, Damon responded: 'Oh, Adolfo, no, she was… she was a great woman. Maybe she didn't get everything right but… what a leader she was! But I'm not asking for your forgiveness,

Adolfo, I don't need it, you're my friend. I - we - don't deserve forgiveness.'

Was 'friend' overstating it? The two men had a good relationship, that was true, but it was a commercial one. Money for Adolfo, sex for Damon. Watching, fondling, boys for the buggering of. That was their 'friendship'.

There was a long silence.

Adolfo reflected: he knew people whose fathers, uncles, brothers, had died on the Belgrano. 323, the whole Argentinian crew, had perished as it headed away from the battle zone, heading home on a bearing of 280 degrees. The foul play of the British convinced the almost friendless General Galtieri that Argentina's foes could not even be trusted to play by the rules of war. The recapture of Las Malvinas was Galtieri's way of stoking up support for his own unpopular government - and it worked. The story of the islands, the Falklands, became associated with the deepest depths of the Argentinian national psyche. Throughout the weeks of the conflict most Argentinian people stood by their unelected military dictator and urged him to victory.

Britannia, it was said, waived the rules - whenever it suited her. There was no better example of this in the whole of the twentieth century, a century which began at the peak of majestic Empire, with Britain dominating the worlds of politics, trade and war and the oceans in between. It ended with a row about some God-forsaken rocks somewhere on the other side of the globe.

The silence continued.

Adolfo finally broke it. 'You know? Two May, Belgrano day, that my birth, too. But I born 19... *ochenta y siete*, 87.' For once in his life Damon appeared to be listening. 'You know what famous thing it happen on that day? Nothing. *Nada*.'

What response was the younger man seeking? Damon was baffled, so responded by merely giving voice to his thoughts:

'All of these business cards, all of these four people - Lee Hardman, Kate Mellor, Paul Roe, me - we were all born in May 1982. All of us. Not all on the same day, but the same month, within two weeks of each other. The same, I don't know, micro-era. Bizarre. Now you, too! But a different year. You're 35?'

'Si.'

'You have your whole life in front of you.'

Another silence.

'Give me back the card.'

Adolfo handed over the last card. Instead of replacing it in his pocket with the others Damon started to tear his own aide memoire into ever smaller pieces. After ripping it into countless fragments he threw the pieces into the air, so they caught on the breeze and fell slowly, scintillating, over the side of the bridge, floating down towards the ground twenty metres below. For a moment he wondered if the pieces, the shards of paper, would reach the ground and spontaneously re-form… They would not, not in a million tries. Such was entropy.

'And then there's you, Adolfo. And six thousand pounds. When I've given Mr Campbell's money back to Lee, I will have nothing left. Except the car. And you're not having that.'

Adolfo shrugged his shoulders. 'But you owe to me. You say you pay me…'

Damon ignored him, turning his back as he took his phone from out of his inside pocket.

'Gosh, look at the time.'

'We go soon?' asked Adolfo. 'Long walk to car.'

'It's not that far. We've come round two sides of a triangle. The car's parked less than a mile back down this track.'

Adolfo looked down upon their intended route. 'But we up here, road down there. We must go back over bridge. Come, we go now, I ready go London.'

'Well, I'm not ready.'

'We must walk back, back that way.' He indicated the way they had come.

'No, Adolfo. We stay here.' Damon looked directly at him and for some reason an image from *Butch Cassidy and the Sundance Kid* came into his mind, followed by *Thelma and Louise*: 'Or maybe we jump?'

'Damon, *por favor*, this no good, no sensible - we go now.'

'Down there is the quickest way home…'

Adolfo could not believe what he was hearing. Damon snapped out of his reverie, realised that jumping was foolish, hardened his attitude, narrowed his eyes: 'You want to go now - OK. We go now. And you… don't get your money.'

Adolfo was taken aback: 'What? You crazy? Why you want stay?'

'You want to go? OK. You go. Look -' he took the car key from his pocket and dangled it inches in front of Adolfo's face. 'You want the car key? You wrestle me for it.'

'We fight? No. You crazy! No.'

'Yep, I reckon I am a little bit crazy. Always was.'

Their stares locked together. Adolfo was unused to the sense of fear.

'Come on! Do you want the key or not?'

Adolfo took a step forward, but Damon held the key high above his head. The smaller man reached for it but Damon snatched it away, teasing, smiling.

A twist of paper tied on a piece of string. That was what Damon used to use, as a small boy, to tease the family cat. The paw struck out, but a twist of the wrist made the paper bow jump out of the feline's reach. Again. And again. The cat never gave up, but never succeeded, either, so long as Damon stayed alert. Adolfo had less patience than the cat: after three vain attempts he withdrew, refusing to keep grabbing at the key.

'This crazy,' he muttered, 'You are crazy man.'

'Here it is,' Damon sang, 'the key. Look, I tell you what, I do like you, Adolfo, and I do want you to have your money. But Lee fucking Hardman is going to drain me dry and thanks to Paul fucking 'Pinko' Roe and that bloody journalist woman, and Charles fucking Mallory, I will be out of a job before very long, and who is going to employ me?' The singing had turned to shouting: 'I'm a rebel, Adolfo, I undermine, I criticise, I don't conform to social norms, I hate soft Tory paternalism, I fuck boys instead of screwing women or having children, I'm only happy when I'm...' he struggled for words, close to tears '- so out of it that I couldn't possibly know whether I was happy or not!'

He cupped his hands to his mouth like a megaphone and screamed: 'By-election alert! By-election alert! By-election alert!'

Adolfo waited patiently but apprehensively. He did not understand.

'By-election alert!'

The Argentine had seen people flip like this before, but normally when they were hammered with chemicals. This was unusual. Damon had been fit to drive, had he not? Adolfo was certain he had not taken anything since they had met up. He interrogated his memory. No, he was sure Damon had taken nothing.

In a voice designed to address a public meeting Damon, the actor, stated 'But you've done nothing bad to me Adolfo, you don't deserve to suffer. I'll tell you what…'

With the keyring hanging from a finger, he put his hands on each of Adolfo's shoulders and drew the slighter man towards him, then kissed his forehead.

'I don't want you to suffer, Adolfo, I won't make you jump. I've kept you waiting for your money for too long. You'll get it. You will get it.'

Nodding, Damon's serious face was close to Adolfo's.

'Look, here's the key to the car. It cost me £40,000, given a bit of depreciation, say £30,000-worth of car. Not bad, eh? You can drive?'

Adolfo hesitated: what was he letting himself in for?

'I no drive England but *si*, I got licence.'

'The car… is yours. Forty thousand pounds. You understand? You can have the car.'

Adolfo could not believe what he was hearing. Damon stood back, outstretched his arm, a simple keyring dangling from a finger, his phone still clasped in the other hand. Adolfo hesitated; he did not understand the teasing. Why was Damon doing this to him? The money the MP owed him was weeks overdue and he had seen scant evidence of Damon's intent to repay so far. On the other hand, though it may be second hand and well worn, the car was worth a lot more than the £6,000 that he was owed. Forty thousand, thirty thousand, whatever. He ought to take the offer. He would drive it back to London, it would be his first time driving on the left, but he could handle it, and he would leave Damon… actually, Adolfo realised, he could not care less what happened to Damon, son of the slayer of his kinsmen.

He held out his hand to take the key. Damon was smiling. Surely he would not start teasing him again? Just as Adolfo was about to take the key Damon flicked his wrist: 'Fetch! Good boy!'

The key was not thrown hard, but hard enough. It sailed almost over the parapet, glancing the stonework as it passed the edge, giving Adolfo no time to reach the edge to watch where it would land, so far below. He lost his temper: 'You crazy man, you crazy, crazy man!' Whether the car was going to be his or not, it was his only means of getting back to London. What was the loco doing?

Adolfo snapped. Shedding decorum, he uncharacteristically flew for Damon's throat. He was not big, but the force of his leap took Damon by surprise and they fell entwined to the ground, jarring the phone from Damon's hand. As they fell Damon stumbled on a stone, twisting an ankle and accidentally kicking off his own shoe as he struggled to regain purchase, but he was up again quickly and engaged Adolfo in a wrestling hold. The two men struggled this way and that for a few moments, grunting and sweating despite the cool of the approaching evening. Damon was stronger but Adolfo lighter, more agile. He escaped the bigger man's clutches and tripped him up. Damon landed on the ground a second time but immediately leapt up towards his opponent. Adolfo side stepped, caught Damon's wrist and twisted it: a loose-fitting, already semi-detached cufflink fell to the ground. Adolfo pushed with all his might - Damon staggered towards the edge and tripped, falling against the remains of an iron bar where the fence used to be, preventing him from falling over the edge. The ancient barrier lurched uncertainly, unceremoniously - but held. Pushing back from it, disorientated by both the blow and the dust in his eyes, Damon jumped at Adolfo, missing him completely as the Argentine once again side-stepped.

Now Adolfo redoubled his effort and went on the offensive: he hooked his foot round Damon's leg, causing the larger man to lose balance and tumble for a third time. This time there was a loud crack as Damon's forehead hit a large stone.

'Oh, Jesus!' yelled Damon, his hands clutching his forehead, 'What the fuck have you done? Oh, fuck! My head! Fuck! I can't see!'

The fight was clearly over, the dust in Damon's eyes and the disorientating blow to the head had seen to that. The struggle had lasted barely 15 seconds, ending with three falls and one submission in favour of the panting Adolfo.

Damon took his head in both hands and rolled over in agony. Alfonso could see no blood, but Damon had clearly taken a heavy, if accidental, blow.

Damon was lying on the ground, holding his head. Now blood was starting to seep through the fingers that grasped his face.

Over the years, through some combination of weather, vandalism and natural senescence the fence had decayed into pieces. Among the remains of the fence Adolfo found a short and unattached length of iron pole.

He did not stop to think.

A memory flooded back from Argentina when, aged 15, Alfonso had killed a dog with a single swing of a spade, a massive, feral dog that was mauling and blinding his four-year old brother, on the ranch where they grew up. Whether he was saving his brother's life or avenging his dead compatriots, the passion was the same.

He picked up the weapon, raised it and brought it down on the bridge of Damon's nose - a solitary blow, as though the pole were a woodman's axe.

Now there was more blood, on the club and across Damon's face, no longer protected by the man's hands. The body was still breathing but no longer talking, taunting.

Adolfo picked up the body by its shoulders and dragged the groaning Hough just a few feet over stony ground to the very edge of the precipice, where he positioned him carefully. There was a hard surface down below, a pile of rocks by the side of the farm track, rocks that had once been part of the bridge's now missing span. He manoeuvred the moaning Damon so that the MP's bloody head was protruding over that edge, his body flat to the ground, lying on his back. Now he turned him round so that his feet (one shoe off, one shoe on) were furthest from the edge. Then he lifted the feet and inched the body forward so that it started to overhang the drop, head first.

He stopped what he was doing. How was he going to get home? He was not going to hang around to carry out a futile search for the car key, running the risk of being spotted. He would have to abandon the car. It might take an hour to walk to the main road, if he walked quickly, it would still be light; but what then? He knelt by the fallen man and felt in his trouser pocket where he found a smart, soft, leather wallet. There was cash, more than a hundred pounds, enough to get him home after a walk and a bit more hitchhiking. He remembered his journey from London, there was a train station at East Midlands airport, close by Donington Park. He would take the whole wallet for now, take out the cash that he needed and dispose of the case a long way from the scene. He would not risk taking it back to civilisation.

Were there witnesses? Way down below was the farm track. Adolfo looked along its north-south axis. There was no one to be seen. East, back along the bridge, the same. West: nothing. It was at least half an hour since they had seen another person. Staying well clear of the drop himself, he again used Damon's feet to edge the body forward, using the legs as the handles of a wheel-less wheelbarrow. Adolfo felt the pull of gravity take hold of the man's head and shoulders, but he resisted its suction; he would not let go until the last moment, trying to ensure that the body landed head first.

He pushed again. Finally letting go of the feet as they cleared the edge Adolfo declared, quietly: '*Por las Malvinas. Por il Belgrano.*'

He had not finished making the dedication before he heard the body hit the ground with a muted crack. There was no more to be done. He turned, saw the lone shoe nearby, considered dropping it over the edge after its owner, thought it better not to touch it. He checked quickly around the scene but could see no blood, other than on his iron club.

Adolfo Bocca started to walk back along the bridge, his weapon in his hand. Blood was splashed around one end of the bar and his fingerprints must be all over the other. After a brisk stroll of a hundred metres, he stopped to peer over the parapet. His estimation was accurate; the gurgling stream was trickling along its path, way down beneath him.

There was still no one to be seen.

He had grown up in the countryside and was well able to judge where a stream was deep and where it ran shallow. He compared the upstream flow with the downstream, on either side of the bridge.

Then he positioned himself above the deepest part, stretched out his arm, took careful aim and dropped the iron bar in a perpendicular manner.

It entered the water with a discreet 'plop' and disappeared without trace.

Printed in Great Britain
by Amazon